TRAPPED MARIONETTES

M. MINJI JACOME

First edition, 2026
ISBN 979-8-218-89264-7

For Taylor, my annoying cat.

CONTENTS

TRAPPED MARIONETTES

PROLOGUE
CRYING CATS

Half a dozen cats stood outside Its door. But like Itself, they were Cats—and, of course, not quite normal *cats*.

The night swallowed the Cats up whole, coldness surging through their small Cat bones. They shivered, their big Cat lips turning blue. Although, of course, they could barely see themselves in the dusty blackness of the night. And they stood in two neat uniform rows of three, on hard stone—the single spot on the ground where no grass grew.

But they did not leave the spot, and only gazed up at a distant small light above them…

It was the light of a fireplace, hugged by the warmed walls of the cabin it was in. Yet, the light seemed to appear dim and cold in the Cats' eyes, for as the flame flickered, nothing flickered in their faces, as if it were a lifetime away, and they were watching it through a sheet of cold glass. Then again, the Cats almost always wore that dry, indifferent, identical face.

Halfmoon observed the Cats from the doorstep. It—Halfmoon—was deeply respected. It was their leader, although It was a bit smaller than most other Cats, and even had slightly different features from them.

But right now Halfmoon was tall. It looked down at them from Its cabin, which was on a small slope about five feet above them, stationed on a little hill. Halfmoon watched in grim satisfaction how the Cats continued to stand silently, black and frozen, not yet daring to disturb It. *Just the way It liked it.*

It studied them, as if by doing so, Halfmoon could find the answers It was looking for.

It was, of course, very familiar with them and their differences from normal cats. After all, It saw them daily (or whenever It occasionally emerged out of Its reclusive cabin to see the light of day, that was). Enough, at least, to know these Cats were not normal cats, although It couldn't say exactly *how*; Halfmoon had only seen normal cats and been to the Human world once.

As the Cats stood there in the dreary cold, their identical black eyes were still empty of any emotion. *But perhaps they did feel emotions, individual, unique emotions,* Halfmoon pondered; entering and reading Cats' minds was something It was still working on. *Perhaps, they were just too frightened to come up or were waiting to be called.*

And Halfmoon was ready to summon them up, but the group was still incomplete. Waiting now, It suppressed the urge to sigh into the silence, or tap Its claws against the cabin door in frustration; It knew *this would be entirely pointless,* and It pulled a serious expression of calm.

Just then, It spotted a small creature, only a few inches tall, trot out from the darkness and up the hill. "Oh, news?" Halfmoon said in the Human language of Japanese. "Tell me where the other two Cats are. I am waiting."

The creature was a small Kitten, not quite a normal kitten, exactly like the Cats weren't cats. But it was not *even* a Kitten, rather something not very alive at all, simply a robot, a camera, one of Its inventions. Halfmoon held it up to Its face level, and as the Kitten Robot's bulky eyes stared into Its own, in that misty eye contact, a shared light shone into Halfmoon's eyes, into Its mind, and by magic, It could see another camera view. The view of two other Cats running, coming near now.

Then Halfmoon set the Kitten Robot down again, and it ran off, back to being another camera.

Although stuck and muddled in Its current situation, Halfmoon smiled to Itself at how much It adored Its inventions, all the different types. It was what It did during those long, driven hours of work inside the isolation of Its cabin. Halfmoon was so proud and looking forward to testing out more. It liked experimenting, when It knew exactly what the result would be, when It knew what It was doing. When It did not let the *magic* bother It—but used it instead. *It was stronger than the magic, after all,* Halfmoon reminded Itself.

The sound of footsteps gave away the others arriving, so Halfmoon took a few steps beyond Its doorstep, into the night.

"Petal. Kamiko," It said. "Why, hello!"

Since Halfmoon was a Cat, of course It did not sound like a Human. It did not have a completely Human voice, although It had made inventions to make Itself sound more and more Human. But Halfmoon specifically sounded *almost* like a Human, unlike the other Cats. The other Cats did not have such a grip as Itself had on the magic. But they all sounded almost normal to *each other* when they spoke. At least, they pretended they did. Halfmoon always tried to make everything as ordinary as It could. *Kept in order.*

"As you hear, I am now speaking Japanese," It went on. "I

am allowing you to understand what I am saying. If you wish to speak too, let me know."

The Cats nodded, and Petal smirked, while Kamiko only smiled nervously.

The Cats could not speak whenever they wanted to. Halfmoon had to help them speak, using magic, and could only do so if necessary. But sometimes, they just spoke. Sometimes they *just* spoke, and Halfmoon didn't understand why. When this happened, It always pretended not to notice.

"Come up to my cabin," It invited them, finally.

All eight Cats slowly marched up the slope to meet Halfmoon. Then It let them all inside, gathering them near the entrance. They occupied one half of the cabin, and It the other.

"As you know," It started, "my dear, precious, *reliable* inventions have informed me of, well, danger. Danger is on its way to us. It is why I ordered you to come tonight." Its voice was unusually quiet and rushed, but Halfmoon kept it high. It knew It had to tell Its Cats what It had seen as soon as possible. It kept Its posture strong too, to hide the way It was shaking—but not from the cold.

As Halfmoon said this, It stood in front of wooden things that looked like shelves on Its walls, and then It pulled off a dark cloth to reveal one of Its inventions, to demonstrate.

It was a strange invention, but the Cats, who stood in frozen silence in front of Halfmoon, could not properly see what it was, as Halfmoon showed only the back. It showed them the orange, square outline of something, with a big screen inside. Then It turned the screen on.

Until now, nothing had stirred in most of the Cats' faces, at least no clear emotion that Halfmoon could make out. But now It grinned to Itself, the looks of fascination and surprise what It always looked for; Its inventions, for some reason, never failed to reveal something new in the Cats' expressions.

The screen now showed an unusual camera view of what appeared to be the corner of some Japanese street, but most Cats were aware of the place it was. Everything in the camera looked blurred, but the forms of two trees could scarcely be made out, which were behind a bench. The bench was right on the pavement, and there was a figure seated on it. But Halfmoon paid no attention to the figure, as Its focus was elsewhere.

"This, of course, is the Portal view," It started. "Some of you may not be familiar with it. But I remind you I speak truth; all my inventions have been tested plenty of times, and you know that I only ever do what is best. For you all. I have been your leader for years."

Most Cats nodded in agreement, yet Petal rolled his eyes.

Halfmoon pointed at a small blue glow on the edge of the screen, surrounded by something that looked like a fence. "This is the Portal. And see this, very far away, is the danger. I have given it a name: *the Terror*. It will be horrendous; it will be *awful*. The Terror—something dark—is coming to attack our island, is going to enter the Portal from Japan, and come here, to destroy us *all*." Halfmoon gave a moment for emphasis, gazing upwards at the ceiling, as It let the Cats around It react and gasp. Except, again, Petal, who wore a firm, focused frown, and Kamiko, who burst into sudden tears.

The camera indeed showed a big yellow blob in the other corner of it. Far, but not too far from the Portal. Terror.

But, of course, the Terror was not the thing that made Halfmoon shake. *It was the fact that, perhaps a little lost and clueless, It almost did not know how to stop it...*

Petal made a peculiar noise.

"Do you wish to speak?" Halfmoon asked him.

It did something with Its mind and the magic.

"How do you *know* for sure that, er, *the Terror* is coming?" Petal spoke, flinching.

Halfmoon knew that speaking aloud was always a discomfort for some Cats. But usually, when they flinched or even cried out in pain, It pretended not to notice.

Looking away, Halfmoon answered, "Well, my inventions, of course. You all know how they work. Mostly my abilities, knowledge, and logic from my brain. And a touch, but only a touch, of magic."

Petal shook his head. "I know—on the camera, there *is* something coming, slowly. But how can you possibly know it's coming to us? I mean, there is a girl sitting on the bench there. Wouldn't something like even *that* be more of a *Terror*? That girl could find the Portal. *She* could enter it, threaten our island. And how do you know she won't? How do you know that a specific Terror is coming? How can you be sure that—?"

"That's *quite* enough, Petal," Halfmoon cut in, a stern look on Its face. "I always tell you, there is meaning, a reason for everything. My inventions are reliable, only too complicated for me to explain. The Terror *is* coming. I am the one who understands the magic!" Halfmoon smirked, relieved that everyone seemed pleased. "Fortunately, time ticks very slowly in the Human world," It went on. "We have time to think. How we can prevent this. I think we have maybe a few weeks."

"So, what would you want from us?" Petal interrupted again.

Halfmoon shot Petal a glare, hoping he did not notice the way It shook. Hoping the other Cats didn't notice either, and scarcely saw an expression of annoyance on Its face.

"I want feedback, ideas."

"Ideas?" Petal said.

"Well, of course, I do *have* ideas already. It is in my Paws, after all. For example, of course I could use magic—"

"Then why don't you?"

"Petal." Halfmoon forced a tight smile. "I do not want to overuse the magic. I want to find my own solutions, use my inventions, for example."

"But your inventions are made of magic anyway," Petal claimed.

"Yes, but only a touch of magic. Mostly hard work."

Petal opened his mouth, but Halfmoon cried, "I want to hear my Cats' voices as well!"

A small cheer erupted among the Cats, and Petal scowled.

Halfmoon commanded, "Silence." *Now they needed focus.*

Halfmoon knew It was running out of options in this situation; *It could no longer pretend. But at least It was telling them the truth about this Terror, and everyone believed in hope.* That was Its favourite part about the Cats: *their innocent ignorance, overconfidence, and easily gained trust.*

Then, Halfmoon continued smiling into the silence, silence that Its Cats left it. "No ideas?" It asked, and still, there was silence.

Except Kamiko. A raw sound escaped Kamiko's lungs. His eyes were wide, a soft tremble coming in.

"What is it?" Halfmoon asked him. "Do you wish to speak?"

And just like that, Halfmoon gave him access to the use of his tongue with the magic.

"Look!" Kamiko cried. Everyone stared towards where he pointed, at the Human figure sitting on the bench.

"What *is* it?" Halfmoon repeated. "That is only a small

Human, and nothing more. Not of importance. A mere piece of the landscape. Let us not get sidetracked, please!"

"But, look, look!" Kamiko spluttered in a painful cry.

Halfmoon raised an eyebrow.

"She looks so sad," Kamiko explained, his voice weak.

As Halfmoon examined her closely, It did spot a frown on the girl's face.

Petal snorted. "Kamiko, that's irrelevant. How can you even *see* that?"

"What is it that you want?" Halfmoon asked, a final time.

Tears were sparkling in Kamiko's eyes. "I'm… so sorry. But she reminds me of my owner, the one I had before. I… could I see her?"

"See her?"

Halfmoon pushed some puzzlement off Its face and pulled a grin. *Kamiko was so vulnerable, so desperate*, Halfmoon knew. It also knew that *desperate minds were easy to please. And happiness brought even more trust.*

"You want to see *that*… girl?" It asked Kamiko. "On the screen?"

"I do… Oh, I really do!" Kamiko again burst into desperate tears, but stood still, waiting for an answer.

"Hmm…" Halfmoon thought.

Then Halfmoon did something. The screen was connected to Its mind, and It rolled back Its eyeballs. It sensed the Cats around it flinch, uncomfortable—mainly Kamiko—but It could now see the view clearly in Its head.

There, in fact, sat a young girl, alone, tears trickling down her face. By the directed look in her eyes, she might as well have seen Halfmoon. But It was looking at her through a camera, and It knew time was so slow in the Human world. She had probably been there for days and days to them. She was probably not going to leave any sooner than the Terror that would come…

And it all came to It. *It made sense.* They could *use* Human *help*, against the Terror!

The plan in Its head seemed simple, straightforward. Unreasonable, but maybe their only choice.

"Kamiko," Halfmoon started. "You can see her, if that is what you want. You can see that girl." It shook Its head and smiled. "I have a plan!"

The Cats cheered. Kamiko cried happier tears.

"It is much easier for a Human girl to stop the Terror rather than one of *us* having to travel to Japan. The girl is so small. She will believe me, trust me, surely, as you do. She will help us. She…" *She could be a tester for Its inventions.* "She can prevent the Terror from even coming, from Japan!"

"But…" Petal spoke up. "How will that *work*? How will she… trust you?"

Halfmoon gave the screen a rather sharp look for a second. And thought. "She *is* sad," It remarked, ignoring Petal's snort.

It studied the image, planning Its move. It sank into her blue eyes, and an idea hit It.

"She's drowning," It claimed. "Poetically. In thought, so lost. My point is, I know how these young Human minds think! Whatever she is sad about, helping us might make her, well, proud of herself." It chuckled, pleased with Itself; it seemed everyone believed Its reasons. *Exactly what Halfmoon needed from them—trust.*

"However," Halfmoon said. "We need to talk to her first. To gain her trust. We *must* talk to her first. We must first bring her here. I know it complicates things—a lot—but it is crucial."

And, Halfmoon thought to Itself. *It could test if Its newest invention really did work!* "I can show her this wonderful place, talk to her, convince her she is the special little angel who can save us all!"

"How will you even get her?" Petal asked.

"Oh…" Halfmoon frowned. "I have an idea."

Again, Halfmoon rolled Its eyeballs into the back of Its head and saw the girl and the bench. It looked for something, anything, and then It saw it.

A pen was next to the girl on the bench. It was her pen. Her almost frozen posture looked like she was about to grab it, even.

And then Halfmoon did something with Its mind and commanded one of the Kitten robot cameras near the girl in Japan to very quickly snatch the pen. It did this in Cat time, meaning it was so fast the girl probably did not even notice. It made the Kitten place the pen near the Portal, between the two trees.

Halfmoon returned to the real Cats beside It. "I just stole her pen. She had a pen with her, and I placed it much nearer to the Portal. This means that when she searches for it, she will be forced to go near the Portal to get it. And from there, well, she will probably see the entrance, and… curiosity killed the cat."

A few Cats shrieked in horror at the phrase, but It shouted, "Silence! Not *you*, not literally! We will not kill her. What I mean is, she might see the Portal, and come closer. I know Human minds; they are scared, scared not to understand. They are so scared if something does not make sense…"

"Like you are."

Halfmoon turned, Its stomach churning. Its face paled.

It was Petal.

"Get. Out," Halfmoon said.

With invisible magic hands, It reached out to Petal, into Petal, his jaw, his insides, and twisted them back into a way that he could no longer speak. Then, with a touch of magic from the air, It threw him out of the door, with a force of Its Paws. An audible crash outside alerted all the Cats.

"So," Halfmoon went on, trying to keep steady. It felt Its whole body shaking, the words having cut somewhere deep, but It would not let them. It hoped Its Cats saw nothing of Its shaking, although It wanted to cry at the pointless comment. "See that force I used on Petal? Well, I had *intended* to throw him out of the door!" It laughed nervously. "There is a force exactly like that at the entrance. So, even if curiosity does not kill the cat, or the girl, I should say, a force will bring her here. This means now we only have to wait a few days, or weeks, for her to notice in Human seconds that her pen is missing. Then, she will come to us naturally.

"When she comes, we will *talk*, and convince her to help us. That is when we must get her back to Japan to actually stop the Terror. We will then take her to the nearest Portal from here. And, er, Kamiko, you will take her."

Kamiko gasped as his eyes widened. "M-me?"

"You wanted to see her, if I'm not mistaken."

"Well, yes, I…"

Even the Cats around looked startled.

"Kamiko, we still have time," Halfmoon said. "While we wait, I will prepare new inventions that track more accurately how soon the Terror will come. You must simply wait. The rest is all up to me."

Kamiko nodded. "Also…"

"Yes?"

He did not meet Halfmoon's eyes. "W-while the girl, you

know, is around, could you please all call me *Koko*? In front of her? I mean, to not call me Kamiko…"

"What? Why is that?" Halfmoon frowned.

"I—" Kamiko sighed, his voice shaky, his eyes teary. "My owner is the one who named me. It's *wrong*. It can't possibly be the same girl that was my owner, but still, I'm reminded of her…"

"But you *want* to see her, don't you?" Sometimes, Halfmoon thought Kamiko was even more annoying than Petal.

"Yeah. And it *is* kind of like the past. But not *completely*. It's still different, and I don't want it to be *just* like the past. If I see someone like my owner, and I'm Kamiko, it's *exactly* like the past, you know? I want it to be different, like this is a better version of the past. Please just—"

"Oh, for goodness' sake!" Petal shouted from outside. "Then call him Koko, if it makes things easier. Nothing really makes sense here, after all—"

Halfmoon silently started to shake again, as It knew Petal was not supposed to be talking. *But after all, sometimes, the Cats just talked.* Halfmoon told Itself this was the only thing about the magic It did not understand.

Halfmoon continued, "Now, get some sleep, er, *Koko*. I can call you Koko. Right. Get some rest, let this all sink in properly. Recover from any… shock."

Koko nodded and hurried away, sniffing.

But as It watched him stumble out of the door and into the darkness, Its eyes widened a bit.

The other Cats around Halfmoon made small grunting and moaning noises, and from outside It even heard Petal ask, to no one in particular, "Do we have a backup plan?"

It laughed and assured, "Doubts? Please, it is all right! *We have time.*"

And like that, Halfmoon dismissed them all too, until only silence rang in Its ears, as Its cabin stood suddenly empty.

Soon, It heard even Petal retreat.

There was no crackling sound nor warmth from Its fireplace, because there was, of course, no real fireplace. It was just a bit of decoration It had added with use of the magic. Now it was a plain, large surface. Untouched by Its inventions. Only some dust fell down from the cluttered shelves above. Now that the Cats had gone, only a blank, dark wall remained.

And even *Halfmoon* felt a bit empty and cold.

Halfmoon stared at the camera, at the image of the distant Human girl and the bench, not daring to, but then It *did,* cry…

Yet, Its distant, tiny sniffles were muzzled by the small wafts of wind blowing through the window. The air itself seemed to shudder.

Then Halfmoon shook Its head, cleaned Its Cat face.

And with this new plan It had made, Halfmoon talked to Itself.

"I must keep myself together, keep it all together. Use the magic effectively, develop my inventions. Or everything will fall apart… perhaps literally."

CHAPTER 1 – LOST, ROTTEN BLUEBERRIES?

S he would not eat.

Steamed rice and an hour-long effort stood beside her with side dishes. Except, she knew it wasn't really an hour-long effort, but pre-made ingredients picked up from the convenience shop nearby and *pretended* to be prepared with effort.

Not that she wasn't feeling hungry… *But she was busy, anyway*, she told herself. *Very busy.*

Her notebook was open in front of her, and she was drawing cats—long ones, with eyes wide and googly, unfocused. They were grey and dull, though not as dull as her surroundings. All slightly different in size, scribbled blobs. They were very long cats.

She was feeding these drawing—feeding them with more rushed pencil strokes and thick, jagged lines that dug a bit too firmly into the paper. All with her small, overused pencil. She was inviting the cats into her mind and letting them eat up all her unnecessary, unwanted thoughts.

Usually, she did not let herself become too absorbed in

thoughts—or feelings. But her left hand rode and drew, solely to avoid having to look at the person sitting opposite her. At the pale-faced ghost who barely even existed.

She knew if she stopped drawing, and met those eyes, she might feel pain and start shaking. And of course she did not want to feel pain.

But then, her ears picked up the sound of a throat clearing. There was a slight weight on her shoulder.

She pretended not to notice. She kept on drawing a new cat. *It didn't matter*, she told herself. *It wasn't there.*

But the weight was the pressure of a hand. The pressure increased.

She ignored it. *It didn't exist. It didn't exist.*

A voice spoke her name.

Amber.

Amber dropped her pencil and was forced to look up.

"Amber," her mother was saying. "Could you go to that Konbini mart nearby and get some more food for dinner?" Her mother's glassy, yet sharp eyes were not even on her, but just gazed at her own fingers, which were counting something from the top of her head. "Some rice, maybe some more bread, oh, yes, eggs would be good…"

Amber said nothing.

"You know, that shop a while from here…"

Again, she didn't reply.

Her mother, noticing her silence, finally looked at her—at which Amber hurriedly returned to her drawings.

"Oh, only if that's OK, of course," she said. "You don't have to."

Amber shook her head. "No, I'll go."

"Sure you remember the way?"

"Yes. I remember."

Her mother looked unsure.

Amber sighed. "I'll keep to the right-hand side of the road for a while. There aren't many turns. I'll recognize them all. Then I walk along the railing above the beach. More turns. I'll know where to cross."

"All right. There's some cash there on the table—you'll be fine then. Amber, you know… Let's talk. I know you're off school now, but how were you doing there? I know that—"

And after that, Amber didn't know what her mother said, for she lost focus, and the next words became muffled and slipped somewhere faded and unimportant in the back of her mind.

Her mother was still watching, she knew. With those tired, yet wide and icy eyes that looked like she'd had too much coffee. A corpse shaken unnaturally alive. Amber did not look.

Instead, she watched the turned-off TV against the wall. She'd spent hours and hours staring at it, only to avoid conversation with her mother, as they lived together and alone. Neither knew what to say to each other. Everything always resulted in buzzing, bustling silence, so why not block it out with noisy, childish cartoons?

But drawing was even easier to get away with.

Noticing her untouched plate, her mother asked something like, *did she not like the food?*

But the town's fish was her favourite. Or *had* been, in the past. And the person—the ghost—in front of her was also from the past. It was the reason she avoided her. The past hurt, so she avoided the meal to further avoid the blue eyes.

After several minutes had trailed by, Amber finally sighed and cut her prickly fish. She cut it into little, mushy pieces.

Her mother went on saying something, but at least the food saved her from having to reply. The taste was duller than she remembered, and all she could focus on was the floppy, saggy consistency.

Her mother was trying to talk about school.

And always in the same low voice. Low and cautious, as though Amber was a dangerous creature, one that could attack at any moment. Cautious, as though dipping one toe into water to test the temperature…

And for a moment, Amber looked up. She even forced a smile. But as she started speaking, her mother shook her head. Denying what she was saying.

… and then, if something went wrong, if the water was cold, she'd always run back. Probably start smirking. If something went wrong in their lives, her mother would *laugh*. She always laughed, so Amber felt she wasn't taken seriously. But she knew her mother was only pretending, never accepting what Amber really had to say.

Yet, it was weird when it was like this. It was weird when her mother pretended, and there was no one there. It was weird, because it was just her and Amber.

Amber swallowed, but a piece of food got stuck in her throat, and she coughed violently.

Her mother stared. *Was she OK?*

Yes. Yes. She stood up to clear away her plate and to get a glass of water. *Swallowed a fish bone.*

When she returned, she continued drawing cats.

Amber drew the enormous face of a cat, so that it filled up an entire page. This cat face was slender, even skinnier and duller than the face of her mother. It was a new thing, with eyes the size of buttons, round, dark, and sickening. They were very big eyes. Its mouth hung open from nearly the top of the page to the bottom, black and empty.

Her mother asked whether *she could stop drawing.*

But drawing was the only thing Amber saw sense in.

Nonetheless, her stomach churned as she grew aware of the horrors she had sketched. *What was she even doing?* She reached for the rubber, rushing to quickly change it all, to force the lines into something new and different. But it all stayed the same; Amber had drawn cats, and they certainly did not look normal. As she stared at the notebook in front of her, the back of her neck prickled. *The drawings were not helping.* The drawings did not stop her from shaking.

Amber always liked to keep her drawings simple and neat. *That was what they were,* illustrations—*not weird, messy cartoon doodles.* But she didn't like it when this happened, when the pencil she was holding moved at its own will, or the will of her feelings—not her thoughts. When all the lines went wrong, and it seemed a ghost hand was drawing, rather than her own.

Her mother tried to say her name again, calling her attention, now agitated, but also exhausted. However, her tongue slipped, and the name she pronounced was not Amber, but *Amaya.* The other name.

The name from the past.

Then a sigh, claiming *a name was all it was.*

But Amber hated her carelessness. This crossed the line. She clenched her fists.

Her mother was laughing it off.

Amber stood up and pushed in her chair. Something hurtful escaped the twitching corners of her mouth.

The laughter faded away.

And for a fleeting second, she *looked* at her mother.

Her face was ghostly pale. The same golden locks that Amber had hung messily around it. Except, these were short, chopped off, with fake, dyed dark streaks in them.

And she *should* have looked like Amber. But she only looked like she had burned her hair.

Although her fake hair concealed her features, in that moment Amber could tell she had tears in her eyes.

Going to the shop, Amber muttered. *Now.*

In a low voice, her mother said, *If she was going out, at least take her bicycle.*

As Amber shook her head, it throbbed terribly. Her ears hurt, too, and she turned her head to look at the TV.

Something flashed across the previously black, empty screen. For a second, Amber saw something that she could only explain by comparing it to her similar drawings. That pale, beefy, saucer-eyed face stared back. The eyes blinked once, almost audibly.

Amber shook her head again as everything returned to normal, and yet, it felt like a piece of the world had broken apart. A faint smile crossed her lips. The eyes were gone.

One glance at her mother, and Amber could tell she hadn't noticed anything.

Amber ran out of the building, carrying her notebook with her, grabbing her sun hat and some cash on the way. She knew if she stayed, if she did not draw, she would snap, and all her emotions would burst out. And she would do anything to avoid *that*.

She ran into the summer day, still avoiding the bizarrely cool eyes of her mother, and the eyes she had drawn.

* * *

Amber walked at a steady pace. She did not look back.

School was off, and ever since her break had started, she had spent her time mostly locked up in her room, doodling, or occasionally watching TV. She knew she was supposed to be studying, but she was sinking and drowning in the new school system, barely understanding a thing.

However, today she was out, and she was going to the shop.

When she did go out, she always went on foot, as she had her doubts about whether her dusty old bike still worked.

It was only when Amber was walking on the pavement, a few streets away from home, that she gave in to her dizzying headache and skin-prickling shudders.

She replayed everything that had happened over and over in her head. Her mother, her drawings…

The horrible eyes in the TV screen.

Had she really seen her drawings, her horrible sketches, there on the wall?

Amber still held her notebook tightly beneath her arm, filled with all the unexplainable creepy cats.

Her thoughts spun around in questions and questions as she continued to shudder. And these shudders turned into an almost sickly, desperate shake and sensation that ran up her whole spine, until she was almost sick. *How she hated unexplainable happenings like this.*

After the feeling had passed, for she convinced herself it was, in fact, just a feeling, she thought.

No, no. She'd probably imagined it. It probably hadn't happened. Yes, she was just obsessing over her drawings too much! She needed to get out more. That was it.

And then she left it at that and told herself she'd make sense of her drawings later.

But what about what had happened *before* she had seen that face? Her mother had called her, called her by *that* name.

After what she had seen on—no, it almost had seemed, *in*

—the screen, it didn't seem significant. Yet, Amber's stomach dropped as she remembered how she had reacted. *It was just a name*. She gulped. *Yes. It* was *just a name; her mother* was *right with that.*

The morning had been so terrible that Amber tried to forget it and return her thoughts to it later. She decided, today, she would not lose hold of her feelings like she had with her drawings, mixing fact and fiction. From now on, she'd keep herself under control.

She continued walking through the streets. To that shop.

Today was one of those usual hot-iron sunny summer days, with blue skies blinded by an electric, white intensity. Even the constant buzzing of the cicadas sounded muffled in the thick air.

Perhaps that was why, as random paths turned into familiar roads, and roads into well-known streets, she aimed her gaze more and more at her feet. Or perhaps it was the same reason that a part of her did not want to go to the shop.

Although it had been months since Amber had moved here all the way from England, some roads still felt twisting and unending to her, and some streets felt weirdly nostalgic even though she rarely visited them. But this only made sense. For Amber had been here before already. She had spent many summers here, before the move or the pain of the past...

And as she walked to the shop she hadn't visited once since moving here, keeping to the right side of the road, passing by houses and houses, plain buildings that all looked the same, memories started crawling into her mind, exactly what she'd hoped would not.

They should have been filled with sweetness. But the faded image of Amber as a little child walking about on these roads with her cute sun hat and her little braids her father had made her… It filled her only with longing and envy.

But no, Amber thought. *Wrong!* The happy little girl on summer vacation in Japan with her parents wasn't *Amber*. It was *Amaya*. Amaya was her first name, what people *used* to call her—Amber was her middle name, which she now preferred. As to *why* she preferred it, she was unsure herself.

Perhaps it was because, after her move, so much had changed that it felt almost wrong for her to still be the same person. Or perhaps it was because, after leaving everything sweet and good behind her in her old home, she was also leaving behind *Amaya*…?

As Amaya, she had always been so sure of herself and her feelings, but she was not anymore.

She could still picture Amaya here now in her free, casual wear. Not any uniform, but her own choice. What had she been wearing again? Comfy shorts, coloured shirts she had chosen for herself, maybe flowy dresses… Amber couldn't remember, now that she was chained and limited to her single uniform outfit. But she did not blame her school. Her school didn't require students to wear a uniform during the summer. And yet, by will, and will only, she did. Like it was with her name, she didn't know why exactly. It was rather that she could not imagine herself *not* wearing her uniform. If it weren't for her recommended outfit, she just wouldn't know what to choose.

As Amber moved down the pavement, she tried to block the memories of Amaya from sneaking into her head.

Nonetheless, they almost always found her. It was as if there was clamorous, noisy music blasting all around her. Something inside her head, yet louder than the shrilling song of the cicadas.

Amber hoped that today she could block out this music and go to the shop.

But, as she crossed a small street, a sudden tune played in her mind.

The summer of Ichigo's death.

One day in July, Amaya woke up to some dreadful news.

Amaya, I'm sorry. Your cat is dead. Ichigo died in her sleep. No one knows why. She was so young. We don't understand. Your father and I are very upset.

Everything else in Amaya's life had been going fine. So, she decided it best to sit in her garden for a while, in the shade of a tree. She managed to stay calm.

People watching had said she looked emotionless. *What a strange girl... Just sitting there, near the blueberry bushes, like she's enjoying the sun. Isn't she sad about her cat?*

But of course, she was sad. There just weren't many tears. And when there were some, they felt natural, not out of control or sudden or unpredictable. Amaya had told herself it was all OK.

That had been her favourite thing about herself; she could, more or less, control the way she felt. Amaya didn't get so choked up over things like others. Her emotions never took control over *her*.

The music stopped.

The cicadas' shrilling swelled.

Amber shook her head.

In front of her there was a brick wall. It was old and faded. It went around a house, guarding the insides from view. The house could have been abandoned and rotten for years, the people inside could have died long ago, and no one would have ever known. Only because of this wall.

And someone had scribbled things all over it in fresh graffiti. *Well, this was new.*

Amber wanted to look inside and see what was behind the wall, but the bricks were fixed stone. She knew it would have been impossible to move one of them without smashing the whole thing down, because the wall was hard with unerasable years.

The wall filled her mind with bustling noise.

One evening that same summer, she'd gone on a stroll by herself, still mourning. She hadn't wanted to cry. All she'd needed was to move her body. And then she found this wall.

Upon gazing at it, it had reminded her of Ichigo and the cat's unnecessarily cruel fate. The inevitable pain that Amber did not want. The things she could not change. The things set in stone and just *existing*, just *there*, in her heart. Too awful to accept. Too awful to deal with.

And even when, in that same summer, Amaya had made her tears go away, when she hadn't reacted and just walked and stood, the wall stood, too. This wall, this old, standing wall, existed there, *too*, and it didn't go away. It glared at her.

And it was glaring at her now. With a twisted smile half-turned upwards. She could almost see a face. She could almost hear it talk to her. "*Hello.*"

These streets were bringing back noise, more dreadful noise, into her head.

"But memories are just thoughts…" Amber muttered to herself.

She increased her pace and took bigger steps around a corner. Now, she walked for a long time, ignoring the memories that tried to claw their way into her mind. Instead, she observed her surroundings.

The town she lived in was coastal and very small. Most

paths she took had a view of the sea, which sparkled and reflected the cloudless sky. Yet, her gaze was typically towards her feet.

Amaya used to love going on walks when she visited. She used to watch everything in the neighbourhood for hours, as if it were a film. She'd enjoy the simple things that were there, and never wanted more.

But now, the streets all looked the same to her. Usually, everything was very quiet, and it had become even more so over the years. Amaya used to skip down the empty alleys as if they all belonged to her, as if this were her kingdom.

In a way, the whole world had felt as though it were made for her. As if her life was a freedom, a gift she had to embrace as her own. Now, Amber felt the opposite. She was here, here solely to… understand, make sense of things.

There were a few small shops along street corners, and people could always be spotted fishing in the distance. There were always stray cats trotting around, asking for food, especially fish. Cicadas could always be heard, wherever you went. But other than that, not much ever happened.

Even Amber's classmates from school—she could never call them friends—lived quite a while away, because it was a long trip to school. But when her mother had inherited the place so long ago, she hadn't been looking for schools. Then, it became a small vacation home. No one had expected them to move there.

But then her parents got divorced. When she recalled it now, it felt like it had happened in a flash. A sudden attack of lightning, randomly striking into clear, blue skies. A clear life, a clear mind, in fact, sure of itself, suddenly torn up into tiny, miserable bits.

Now, Amber could not help but find these streets boring.

Dull, dry, everything drenched and soaked in feelings that she didn't even dare feel, memories made only to be forgotten. She trudged along the pavement, her feet barely lifting off the ground. She passed a corner shop and came to a bridge, one with a big view.

And… she could not help it. A salty wave of fresh memories washed over her as she remembered how Amaya had loved this place.

For a moment, as Amber dared peering out at the view of the ocean, the air blowing into her face, she held onto the railing. The sea was right beneath her, roaring and crashing against the shore. And she allowed herself to remember, for only a second.

She had always stood in this spot, sometimes on her father's back, to see even more.

Amber remembered the rush of wind on her face. The way her eyes had lit up, perfectly reflecting the colour of the waves, not unlike the sky. How, when watching the ships in the water, her heartbeat had quickened, excitement and anticipation in her chest. Life had always been so beautiful. Amaya had been so immersed in her surroundings.

It also reminded her of something else… She remembered how Amaya had had an unusual love for berries. She had loved sweet, plump *blueberries*. In her old home, in her garden, many grew. Every day after school, she raced home immediately just to taste a handful of them. Juicy and fresh, she licked the warm sweetness off her fingers. Amaya had always been so passionate. About simple things. Like small feelings or flavours. *And she had been so sure of everything, sure of herself.*

But now, as Amber gazed into the distance, she blamed herself for even doing so, trying to recreate such a feeling.

The seaside air washed over her, but she couldn't smell it. Even the cicadas' song had now dimmed. She could hear the scream of seagulls, but she wanted them to drop dead like flies, into the swirling ocean.

She continued walking, trying to shift her full attention to moving, and pinched herself. *There was no sense in what she was doing, recalling things from the past, feeling pain.* She shook her head, walked on, and kept herself busy.

But the reason she felt pain wasn't because of the pain itself. It was because of the confusion, the puzzlement and doubt in her pain—what had happened to her? When had she stopped being so sure?

She found it hard to give one answer.

She came to a sudden stop again.

The streets were all still empty; Amber was alone, walking along the railing, sliding one hand along it.

She was unsure exactly why she had stopped, but she felt the back of her neck prickle, almost as if something was not right. Again, that cold, unpleasant shiver up her spine. A ghost going through her.

The unnerving feeling that had unwelcomely settled on her back was still there, but she ignored it. For the feeling reminded her of the horrors she had sketched today... Those drawings of the eyes.

Amber shook her head, dismissing it as a small, peculiar feeling. A feeling of little importance, like her memories.

But then she realized what was wrong.

She looked down at the grey pavement but could not help noticing how unusual the day was. It was midsummer, and yet... She could even see the intense golden rays of sun beam all over her skin. And her uniform, though it was a skirt and a sleeveless blouse, was sweaty, cut for all seasons except for extreme winter. She was surprised when she reached up to her forehead and felt it was moist.

However, although she had been walking for a long time, she did not *feel* hot. Not at all, not mentally. It was that same feeling of unexplainable strangeness.

Amber *hated* odd happenings. She especially hated the unexpected and preferred everything to simply remain in order. Even Amaya had cried, and that was the only time she'd *really* cried, when something was out of the ordinary. She—both Amber and Amaya—liked to be sure, and understand everything about everything. And she had a good idea of why she was not hot. She was bored; that was the reason. The entire summer, this entire year, she had slowly developed a sense of boredom, sometimes numbness. Trapped in her room, letting hours and hours pass, and drawing. Never immersed in life, as before.

Amber stopped her thoughts and pinched herself again. *That did it.*

She let go of the railing.

The cicadas in the background resumed their chorus.

She ran.

And then her feet steered and steered her over the burning concrete ground, heels kicking off over the hot coals. It was almost like her body took her, against her mind's own will, and she couldn't stop her running legs, her legs that ran and ran her to that shop, wherever it was now.

Her body, her feet, wanted to remember, *wanted* to let her memory guide them, but her mind—and her feelings—did not. Her feet ran to the shop, although her feelings screamed and cried out with the memories evoked.

Except, of course, it wasn't just her feet steering her, but also another part of her mind. The part that, when her mother had asked if she knew the way, had made her nod. The part that had insisted on going, to show, make herself see. *See? She could leave the house. See? She could fight memories. They were just stupid feelings.*

But now Amber *had* become absorbed in her feelings, and there was no way back.

Her feet had puzzled her; she was tripping over her own feet, which were tripping over her laces…

Amber fell and scraped her knees on the concrete road.

Getting up, she could feel a throbbing in her ears, and it was like she had fallen into a new street, one that she did not recognize as she stood up.

Perhaps by accident, she had reached a spot.

It was a bench. The bench she'd sat on so many times.

Amber sighed. Amaya had adored cats, and she had fed them here, by *this* bench.

Then, she noticed something different: there were no cats here now. In fact, she hadn't spotted any the whole day. She looked into the distance, past a house, and found the beaches empty; it wasn't even a normal fishing day. Her neck prickled, but she gave a small laugh to shake off the feeling, as she knew cats were such funny creatures.

The next moment, she had convinced herself that everything was fine.

Nonetheless, a feeling, a distant memory, had burst inside her.

The summer Ichigo had died, she'd gone on that trip to Japan. It was at this exact bench where she had fed a kitten. Light, fluffy chocolate-brown hair and doe-wide eyes. She had named him Kamiko. But Kamiko had been more than a cat to her. To Amaya, he had been a special friend. She had always taken care of him, and fed him blueberries. All by *this* bench.

That summer had been just that point, that edge of a cliff, right before things had started to go wrong…

Amaya had almost sensed it; it was that same feeling of wrongness. It wasn't pain, or anything *really* wrong, but something very slight, like a warning whisper to her ears. Back then, she'd felt that same empty feeling, the need for something—a cure, a distraction, perhaps—without understanding why. And in that summer, Kamiko had been the thing that had helped her. Her cure.

Without thinking, she sat down on the bench, proving to herself that that the bench did no harm. Pretending. Trying to control the way she felt, like she had used to…

Amber realized she'd been clinging to her notebook the entire time while walking, the black cover moist because of her sweaty palms. She hated the way she had behaved today, and gulped, swallowing it all up and away.

Then she opened her notebook. *Maybe now was the time to study her drawings and understand them.*

She observed the cats, then the enormous face she had drawn today, the face's eyes she swore she had seen in the TV.

But the more she stared, the more she felt that prickling on her skin and the more she felt that *she* had not made these drawings.

Amber drew. *Only a few lines*, she thought. *She was only going to draw a few lines, and they wouldn't turn into anything.*

She bent down and stretched her arms down to her long socks. She put her hand into her left sock, searching, until she got it; she pulled out her black pen, the one she'd been walking around with all day. The one on the paper.

Her hands moved and moved, or perhaps her pencil was moving. She couldn't tell the difference now.

But then, her lines became rounder, and the next thing she knew, she was drawing two wide circles, eyes much bigger than her own. She wanted to stop, but this time the eyes filled the whole page, and the iris *was* the pupil of the eye, all in her wacky Japanese-cartoon style that she always tried to simplify and soften. Her style was all cartoon, probably inspired subconsciously by what she watched on TV, but sometimes she surprised herself with how realistic her drawings could look. How creepily lifelike. She'd always rip the page out when this happened unexpectedly; this, she knew, couldn't have come from the shows she watched.

She stopped.

As Amber stared at the eyes before her, at the petrified expression, she knew that the eyes were *trapped*. The eyes were trapped. She did not understand yet, but she knew—she felt a terrible certainty—that the eyes were, somehow, trapped on the page.

And… *they were exactly the same as the ones she had seen on the screen*. Trapped in the TV screen.

Amber shivered as she saw what she had done.

That was when she realized that all the lines she'd drawn were digging deeply right into the paper, as she had pressed with too much strength. She realized that all the feelings she was trying to suppress were now only a single memory in her head. Of that summer. Of taking care of that small kitten. Kamiko.

Almost automatically, her eyes scanned downwards and spotted something by her feet: a blueberry. It was bruised and discoloured. She stomped on it as hard as she could.

There was no sense in what she was doing, she reminded herself. *Her mind had slipped again, remembering things by accident, because she wanted to* feel *again. Feel immersed.*

Happy. Because she wanted to be as sure of things and under-stand as much as Amaya had.

But Amber was sure of only one thing now: she had lost her way to the shop.

* * *

After a while of sketching and doodling, Amber brought organization back to her mind. She knew her mind had slipped, on unwanted feelings and memories, things she hadn't meant to remember, but she had to keep going. She would not allow herself to slip again.

She got up and decided the day had tired her. She'd go to the shop later, unless she happened to stumble over it on her way back. *Where was it again?* Amber was sure that, when she'd said she knew the way, there had been a map of turns and streets in her mind, but it all seemed jumbled and nonsensical to her now.

She passed by more houses and houses, trying to find out where she was, but still with no clear direction. The thought that she was moving blindly along the streets startled her, and so she turned, trying to retrace her steps, at least to places she'd been to today. But she grew unsure where she'd even come from.

Amber decided to cross a road…

The road was longer than usual, and wider, too. Her eyes trailed upwards, and she spotted a traffic light. Red.

Amber stumbled back just in time with a yelp as a car zoomed straight past her. Puzzled, and with little thought, she waited for the green-blue light before crossing properly.

But… Her body froze. She knew very well that *there were no traffic lights in her town.* She felt sick.

That moment, she heard familiar voices. Amber turned, and her stomach lurched as she saw them. She had never expected to find them here. *This was what happened if she wandered around with no direction.*

She scanned their cold, deadly faces, as if to make sure it really was them. But of course she recognized their swaggering movements, their chins held up proudly to the sky. And one of them—Amber did not even know her name—walked in front, as always, the other two—or maybe it was three or four—following, not unlike slaves. It was *the* Gang.

Amber glanced around, trying to ground herself in some familiar landmark. She was standing in front of a tall house, in an unknown neighbourhood. She cursed herself. *How far had she walked?* There were many more foreign buildings here, and the ocean was suddenly nowhere in view. She caught sight of small children walking about on errands, and people having lively conversations, something she rarely saw in the small area she lived.

Standing in the shadow of the building, her hands hidden behind her back, she tried to stay unnoticed. But she was wearing her uniform from school. And with her messy, long golden curls and sea-coloured eyes, she knew she couldn't escape. The Gang marched towards her, pointing.

Still, Amber pretended she had not seen them. Although her insides were screaming, she slowly strolled back into the somewhat quieter street she had come from.

But they followed.

As they reached her, she knew she had no choice anymore. She did not run.

She opened her notebook, pretending to be reading something, as she stared at the cats and the eyes she had drawn. She pretended this was something not really happening to her, a dream, perhaps, in her head.

But a shadow came over her. With cruel, wide smirks on their identical faces, they grew together into a single thing, and trapped Amber at the wall.

The nearby sounds of chatter and children's squeals grew distant, muffled. For she was on the other side of the house. It seemed the single wall separated her from the outside reality, and now it was unreachable. She was only *here*.

A well-known panic filled her, and she let her arms drop by her sides, in helplessness.

The Gang started their game by commenting on her uniform. *It looked so ugly on her, did it not, and why* was *she even wearing it?* They giggled in their own bright, flashy clothing of fashion trends that Amber could never understand. She preferred her uniform, anyway.

And then they talked some more. The Gang spoke words with their glittery red-smeared lips, and the words were all meaningless to Amber. *Words were all they were.*

Words she could ignore, if she wanted to.

They gave smiles that were fake before their faces went back into the shapes of monsters; long, sinister-looking eyebrows facing down like knives, cackling in their high-pitched, fake way of speech.

They were a messy cloud of muddled laughter and faces, seemingly millions of eyes staring at only her. She didn't know any of their names, if this monster even had one at all.

One of them said something like, *Let's take her to the Konbini mart. Make her get us some gum.*

Amber didn't look at them. *Words were all they were.*

But the next thing she knew, she was being pushed, pushed

through the crowd of the monster's hands, into a new turn. As she was pulled, stumbling over other feet, she couldn't shake off the fact that, for the first time that day, she was going an actual direction, not wandering aimlessly. She was almost glad.

You're coming with us, coming with us. The monster snickered.

Leave me alone. But the bare weight of the words in her mouth drowned her, and Amber couldn't even speak or fight the current. What could she do but let them?

And the next thing she was aware of, they had brought her to a convenience shop.

It was the shop she'd been searching for all day.

But Amber knew now was not the time to do her shopping.

The front row at the counter was neatly lined up with all flavours of chewing gum: strawberry, lemon, raspberry, apple. Blueberry.

Will you get us some? The monster asked.

She squeaked out something about not having any money, although she carried a five thousand yen note in her pocket, the cash from the table at home.

Then, the monster said, *steal.*

Why?

But as she looked at their faces, it was clear she could not understand this monster, ever. Before, she had tried. But no, she could never understand them.

Steal, they repeated.

I can't steal. She gulped.

Why not?

It's wrong.

She didn't know what made her do it. Maybe it was a slight feeling, those wretched memories. Maybe it was Amaya, for only one second.

But her feet steered her away, and she ran out of the shop.

She nearly tripped again as she stumbled away, trying to reach a place somewhere, *anywhere* else…

Yet it took only five seconds until the dull thud of many sneakers followed.

Approaching from behind, the current of monsters and laughter picked Amber up again. This time she didn't even try to protest.

The next moment, they were back at the wall.

When she had first joined the school, everyone had been curious. Interested, ignorant. She was something new—nothing ever happened in this small town. She had been something scary, something confusing, something to pick on. A creative outlet.

Amber was used to it. Nasty comments, provoking smirks curled into paper balls flung at her desk with things written on them that she didn't bother to read. It was annoying. But it did not *hurt* her.

Sometimes, she even liked it. Sometimes, it distracted her from other things. So, usually, it didn't hurt, and was just boring. At least, that was what she told herself.

And for a moment, one face shrank back a little, the smile dropping, the face softening. For a split second, Amber caught sight of the smallest hint of something darker in the eye. Something poor, something scared, something trapped. Trapped, like the eyes in her drawing.

She recognized the expression, yet pretended she never saw. She pretended she never saw the own *fear* in the Gang's eyes.

But this time it was different. And as much as Amber pretended it was not, her feelings were different today.

Because they saw her notebook. And they snatched it from her hand. She lost the grip on her notebook.

Amber's stomach formed a huge, thick knot and her chest started to feel very heavy when she saw her drawings a foot away from her. One of them had a water bottle, and another opened it.

Oh, she should have done what they had said!

The monsters destroyed her order, the thing that kept Amber together, causing chaos in the air. And this time everything was different, because it had been unexpected, because she grew confused. She lost sense with herself and her surroundings. For a second, everything felt distant and unreal.

They had destroyed her drawings, and this time, she snapped.

For the first time, Amber was hurt. Something hurt, because she didn't know what to do and they were all looking at her and her notebook was dripping. For the first time, she cried, she really *cried*, and she let all those memories, those vulnerable feelings, out in their wet, hot, horrid nakedness.

She felt lost now, like she had no grip on anything anymore. Not even her notebook…

Again, she ran, with no proper direction, not even with the Gang's.

Again, she sat feeding the cats. Feeding her thoughts into cats.

Except, Amber was drawing them on herself. On her palm, knowing she could wash them off later, as long as her mother did not notice. She was back at the cat-less bench from earlier. She had a few tears running down her face.

Amber knew it was nonsense for her to sketch such creepy cats, but it wasn't like she could help it. She knew it was a bad habit, but she told herself there was nothing extraordinary about it, as it set things *right*. That was her reason; drawing made things seem right. And the cats seemed to come to her.

Again, she asked herself how she hadn't seen a single real cat today. *But maybe it was because this place had changed a lot since she had last come here. After all, this bench was not on her usual way to school. She had only visited it three times since moving here.*

And it was summer. The cats were probably all sitting lazily in the sun by the docks. Cats were such bored, funny creatures. Bored, but careless. Amber wished she were like them; she was bored, but she cared, even if she never admitted it.

After the unexpected meeting of the Gang, she had immediately fled, leaving her ruined drawings behind. She knew that, next time, she needed to stop them. She couldn't say exactly why she hadn't this time—why she hadn't tried, at least, to stop them.

Amber placed down her pen onto the bench and sighed. *This wasn't helping at all.*

She thought of how she had let her memories, her feelings, take hold of her far too much today.

But she knew *why* she kept thinking of the past. It was the one thing she understood.

It was because she had once been so sure of the world. Of the logic in it, her place in it. She had felt so deeply, and so properly. And yet she'd been able to control her feelings, not let them control her.

But now she couldn't. After her parents had broken up, and the move, she'd left her carefree life behind, and it was like her controlled, firm feelings had slipped out of her grip... and her whole world had fallen apart.

Amber had tried for *so* long to ignore this, to set things right, to understand her confusion. But now she grew tired of trying to understand. She couldn't understand the Gang, couldn't understand how much she'd changed, not even her own cat drawings.

And sometimes, of course, she wished it were like before.

Amber hated the way she had reacted earlier. Still, she wished, wished for... *something to change.*

In the most realistic *way.*

But she knew it was impossible.

After a while, Amber knew sitting here was pointless, and

she decided she would escape this uneasy place. The bench faced that same ocean view but was on the side of the street. She started walking away when she realized she'd forgotten her pen.

She could not find it on the bench. As she crouched to look for it on the ground, she realized something.

This bench had been her favourite spot. Somehow, she'd forgotten it all.

The spot backed onto buildings made of stone. In front of them, right behind the bench, grew a thick cluster of bushes.

Amber frowned. She had paid no attention to these bushes today, as she'd forgotten what they were, perhaps because they were so odd. They were, of course, blueberry bushes.

This had been her favourite spot. But not *only* because she liked blueberries.

Rather, it was the strangeness of the place…

Amaya had always known it was odd for blueberries to grow on the street—she'd *felt* this fact; a crawling beneath her skin. But here they did.

The bushes looked unhealthy and grew out in a wobbly, wild shape, with not even a fence to separate them from the bench. They simply grew *behind* the bench, and it looked like they were growing *out of it*. And she knew right behind them were the very edges of two houses, an odd design she'd also never understood.

So, this place, the bushes, had always made her skin crawl, the back of her neck prickle. There was just something about it, something perhaps unexplainable, about the way this was the only bench in the street. The way that a berry plopped down sadly every few minutes, and thorns and twigs poked into anyone sitting there.

But Amaya had seen this as a sort of challenge. One thing

she never listened to was her intuition. The reason that this place *felt* strange had never been something she liked. So, she always came here to feed cats, ignore the strangeness and enjoy the bushes, showing off how the bench was fine! Or perhaps it *had* scared her somehow, and she'd just never wanted to admit it.

But now Amber didn't know what was happening to her. She knew she did not have her intuition out of her way completely, like she used to. She found it harder to ignore her feelings today.

She wanted to leave, but as she stared through the two bushes, she spotted that between where the two houses ended, there was a gap. And in that space, on the ground, almost hidden by the bushes, was her pen.

Amber groaned. But she knew her pencils were at home and all now the size of her little finger, and her notebook, of course, was as good as gone. She loved that pen.

She bent down beside the bench and got on her knees. Reaching out her hand wasn't enough, so she half-crawled under the bench, nearing the gap… She could see it now. She grabbed her pen.

Getting up, Amber was about to walk back in the direction she had come from when she felt a desperate tug inside her.

She was so tired of trying to understand…

And yet, and yet.

She shuddered at the way the fat, juicy berries gleamed out memories in the afternoon summer sun. She couldn't understand why this made her unable to look away, and feel unusually… *cold*.

But she had to set things right in her head. *She had to show herself that there was nothing wrong.*

And… perhaps this was her chance, her chance to prove

that she wasn't any more afraid than Amaya after all. That she could understand as much as she used to.

All she needed to do was see what was behind the gap. See that there was *not* anything scary.

Besides, now Amber knew she could not go off and leave this place, tolerating the odd idea she had of it in her head. Now, it was too late to leave.

With a sigh, she turned to see no one was looking. The streets remained empty. She left her pen on the bench.

She had no other option but to squeeze between the bench and the bushes and duck *under* them, lying her whole body on the ground. The soft texture told her it was grass, even though she could barely see her hands in the shadows of the bushes.

In this way, she wiggled through them. Twigs and sticks occasionally scraped her head, and she even felt a blueberry roll onto her. Strangely, there was a small distance *between* the grassy ground and the bushes, so she could fit.

She travelled through. Now she could no longer feel any grass, only normal street pavement.

Lying on the ground, hidden behind the bushes, Amber felt extremely stupid. Both walls of the houses were next to her now, and she was facing the gap, open, great and blinding. Great and... *blinding*. There was a light stinging her eyes. Dazzling, like when you stepped inside into the dusty blackness of buildings after having stared at the sun outside. Amber couldn't pinpoint where it was coming from. But there was something, something very *new*, that the gap led to. Something that she still couldn't see.

She rose to her feet, pushing herself even further through the walls, with half-closed eyes.

When she opened them again, she winced, a splitting pain

in her head. The light was crisp and white, intenser than before.

It soon seemed to her that she had got into a new neighbourhood. *But not quite.* All she knew was that only houses and houses surrounded her, and that she must have been in some narrow, hidden street corner, or a tight passage leading onto somewhere. Surrounded by what seemed only walls, which almost seemed to close in on her, she lost a bit of her breath.

Amber soon saw that only one foot away, the hard street ground stopped and something soft and green that looked like grass started again. *But, very different.*

Although Amber had thought it was boring, for a moment she missed the ocean view, the fresher air. *This was another place, a place somewhere else.*

She observed the grass but could only frown at it. She tried looking back at the gap to figure out where it started but saw a definite, almost straight line dividing the grass from the pavement. Except the line was more *wonky* than straight. It wasn't quite right.

She reached out her hand and touched it. The softness surprised her. It did not look like normal grass, but was the colour of crocodiles. Something else about the ground resembled crocodiles too; it was the unusual, sharp, snappy way the blades of grass ended in their stems, although in a smooth, stylish manner.

Amber shook her head again. *It was just grass.*

For a while, she stood and let her gaze focus on nothing in particular, allowing her eyes to adjust to the light. Or perhaps her body was too frozen to move. It was shaking with that same feeling of something being wrong.

But, still, she needed to show herself that all was all right.

That light remained in her eyes, but, swallowing, Amber studied the shapes of houses she could make out. She was, in fact, surrounded by houses, and houses only. But only the backs of houses. On all sides were the empty walls of houses, windowless walls that touched. It was like she was in some kind of backyard, a space in between neighbouring houses. But this made little sense to her; this space was only reachable through the blueberry bush entry. There was something about the way this spot was so *private*, the way there were no windows or doors, that made her feel sick.

As she looked up, she realized she couldn't see any roofs. Only walls, reaching up… and then cutting away. Either the buildings had no proper roofs, or she was placed in a very big box.

Amber thought this assuming the walls were of normal houses, but the more she looked, the more the nausea rose in her stomach.

There was something drawn on the back of the houses, in colours and strokes so soft that the white light prevented her from seeing properly. She still couldn't even figure out where it was coming from. Not from above, she knew, as the sunlight wasn't so bright here. There was a bursting whiteness in her field of vision, perhaps something *in* her eye.

But from what she could make out, the walls of the houses were… painted. As she stood observing for a few minutes, she found the white light grew weaker.

And she saw that the walls were blue. Swirly, pearly-white clouds looked like they had been dabbed with some fine brush onto what looked like the exact shade of the sky.

A whole new panic set in Amber's stomach as she took a step back and examined the walls. Left, right, on all her sides, and above her, was the same blue sky.

For a second, she questioned everything. *Which side was left? Which sky was the true one? Was she the correct way up herself?*

There was something else.

On the wall of the house straight ahead of her, there was a drawing. It was two lines crossing over each other, forming an X. It looked like someone had spray-painted it onto the house, and… very *neatly*.

Amber scratched her head and asked herself what she was doing in this place. *She really, really was in a place somewhere else.*

For a moment, she sat down on the crocodile ground. Her lip quivered. Her mind was buzzing, and she tried to come to conclusions, tried to think, but her thoughts turned blank, and all she could do was laugh, tell herself it was fine. *Fine.* She'd come to reassure that to herself, after all.

But in that moment, she couldn't help asking herself why she *had* come here.

Amber shivered. *She had thought, thought that maybe, if she could show herself there was nothing behind the gap, nothing, at least scary, all would be fine. She'd have conquered a fear that even Amaya couldn't. She'd have been better than Amaya—not worse. But now she was here.*

Then there was a noise.

There was a feeling.

Amber got to her feet, having known all along she would soon need to return home.

Yet she was already there, and she could already feel it.

It was like a hidden force, not just her urge to understand, but something more, something physical, pushing her closer to the wall in front. What felt like two heavy blows of wind hit her face, making her yelp out in pain.

The spray-painted X on the wall appeared to be getting bigger, like the drawing was being peeled off the wall. It was coming to life.

Suddenly the colour in her vision intensified, the strange light hurting her eyes again, and when the unpleasant feeling stopped, her eyes still stinging, everything looked crystalized, somehow doll-like, less realistic.

The X sprang in front of her. Amber could not tell whether it was still stuck to the wall, or gliding in the air.

Behind the X, she saw more trees and more grass. Behind the X there seemed to be a new *scenery*. But the X was a cutting line.

Amber screamed, because she knew this was not something she had meant to see. It was something terrible, the worst horror, the unexpected.

And in the centre of the X hung something dark, grey and fuzzy.

She could see something else. Behind the X, next to the trees. She could see *things…* she caught a glimpse of *something…* but she did not know what they were.

Her stomach lurched and Amber gasped, but it sounded more like a question. *What? Was she meant to be here?*

She tried to turn, but somehow she was still eyeing the X out of the corner of her eyes, and the force grew stronger.

She fell onto her knees on the stupid, stupid crocodile ground.

There was nothing she could do; she was facing it, right there.

"*Uhhh…*" Amber stared as the X came closer, closer.

It reached out to her.

And there *was* a time for her to run, like with the Gang. For a second, she *could* escape.

But she was startled, she was frozen, and tears ran down her face, because deep down, she *had* to see, see what this was all about.

The world had stopped, and everything was shaking, and she wished she had never come here.

But the grey thing, whatever it was, choked her and held her by the throat. It looked like the hand of an old man, with fur on it.

The hand pulled her. She fell into the X.

Thud. Her eyes turned dark.

* * *

Amber was sleeping in her bed.

When she awoke, she still kept her eyes closed. She didn't want to see, hear, or face anything. She wanted only to feel the cushiony softness of her bedroom mattress, and feel it forever.

And she lay there for a while.

But soon, she could not ignore the pain in her ankle. Soon, she could not ignore how her bed felt different, harder than usual... her bed was a bed of grass.

She was not at home.

Amber was *forced* to get up, her legs aching, because she could no longer pretend.

And she had never seen anything before. Nothing like this.

Everything was lit by blue angel skies that were all in place, with not one cloud. Beside her was a smooth wooden path, bridge-like. It was half-buried into the ground, and took a turn to somewhere she could not see. Amber thought it would be safer to know where it led, but she couldn't move anymore.

Something was swinging in the breeze. *Were they... trees?* They were round, and smooth, almost... *slimy*, and glossy, as if they were oozing with sap. But they weren't shaped like trees. Instead of proper, distinguishable branches, they had other abstract shapes sticking out of them. Soft little balls, or antenna-like bent sticks, in an almost zigzag pattern.

Amber stared at them, trying to understand what they were, only to realize she had been looking at them for minutes. Assuming they *were* trees, she observed how they danced above her, trying to push out any emotions—then, she noticed that they weren't above her. In fact, everything in this place was *miniature*. Everything but that same thing that was just grass, which, ironically, now grew to her knees. It was soft. So, *so* soft, softer than cat fur… She was really trying everything to distract her mind from breaking down. She clenched her teeth, trying to detect the slightest unseen details. And there were many.

But as the warm, alien scents made her face hot and break into a cold sweat, and the terrifying noises in the distance told her blood-curdling stories, her mind slipped and could no longer concentrate on the lovely flowers and the ethereal scenery. She felt dizzy.

It wasn't even like the place she had discovered before the X had got her. It was beautiful, *yes*, the most whimsical thing she had ever seen, but it was too perfect. *Exactly her taste, perhaps.* But time had taught her how foolish she was, how foolish her fantasy-daydream-wants were. That something like this was impossible.

Her eyes fell on the wooden bridge again. She peered around, but she could not figure out how she had got here. It wasn't that she *wanted* to go home, but she *needed* to get back.

Perplexed, Amber explored the bridge. It started here, but she couldn't see the end. On all sides grew more trees and plants.

After a long while, Amber had to admit to herself that the only way she could get back was to regather her knowledge of her surroundings—and follow the bridge. Her legs seemed to be working again, and so she walked, her glance down, only at the long socks peeking out of her shoes.

There seemed to be life here. She could hear it, sense it, in the distant chatter. Again, it sounded perfect, in some way, too good to be true. But it didn't sound so happy.

There was another background noise. Amber knew the sound. Her mother liked to take videos of her on a camera, but when she played them, the sound didn't sound like real life, for the sound was stuck in the camera. It just couldn't quite sound like the actual thing. These sounds were the same; it was as if someone was playing a video of the place.

She halted. In front of her there was a sign hanging about two feet above the top of her head. It read, *A very warm, fuzzy welcome to Catslaughter Island!*

Amber shuddered and whimpered. *What did Cat slaughter mean?* She already hated the thought of it. She hated this place.

She walked further past the sign. The path had ended, and the tall grass had died into a short moss-like ground texture.

Although her legs felt numb, she turned.

Then, she saw it.

It was the most grotesque thing she had ever seen. Yet, something about it was almost fine.

It was that *same*, almost wrong feeling. She could sense it.

Her eyes widened to try to understand it. It was tall and long-limbed, with distorted features and great, goofy, googly eyes staring dead into her, unblinking.

It was nothing like a cat. But it looked like a cat. And

suddenly she could not remove the image of her drawings from her mind.

"OK..." she said. She fell over backwards as her knees knocked into each other.

Then she heard the noise it was making. But she couldn't quite figure out whether it was laughing or screaming. Or whether it was communicating at all. *What had she* done?

She looked at it for a few seconds, but then her feet picked her up again and stumbled away, before her heart could.

The sign was right; this thing was fuzzy, and it certainly looked like a slaughtered cat.

Even when she was hidden between the tree-like plants, which felt sharper than before as they rubbed her skin, she could still feel its dark eyes, comical and empty, boring into her back. Somehow, they reminded her of an open window exposing a hideous living room.

Amber flinched and felt her heart thump violently against her chest. Part of what had appeared to be a beautiful tree—the part that she was touching—was prickly. *So, this dainty place, this ethereal beauty, was here only to disguise the horrors awaiting.*

Her breathing grew rapid and much too short, and she wasn't getting enough air...

A menacing question sneaked up her spine. *Were there more?*

Walking back, she found the bridge, and then she looked for the X, the grand X she'd stupidly fallen into. Surely, that odd opening—that *portal* she had come from—was still there, as much as she hated the idea of what it was. But she couldn't find it again. She couldn't find her exit.

The back of her neck prickled. The sounds returned, and *they were here*, for she could sense it. Somewhere above her, maybe up in a plant, she heard rustling, like she had before, *before*...

She kept running away from the bridge, in the opposite direction—

Amber was gone. She stood back below the sign. Trapped.

Then, she saw them. *They* were taller. Amber gagged.

And it was that same feeling. Of confusion, of losing it all.

CHAPTER 3 – WE WANT YOU

She didn't know how long she had been standing there. The cat-thing from earlier was still looking at her, with dozens more standing behind it.

Groan-like growls and whispery hissing noises sent dread into the air, almost sounding like cats.

Amber felt like she was being choked. All the air was being sucked out of her.

And these beings *looked* almost like cats, but more like humanized ones. More like cats that had fallen off cliffs, cats that had been squished and slaughtered beneath rolling tires, cats that had been drowned. These cats were not cats.

And then they sang. They hummed. It was slow.

Her knees weakly started to give way in a slow, silent scream as she looked at all the distorted faces. All the horrible, *horrible* faces… How she wished to understand them.

They had round, watery blobs for eyes. Small, sharp bumps in the centre of their faces. *Possibly noses?* But no, this couldn't be, for they had no slits for nostrils. *Perhaps that was why their mouths hung almost constantly open—to breathe?*

But no, their mouths only seemed open because there was something fat and bulgy growing around them, blocking space for intake of air. *Maybe cats had lips?* But no, their lips were certainly human-like, and even more swollen and blistered than human lips. And they had slim, human-like bodies with limbs that looked like arms and legs. *Maybe it wasn't too odd for cats to stand on two legs?* But no, no. They could not be explained.

Amber forced herself back up again, lightly punching herself in the ribs. It was as if she were in a nightmare, where she knew where the monster was, she knew she had to scream, but she couldn't get the sound out properly, and it only sounded like something stupid, as her legs stood still. Like she felt with the Gang.

She wanted to run. But she was trapped. She wanted to close her eyes. Maybe if she couldn't see what was happening, then it wasn't happening. But Amber couldn't close her eyes.

So, she did the next best thing: she raised her tight, sweaty hand and held it above her eyes, shielding her face with her palm.

She could still see them out of the corner of her eye and through the spaces between her fingers. *Peekaboo.* But maybe they couldn't see her.

So, Amber stood there, like a ridiculous baby, playing peekaboo with them, as she heard them communicate.

It was perhaps her concentrated listening, but slowly it seemed to her that they weren't hissing or groaning at all but *talking.* She shuddered. They spoke *words*. Except they swallowed the spaces between their words, slurping them up like a bowl of noodles.

"So, isthis *the* Girl?"

"I thinkso butis shedangerous?"

"She's notevenJapanese…"

"*Halfmoon* choseher."

"We've beenwaiting forweeks!"

They spoke in a very, very strange way. Like their throats and mouths were stuffed with lots of wet, filthy cotton. Amber's ears could not even quite pick it up.

But whatever was going on, they knew *more*.

Suddenly, all the talking and the hissing were silenced. Silenced by a single figure—Amber dared remove her hand, and she looked to see a smaller creature.

The other things were all dim, and their colours were all murky, rotten. And their eyes were enormous, shrunken, googly, and empty.

But this one had fur *actually* grey, and shiny, like light upon gems. With smart blue eyes, it seemed to be their leader…

It stepped in through the waves of slender cat-creatures, and they moved around it—not one touching it as it casually walked through.

The things even seemed to bow before this new thing, and screamed, "Bow before the Great Moon! Before theGreat-Moon! BeforetheGreatMoon! The GreatMoon! Bow before Its majesty!"

Amber waited, wanting to know finally if she was going to get eaten or not.

"Stop speaking," the new Thing commanded, waving up something that looked like a hand.

All the other things stopped their noises.

The grey cat-creature fixed Its magnificent eyes on Amber's and muttered the words softly, "Follow me, girl." She did not hear the squeak or the hiss sound in Its voice. There was something about It that made It look and sound more *human* than the others.

But she did not follow. She stayed, staring, trying to shake out the rest of the things in her vision, and focusing only on this one.

The Thing turned Its head to look at her properly again, and her stomach churned as she saw the others were mimicking It. All the cat-creatures tilted their heads slightly at only her.

She just stood. And stared.

Amber could not help herself. She giggled, without meaning to. She giggled into the white noise-like silence, the weird noise, without really feeling amused, only bewildered, at this nonsense. Perhaps to soften or sweeten what was in front of her.

A wide, toothless-looking grin also spread across the Thing's face. "Girl! Girl! *Now*, child!"

She did not react.

"But come, come! We all have waited."

Amber laughed, not knowing what had got into her. She laughed because now she felt amused, and these creatures looked so funny. The child-like noise reached the air and everyone's ears, fragile, but truly clueless. The slender things were odd. She knew they weren't right, yet found they were just so *funny*.

She laughed, not noticing the prickle of tears forming in her eyes, running down her face, or her legs slowly giving in.

And then it happened.

The cat-creatures laughed back, but this noise made Amber stop. She stopped moving, stopped laughing, stopped breathing. Because the creatures, as their lips made hideous, head-splitting sounds, made Amber feel unsure again whether they were really laughing, or making other sounds.

Their lips moved and moved, and their eyes focused on nothingness, the pupils rounding, the faces tensing, as they stared up at the sky and laughed and guffawed and screamed. The lips expanded too, as if starting to form something new, something perhaps alive itself, just within their features.

A few feet away, Amber observed passively, her own lips forming a small "Oh" sound as she saw some tumble over with the commotion and fall into each other, screams filling the air with their sharp pain, so that her lungs almost hurt in response as she breathed in. It was as if she were breathing in their poison.

The leader seemingly thought it had gone too far, and screamed, "SILENCE!"

The things replied with more cheers of "Great Moon!" and kept screaming all at the same time. But one second later, they all suddenly stood silent, with blank expressions on their faces, as if they *could* no longer form words. As if with the small hand movement, they were unable to speak. As if the Great Moon had turned them off.

The Thing that they bowed to and called the Great Moon looked at Amber and said, "Child, you come."

She still felt lightheaded, and her feet felt out of place. She looked up at them to realize she had fallen to the ground and had trouble getting up. Somehow, she regained her voice, but it was hoarse from laughing, so she cleared her throat.

"Uh—sorry, b-but… it's *Amber*," she burst out to the Thing.

It stared. "Sorry?"

"My name is… Amber?" It was as if she were unsure of her own words.

"Oh. Well, come, Amber."

And then It led her away from the cat-creatures and the entrance; she obeyed, wanting more than anything to leave what was behind her—even if it meant leaving the entrance, the X.

Amber decided to let It take her. She didn't know what else to do. Her insides screamed and churned.

Slowly, she drew breaths again, but they were still shallow as she awkwardly paced behind.

Mossy, yet sandy ground was everywhere they walked. Small wooden buildings that looked like moss-covered houses with half-open roofs stood even higher than where Amber and the Thing were walking, on what looked like an elevated jelly platform. The platform went on in a wavy, zigzag pattern, a miniature mountain range, up and down. On the highest point of each mountain, there was one house. Then, when the mountain dropped like a wave, an empty space, then a house again, and so the pattern followed, lining the edge of a huge camp.

This was their *camp. They lived here.*

But there was something more to these houses. They could have been any type of oddly-constructed wooden buildings, but somehow, as Amber saw them, she knew they were *bedrooms*. It wasn't only their one-room size, but something else, more like a simple feeling to them, that told her these were for sleeping. It seemed as the sun shone stronger in the sky, the jelly platform wobbled a little unsteadily, rocking the houses like little cradles. She pictured these funny, vicious cat creatures inside them, snoring away lazily in the sun, *drool dripping from their blistered, horrible lips...* Amber shuddered.

Great Moon turned Its head for a second, as if having

noticed something was off, and gave her a bright, stomach-churning smile. Then It turned away again.

Amber kept up her pace behind It.

In what appeared to be the midpoint of the camp stood a long table. The table—she squinted—appeared to be *floating in mid-air*. But she wasn't sure, as it floated at a low height. Amber hoped it was a trick of her eyes. Otherwise, she didn't think she liked it.

The leader stopped in front of a cabin and opened the door.

Amber was unsure whether she was meant to enter, but a nod pressured her to squeeze in. She accidentally knocked over several bottles and glass containers from the shelves that were inside.

She hadn't even regained her voice to apologize, but the Thing did not seem to mind, anyway.

"Forget that."

Amber spotted a chair in the corner of the cabin and made her way towards it, ducking her head to avoid the ceiling. But as she walked, she realized the ceiling was quite high after all. It was as if everything in this place was unsure of her height. Nothing felt certain.

She noted she was bigger than this grey Thing, and she could probably beat It in a fight. Or maybe it was something about Its eyes, eyes unlike others, that made her feel less uneasy. The eyes were... *kind*. They reminded her of an aged, soothing grandfather.

But she would not judge Its eyes. So, she still laughed.

She waited for some sort of explanation. *Or finally, her warm, fuzzy welcome.* She waited for It to talk, waited for answers...

The Thing held out an unexpected hand—or whatever it was—towards her.

Amber dug her nails into her right hand. She knew this creature had somehow brought her here. She had somehow been brought into Its place, into Its wacky bubble of a world.

And it was something that had never been meant to occur. Something by a very slim chance, a thing that should only have happened in a parallel universe. But never like this, not to her.

Unable to form her own words, she let It talk. All the air had been sucked from her lungs, and she stared at It as the blood left her face and her breath seized, not being able to blick away tears.

The Thing grinned. Amber's stomach dropped, noticing that the grin literally met Its ears.

"Are you quite all right?" It asked.

Amber grinned herself, but in panic, not knowing how to act.

Then It gave her those seemingly soothing eyes, those full of goodness and understanding.

She waited, and after an empty minute had passed, the Thing scrunched up Its face oddly, almost as if It had expected her to introduce herself.

Then, It started, "Why, hello, child—or, *Amber.* Please forgive me for that."

Amber raised her eyebrows, yet they rose a bit higher than she'd intended. It was like she could not control herself.

But she wanted answers.

"What—what am I *doing* here?!" she demanded, taking advantage of the fact that she wasn't being attacked.

"Patience, patience," It replied. "First, let's finish off our little introduction, shall we?"

And then—Amber had no other way to describe it—It reached *into* Itself, into Its fur, as if Its body was a place for storage, and pulled out a handful of peach-coloured sweets. At least, that was what she thought they were. They were about the size of hazelnuts, in soft, dainty wrappers.

She recognized them as Japanese candy that was sold at the Konbini mart near her house. Or, at least, they *looked* like them… There was something about the fine, intricate details of their wrappers, their slightly stickier, fatter-looking shapes, the way they looked in the hazy sunlight shining into this cabin, that seemed different…

The creature held out Its hand—or whatever it was—full of sweets to her, closer, closer, as It grinned again and met her eyes.

Amber's eyes prickled with tears. She wasn't sure if she was meant to take one of these sweets. These sweets that were *almost* like the ones in her home, yet different.

But the creature didn't wait for her to take one.

Instead, as It held out Its hand, It said, "I am Halfmoon. I am *It*; the Great Moon, as Cats also call me. It is my role to lead and protect this part of the island. I *care* for everyone."

Then It pushed the sweets closer.

Amber was somewhat relieved that she was finally getting her explanations.

Her whole body was still tense, but she decided to take one.

Halfmoon grinned.

She unwrapped the sweet. As she had thought, the wrapper was thinner, and more transparent and crumpled than the ones in her town.

Amber wasn't at all scared that it could be poison. There was something about it, something about it being almost the same sweets, that assured her it was not. Or maybe she was too terrified to resist.

She put the small, soft, rosy ball into her mouth. It was exactly the same taste as the ones in her town… *And yet different.*

As Amber chewed and chewed, she became aware once again of where she was and what was happening. She swallowed, then asked, "But why *can* you even speak? You and… and your—your *things*—?!"

"My cats. We are Cats, just *cats*."

Amber thought. "And this is *Cat slaughter* Island?"

Halfmoon exploded into laughter, and did not stop chuckling until It saw the seriousness on her face. It placed the rest of the sweets on the table in front of her.

"No. This is Cats*laughter*. Cats' laughter! We are simply Cats, cats that laugh. I asked my Cats a long time ago what we should call our island. And they gave me the sound of laughter, so I decided on that."

She studied Halfmoon. *It had sounded more like screaming.* "And you have hands."

"Just call those Paws. There are a lot of things on our island that—how should I say? … *Are just called.*"

"Why—?"

"Shh. We do not ask so much. Our existence is *completely* logical! We all live in another place, a place parallel to Japan. Want another sweet?"

But the words sank in. *A place parallel to Japan.* Amber didn't want another sweet. "Japan… Japan exists in another *world* than—than Catslaughter Island?"

"Put simply, we are in another realm than Earth."

She grinned. *This wasn't possible.*

Halfmoon seemed to mistake her grin. "Very impressive, right? One would never find Catslaughter Island on Earth."

She almost replied that she had, in fact, found it on Earth.

But she remembered the X. *And she had not found the Portal; she had been* brought *here,* taken *by these Cats, by their force.*

"We are Cats. I have to apologize actually in advance for my Cats. I see they startled you. I try to silence them with magic when exciting things like these happen, but they speak a lot—"

"With… magic?"

"Yes, magic. *Mahou energy*, as some also call it. But I think that sounds too fancy, *too much*. I say magic. Talented as I am, I am the only one who can use the magic properly. I am the one who allows and decides when my Cats can speak. Sometimes, I give them free will of speech, but otherwise… Well, you never know what might come out of a Cat's mouth!" Halfmoon gave a goofy laugh, and it was as if It had told a joke Amber could not understand.

"Anyway," It went on. "I was saying… We are Cats, Cats that have come through the Portal, the very one *you* entered to find this place. It is the thing that links our two realities. The very Portal that you saw in Japan. We came a long time ago, long before this generation of Cats. I am the oldest alive here. Over time, we have adapted magic and abilities, as well as some intelligence, at least for *some* of us, in this realm. I, for instance, am blessed with power and knowledge. And we created land."

Amber shook her head. "But, er—"

"Amber, how do you feel? Yes, I appreciate your concern about the logic in our bare existence, and I do worry about that constantly, but you may leave it all up to my decisions. Trust in me, as everycat does. Everycat trusts me. Everycat trusts me."

Amber felt unreal, talking to this Thing. Words spilled from her mouth, completely beyond her control.

Then, Halfmoon clapped Its Paws together and let a huge smirk run across Its face. Amber found that Halfmoon let Itself get quite enthusiastic, but never expressed more emotion than was needed.

"As I mentioned," It went on. "I am amongst the most talented of Cats. I do not even have the regular Cat's lifespan. I invent and create very often. In fact, I have made many inventions. Many, as I call them, Gadgets. I'd like to show you."

Still not knowing what was going on, Amber watched Halfmoon turn to Its many shelves. They were, in fact, filled with inventions, filled with outlandish objects and technology that looked as if they were from the future. But she could not focus. It was as if there was a force, a force in front of her that pulled her face, did not allow tears to fall, did not allow her to scream, but just sit passively, suffering, smiling, and letting this happen.

She watched Halfmoon. *Halfmoon made inventions using magic. It created strange Gadgets and was talented. Everyone —everycat—liked It. Halfmoon was the leader, at least of this part of the island. This part of the island must have been the entrance of the realm, as the Portal—the X—transported anyone who entered it to this specific place.*

Amber watched Halfmoon go on. Everything was too overwhelming. It pointed at multiple strange objects on Its shelves, mostly bragging about what good quality they all were, how much work It had put into them, and how everycat loved them.

Still not being able to focus, she muttered, "What did you say this has to do with me—er, *Sir*?"

Halfmoon stopped and smiled. "My Gadgets, these inventions, have shown me something terrible."

"Shown... you...?"

"One of my inventions, for instance, is like an invisible

eye. I have a lot of them. I call them my *Eyes*. They can see far into places that are not where I stand physically."

"Like—like a camera?"

"Precisely. They also show the magic energy around us. I have one of these cameras, I should say, guarding the Portal, right outside of Japan. Because the Portal brings anyone who enters directly to Catslaughter Island, I, of course, do not want evil to come, so I watch it regularly, making sure that no Human enters. In the past, there have been wars, even, as bad Humans have tried taking over. But nothing of the sort has happened in a long time, as Humans these days, they only care about their own things. Besides, I have power and control over… well, a lot. I do. However, about a week ago, my Portal view has shown me danger. Terror. Terror in the distance that is planning on coming. I assume it is a bad Human. The Terror is coming. The Terror is on its way to enter the Portal."

An evil person was planning on attacking this island.

"I just know," Halfmoon insisted. "I just know. My inventions are very reliable. They would never lie. And I know, in not too many days' time, the Terror will enter the Portal, to Catslaughter Island."

"So," Amber mumbled, feeling dizzy again. It almost hurt her to speak. "You want me to stop this… *terror*?" She gave a little laugh.

Halfmoon gasped and looked at her for a moment, as if she were very clever. "Yes! Fortunately, there is a time difference between the Human world and this realm. Time ticks *much* faster here, meaning we have time before the Terror arrives from the Human world."

It went on, and she let It, "My Eyes have shown me that danger is coming. But *another* one of my inventions showed me how to stop it."

It produced a sphere-like Gadget that resembled a crystal. Amber could see her own reflection in it.

"This tells destiny," Halfmoon said. "It is different from a time-teller, which, er, does not exist. Anyway, it tells destiny. It has shown me that *you* are the one; it is your destiny to save Catslaughter Island from its doom!"

It made it all seem like a fun game, speaking in a tone as if to a small child.

Amber looked at Halfmoon, and then she laughed. Spluttering, she tried to stop but failed miserably.

Halfmoon's enthusiastic face dropped. "What amuses you? See, your face is even inside it."

"That's my *reflection*," she explained.

A destiny, a clear, chosen path, was too unrealistic to hope for. That was what she knew.

Halfmoon looked dumbstruck. Again, It gave her that look, as if It had not expected her to understand the truth.

"Excuse me," It said in a smaller voice. "The average intelligence in Catslaughter Island is very low. I did not expect you to get that."

It looked away for a moment, as if in thought, and then explained, "Sorry, but it is not common for me to lie. Everycat trusts me, I swear, everycat trusts me. You are right. It is not destiny; you are not chosen. But I choose you. Out of all the Humans in your area, in your city, in Japan, we want you. You may not be chosen by magic, but I guess I could say you were at the right place at the right time. Quite literally. I have been *waiting*. I still would like your help. Yes? It is logical. You, a Human, can prevent this from happening, from the outside of the Portal! Want another sweet?"

"What do you mean, you've been waiting?" she asked, ignoring Its last offer.

"Well," Halfmoon started. "It is a bit… complicated. But over a week ago, I saw you in the camera. I saw you sitting on that bench outside of the Portal. For you, that was only about half an hour ago. And in that moment, I knew that you could help us. It is simple logic to have a Human stop another Human from coming, without us Cats having to get involved out *there*. I… please forgive me, stole your pen, placed it closer to the Portal, and then sent a magic force… And so, we waited—several weeks, in our time—for you to notice, drove you closer to the Portal, and now you've come!"

"Oh. A trap—?"

"But not a trap! Amber, are you all right?"

"What do you mean?!" she replied.

"*It* is all right. This is what you can do. Your life would be better. This is a great thing."

Amber could not think. She did not even cry or laugh anymore, and there was nothing she could do.

"You need to travel back to Japan to do this, naturally."

She shifted her attention to these words. "So, I-I just go back and *enter*… the Portal… again?"

At this, Halfmoon winced. "Essentially, yes. However, be aware, the Portal is only one-way. The Portal in Japan, the one you came from, the one I received you from to tell you all this, is only from Japan *to* Catslaughter Island. But there is no Portal *on* Catslaughter Island. To return to the Human world from here, you need to travel to another island that is near, where there *is* a Portal leading to Japan."

"Uh—" she shook as it all started to sink in. "A-alone?"

"No. One of my Cats will guide you."

At that moment, the door burst open, and a thing entered. Amber shrieked, having become used to Halfmoon's more neutral features. She recognized it as the first Cat she had seen when coming here.

"Speak of the devil!" Halfmoon shouted. "This Cat will take you, Amber. This is, well, Koko."

Amber gave a crooked smile. "Th-this?" She pointed.

Halfmoon must have noticed how she started losing her breath, for It shooed Koko out.

But Amber had already bolted out of the door.

Outside, her nausea returned, as well as her shivers and everything else. She ran, not sure where she was or where she was going, what or who could be watching her, but she wanted to hide.

She found a tall, spongy tree-like plant with long, concealing branches, and hid behind it. Somehow, as she crouched there, she hoped it would be Halfmoon who found her, and no other Cat. Now tears streamed down her face, and she felt like the ignorant thing she was.

She did not feel time pass, but when she looked up, Halfmoon had found her.

Amber couldn't deny that, very strangely, she felt a little… comforted. There was something about Halfmoon, and about the way It spoke words, that she liked. All those explanations.

"Fine," she said. "Fine."

It smiled from ear to ear. "Let us do it, let us help you."

She nodded, not being able to form straight thoughts with all this chaos, without any guidance. Shaking, she stood up.

Halfmoon produced more sweets and handed her some. Amber stuffed them in her pocket, not knowing what else to do.

"One more thing," Halfmoon added. "I will give you a special invention of mine to take on your journey. It is a Gadget. It has been tested out many times. I also must pack you a bag with, er, Human food, and Cat food. Now, I must check that all my inventions work well before you leave. In the meantime, do enjoy a small tour around this part of the island. Enjoy the, er, Cat food. Meet Koko properly."

Although, of course, she hated the strangeness of this place, somehow Amber felt such an overwhelming *relief*—it was the first time in her life that someone had explained things to her.

Koko showed up behind her, nodded, and took her.

When they were alone, Amber didn't dare look at the Cat.

They silently trotted towards the camp and back into the unexplainable.

CHAPTER 4 – A WORLD OF NONSENSE?

Amber was very tall. She was tall for her age, and compared to her peers at school even more so. But these Cats were taller.

The tricky thing was that everything in her vision was shaking (maybe because she was trembling) and the dreamlike atmosphere hadn't quite stuck in her head. It was as if every few seconds she forgot she was there, and then was reminded by the horrors. As if she noticed that the Cats were tall, but her mind couldn't quite work out exactly *how* tall. Everything around her seemed to change every second. Nothing seemed *certain* to her eyes. And she had never felt like this. She had always felt out of place, too tall. But now she felt tiny.

Silently, the girl and the Cat Koko trudged in random directions. Amber wasn't sure where they were going but had no choice other than to follow the tall beast. After all, that was what Halfmoon had told her she should do. Around them, Cats moved about. She wanted to understand them and their strange way of life. But she couldn't look at them at that moment.

It was all very odd. But Amber really wanted to be able to trust her eyes and hoped she could believe Halfmoon. For now, in this new place, Halfmoon was the only thing she *could* believe. And she *wanted* to believe Halfmoon, she really did, the Cat who had all the explanations. But she also wondered. *Was It right—about everything? Who else agreed with It?*

They walked down a small slope. Her mind spun through thoughts and thoughts, so fast that it almost hurt. Her body felt frozen and tense, but also numb, like her head might slide off her neck at any moment. She watched Koko, her eccentric companion, out of the corner of her eye. It did not look at her, only stared straight ahead, as if it were hypnotized by something in the distance. There was something about its quick intakes of breath that suggested it was having trouble breathing. This made Amber's stomach churn. How desperately she wanted to understand it. How desperately she wanted to know, at least, what *it* thought about Halfmoon. But perhaps she could find this out.

Koko stopped.

Amber realized they had walked back the way she'd gone with Halfmoon. They were almost at the long table, which was now crowded with Cats. Amber and Koko were still a few feet away, but from what she could make out, the Cats were... eating. Her stomach felt twisty.

At least two dozen pairs of eyes were watching them with round-shaped pupils. Yet there was no trace of any particular emotion or interest in them. These Cats could have felt repulsion, eagerness, or dread, just the same.

Amber noticed that the Cats were watching her differently than when she had arrived. Before, regardless of what *kind*, whether they had laughed or screamed, they had obviously found some interest in her. But now, she couldn't even tell *this* from their blank, complex stares, and Amber wondered if they were already bored with her.

Except for Koko. It wasn't meeting her eyes, and as she looked closely, she saw its lip was quivering. She took these as distinguishable signs that it was… nervous. *But no, that couldn't be right. There was just something wrong with it.*

That almost painful, unbearable feeling of horror in her stomach was mixing with a deep want, a want to *know*. Even if it was to prove to herself, somehow, that these Cats weren't *so* bad.

Koko's eyes, still distant but never empty, became fixed and sharp as it looked up to another Cat trotting towards them.

This Cat drastically stood out from the others. Amber's eyes left Koko.

Unlike any other Cat, even Halfmoon, this Cat was wearing clothes. Not a full outfit, but simply a coat. Sturdy blue material, leather-like, swung loosely and almost carelessly over the Cat's shoulders, as if someone else had put it there. Amber wondered if the coat was actually made of real leather. It was somewhat odd to imagine a Cat wearing dead animals on its body.

But even its fur was different. Its fur was white, or at least looked like it was white beneath the murky, rotten-looking usual colour of the Cats' appearances. Yet its fur sparkled out a little. *It was as if it were almost white,* Amber thought. *Most of the Cats were dull, Halfmoon was actually grey, and this one was almost white. And it was wearing a coat.*

It walked with its chin up, and its posture was far less slumped, less slouched and saggy than most Cats'. Its eyes were not as miserable and goofy as most. But they still made

Amber feel like her body was frozen, dead, as its eyes were very cold.

She *heard* Koko beside her open its jaw, which was disgusting, and say something like, "Hiya. Petal."

Amber flinched at the sound. She remembered Halfmoon had said something about giving the Cats permission to speak. *Apparently, It was allowing Koko to speak at that moment.*

Petal spoke too. "Come on, it's not sohard to speak Human! Don't exaggerate!" It spoke in a mocking yet playful way, and unlike the others' similiar, strange, almost uniform voice. She could not ignore the fact that she heard a firm, *unique* male voice—it was like Petal was speaking for himself. Almost like he was a bit more naturally alive than the rest. A bit more *human*, as Halfmoon was.

"You'rewearing yourcoat again today," Koko acknowledged.

"So? Am I not allowed to?" Petal replied.

"No, that's notwhatI meant. It… it looks goodonyou."

Petal smiled and looked away, and Koko's gaze became fixed on the ground as the three continued walking.

"So, what are you doing with it?" Petal asked after a moment.

Koko looked away, then stammered, "The—the Girl is a *she*. Andher name is Amber. But I dunno…"

"You're so useless." Petal scoffed, but smiled. "I listened in, and Halfmoon said to give her a tour. Or to feed the girl, or something. Feedher!"

Koko turned a (dull) shade of red, and awkwardly led Amber to the table, as Petal had suggested.

Almost losing her sense of self again in this dreamlike place, Amber grounded herself back into what was happening.

They were talking about her. These Cats were talking about her. She would be working with one of them. With Koko. Soon, things would happen, and she would go on some journey. But before Halfmoon had packed everything, and before she could leave with Koko, they had some time to look at the island. And the Cats wanted to feed her.

As she had with Halfmoon, Amber obeyed and let Koko take her.

As they approached, she saw the table was indeed levitating over the ground—as she had wondered before—and filled with dishes. She realized she was trembling.

She forced her body to follow along and sit down on one of the table's odd mushroom stools. In front of her was an empty plate. She stared at it as her heart raced. Her chest hurt. Every intake of air was sharp. She hated it when these Cats spoke and didn't understand why they did. There was so much about them that she did not yet understand. All the Cats' lips were swollen—except Halfmoon's—and how they spoke was odd, distinct from how people spoke. The voices sounded raspy, muffled, and high-pitched at the same time, or simply... *wrong*, and she could not follow what they said.

Sitting at the table, the same table where all the Cats sat, she realized what a good opportunity this was. Koko was beside her, and *there was nothing stopping her from asking all the questions she wanted to.*

But when she opened her mouth, when she turned slightly towards Koko, all those horrible sensations came to attack her body again, and her voice was lost and gone.

Amber stared at the food on the table. *It did not look like food.* She gagged at the sight of the Cats eating. They opened their broken jaws very widely and chewed with their mouths open, most of the food falling back out again as they did, and making loud, wet slurping noises. She didn't feel like talking to them.

There was only one type of food to be seen—pink, fluffy, tube-like things. The texture was hard to make out. The food looked fuzzy, and at first the whole table seemed to Amber like a big feast of a giant, shared candyfloss, but she soon realized that within their strange organic shapes, the tube-things were compressed into individual hard shells of unique shapes and sizes—though most were like capsules. One thing was certain: it was not normal food, nor normal Cat food.

Amber shut her eyes and bit her tongue, trying not to be sick. *There was so much she wanted to know and so much she wanted to understand,* but all she could do was sit, waiting and waiting, perhaps for the big, ugly lump beside her to introduce itself. It only looked away. Instead, she felt many other eyes on her, staring, as they munched and munched and munched…

In that moment at the table, all she wanted was to leave this place. But there was nothing she could do about it.

Minutes passed, and Amber did not look at anything but her shiny plate. She expected Koko beside her to burst into speech at any second, to tell her something, or at least to talk with the others beside it, but it went on eating and eating.

Then finally she heard the name. *Halfmoon.* Amber turned.

She watched Petal stand up, his Paws on his hips in an awkward way, as he talked to a thing seated next to Koko.

If Koko and Petal were Cats, then this was a Kitten.

It was skinny and tiny, barely able to sit upright. *Cats weren't meant to sit upright, after all.* It was all shrivelled-up, ugly and naked, but somehow cute at the same time, Amber thought.

And it seemed to be Petal's younger sibling. Like every other Cat, it had that exact same bored, grey expression on its face, as if it had not a care in the world, or it was impossible to know whether it had a care in the world.

Petal cried something out to it, but it rolled its eyes.

"GreatMoon do it! Great Moon should do it!" she heard it say.

They were talking about Halfmoon. Amber found her eyes drifting towards them.

"Now, Frog." Petal looked crossly at the thing that was Frog.

Just then Amber saw that Frog was staring at something. It was gliding in the air, a foot above Frog's head. It was big and square, and she caught sight of what looked like the small screen of a TV, Frog's eyes glued to it. She wondered if it was one of Halfmoon's inventions, as it looked like the things she had seen on Its shelves.

Koko gave a toothy smile. "Frog, listen to your brother."

Petal smiled at it, but still looked stern. "As much as, really, I appreciate your support, I… *leave it to me.*"

Amber watched Koko's profile redden again. "Youappreciate… my support?"

Then, it shyly returned to its pink meal.

Amber again tried not to gag.

Petal continued to look his sibling in the eye. "Frog, Frog, look at me!"

But Frog ignored him.

Petal lowered his voice. "Frog, we've talked about this, right? Right?! *Put the Teleclock away when I'm speaking to you.*"

"But…" Frog's voice was small and sniffly, like a little child with a cold. "Halfmoon saidI'm testing thisinvention." Its words were hard to make out.

Petal rolled his eyes. "But not when I'm *talking* to you.

Halfmoon's not here. Look, during this meal you've eaten quiteabit. You've eaten ten pieces offood. My point is, food is not infinite. I can see you have overeaten yourself, and it's not just food—"

"Food is infinite!" Frog roared. "GreatMoon makes *loads* offood! Halfmoon make asmuch as wants!"

Petal gave a long sigh. "Well, I guess thatis true. Halfmoon doesmake a lot of food. But mypoint is, you must also care for yourself, learn to organize yourself. You know how I raise you—"

"Not to gettoo influenced by othercats, blahblah!" Frog hiccuped and returned to the invention screen. "GreatMoon can organize."

From what she was hearing, the other Cats did, in fact, trust Halfmoon. Apparently, too much. But Amber wanted to know more.

Petal sighed again and started chewing his own food.

Amber decided to speak. "Er..." she started, shaking all over. "Petal?"

Petal turned towards her with something like surprise. "What?" He looked at Amber as if he had never seen a human —or, *Human*—ever before. *Before today, he probably hadn't.*

"Can I ask... Why are you wearing a jacket?" she said.

Petal didn't reply and stared at her with an expression of indifference.

"He wears itbecause..." Koko cut in. "Petal likes to be *individual*. He says the other Cats are boring."

"That's... right," Petal said. His eyes got a new gleam to them. "They don't care about anything. Idon't think they even *think*."

Amber nodded quickly, as if this made perfect sense. Then, she said, "I want to... know about things."

"You want to know stuff?" Koko asked, facing her for the first time, eyes now shining slightly like Petal's.

"Yes." It felt like something dropped into her stomach, so she forced a smile, but instead pulled an ugly grimace.

"Yeah. Then *you* go on, talk," Petal said to Koko. "You heard her. The girl doesn't knowstuff."

"Why me?" Koko's face flushed a little.

"The girl nose stuff?" Frog said.

"No," Petal scolded. "Not *nose stuff*, Isaid *know* stuff."

"What knowstuff would you like to know?" Koko asked.

Petal rolled his eyes.

"I'd like to know about Halfmoon," Amber said. "Halfmoon told me a lot of things. But, I just want to see if It was right."

At these words, something shifted or dropped in the air. Something happened between the Cats, like a secret communication or a shared emotion, that Amber didn't understand.

Frog gave a head-splitting squeal, Koko coughed violently, and Petal's eyes trailed downwards as he frowned, as if ashamed. The Cats around them all stared once again, this time making small moaning noises.

Then, as Amber started feeling dizzy in all the confusion, the Cats broke into a gasped, raspy chant:

"We do always listen to our leader,
Who cares for us small-Cats, poor desperate creatures!
O the Moon is not a vicious meat eater—
But an all-knowing thinker, for all of us believers!

On our lovely island, safety never slackens,
For the GreatMoon, O the powerful, robust
GreatMoon... will know of anything that happens.

GreatMoon thinks, GreatMoon knows for us!

We don't mind the world outside our fuzzy welcome
  sign
After all, we are only small-Cats, and we
Have all we need, inventions of genius design!
O toothsome food, land, and snuggly homes, all free!

In this place all is right, and never wrong
And that's why GreatMoon makes us memorise this
  song."

She noticed every time the Cats said *O*, their whole jaws and faces stretched out to fit the round shape, so that their eyes had little space and nearly popped out.

When the song had finished, the back of Amber's neck prickled, and in the frozen silence that followed she felt a burning flush to her face, as if *she* had done something odd. The Cats' frequent blinks were almost audible.

Amber noticed that both Petal and Koko had gone pale, and neither had joined in with the song.

After a moment, she laughed. "But…" she said. "But, what does that *mean?"*

Petal shook his head.

Koko opened its mouth, then closed it again.

"OK." Amber's eyes retreated to her plate. Then, without understanding why, she shuddered. She didn't want that silence, or to hear the Cats sing, ever again.

"You gottaeat," Koko mumbled, probably to her. She ignored it.

Amber felt Frog's attention shift and it fixate its dot-eyes onto her as it asked, "Whyyoublonde? WhyyouHuman?"

She felt colour and panic come to her face and didn't have a reply. Frog snickered.

"Oh, shutup, Frog. Leave the poor girl. She only just now discovered our existence," Koko chimed in. Then its face tensed as it realized what it had said, and that it had spoken English perfectly, almost as if it could not believe it.

"Koko…" Petal started.

"I'm sorry! I'msosorry!" Koko's voice broke.

Frog, who had looked emotionless seconds ago, started to scream, and Amber covered her ears at the horrible sound.

"Sorry…" Koko mumbled again. "Didn't mean to, um, provoke."

Amber sat with her hands over her ears as Petal tried his best to calm Frog down.

Cats around them seemed to scowl, but no Cat actually cared.

She felt Koko twitch unnervingly, its eyes staring right through her. She didn't like the feeling.

After a while, Frog had fallen asleep in Petal's Paws, snoring deeply.

Koko spoke, "Petal… leave it… I think youshould leaveit."

"No, I won't *leave* things thisway! I know you like to follow the crowd…" Amber could not tell if Petal was still speaking in that mocking, playful way or not.

"What are you talking about?" Koko sounded hurt now, its eyes prickling with tears. It seemed to have taken Petal's tone personally. Then, it continued staring at Amber. She wondered if it had been staring the entire time. "And… why aren't *you* eating?"

"Uh…"

She could not eat. Not here, not like this.

Instead, she wanted so desperately to understand.

Petal sighed again. "I won't leaveit. But *ugh*, these Gadgets…"

"What *about* the…?" Amber started when she realized she could not finish her sentence. She didn't want to hear more Cat songs.

But Petal considered her. "Well… Frog has Halfmoon's new Gadget. Catsalways test unfinished Gadgets out, test Halfmoon's inventions before It finishes them. Frog istesting. But I am *not* so keenon thisinvention. Honestly, it's quite useless. It'sso… distracting."

Distracting.

And she recalled Halfmoon had mentioned that the Gadget It would give her was already tested out. *It had probably meant another one.*

For a moment she looked around, wondering why no Cat was protesting at what Petal had said, for he was the only one speaking into the silence left by the song. After all, they had just sung about Halfmoon's inventions having *genius design.* The contradiction of it made her head hurt.

All Amber knew was that she believed Halfmoon more than Petal.

When she looked at Koko and caught it staring again, her stomach dropped. Its face was all scrunched up and twitchy with anxiety.

It turned to Petal. "She's not eating. My—fault. If she dies. Halfmoon won't trustmeanymore…"

As if expecting her to drop dead at any second, its eyes grew wide. "Eat!" Suddenly, it stuffed Amber's face with food.

Her whole body prickled, especially at the taste and weight now in her mouth. It felt like she was taking a pill.

Koko and Petal looked at each other. The taste was *disgusting,* sweet and sickly, and she had swallowed the tube-shaped thing in the wrong way… She felt tears prickle in her eyes and she panicked when she could no longer breathe. This was Cat food, but not the usual kind.

Amber choked and shot up from her seat. Several plates clattered and fell at her movement. The Cats gasped.

She ran off. The pink tube travelled back up her throat, and she was sick all over the grassy, sandy ground, with disgust at these creatures and their nonsensical actions. There were so many things she craved to know. She could not understand a word these creatures spoke.

She heard Petal in the distance, and they *all* stared. "Ithinkyoubrokeit."

* * *

They were all so terrible, such things that she could never have imagined.

It was something, a reality, that she wished did not exist. She just *wished it did not exist*. But she kept her feelings inside, for now.

Amber felt self-conscious. She was there, present, right in the moment. Or lost.

Her human body felt so wrong in this place. She felt self-conscious of her skin. Of her every single skin cell, every hair that stood out on the back of her neck.

She felt any usually distant sensations ten times stronger now: every tremble made the whole world shake, every slight uneasiness made every inch of her *crawl*, every shudder nearly made her break into convulsions.

As she walked, she was very conscious of how she, a human, an innocent girl, walked along the grassy camp and saw Cats that walked on two legs with human-like eyes and faces. *How funny, how very funny.*

And her surroundings did not have a proper form. They could not be described in words. For these Cats, the camp, seemed to *shift*. One moment, Amber thought she understood something, and the next, all was different. It was like a blurry dream brought into vivid real life. As if nothing she saw stayed fixed in her head. But unlike a dream, she was conscious of it all happening.

Conscious. She gulped. *Yes. She was a conscious being. For the moment, she did not* need *to understand. All she needed to do, while she waited for Halfmoon, was to stay conscious, stay alert, observe her surroundings (but not too much, to the point of confusion or insanity), not let anything go wrong, and just keep, keep breathing...*

Petal and Koko had stopped arguing about Frog and the Gadget.

Amber hadn't received any proper answers to her questions, but she was not going to ask again. Something strange, in the uncomfortable, frozen silence, had occurred at the table, and she didn't like it. Something had escalated, but she had to focus on something else.

Before she needed to leave, they still had time to kill. So, to keep busy and have something to do, Amber, Koko, Petal, and Frog decided to walk to the beach. Amber would observe and walk and get a few simple explanations if she was lucky, if Petal was talkative again. At the same time, there was a part of her that didn't want—that dreaded—to hear more.

As she shuffled her feet, trying not to stare at everything that walked past her, Amber, again, felt oddly conscious.

This camp was like a large beach ball—with the Cat

houses or bedrooms on the sides, on the see-through, wobbly jelly.

"Absorbsheat," Petal explained to her, to both her relief and a prickling on the back of her neck. "The sun comes in through the open window."

Amber wouldn't have called the roof a window. Apparently, the Cats liked the heat.

But this was all round, she told herself. *This camp was nothing more than a beach ball.* "A beach ball…" she muttered to herself. "A shape. New land."

Koko apparently heard this, and startled Amber as it turned towards her. "It's not abeachball, actually. If you mean the shape of this part of the island. Thispart of theisland is the Leftear of the Big Cat. The whole islandforms the shape of a giantcat."

She didn't know how it had known she meant the camp shape, but its words somewhat made sense, as she imagined the whole of Catslaughter Island in the outline of a Cat, with the entrance being in the Left Ear. At least she understood this.

Around her, Amber saw uniquely shaped plants. They were of all sizes and colours. They gave her the same unpleasant alien sensations as the Cats did. *Just trees,* she reassured herself.

The ground was covered with the same crocodile grass. She heard something prowl about in it nearby. Something was moving. A Kitten sprang out, landing a few feet away.

But as far as Amber could tell in that brief second, it wasn't an ordinary Kitten. It wasn't even like Frog. Frog was a Kitten, exactly like Petal was a Cat. But this Kitten looked robotic and not even alive at all.

She had only caught a glimpse of it until she saw it run up

a tree-like plant. The trees were full of horrifyingly tiny holes. The Kitten Robot scuttled into one of them.

"W-what was that?" she mumbled, as if to herself again.

"One of Halfmoon's Gadgets. Nota real Kitten."

Petal and Frog were next to her. Again, they had heard her muttering. She wondered if she was speaking aloud all the time.

Petal smirked. "We call them Halfmoon's Eyes."

Amber remembered Halfmoon mentioning *Eyes*. "What exactly *are* Eyes?"

"Those Gadgets that look like Kittens," Petal replied. "Halfmoon has loadsof them. They run around everywhere, always hiding in plants, so we rarely see them. They record everything they see and report back to Halfmoon. But Halfmoon can also move them with Its mind, control where they go. We think they're connected to Its mind, but whoknows? Halfmoon would doanything to keep us safe."

"OK." She forced a nod.

Whatever she did, she would not let herself snap again, so Amber forced her gaze and the corner of her lips upwards, keeping her pace steady while walking. But somehow the idea that everything was being watched by Halfmoon also calmed her.

"Why are we going to the beach again?" Frog asked in its sniffly voice.

"To show Amber," Petal replied in a kind voice.

"To drown her?" Frog suggested.

Amber gasped, and Petal did, too.

"Frog!" he scolded. "*No*."

Frog made the same crying noise, nearly making Amber's ears bleed.

Petal shushed the creature and ran with it off the path to stop its noise, leaving her alone with Koko.

They walked silently, but there was never actual silence. Amber heard the noises that she had heard when first arriving, but realized they had probably been in the background all along. There was always a static, almost bustling noise somewhere in the background. Like someone was playing a video of the place.

Like this all was recorded.

They were almost at the beach now. Amber made her way out of the last branches, racing into open freedom, and now that she saw it, she felt a powerful desire to keep running, for it almost felt like she was finding a way back to Japan. But Koko was here, so she slowed down.

Like the rest of the island, the beach was plain. But it looked like it had once been beautiful, in a video. A video that was playing now, with worse quality than something real.

Somehow, it triggered the past Amaya in her. Her very, very old feelings. She felt nostalgic, and within a few brief seconds, she wanted to run along the sand again. She wanted to be in her old life—to be anywhere, anywhere but here in this place at this time.

And for a second, in this scenery of fakeness, she pretended. She pretended the dull blue skies were beautiful, that they could show off their beauty and glory, where there were no trees.

There was no salt in the air, but the waves swung playfully, the ocean clear like the sky, clean and entirely untouched from the terrors she had just seen. She took off her shoes and her feet sank in.

She felt the slow rhythm of everything, knowing something was nearby. But for a split moment, she forgot what it was. She forgot where she was. Everything felt so unreal, so fake, so recorded, so much like a distant memory, that she could *pretend* for a few seconds, that this was not real.

Her skin was comfortably warm, but not too hot. Nothing here matched the season Japan was in…

"Time difference."

Amber craned her neck and came back to disturbing reality as she looked at it. She remembered it was Koko, she remembered this was her reality.

"Time difference," it repeated, reminding her that there even was one. "Thirty seconds in the Human world is a day here. Seasons don't exist, and things are always warm."

There again, that shocked expression on its face, like it was taking itself by surprise by its own ability to speak.

Thirty seconds in the human world was a day here.

Amber grew ashamed and stared at her feet. Hurriedly, she put back on her wet socks and slipped back into the trees, away from Koko.

When she stood somewhere between the beginning of the bridge and the beach, she heard Frog's sobbing noise. She didn't know where it came from and hid behind a plant with thick thorns. Then she spotted Petal and Frog near the entrance.

"Shhh, sheleaves soon."

Cries between words. "Don't…wanther… here. In home."

Frog spoke impressively for a Kitten, and Amber wondered if Petal had raised it.

"This isn't home," Petal replied. "Like I always promise, oneday we'llsee Human world again, like when I was younger, beforewe camehere."

For a second, Amber saw a glimpse of Petal, as something more than the Cat he was.

Maybe *Amber* felt as wrong to the Cats as they did to her.

But again, Koko, behind her, ruined it. When it stepped near her, she almost jumped in alarm. She looked at its face once more, and still, she could not make sense of the features in her head.

She walked ahead and returned to the camp. Koko followed behind, and she still laughed, still felt self-conscious about every inch of herself and conscious of all that was around her, still let the world around her sink in, before she finally broke down in her own confusion.

CHAPTER 5 – A NEW PLACE??

Amber liked to understand. She liked to know everything about anything, or, at least, not be confused. She didn't like to be confused, because then, it seemed she had nothing to hold on to… Nothing at all.

Tears were running down her face. She didn't even notice.

She didn't even know where she was exactly, as the whole camp—the whole world—seemed to spin, and spin around her.

And those things that weren't cats were all here, too. They could not keep their wide, googly eyes off her.

She tried to walk, but her vision blurred. She could not tell if the grey thing she walked towards was Halfmoon, or something else.

They all looked the same. They all seemed to smile.

She wasn't even sure where Koko or Petal had gone. If she could believe them. Or what she could believe at all.

She heard strange noises around her. Recorded, a video played, of a distorted children's lullaby. Everyone seemed to laugh.

And she didn't know why they did.

But then the grey thing—*Halfmoon* indeed—shooed the Cats away. It came and asked her if she wanted to sit down.

Sitting now, Amber wished this would not exist. She hated, hated the fact that such a reality existed, that it was alive. That it felt so real.

It never happened. It never happened. It never happened, she thought or muttered to herself. *She never came here. This wasn't real. This wasn't real. This wasn't real.*

Halfmoon seemed to notice this. "Oh, but it might be real, Amber." It chuckled. "Those strange, unreal noises you may have heard at the beach, I made those, purposely. They sound fake, don't they? I made them for this all to appear less real, to be easier to process!"

Amber looked up. "You made them?"

"Yes. However, it may not help. As, obviously, we *are* real."

Amber did not understand exactly what It meant. She knew only that she still did not want to believe. She did not want to believe, unless she could understand.

"I don't like this," she said a moment later.

"Oh?" Halfmoon smirked. "You don't *like* this because you don't understand, but I will make you understand. And I promise I will."

It pulled out one of Its strange inventions. There was no doubt that it was the same Gadget that Frog had. It was covered in numbers and buttons. It had that same TV screen.

"For your journey. Amber, this is a Teleclock, my newest Gadget. In many ways, it is an ordinary clock. But it is a better clock than Human ones. These numbers on it, they re-set themselves every few minutes, calculating the most accurate time that the Terror will come in. It tracks how much time you have. On your journey.

"But you should not worry about the numbers. Ignore them until you are ready. You will understand later, I promise. And the Teleclock is more than a clock. It is also like a... telephone... and more."

Amber nodded, although she didn't understand all of Halfmoon's words. But somehow, listening to It speak with such certain confidence was a comfort.

"I see you feel bored with life, perhaps," It added. "Boredom is a weakness. This helps boredom; it is entertaining. Plus, it is a form of communication."

Amber watched as the Teleclock glided and landed by her shoulder, as if acknowledging her. Then it went higher and stopped in the air.

"This Gadget naturally follows you," Halfmoon explained. "And here is your food. I also packed a map. Some other supplies as well." Amber saw It was carrying a small sack, which It handed to Koko, who sniffed it. She could only dread the pink food that was probably inside.

"I didn't like the Cat food," she burst out. She tried forcing a laugh, but it turned into a hysterical, nervous giggle.

Halfmoon didn't say anything. Instead, Its grin widened, though the grin didn't reach Its ears in the creepy way like last time. As Amber studied Its face, she appreciated Its more neutral features more than ever. *True, It did not look like a normal cat, but Its appearance didn't make her lose her breath. If she only listened to Its voice, without seeing It, she could almost believe It was human.*

After considering her, It said, "You won't need to like the Cat food. I packed Human food just for you. Here." With a flick of Its Paw, the sack opened, and what looked like an ordinary sandwich drifted out, into her hands.

Hesitantly, Amber took a bite. Lettuce, tomato, and some cheese. *It was just a sandwich.*

As she continued chewing and chewing, the simple, ordinary taste made her feel better. She could almost close her eyes, listen to Halfmoon's almost-ordinary voice, and pretend she was still in Japan.

"Are you ready to make the journey, Amber?" Halfmoon smiled. "All you need to do is travel to another island with Koko, who I am confident will take good care of you. Then, you must travel back to Japan and prevent the Terror from coming. On the way there, I will regularly contact you and explain more if needed. I promise, I promise, you will understand. Soon, everything will make perfect sense."

And suddenly she realized that, were Halfmoon not here, she really would be losing her mind.

Amber knew now that she *could* believe Halfmoon. Perhaps Petal disagreed with It over some things, but after all, Halfmoon was the Cats' leader, and they all followed It. No one listened to Petal. And Amber had tried to find out what the others thought... but with Cats as strange as these, it wasn't that easy.

"*That's* it! The plan isthateasy!" Koko shouted, smiling broadly. Its smile was crooked and, unlike Halfmoon's, did reach its ears. Everyone stared, and Koko reddened, regret on its face.

Amber ignored it.

But Halfmoon, *Halfmoon* was her single anchor in this world. The one thing she could turn to when unsure, the one normal thing with the semi-normal face. It was the creature with all the plans, knowledge, and explanations.

"Oh, yes, I'm ready," Amber mumbled.

They would travel by boat, the plan was explained, so Petal

and Koko nodded at the same time, ready to guide her to the other side of the beach.

But before they left, Amber looked back at all the other Cats, now arranged in two rows, faces still goofy yet somehow vacant of direct expression, eyes simultaneously watching Halfmoon, and blinking less than occasionally.

There was something so... *sad* about them. Amber couldn't put a finger on what it was.

Maybe it was that they all looked the same. Except for Petal, they didn't even wear their own coats.

Yet Amber had no more time to think about them anyway, because Halfmoon, Koko, Petal, and Frog started walking, and she followed, the Teleclock drifting above her.

"This world is a funny place, Amber," Halfmoon said, as if it really were so simple.

Funny, Amber thought. *Yes. This whole thing did seem so, so funny now.* At least as they walked, she could tell herself this.

Then, she laughed. As she did so, she sounded like them— unnatural, fake, wrong, and recorded. Maybe she was a recording of her future self, finally completely mad. But Amber could not deny that at the same time, she also liked the fakeness. Because it was almost like she could pretend this was, in fact, not real. *It made it, as Halfmoon said, easier to process.*

She laughed and laughed, spluttering and spluttering. *This was such a funny place.* Although she could not breathe for laughing, she did not stop. She wanted to stop, but she didn't, not until they arrived.

The beach on this side looked almost the same as the other. It was the same snow-white sand and crystal water. The main difference was the thing that was peacefully floating *in* the water. Smooth, dark wood and a strong mainsail, all in mini size.

"What on Earth is this?" she said.

"A boat. We're not… onEarth," Koko chuckled. No one laughed.

"Get in, sail to the island, andenter Portal again," Petal told Amber, but smirked at Koko.

She reminded herself *she only had one option, as she needed to return to Japan, home, anyway.*

"You must leave now," Halfmoon pressured.

"Twas nice to… have meetyou," Frog squeaked.

"A Kitten named Frog," Amber laughed nervously.

Then, without looking at Koko, she got into the boat, and it followed.

They started sailing.

"GOOD LUCK!" Halfmoon shouted after them.

Amber failed to see how it all made sense, but still, she chased things she could not find, trying to wrap her mind around it all, as she kept her face straight. For as long as she could.

* * *

They had been out at sea for quite a while now, unfortunately not seeming to be making too much progress. Catslaughter Island was no longer in sight, but their next destination wasn't either. Amber was starting to think they would spend the night on this boat. But then again, she barely knew anything, and she wouldn't know what *progress* even looked like, because everything was just sea and sky.

Except, of course, it wasn't normal sea and sky. She tried her best not to look, but when she observed the rising waves for more than a few seconds, she could see a bubbling, rippling effect, like there were fizzing, miniature waves within the waves. It was like the entire ocean was an enormous witch's cauldron, and she was one of the ingredients. And the sky—it was just blue, but there was something about it that looked *too* perfect, too cloudless.

It took her a while, but she soon noticed that no one was steering their ship. The small sail seemed to steer itself, advancing along the waves as if someone were pushing it. Suddenly, she doubted everything. *Were they even going in the right direction? How long would they be at sea? Could they get lost?* Her stomach felt twisty again in that strange way.

But when she looked at Koko, its expression suggested it was shrugging this off easily, as a simple, simple fact. Or perhaps it had not noticed.

Still, Amber somehow couldn't find her voice to ask about the boat. They had not said a word since leaving Catslaughter Island. Each of them sat separately at opposite ends of the boat, though it was small. So, she decided to accept this as a fact, too. Accept everything she had seen today. *Yes, the boat was steering itself, but that was fine. It was probably part of Halfmoon's plan, and that was fine as well. They were most likely going in the right direction.*

Now Amber sat and gazed at the endless water surrounding their tiny boat. Her eyes looked transparent in her reflection. They were the same colour as the waves. She barely recognized herself but was unsure whether this was because her eyes had been watching those terrible creatures all day, or because she rarely looked into mirrors. Her reflection was from the past.

Koko looked odd. It always did, with those wide eyes that looked like they could start crying any moment. It made

Amber uncomfortable, how it obsessively watched her, especially how its jerky movements showed it was restless, probably unable to stop boredom from attacking its mind. That was all that these Cats were, after all: dull, bored, funny. And Amber couldn't suppress her annoying laughter that kept coming up.

She stared at her hands. She felt an urge to draw. Then, she remembered. Amber turned her palm, and there it was; a strange cat illustration. The face.

After a moment of staring at it, she shook her head. *No, it couldn't have anything to do with* these *creatures. It was a pure coincidence*, something she didn't want to think too much about. Pure chance.

She wanted to dip her hand into the sea, wash off the ink, but hesitated as the water was gurgling.

Amber also wanted to try out this intriguing Gadget that Halfmoon had given her, which was now floating above her. But she did not dare to move and would avoid Koko as long as she could.

So she avoided conversation for hours.

After a long time, she felt a little restless, too. Not because she was on a tiny boat out at sea, but because the sun was setting, and soon it would be dark; she would not be able to see what was around her. She didn't like the dark.

Amber watched as Koko had its head stuck inside the sack of food. She could hear it munch whatever it was that it was munching.

When it lifted its head out, she saw its mouth was covered in that same fluffy pink stuff she had seen on the table.

Amber groaned without meaning to.

As Koko shot her a questioning look, she couldn't help but say, "What *is* that?"

It swallowed. "Oh, these? You've seen them before. They're CIPs. Cat Improvement Pills." She noticed its voice was strangely clearer than it usually was, a bit more like Petal's.

Koko made a crunching sound. Amber didn't think it was good to crunch on pills.

Noticing her still furrowed eyebrows, Koko explained, "This is… special Cat medicine. It helps us *speak*." It looked at Amber as if to see if she was still confused, if its vague reply was enough and it could stop speaking.

But her eyebrows remained furrowed.

So, Koko explained, "Cats don't have a big vocal range like Humans. They physically can't speak Human words. But Halfmoon… It can do it all. With Halfmoon's Mahou energy, It does something to our insides. It says, *It makes them better*. It stretches them, so our vocal cords can pronounce Human language.

"But, well… Our insides aren't *supposed* to be stretched. Although Halfmoon makes us able to speak, it often still sounds… off. We swallow words. But we *need* to speak, so we take this medicine, or, *food* Halfmoon makes. Thanks to Halfmoon, the Cat Improvement Pills—uh, *fix us up again*. Help our throats stay… healthy…" Koko looked away. Again, she spotted that regret on its face, as if it had spoken too much by accident. "Halfmoon speaks to us in English and Japanese. We rarely reply. But we have to talk for *you* to understand."

It left it at that.

Amber could not help but wonder if speaking were the reason the Cats did not look like Cats. Or if there was any reason at all. Either way, she shut her eyes, trying to make the image of Koko melt away into blackness.

And the blackness came. The moon was up. Koko curled up on its side of the boat.

The stars did not give off much light. In the dark, although it was barely visible, Amber was surprised at how small Koko appeared to be now. It was the reason she hated the dark—it played tricks on her eyes.

The whole day, Koko hadn't done anything bad, her thoughts spoke. *Nothing bad had really happened.*

But at the same time, the knot in her stomach told her it had. *Things had happened so unexpectedly, without her being able to grasp any of them.*

Amber heard the noise of something clattering and moving towards her.

She sat up, heart beating fast, expecting a new creature of some sort to be there. But in the dark, she could scarcely make out that its outline was the size of her hands clapped together. It was a small bowl.

The noise became quieter as the bowl settled, the waves slowing. Amber couldn't understand where it had come from.

She studied the outline of the bowl as her breathing returned to normal and she felt slightly calmer. Then, she noticed the flavourful warmth spreading up to her face from the bowl, and the distant smell of some dish from her town. It was a bowl of noodles.

Her stomach felt light and empty, but there in the dark and next to Koko, she didn't dare to touch it, not only because she feared she might wake Koko up with the noise, but also because she didn't like not knowing where the bowl had come from.

Amber lay back down. After a few minutes, she heard the bowl clatter away again.

Turned towards sleeping Koko in this position, she noticed something else out of the corner of her eye—spiky triangles in the sky. They looked a little like stars, but somehow, there in the dark, almost all alone, something kept her from looking. She'd had enough, seen enough weirdness for today. For a lifetime.

Amber tried to rest. But the night was cold and unbearable, especially lying on wood. Her bones felt chilled and weak, and all she wanted was to be hidden safely beneath a blanket. She stayed up nearly the whole night, restless, but too frozen in shock to move, yet still feeling she might need to defend herself.

She didn't feel time passing. She could not feel anything in those long moments. All she knew was that something was about to happen, and she didn't yet know what it would be. All she knew was the swaying of the waves and the slight metallic taste of her having bitten onto her tongue a little too hard. All she knew was that she could not even cry, and could only stay frozen and awake.

When it seemed like early morning, Amber decided to take her chance. She hadn't been able to use the Gadget around Koko, as she had no idea how Koko might react, but now it was still sleeping, so she pulled the gliding Gadget down. She got a good look at it.

There was enough light in the sky now for her to see clearly. It was quite odd; twisted and uneven, the Gadget's jiggly lines curved out its oddly shaped frame. It was bright orange, the colour of a ship's life belt. The tone was a little too exhaustingly vibrant, so that at first sight it blinded her eyes unpleasantly, even in the mellow rays of the warm morning sun.

It almost looked like an ordinary… Amber couldn't quite

place a finger on what it *almost* was. But it was a bit like a telephone. It had a receiver at the very top.

Except, it was also a clock. *And* something else.

What was the word Halfmoon had used for it? A Teleclock, one of Its Gadgets.

In the centre of it was a screen, not yet turned on. Buttons and numbers circled around it.

If she only observed the numbers, she found the Gadget looked almost like a clock, except that it had a screen in the middle instead of clock hands, which was surrounded by the numbers one to fourteen.

Amber found she could view the Gadget as either a clock, a TV screen, *or* a telephone. But not all at once. She could focus only on one of its features at a time.

But Halfmoon had told her not to worry about the numbers. Amber decided to ignore them for now.

What she really wanted to explore was the screen. Amber spotted a small button. Although there were many buttons, somehow she knew that this was the one to turn it on.

She clicked, and the screen turned white, the light stinging her eyes. Then, the screen filled up with curious images and symbols.

Amber swayed, and sat back a little, dazed, overwhelmed by all the colours and tones in front of her. *They looked like strings.* Strings pulled into different shapes and sizes, making buzzing sounds.

She remembered what Halfmoon had told her about it. *I see you feel bored with life, perhaps. Boredom is a weakness. This helps boredom; it is entertaining. Plus, it is a form of communication.*

The strings kept changing until they started to form fixed images. But again, she saw they weren't fully fixed. They were a bit like Catslaughter Island; dreamlike, brought into consciousness, shifting, unreal.

Boredom is a weakness. She thought Halfmoon might have meant being bored, not ambitious enough, during the journey. It would only slow them down, if she was unsatisfied, after all. But somehow, this was meant to be entertaining.

Amber stared at the strings for a while when she noticed they had taken the shape of her face. Many miniature moving, squirming forms lined her features. It was like a reflection in a distorted texture and drowned in over-saturated colour. For a moment, she felt scared of what it knew about her. But she believed it. And she liked it.

This device gave her the same unexplainable satisfaction, the same outlet for confusing feelings as when she tried connecting lines with her pencil, or when she tried making things work in her head. It was like drawing. Instead of drawing Cats, she was drawing these strings.

But this was better than drawing. It demanded less force, less strength. It did not leave her hands shaking. Yet, it felt like it was somehow connected to her mind…

She felt a sensation she couldn't quite describe. It was as if the strings were sending her a *message*. They put thoughts right *into* her head.

Hello, child. Amber. She swore she heard Halfmoon's voice, giving her instructions. *To use this Gadget, the receiver part is to be held to your ear, like a telephone. This makes it easier for it to take your thoughts, sort them, and display your mind visually on the screen. It will also tell you things of its own. All you need to do is watch. Just watch.*

Amber shook her head and turned the Gadget off. She had somehow *heard* Halfmoon's voice in her head. It had *communicated* through her thoughts.

The Gadget, Halfmoon, the *magic* behind it, could tell her things.

And she liked it.

Everything was all planned out. The Gadget had explained to her how it worked. It could tell her things, things that perhaps made sense… Amber started beaming a dreamy smile, as *perhaps, this all could work.*

Koko was awake now and groaned beside her.

Her stomach dropped at it.

As Amber turned her head, it took her a moment to realize how cold it had become. In fact, she was freezing, teeth chattering and shaking, within a single second.

Their boat bumped against a hard rock surface, indicating their arrival.

Amber got up and watched the new, to-be-discovered island unravel before her eyes.

"Why is it s-so *cold*?" she gasped, folding her arms over her chest. "It's freezing."

"That's why wecall it the Wacky Winters."

"Wacky…?"

"Thisis the island of the Wacky Winters."

Koko's words were untouched from any shivers, yet its body still shook lightly, although that might have been out of fear.

Fear streamed through her own body now. But she remembered something, and there was a spark in her. *I will make you understand.*

In front of them was land slowly lifting out of the water, covered in a white blanket of snow.

Amber had to jump into the water to cross over to it. The ice felt as though thousands of tiny needles were stinging into her legs, and she shuffled and pushed herself until she stood gasping and shaking in the snow.

Koko crossed over effortlessly, having a bigger body than her.

For a moment, she looked back, wondering about their boat and whether they would leave it there.

"I wanted to ask," Amber started. "What's *with* our boat?"

Koko looked at her for a few seconds. Then it shrugged.

"Halfmoon… Halfmoon must have been steering it by magic?" As she said this, she convinced herself, answering her own question.

"I guess," Koko mumbled.

As it continued to say nothing else, Amber added, purely to comfort herself, "Yes. Magic. *Mahou energy*. That must be it. We seem to be on the right island. We went the right way." She knew she couldn't get Koko to explain things properly, at least not the way Halfmoon did.

"B-but the boat is safe here?" she said again to Koko, with a shiver from the cold.

It nodded. "Ithink it'll stay there."

She sighed.

Amber felt heavy and exhausted already, only by staring at the path ahead. Except, there *was* no path ahead, and just white nothingness.

But she knew there were far worse things than nothingness. As she started trudging through the heavy cold, she hoped that the land ahead really was *only* of emptiness and cold—and, of course, the Portal—and that no other thing could be lurking.

However, as much as she tried, she could not pretend that this was Earth. For the talking thing next to her showed they were not on Earth, and she could not deny that this was a new place. Something frightful.

CHAPTER 6 – HOME WITHIN STRINGS

They wandered through what seemed like a light snowstorm. The air rushed over her weakly bones, which were dressed only in her airy, summery uniform. Amber's whole body was covered in goosebumps.

Just this morning, it had been hot. When she'd walked in her town, her uniform had clung to her skin, sticky with sweat. But now it was no more than a thin strip of hopeless fabric.

Shivering, she crossed both her arms over each other as tightly as possible, to keep the warmth in her upper body. Although she couldn't feel her legs at all anymore, she kept walking.

Yet, it was all different. This was not like being cold in Japan—or anywhere in *her* world. Instead of making her feel more alert, or even sharp pain, the coldness… blinded her. She felt confusion, dizziness.

Soon, Amber did not know in which direction to go. Here she really was as good as blind, and everywhere she looked there was only white, nauseating her, and the world started spinning again.

Trying not to appear lost, she looked at Koko. Perhaps for some further clue of the plan, or to ask about their time of arrival. She didn't like the idea of a whole alien land and knowing nothing of it. But she could barely open her mouth.

And yet, Koko seemed to understand. It sighed and opened the sack of food that it had hung over its shoulder. After sticking its head inside it for a few seconds, it carried out what looked like a thick slip of paper between its teeth.

"This isamap," it said. "Halfmoon packedus one."

Koko held it down towards her so that Amber could see the outlines of different islands. The one labelled the *Wacky Winters* had a red dot on it, which she assumed indicated the location of the Portal.

It still looked miles away, but they seemed to be going in the right direction. Amber followed Koko's lead, although they were walking in a straight single line anyway.

It was hard to see ahead. A few boulders pierced out of the white ground. There seemed to be more and more the further they travelled into the island, and Amber could feel the temperature dropping even more. Soon, she could no longer feel her face aside from a distant prickling on it.

Still, she told herself nothing was wrong. *Nothing bad had happened yet today. Koko knew which way to go. They would soon find the exit. All she had to do was try not to freeze to death.*

But there was something strange about the way Koko behaved as they walked; it went through the chilly winds with no apparent effort, treading silently, like a cold ghost, though it was still carrying the heavy sack. Koko did not seem to mind the cold, although it lived in a place where Cats had their windows half-open to let in extra sunlight and warmth. While Amber's lips were turning blue, Koko held itself in a steady, unbothered posture, while its dull, slightly brown fur-covered body glowed almost reddish in the cool light.

"Er, Koko?" Amber asked.

Its face scrunched up.

"Koko, h-how are you not cold?" she stammered.

Still, it gave her a wary look.

"Your name *is* Koko. Correct?"

At this, it shook its head. "Yes, yeah, of course. My name's Koko. Sorry. Yes, that'smyname." It gave Amber a nervous smile that made her uncomfortable.

After a silence, Koko sighed. "I'm sorry. Yeah, Koko's my nickname. I guessI'm not very… *used* to hearing it."

"Oh."

"I prefer you to call me Koko over my real name. It's just… a feeling."

"A… feeling?" She felt odd. "I prefer *you* to call me by my middle name. My first name is like from… a different time."

Koko nodded, and Amber took a few steps ahead, not knowing what had got into her. Usually, she did not like having *just a feeling* as an excuse for something. Usually, she would have felt annoyed.

Koko then shook its head. "So, yeah. I'm notcold. I've enoughfur."

There was no silence when they stopped talking, for the winds audibly clashed against Amber's skin.

When the wind gushes calmed, and she got the impression that whatever snowstorm had been forming was now past, her eyes found something.

It looked quite stray, placed there in the middle of the white sheets.

It was an odd plant, one she did not recognize; thin, thorny, dark branches drooped down sadly, yet offered many blue, juicy berries. *They looked like blueberries.*

Amber gasped and stopped in her tracks.

Koko looked confused. "What'sup?"

Why were there blueberries here? Amber shook her head. But there was more. She saw something white, something white that was not snow, exposed and eating the berries.

It gave the impression of being a tiny little creature, lying right next to the gigantic food source, covered in the wide blanket of snow. Licking off the last drop of a berry.

It was a fox, or at least appeared so. But the closer Amber dared to step, the more she believed she was wrong.

It was a Fox cub, a Fox that was not a fox. It had thick, white, fluffy fur to protect it from the cold, speckled all over in a tone of baby blue. Ethereal, shimmery angel wings sprouted from its back, fragile. And of course, it had googly eyes.

But as it appraised Amber, its eyes grew wide with fear... and something else.

Amber was five feet away from it now and turned to see Koko behind her.

For a moment, or a second, or perhaps no time at all, Amber's eyes met the creature's. It was clearly horrified, but Amber did not know of what. It let out a small warning cry, then trotted away.

"What wasthat?" Koko's voice came from behind.

Again, she shook her head. *That was just a fox,* she told herself.

They continued walking, pretending Amber had seen no fox. She ignored it now. There was nothing wrong with a fox —even with a *Fox.* She simply did not like it.

Having started with that single strange plant, there were

now a few others, of all types, slowly forming on all sides. She ignored this too, and they kept up their speed.

A while later, she heard Koko mutter something she did not catch.

She watched it and saw only the back of its head. It seemed to be whispering to itself. Then, she realized it was holding something in its Paws.

Amber stepped closer, and Koko noticed her stare. "Oh!" it said. It turned towards her to hold up… a Lizard. It was small, seemingly having too many fingers, and licked its lips.

"This is my friend," Koko explained. M-my—my best friend! From… Catslaughter Island!" Its face twisted into a huge smirk that made her skin prickle. "A friend!"

"Your friend." Amber gave a smile.

Koko hid its Lizard back inside the sack.

They continued walking and found the snow became thinner beneath their feet. Amber was on the cusp of feeling quite steady, knowing a lot about their surroundings on this island now, when she saw it.

It was something in the distance. Moving rapidly and racing towards them but keeping a good enough distance for her to see only half of what was happening. It was shrieking, screaming its head off.

Amber recognized it—the small figure running about was the same Fox cub. But… *she thought it had gone in a different direction.*

It gave one last dizzying spin and weakly trotted to the side, tilting its head. Halfway towards her, its wobbly knees gave way, leaving the creature splattered helplessly on the ground.

Amber's stomach lurched as she heard a last blood-curdling screech.

It lay there—as the snow was, in fact—tinted bright red.

Amber didn't know why, but blood was dripping from its mouth, for no apparent reason, and its eyes rolled into the back of its head.

The dead, horrible thing lay on the ground, and it made no sense to her. *It all seemed so random.*

Feeling shaky, she plodded towards it, almost to convince herself that it could do no harm. *To prove it had simply injured itself, but at least this was* natural.

When she came closer, the image startled her more than she would have admitted.

And then she watched in horror as the body was lifted into the air, and suddenly the limp Fox was gliding stationary a few feet off the ground.

Amber looked up, her lips trembling not just because of the cold.

She wanted to understand it. She needed to know what was happening.

Without warning, a tremendous gust of wind surged through her, and she nearly tumbled down at the coldness. She was sure by now her face had drained of life, and her lips were purple-tinged, but she looked up.

Now there were more. The Fox cub was *duplicating*; more dying Foxes hung motionless in the sky, blood still running onto the ground. They were bleeding straight, fluid lines all around her, and she felt there was nothing to do to stop this.

More and more Foxes appeared in thin air… until she really was surrounded.

Then, as she couldn't understand them, as she knew she had failed at understanding anything, she buried her face in her hands and slowly started sinking to the ground. To the cold, cold snow. The cold took all her warmth and energy, and now again not understanding, she wished and pretended she wasn't there. That this was not happening.

And the bitter cold swallowed her up.

* * *

She awoke to a smoky smell.

She was lying on a soft, fuzzy blanket made of grass. A fire crackled beside her.

It was then that Amber remembered that she was not alone, that Koko was here.

Koko was also sleeping around the fire, closer to her than she would have liked. It seemed to have *made* the fire. This was odd, as Koko didn't seem to mind the snowy weather, so she couldn't think of any reason why it would want to keep warm.

Now remembering all that had happened, Amber sighed. *She hoped she hadn't passed out in the cold.* Her thoughts were still muddled with her own confusion and the Fox cubs.

A few tree branches sheltered their spot here, and they were right next to a forest. But they were not in the deep depths of it yet, and it was calmer here. There was no longer a crazy, soaring wind.

So, Koko had saved her. It had saved her from the cold, but she knew it had, somehow, saved her from something else. She shuddered to recall the Fox and the nonsense she had seen. She knew something more had happened, that there was *more* to the Fox… But she didn't want to think of it anymore.

The fact that Koko had saved her managed to make her feel slightly less tense. *They were working together and would soon find the Portal.*

It was strange to think that unless they found the Portal

within the next day, the days were bound to stretch on. And her mother, her life, would still be on hold, waiting…

Amber sighed and came up with an idea. She could use the Gadget. Now was probably her last chance.

Sitting up, she saw the Gadget was still with her and carefully got it down, not wanting to make a sound.

She turned it on, this time pressing her ear against the receiver. Once again, her eyes watched the string-like images play before her. As they moved, she pictured that they were retrieving things from her head and playing out her thoughts.

The strings turned grey and started twitching convulsively, reminding her of a mannequin being animated to life. They showed her images of Cats; they formed Fox cubs and other things she so dreaded, yet distorting them even more than when she'd seen them in real life, giving them a whole new starker colour and shape.

But somehow, as Amber saw all the horrible things, she felt better. She almost let out a genuine smile. It was as if those dark things had been living inside her, as if those feelings and reactions had been sucked up, but now were displayed, released. Were taken, sucked away from her mind, and instead expressed through image.

The strings formed other monsters, they formed nonsense, things that appeared by randomness, without reason. But in them now, this way, Amber could see reason. The strings were, in her current situation, her temporary *home*. A safe place. And she felt happy, for a moment.

* * *

It was the dazzling, wintery morning light that opened Amber's eyes. She couldn't recall when she had decided to get some sleep, or if she had even decided it at all. She only knew she had stared at the Gadget for a long time, and it was now again above her.

The morning light really did look dazzling; it was the crisp, piercing rise of the sun. Somehow, as she breathed in the cold air, her reality felt sharper. It was almost like, when she stopped using the Gadget and properly studied her surroundings, she awoke from a sort of technological dream, feeling a little dazed at first. Her eyes hurt not unlike when she had discovered the Portal in Japan.

She decided to get up and clear away the remains of yesterday's fire.

Then, she lay for a while with her eyes open, waiting for Koko to wake up. She tried to prepare herself mentally for the day, hoping for success.

When Koko woke up, she heard it mutter something a bit like, "Breakfast…" and check if she was asleep. She quickly shut her eyes.

"I'm goingtoget someofthoseberries," Koko mumbled.

Amber sat up at its horrible voice and looked at Koko. *Its face was more swollen and wrong than yesterday.*

Koko shook its head and cleared its throat, slightly straightening its features. "I mean, I'm gonna get some of those berries we saw yesterday. Catscan eat berries."

But as it left their camp, Amber called out, "Can we not see if, er, Halfmoon packed anything?" Her voice was small. But she did not want *those* berries. She didn't want to duplicate and die and bleed from the sky after eating them.

Koko's facial muscles tightened, and its mouth opened in a half-formed protest, as if it wanted to search for food by itself without relying on the sack. But this lasted only a second, and then Koko's shoulders dropped, and it mumbled, "Let's doit the lazy way then." It handed her the sack.

Amber was about to open it when another one of Halfmoon's cheese sandwiches glided out by itself and landed in her hands, along with some pink Cat medicine aimed in Koko's direction. She tossed the sack back to Koko, satisfied.

When they had finished their meals, they left the camp into the unknown wilderness. *Today she would get back home.*

CHAPTER 7 – SPACES IN-BETWEEN?

The forest was at first a little dark. Pitch-black shadows were cast here and there on the woodland's ground, everything unilluminated except for the last rays of daylight still gleaming in from the December-like sky. There was less snow here; instead, there was an unsettling, howling wind that still kept the temperatures quite low.

They were deep in the forest now. It seemed normal and only slightly out of place at first, like everything did in this world, but after a few minutes, Koko broke into a cold sweat.

The trees started looming closer together, and it got even darker. Amber had to squint her eyes to see the path. Yet, it was simple and straightforward, and she was willing to do anything to finally leave Koko and this place behind.

They had been walking for a long time now. Whether that meant for a few hours or the whole day, Amber was unsure. She had no way of keeping track of time.

The sky was darkening. Her legs slouched beneath her. According to the little red dot on the map, they were very, very close to the Portal. All they had to do was walk straight ahead.

It was like they were in a tunnel—a dark, faint tunnel with sides that came closer together. One that Amber rushed through in small, heavy steps, Koko stumbling along beside her.

Around them, there was barely any snow left, only needle-like frost. The space on the path was getting narrower and almost claustrophobic now, and Amber thought they might soon not fit through anymore. Then she noticed that the trees actually always stayed the same distance from each other, and the path was peculiarly neat.

Almost halfway along it, she heard a sob.

"The trees… they'resoskinny!" Koko gulped.

"They're just… *trees*," she said.

"I don't know how I feel about them, thosetrees…"

Amber let out a joyless laugh, perhaps to fill the eerie silence. "Well, I *love* them." It was the first time she had heard complete silence since entering this realm.

"They're… *too* close together…"

It was right, she had to admit. The tall trees, starting to resemble no more thickness than her arms, were forming lines at the sides. Perfect, straight lines. And they made Koko cry.

Amber herself felt a bit like she had on Catslaughter Island. She felt terrible emotions floating beneath the surface, but she let them stay there for a while. She hated this place, of course, but she could hold on a little longer, let things happen. Besides, *she had the Gadget*. It made her feel much better, she knew that, and it seemed to remove all the feelings that these places triggered. If she didn't find the Portal soon, she could always use it.

This time, on this day, she would not break down again like she had yesterday. *It really was just utterly* inconvenient, and it would result in her spending much more time in this realm. She needed to stay in control—until she could get out.

This time, she would try to stay focused, telling herself *this was just a forest*. She would not burst out into sudden tears, like Koko had. She would ignore the strangeness that hung in the air.

Soon, from what Amber could make out on the map, they needed to get into one enclosed little space with trees on either side, leading on to a tall, dark figure that was not recognizable yet. And there would be the Portal.

Koko mumbled something, and she only caught the last word. *Anymore.*

"What did you say?" she asked, dreading the answer, that something had gone wrong.

"I don't feel... *real* anymore here. It's like timedoesn't exist. This place is so strange," it said with a shrug.

She could relate to the feeling, although she wished she couldn't. She knew, after all, *it was just a feeling, a sensation, nothing more.*

As they walked through the narrow space, through the scenery that looked so perfect that it almost looked fake, she felt... *distant.*

It was the same detachment she had felt two days before, in Japan. The one she felt daily. That distantness that came when she tried too hard to keep her feelings under control, or when she tried to disconnect, and it worked. But now, she was forced to face it directly.

It was a numbness, the opposite of real pain. It wasn't always a bad feeling. She liked feeling distant when it kept her *away* from the pain. But Amber's chest felt tight and her palms began to sweat, when the distantness came *unexpectedly.* Because then, it really felt like she was not real. It was a bit like the feeling she had got on Catslaughter Island. When things felt so intense, so real, they no longer felt real at all. Because then, when she hadn't *meant* to feel distant, it felt as if there was nothing she could do to her surroundings. As if she had no influence on them.

As she walked, it felt almost like this reality just happened to exist, and she happened to exist in it. And apparently, Koko felt it, too.

Amber pinched her skin to snap herself out of the feeling; she knew she had to focus. *It was just a sensation. Nothing was wrong.*

But as they approached the ambiguous black outline where the Portal supposedly awaited, and she recognized the outline as a small brick house, she stopped.

There was a house here. A brick house with a simple roof.

Koko marched ahead, still shaky, but Amber fell behind for a moment.

She could no longer pretend that she understood everything about this place. Because the house was wrong. The House was *wrong*.

Amber knew it was foolish, but came closer to knock, if only to see, perhaps, whether it was as terrifying as she thought it was. To understand.

"Wait!" Koko whispered, but she had already done it.

The House flickered.

It happened in a matter of seconds. But Amber saw it, and she couldn't forget it.

For a fleeting moment, the House gained eyes. Real, human-like, yet at the same time cartoonish eyes, and a toothy smile had curved its lips.

"Hello?"

Both Amber and Koko went still. The mouth had moved—

when it had been there—and Amber had heard a voice, but she wasn't sure if she really had, and where it had come from.

"Who's there?"

She couldn't find the source, the person, the real, normal beating heart that should have been behind the voice, and her own heart spun around in circles.

Koko stepped forward. "We're hereforPortal." Its voice was steady, yet there were tears in its eyes.

The face and the voice again. "Come inside, if you must."

Then, the face disappeared. *Had they imagined it?*

For a while, Amber was speechless. She wished, as always, that she weren't so *ignorant*. She felt so stupid, so tiny here.

"Amber," Koko beside her did not seem so terrifying anymore. It gave her a weak smile. "That House… I have anexplanation for it."

"An… explanation?" Its words caught her by surprise. She wanted to forget this House, but Koko seemed to *know* something.

"There's something about themagic that we haven't toldyou," Koko started.

"Yes?" Amber said.

"They're called illusions." Koko's face brightened as it noticed her interest. "This is something… I guess Halfmoon's been tryna hide, and has hidden, from most Cats. But it's something I've kind of figured out myself. The thing is, the Mahou energy in this realm, at least I think, is constantly tricking the eye. So many weirdthings happen here, and trust me, you shouldn't let yourself believe them too easily. Maybe, you can't know what is real—"

"Stop it," Amber cut in. "Of course I can tell what is real." This was not what she had expected Koko to say.

She knew tears would be pointless, so she didn't allow

herself to cry, although in that moment she wanted to. It was as if it were robbing her of all hope, all meaning.

"Amber." Koko never seemed to understand what *kinds* of things made her upset but somehow seemed to notice when she was. "Look, what happened yesterday… I think, those images… you let yourself get too influenced into believing them."

She did not look at it. *It was saying that the Fox cub yesterday was fake. That she had let herself believe a lie.*

"Did you know," Koko went on. "The snow, the ice, all this coldness on this island isn't real? I think you don't want to hear this, but I'mgonna be honest. It's an illusion."

"*Oh.*" Amber didn't know what had happened to the shy, nervous Cat that she had accepted as Koko, but now it was opening up. It made her feel real pain.

But she remembered she had to focus. She shook her head, forced a small smile on her face—like she always used to— and said, straight-up, "I don't believe you. You must be wrong. Everything has a reason, in any world. I *am* careful in trusting things; I don't blindly trust anyone or anything. I know how to tell how things work. Or at least Halfmoon does. It says It has the magic all under control. I bet *It* can spot illusions! I—I believe It."

She wanted to reject the idea of illusions completely, as it seemed nonsense to her. *But it didn't matter if they existed; Halfmoon could surely spot them!*

Koko looked at her, biting its lip, as if it wanted to say something but didn't.

Then its eyes swelled all round and brimmed with tears. "Are—are you saying youdonttrustme?"

Amber nearly rolled her eyes. *It didn't need to make this emotional.*

"Let's just *go*," she said, trying to shrug off everything that had happened.

Koko sniffed.

"Well?" Although her insides and feelings gripped squeamishly at each other, she wanted to enter the Portal. "The Portal must be in there. I need to go home. Who's going inside first?"

"Iwanttopass, to be honest—"

"Fine. I'll go look for the Portal. I'll be back to tell you what I saw."

"Nice…"

Without further thought, Amber tried the door handle. It came unlocked, and she rushed right in, her eyes shut. She tried to get this over with as quickly as she could.

* * *

That same feeling was in her throat and her chest again, stealing all the air from her lungs. She grasped her hair as a slight comfort and took a deep breath, but it sounded strange. It echoed.

Hadn't she thought this through? She had been running for a while now.

Now she was alone, lost. The Gadget must have been above her head, but she couldn't even see it.

The next thing that came out of her mouth was a shout, a cry. *She was afraid of the dark.* She couldn't deny it now.

She was so foolish. Running straight into what scared her to prove it wasn't scary.

Amber turned around to see if she could still spot the open door, but she'd run too far now. Everything was black. The

House she was in seemed bigger than it looked, *if that was possible.*

Then, she heard something. It came out crawling, low and quiet, from a corner. A distant echo, a faded melody.

It was a funny tune, but somehow when she heard it, she saw light. She saw it, rather than heard it. Or she was listening to light.

Whatever it was, it was straight ahead, and she had no choice. She was here for a purpose. So, Amber closed her eyes and moved towards the sound.

She could still see the light even with her eyes closed—or hear it. Then, she tripped and fell forwards onto the ground. Amber had expected tiles, or maybe rock, since this appeared to be a sort of cave, but was quite staggered to land on grass. And *something else.* Something that felt like plants. Plants in the dark.

Then, that tune again. It rang into her ears, loud and clear.

"Don't let my walls fool your open eye
They could squash and squeeze you
Into a lovely pie!
Into wrong places in-between
Where you suffocate unseen.
Are you scared? Yes you are!
Trapped in darkness, in my jar..."

It sounded a bit like the Cats' voices. But it wasn't them. It was low, hummed and sung by someone she could not see or find. The voice didn't sound human, anyway.

She froze for a moment, dazed. And still, she had no explanation. It did not even seem like there was anyone or anything present with her.

She couldn't make sense of the lyrics. For a moment, she wondered if it might have been an illusion, but instantly put the thought away. Instead, she told herself, *the voice didn't matter, anyway*. There was no one confronting her now, so she could pretend she'd never heard—or *seen*—it. Amber tried to erase the words from her mind before she came to any other conclusions. *They didn't matter. She needed to get home.*

She got to her feet.

Then, she recognized a blue light.

She did not come to it, so much as *it* came to her. And it illuminated everything, revealing walls crusted with ice.

It was the Portal: a glowing X.

Before she entered, Amber decided to go back and tell Koko, so that it could confirm to Halfmoon that she had done it. Or perhaps because the light blinded her a little, and she wanted to leave the song behind her, not wanting to find out what else the dark held for her before she was sure how to enter properly.

When she was back outside, the chilly breezes made her tremble and shudder as she got Koko. The weather seemed worse than before.

They went back in.

Amber ran through the dark, Koko now following. Somehow, she had to run for longer this time, but they came to the same light.

"This is it?" she gasped, exhausted.

"Yes!" Koko exclaimed. "I think we've found it!"

"So, I just walk into it? Reach my hand in first?"

"Yeah. That shouldwork."

Then Amber saw Koko's face in the blue light. It studied her awkwardly for a moment, as if it realized it would never see her again. As if it would miss her.

It looked terrifying.

In its gaze, there were many things it wanted to tell her. But Amber didn't want to hear—she wanted to get this *done*.

So, she gently reached into the Portal, waiting for a force to suck her in. But no force pulled her.

In fact, as Amber reached her hand right into it, she felt a blast, a light, and she was pushed *away*, against the wall.

Groaning, her head ached in confusion. She tried again. She ran straight in, ignoring what had happened.

Again, she was thrown back.

And then, as she tried to look at the Portal properly, she realized that, not unlike what had happened with the Fox cub, there were two Portals. No, three.

Something strange and wrong was happening, and Amber found it hard to deny.

CHAPTER 8 – TRAPPED??

She tried again, and Koko seemed to be cursing under its breath, muttering something about *stubbornness*.

Amber forced herself to smile. *This was fine, this was fine. This all made sense.*

But the Portal was not like the X she had encountered in Japan. All the light inside the House now revealed something that—she hated to admit it—reminded her of the Fox cub; they were all strange, duplicated images, out of place.

Before her, there were multiple Portals, but her view was unfocused as she walked towards them, shaking and swaying. Trying to ignore their strangeness, she picked a Portal and ran into it.

It did not work. She could not enter.

Now, standing there, the Portals reflecting in her eyes, she felt numb again. Numb, useless to her surroundings, like there was nothing she could do to them. As if she were a tiny, stupid creature.

Amber wanted Halfmoon. She wanted Its order, Its ideas, Its thoughts.

"K-Koko..." she muttered. "What do we... do?" She giggled nervously into the silence. Even the low hum had gone.

Koko shook its head silently and shrugged. "I... dunno. It seems it's kinda impossible to tell if this is real."

Amber laughed at these odd words. She would not give in.

She needed Halfmoon. She needed suggestions. She needed order.

"Look at it this way," Koko stated, its voice happier than it should have sounded. "Halfmoonwants us to go thisway, but what if we do something else?"

It said this in an exaggeratedly casual tone, though the Portal's light inside the House showed its face was serious.

The words did not make sense to Amber's ears. "*Something else*?" she said. "What can we possibly do? This was our plan. This was supposed to be my exit..."

A voice hummed into her ears. Again, she heard light, or saw a low, childish sound. It was a musical tune... of barks. She dreaded the worst. Something was coming.

Koko shrank back and made itself flat against the wall, whimpering.

Amber froze, not knowing what was happening.

She could not spot the danger yet, as it was concealed by darkness. So she had to wait in painful anticipation, relying desperately on the blue light in front of her, until she could finally see.

Through the dark they crept, big and bushy. Silky, sleek, plush fur, the colour of moonlight, grew up to their pointy ears. Their lips were pulled back in a menacing snarl, and their teeth were bared—in a smile.

They looked like seahorses, thought Amber. They had no

proper legs, but instead something that looked like a small cartoonish cloud, a scribble, drawn in the air.

If she had squinted her eyes and hadn't been so terrified, she could have assumed that they were very big seahorses. Big seahorses that lived on land and could levitate. Maybe she could even have believed that they were seahorses with icicles growing on their backs, who were smirking.

But they were not seahorses. Something about them was very, very wolfish. And strange.

She should have screamed, but the frosty air swallowed her voice; there were at least five of them, though she felt too dizzy and weak to count. They floated closer and devoured some ice that lay on the floor of the House.

She was next to one of the walls. Koko was beside her, hissing.

"What are they?" she asked it, as they all lined up to stand guard before the Portal.

"Um—Doodles. Halfmoon saw them once through Its Eyes, as It has Eyes here too. Halfmoon was reminded of tiny Humans' drawings, and so namedthem Doodles…"

She saw it, *exactly*; not unlike the Cats, they were odd, almost comical, like their proportions were wrong—though not just wrong to Amber, but *objectively* wrong, as if something a five-year-old child had drawn had come into real life.

The Doodles were barking. *Poor dogs*, thought Amber. *Dogs drawn wrong!* But, of course, she hated them. They were all childish nonsense.

Every time they made a sound, barked, howled, or sneezed, ice and snow sprouted from the air.

She looked away at precisely the same moment the Doodles shifted their focus, almost in unison, to face her and Koko.

Amber wanted to stay because of the Portal, but the next thing she knew, they were being chased, blindly running all the way back through the House, and soon stood gasping outside.

Koko ran out of the enclosed tree path, and she had no choice but to follow.

With their gaze on the empty path behind them, they stopped for a moment. "The plan didn't work out," Koko said.

Its face looked so surprised.

"Oh, I didn't *know*!" Amber snapped. But she knew Koko had done nothing wrong. "We… have to go back," she spluttered. "Do what… Halfmoon told us to do."

"Amber, no." Koko seemed to be trying to soften its voice, as if softening the truth. "Like I said, Ithink it's, uh, impossible."

"Impossible?" She didn't want to hear it.

"Yeah? It is!"

"What do you *mean*, it's impossible?!" Her voice broke. She didn't want yet another surprise, another plan. She wanted to get back and escape this place forever.

At that moment, there was a hair-raising feeling in the air. They heard a familiar voice, almost a musical hum.

"Out, out, out you go."

Amber glimpsed through the trees and saw a face staring back at her with big eyes, for only a second.

The ground shook as the door creaked open, and then came the sound of many things running. Running, yet not on the ground.

Koko grabbed her tightly in its Paws, pulling her along with force. Taken aback, she went with it.

They sprinted down the rest of the forest trail, carefully dodging fallen trees and prickly winter plants. Somehow, the path looked less neat now, and more open, too. Now, it felt like she had been lied to. The path from earlier had completely changed.

They ran and ran, and as Koko carried and pulled her along, with the speed it was going, she could not tell where they were.

But they were not in the forest anymore, and she couldn't see any more trees. Amber wanted Koko to stop, for them to go back, for Halfmoon to be here, but she found she had left her voice behind at the Portal.

All she saw now was the same sheet of white. She barely heard the monsters in the distance.

Soon, Koko set her down again, and she had to use her own legs to run. But then, as she looked back, she saw the Doodles were catching up with them.

Perhaps unwillingly, Amber stopped in her tracks. They were here now, and she could not close her eyes to them. Yet, she did not escape.

The Portal. It had been Halfmoon's order to enter it. *Wouldn't giving up on the Portal mean that the magic was out of their, even Halfmoon's, control? That they absolutely* could *not enter?* She couldn't accept *that.*

She realized Koko was pushing her along again.

"Amber," it mumbled, "whyaren'tyourunning?"

In that guilty moment, she realized her torn thoughts had frozen her to the spot.

And now it was too late.

The Doodles encircled them.

"OK…" Koko whimpered. "OK. Trust me…" It reached into the sack it was carrying and pulled out its Lizard friend. It held it up high into the air.

The Doodles stopped. They peered, interested.

The almost full moon was shining, shining on Koko. She didn't know what it was doing.

Amber edged closer to see better, but Koko, its claws still out, pushed her away and shrieked, "Stay away!"

It lifted its Lizard. *Like a sacrifice.*

The moon beamed down onto Koko's exposing Paw. It was pearly, milky, and much paler and brighter than the moon Amber saw on Earth.

In that brief, frozen-still moment, the sight of the likely very confused Lizard beneath the glowing glamour of the moon felt like an invitation to heaven, the light slowly spreading and falling onto everything, as if stroking the entranced, moonstruck Doodles.

Amber still couldn't figure it out.

But then something went wrong. One Doodle lost interest and started watching Koko, its jaws widening and a low growl escaping it. It was about to leap on top of Koko.

Koko, who noticed this, mouthed, "Help me" to Amber.

But she had never been asked to help anyone before. She started to think. *What could she do?*

Koko was trembling. It looked up at the Doodles, their horrid anticipation.

Something fell onto the ground.

The Doodles started eating it.

Amber couldn't see what it was—only that Koko was no longer holding its Lizard.

Moving towards her, Koko cried out, "Let's go! We can't save it! *Trust* me!" And it, of course, was crying.

Amber could see now. They were only eating the tail of the Lizard, nothing more. *So where was the Lizard?*

A pain shot through her foot, and she saw a Doodle had its

wide jaw around her ankle. Amber lifted her foot, shaking off the snarling beast.

A flat, squashed, blood-splattered Lizard fell off the sole of her shoe.

The Doodles had finished eating. They sprang at Koko, then stopped abruptly, their eyes gleaming.

The furred beasts all let out a clear, long howl as sharp, needle-like icicles shot into the air. All pointed directly at Koko.

Koko hissed at the incoming assault as Amber tried hitting them out of the way, but it was too late; the icicles moved with singular purpose as if guided by the ghostly hands of the cool wind.

Two of them hit Koko on its hind legs.

The Doodles stopped to watch.

Koko's breath seized as it hissed out and spat in pain. It tore its eyes open to the fullest as the rest of its face screwed up in terrible agony, and it grunted and screamed. Its wound was leaking blood, which was freezing beneath the ice.

Having only a single option left, Amber picked Koko up and dragged it along, finally running and escaping from what was behind her. Escaping from the monsters.

Holding Koko's body in her arms, it felt smaller and lighter than she would have ever thought.

Perhaps because Koko wasn't conscious, she released them —her emotions: the human feelings of shame, pity, and compassion that she knew she should have felt more of. Of fear.

She released the tears from her already burning eyes and let them cool and trickle down her cheek, the curve of her nose, over her mouth, down her neck…

As she ran through the storm, she saw it again. The Fox cub.

Its fur was ruffled in the strong winds. But it didn't seem bothered one bit. In fact, its eyes stared colder than the weather.

Amber tried to keep her eyes half-closed, not wanting to see. Her stomach dropped as she heard that same voice. She knew it was coming from the Fox cub.

She did not want to hear what it was saying—if it was even speaking. She had tried to understand it but failed. So now, Amber did not want to meet it *at all*.

And maybe she could *not know what was real.* Maybe she had to admit it now. *Maybe it was all just too scary for her to understand.*

She had tried. Tried to understand the Cats' nature, to understand the Fox cub, the skinny trees, even the Portal. But now, as her final option, as she had failed to detangle all the nonsense in this world, she wanted to escape it completely, as she could not make the horrors less scary. As she could not escape physically.

Nearly tripping along the rocky beach, Amber made it to the boat and leapt into it with Koko, not knowing what to do now.

CHAPTER 9 – HALFMOON

Koko was awake again. She heard it move around the boat nervously. From what she could feel while lying on the boat, they were not sailing yet and were still by the Wacky Winters. But she avoided any thoughts about whether or not she was cold, and any thoughts about the snow, as Koko had said the snow had tricked her.

Amber pretended to sleep. She pretended not to care.

Eventually, she felt the weight of a blanket being put onto her, at which she almost opened her eyes.

But she did not want to face Koko. She could already picture in her mind its now especially red, watery eyes and fat, trembling lips.

Although she felt restless, she continued to lie silently with her eyes closed to the world around her. She did not know how much time was passing. She would not have known if it were minutes, hours or days, but she wanted to stay like this. She tried to force herself into sleep, drift away into a careless dream, forget everything, forget herself, but all she saw in her head were things that would surely make nightmares.

And she would have stayed there, continuing to procrastinate and lay, blind and still, forever, but soon she could no longer control the urge she was trying to fight. Of using the Gadget.

Koko had its back to her but turned around instantly when it heard her sit up. Its eyes were indeed wet and puffy. "*Why* did you do that?"

Amber didn't reply. This was just what she had dreaded. Koko's reactions only made everything worse. As did its terrifying face.

She gulped, not looking at it, trying not to reach for the Gadget. She knew, really, she *needed* to let Koko talk for a while. So, she let it, but she avoided its eyes; she avoided most of the meaning of what came out of its mouth.

"They *hit* me," it croaked. "Becauseofyou. I had this plan. To distract the Doodles, but—butyou… *Why* didn't you help me?! I needed youback there! Because ofyou, I can barely move my legs. My Lizard wouldn't have been lost…" It started to sob.

Koko did not know *she* had killed the Lizard. Amber remembered that it had wanted to distract the Doodles by *tricking* them, making them think they would get the Lizard, but then the Lizard had launched its tail at them. In that moment, however, she hadn't understood what Koko was doing. And then, she'd just *had* to understand, accidentally stepping onto the Lizard while doing so. It was a further reason she wanted to avoid talking to Koko.

Koko was a horrible sight when it cried. Its usual appearance was already enough for the palms of her hands to get all sweaty and her heart to beat all wrong. For it was wrong. She knew something like it was not *supposed* to exist. Normal cats were just cats, something warm and familiar. Something that,

if she took the time to think back—which she avoided doing—
brought back memories of love. *Cats were small creatures,
and most certainly not any bigger than people. Besides, there
was never anything menacing about even slightly larger cats,
as it was easy to tell exactly how big and strong they really
were. They came with no surprises and always stayed the same
shape and size. They did not talk. They did not talk of the
unexpected.*

But this one did.

And she was all alone with it. Still.

She watched Koko burst into tears as it spluttered it all out.
It always spat out all the sickening pain, all the words she
avoided, that came crawling out of its grotesque jaw. It was
just… too honest.

And it was speaking—*screaming*—there in front of her
now. It yelled, and it talked, and it muttered, and it whimpered.
It drowned her in words. The words of what had *happened*,
what it all *meant*, what she needed to *do* in the future, what
had gone wrong…

"Just accept it! Just accept it!" it cried, when she only
shook her head.

She wished that for a little while longer, she could go off to
a temporary safe spot, in the Gadget, or in her sleep. But she
knew she was not safe. She knew, deep down, in this world
there was no escape. Not for long.

Her mind drained out its voice, all the words, the tears.
*Aside from, perhaps, the Lizard, nothing bad had really
happened*, she told herself. But she knew a hidden, appalling
truth, something *else*, was hidden from them—very near, yet
always out of sight.

Because Koko was saying, "We needto see if there's anoth-
erPortal. The other one's not working like Halfmoon should be

making it work. I know youwant to go back, but something's wrong, and if you don't get out of this world through a Portal…"

She would be trapped.

Amber knew.

She would never get back to Japan.

The small Amaya side of her still thought nonsense was only… amusing. Yet, even laughing now would be pointless, and she felt her ability to laugh was gone. She was tired. Of laughing, of trying to understand this world.

But Koko was still crying. "Whyareyou *ignoring* me?"

She replied, "Sorry, Koko, I—"

Then, something froze her voice, kept *it* trapped, too, inside her throat…

Amber's eyes widened as she stared at them.

By the edge of the boat, there were slender monsters.

She didn't know when they had got there, and if they had been watching her this whole time.

They appeared worm-like. Sad-looking, slight, snake-like things, except with no distinct transition from their heads to their worm bodies. They didn't have proper mouths—only small slits below their bulky eyes, which were hollow but filled with a worn, exhausting blackness, as if grieving or lost in dark thoughts. Their expressions reminded Amber of the Cats' eyes.

Unlike the other creatures she had encountered, there was something about these Worms that looked… *simple*. They had no unique, spine-chilling features like the Doodles or the Cats. They were *just* sad Worms

There were three of them, a foot away from the boat, heads slightly tilted depressively. Amber had no way of telling how tall they were, and how far their bodies reached into the sea.

She didn't know what it was, but something about them made her pinch herself even harder than she had before. *They were simpler than the other creatures, yet somehow this brought up an even worse feeling.*

Something about their eyes.

It was almost as if Amber's own tiredness, her own fatigue and frustration of failure and trying to understand were *reflected* in their eyes, and she was staring at a skinnier, sadder, smaller version of herself. A version bored with trying and bored with life.

Koko screamed, and the dreadful noise made Amber bite her tongue so hard that she could actually taste blood. She had never expected Koko to react this way to creatures of its own realm.

Perhaps it was thinking the same as she was about them. Perhaps it even felt bad in some way for the Worms.

Koko gulped and made more coughing, laughing noises. Amber knew it was not really laughing, but told herself it was. *Yes, laughing. These monsters were funny. And they weren't different from anything else in this world.*

But after a moment of silence, she realized they weren't attacking after all. The Worms were only watching carefully.

Amber suppressed a few horrid shudders and turned her head away. Staring would be pointless.

She decided to get the Gadget down. Now was her chance. She turned it on and held the receiver to her ears. That same comforting feeling of protection came to her; she felt a bit safer in this place. This would, she knew, remove her current feelings, leaving only pleasant nothingness. Now her eyes were fixed on nothing more than the strings, the coloured cords. They formed nonsense. But she knew they were also removing all the things she had not meant to see from her head, sucking them away from her, finally.

She felt the memory of the talking House glide away. She felt the weird lyrics from the humming voice vanish from her mind. She felt the Doodles sizzle and evaporate, the nonsense of the past hours almost completely perish.

The Gadget was keeping her away from reactions, away from decisions and actions. At least for now.

Deep down, another subtle feeling came up. It was a feeling of guilt. It whispered to her that *she had to go. That she could not escape for much longer. That there were things she needed to do.* She ignored it. For a little while.

But then, she recognized a new sensation. From the Gadget, a message into her mind. Halfmoon. Halfmoon!

Hello, child, kiddo. I'm glad you are liking the Gadget. Always helps to disconnect, does it not? Then It told her something that changed her feelings entirely. *What happened today should have been expected, my mistake. There is another way, there is another Portal. Do not worry. There is still time.*

She let the words sink in. There was another Portal.

Another *Portal*!

There was another way back. She had her ticket home.

There was an electric, blaring noise. Amber heard Koko gasp. The noise was coming from the Gadget, but was not something that only she could hear through the receiver—instead, it was loud and clear, and seemed to erupt from within the Gadget and transmit onto everything all around, so that Koko heard it, too.

Halfmoon was calling her. But this wasn't an ordinary telephone, and she *already* held the receiver in her hand. There was nothing to pick up.

Yet, it seemed the phone picked itself up, anyway; the

screen changed slightly, now also showing the wobbly image of Halfmoon. She saw It sitting at Its small desk in Its cabin, smiling broadly and apparently being able to see her as well.

"Hello," It greeted through the screen, a joyful look on Its face. "Amber, I see you have figured out how to use my invention. Yes, I can send you direct messages through the screen. But I can also speak to you aloud this way."

Amber liked how although Halfmoon probably knew what had happened with the Portal, It did not bring it up immediately.

But, after a moment, It finally said, "So, Amber, how was it?"

She was relieved that It hadn't asked something more direct, like, *So, Amber, did you find the Portal?* but felt her body become tense.

"Well…" She recalled everything. The bleeding Fox Cub, the House with eyes, the plants in the dark inside it, the voice with obscure lyrics, the blocked Portal, the Doodles…

"Well, it was very cold," she said.

Koko looked at her and it was hard to tell if it was about to laugh or cry.

"Why, the Wacky Winters *are* very cold," Halfmoon replied, with a neutral expression. "It is good I gave you those jackets."

"Jackets?" Amber asked. "What jackets?"

"The ones I packed you."

As she still looked clueless, Halfmoon's eyes narrowed and moved to Koko's side of the boat on the screen.

"Koko. You had the sack. Am I right?"

It coloured instantly. "Yes. YesIdid."

"And the jackets? Did you not give Amber one? Did you only take one for yourself?"

It looked away and muttered, "I didn't take out or find any. Iwasn'tcold."

"Oh…" Halfmoon shook Its head, Its voice a low growl. "Selfish Cat!"

Koko's lips trembled, and its whole face shook.

Halfmoon sighed. "Do not cry, Koko."

Tears spilled from Koko's fragile eyes.

Halfmoon let out another long sigh, which made Amber wonder if It was also just incredibly exhausted. But then It retrieved Its usual slight smile.

It went on, "I have Eyes around the island. And I have seen… you have been *injured*. Koko, terribly wounded, and Amber, bitten on the leg. Are you… all right?"

"Oh." Koko's teary eyes widened further, and then both Amber and it smiled, as they had almost forgotten their injuries because of the Lizard event itself.

"You have simply experienced shock. The cold temperatures do make things seem funnier than they are, right?" It forced a chuckle. "Doodle injuries are fine after a couple of hours. Be patient, and you'll be all right."

Amber nodded. "Yes. Shock is all it was."

"*Yes*. And so, perhaps it *is* better you do not go back there," Halfmoon advised carefully.

Amber nodded again. Halfmoon's words were simple, stronger than her own, urging her to listen.

At that moment, she realized that a wooden bowl was set beside her with ramen, still hot and sizzling, with a fried egg and pieces of fresh ham on top.

As if knowing just when she saw it, Halfmoon said, "You may have noticed before, but I always send you meals through the sack. The sack is amongst my newest inventions. It is a type of Portal, except it cannot transport living things, for everything that enters it becomes frozen in its state—anything alive would die. It is also the reason why, when I send you food, it will stay warm forever, at least until it enters your mouth."

Amber didn't know what to say. She picked up the steaming bowl in her hands, although it slightly burned her skin. "Thank you."

Halfmoon's expression shifted. "Now, there are some things I do need to speak to Koko about. Privately. This will be short. Please, Amber, could you give Koko the receiver?"

She did so.

Koko looked puzzled. Taking the receiver, it shot a look at the sea, to where the Worms had been a moment ago. They had completely disappeared.

Amber half-convinced herself she'd imagined them.

Hesitantly, Koko nodded. "OK."

Halfmoon's image vanished from the screen, and for a while, the next few words It spoke were barely audible to Amber.

Nonetheless, it was not an ordinary telephone, and Koko did not have human ears. It held the strange phone in a strange way, and somehow, Amber was able to pick up a not-so-quiet squeak of words, sometimes growing louder.

She understood they were discussing the events of all that had happened on the Wacky Winters and preferred not to listen. However, she could not help but catch a few gruesome details of the Doodles and their oddness. Koko sobbed.

Halfmoon seemed uninterested in the Doodles, almost as if It was shrugging them off. And then she heard It drop Its voice and whisper something as if to ensure Amber would not hear.

She would have simply eaten the bowl of ramen and

pretended all was well, but she felt an urge to listen. Slowly putting the bowl back down, she caught a few fragmented words.

"Koko, really… must stop yapping nonsense… not scare her with ideas… with illusions… all is nonsense… as if I did not… as if… no order… have you forgotten how to behave? … wish you were different… If you want her to be happy… and… *nothing* is wrong… also… keep your emotions together… new Portal… Teplaytides… with your clumsiness… control yourself…"

What was nonsense? What was It talking about? She ached to fill the blanks in her understanding, but she knew, somehow, that Halfmoon had it all set for her. Maybe not understanding was all right—and for now, she didn't *need* to know everything?

A sudden warmth filled her. Or rather, not a warmth, but a block of that guilt she had felt when she'd used the Gadget instead of creating a new plan.

She still didn't know what was going to happen, but she knew Halfmoon did. She knew now It *did* have new ideas, *and It could steer her*!

Amber picked the bowl back up again, and started mixing the egg in with the noodles, blowing to cool her meal down.

They were figuring out a plan—for her—*and she would go in a new direction* with their guidance. Halfmoon would guide her, and all she had to do was to allow It.

She had been lost, but now she would follow!

Amber realized that Koko was staring at her. Halfmoon's voice was no longer heard. The talk had ended.

The invention had sucked away most of her previous feelings, and she turned away from it to face Koko instead. She smiled for only a second, and cried, "OK, OK. We need to do this in a new way. To get to Japan, I mean. Since there *is* another exit. You can now tell me the *new* plan."

CHAPTER 10 – STEERING STARFISH?

While she waited for Koko's reply, Amber calmed herself by starting her ramen.

Koko didn't say anything. She kept swallowing spoon after spoon.

Then, Amber turned again. It wasn't a sound that made her do this, as the creatures stared in silence like before, but it was as if she had *sensed* that the Worms had returned. They were here again.

She also realized that everything was moving; their boat had started to sail. But Amber was *fine* with this, she told herself, because there was no need to go back to the Wacky Winters.

The Worms' long, stick-thin bodies remained in fixed, unmoving positions but followed along smoothly as the boat sailed on. They were here for the ride, seemingly *attached* to the boat somehow. They still looked quite melancholic.

But again, Amber felt fine with them. Because she knew they were only watching, and she no longer felt any pressure to understand them or interact with them in any way. Halfmoon had lifted that pressure. The Gadget had lowered the *true* levels of terror. The creatures were terrifying, as this world still was, but there was a new direction, and it was like she was *allowed* to eat her ramen and pretend they were not there.

For a moment, the steaming spiciness made her eyes water and her mouth burn, but then she realized how much she loved the taste. She loved it, mainly because its sweet-spicy intensity and flavour kept her from speaking.

Koko was staring at her. It still looked very upset, though its expression was hard to read. Things seemed to be happening, bursting and swirling in its own mind, not unlike her own. "I don'treally want totalk," it squeaked.

For a moment, with the Worms there and Halfmoon's voice gone, it all almost seemed very funny to Amber again.

"K-Koko," she stuttered, grinding her teeth. "All I need to know is where we are going now. A simple overview. I don't even need lots of details." She knew she needed to be cautious, simply get the information she needed, and not ask for any more. Without getting scared or confused. And without upsetting Koko.

Koko studied her. Its eyes were still teary, and it gave her an apologetic, yet hurt look that said many things, things it would not put into words.

She was about to snap. *Why was it being so complicated? And right when she had wanted to hear the plan. Right when she was no longer so afraid of new ideas.*

"Doyouknow what happened to my Lizard?" it asked, keeping itself steady.

Amber gulped, feeling the burning pressure of its eyes on her head. *So this was what it was about.* "Yes. I mean, no." *Guilty.* "Koko. Can we please talk about this when I know the plan?"

The Worms were gone again. Amber set her ramen aside for a moment.

Koko continued to study her, but as soon as she met its eyes, it looked away, quickly breaking its gaze. It sighed.

"Please, Koko?" Amber asked.

Fortunately, Koko seemed to want to avoid the truth of its Lizard's death anyway, and shook its head, indicating she should say no more.

"You're right. I don'teven want to hear about thatnow," it started. "Let me tell you the newplan. But… it might be kinda complicated. You mightneed *this*." It reached into the sack and pulled out the map.

Amber raised her eyebrows. "Just tell me."

She realized she had never properly looked at the map before.

It was all sketched out in thick lines. Four islands were to be seen, each with its name, yet with hardly any detail on them besides red dots indicating the two Portals.

Koko took a large Cat Improvement Pill from the sack to clear its voice. It pointed at the red dot on the Wacky Winters. "So, we weren't able to enter this Portal, obviously, because of, uh, well, *complications* and not being able to tell whether—"

"OK. I understand that. *What are we doing now?*"

"There are two Portals in this realm that lead to Japan. One of them being on, well, the Wacky Winters, and the other is on this island called Teplaytides."

"Te-play-tides?"

"It's… It's the… I don't know how to describe it. It's the *funniest* island, Halfmoon says…" Its voice trailed off.

"The *funniest*?" Amber scrunched up her face.

"Best ask Halfmoon. It says it's a… what was it? A folly!

The… Folly Teplaytides! It keeps a lot to Itself, but sometimes It tells us Cats stuff. Sometimes, It tells us things It has seen with Its Eyes. Legends, you know, of other islands."

"What legends?" she asked carefully.

Koko was about to open its mouth when she muttered, "If you're going to say something terrifying, then never mind. Just —just go on."

It nodded. "What I was saying is that when Halfmoon talks about Teplaytides, as much as It laughs, we know it's being sarcastic. It almost pretends it's like… I don't know, child's play. From what I know, it's a terrible place that really can confuse you. Awful—"

"I don't need to hear about it," Amber cut in.

"OK, no details… It's just *bad*. But unfortunately, that *is* the place we have to go to." It adjusted its face, looking down. "But we can't go directly from here to Teplaytides, anyway," it went on. "Strong currents. *Very* strong currents. Trustme. There's this… river. It does a half circle around Teplaytides. It's impossible to get directly from here to Teplaytides *without* meeting it.

"The only spot on Teplaytides that is not surrounded by this river is much further north, but it would be too risky to sail all the way up there. Halfmoon tells us some scarythings about the river, not to go near it. Trust me. I probably shouldn't tell you about it…"

"OK." Amber nodded. *She was better off not knowing.* "What are we doing?"

Koko pointed: there was another island on the map. It was labelled 'DragonFree Haven' in English.

"Halfmoon says…" Koko paused for a moment, frowning, as if to recall Halfmoon's exact words. Or maybe it was frightened by Amber's intense gaze. "We're taking the longway.

Yes. We're sailing back, all around the *other* side of the Wacky Winters, west, you know, that doesn't face Teplaytides. Then, once we've completely passed the Wacky Winters, we can approach Teplaytides from a river-less angle.

"But before we get there, we should… stop by another island. Halfmoon says we should stop by at DragonFree Haven. The river starts somewhere *around* DragonFree Haven. So, Halfmoon says it's easier to first cross land. Before, then, going to Teplaytides. Trustme."

She kept her eyebrows furrowed. "I'm… not sure if that makes much *sense*."

"What don't you understand?" Koko asked.

Amber clenched her fists at its blank, still tear-stained face. Even Koko *looked* a bit lost.

"I do understand it," she snapped, "but can you *explain* it differently?"

Koko gave a quick nod, ignoring her harsh tone of voice. "We need to get to Teplaytides for you to enter a different Portal that still leads to Japan. We can't go directly from here because of dangerous currents, so we're going the other way around, passing by the whole of Wacky Winters first. Then, we're stopping by at DragonFree Haven."

The plan, to Amber, sounded overcomplicated. An unnecessary detour. But she knew it was in Halfmoon's safe, stable grip.

"I understand," she said.

They would visit another island before visiting the final one. The thought made her feel shaky. *A whole new island.* "But *why* did you say we need to stop by… DragonFree Haven?"

Koko gave a weak smile, which she did not manage to return. "It's easier to get around DragonFree Haven by crossing on land. But, actually, it's also because… DragonFree Haven is like a, well, haven. A temporary one, anyway. Because Halfmoon says Teplaytides can be… *strange*."

Amber slowly looked up. "Strange?"

"Forget it," Koko muttered, clearly noticing a shift in her behaviour. "Trust me, forget it."

"No." Amber's jaw tightened. Suddenly, she, once again, found herself wanting to know. Clearly, there were many things they didn't tell her. *This was OK.* She believed Halfmoon *had* things figured out, and she did not fully need to know the plan. *But she didn't like the word Koko had used.* "What do you mean?"

Regret flickered across Koko's face. "No, really. I'vetalked too much. Stopit." It made a hideous coughing noise, a sign it had indeed manipulated its throat too much.

"What do you mean?" she asked again, unable to let it go.

Koko's face darkened. "Teplaytides is simply a strange place, OK? We're stopping by on a safer island first for a… break."

"A break?"

It was like Koko thought she was doubting it personally.

"Trust me!" it threw its Paws up. "The thing is, the Mahou energy—it's just strange! It's hard to understand!"

Amber gulped, but faked a smile. The only reason she had talked to Koko was because she knew the Gadget could suck away her feelings afterwards. So, when she felt all those escalating emotions—the ones that made her stomach knot and her mouth go dry—she tried to keep herself together. "I see. Well, I guess you are right. Halfmoon *would* tell us anything worth knowing."

Koko sighed. "We're just going to DragonFree Haven first. As a small stop, before Teplaytides. Trustme."

"Koko. Why do you keep saying *trust me*?" she burst out.

It shot her a wobbly, unsteady look, and then its tears came. This time, she had almost expected them.

"What did I say?" she asked.

"Forgetit," Koko mumbled.

Amber had already heard enough of the plan, so she turned on the Gadget, with the receiver in her hand, before she was able to break down into tears herself. Even as her attention shifted to the strings, she could hear Koko crying. *It was such a confusing creature.* She ignored it.

Nonetheless, Amber knew there was *something*. Something that Koko was afraid of. Even if she didn't know what. She had her own things that scared her too.

With a whole new journey ahead of her, she decided to make her own new plan…

She would stop persuading herself that things were not real. For Halfmoon and Koko were equally as real as the Doodles. Otherwise, things were hard to make sense of… Amber sighed. *Either it was all real, or it all wasn't. And anyway, Halfmoon was what she believed in. Halfmoon was the one she wanted to believe.*

After forcing herself into this mindset, she sank into the hypnotising strings of the Gadget, the back of her mind reflecting on what Koko had told her, and thus avoided unpleasant thoughts. She wasn't even hungry for her half-touched ramen anymore.

The Gadget made everything less real. She watched as tones of sea-blues and deep purples formed oceans and snow-storms. She watched as waves clashed down onto the shore, but the waves seemed tiny compared to what lay in the depths of the waters (the strings did not even show her). Amber grew uncertain, although she knew she was still safe in the

Gadget. She tried to ignore that she really *was* surrounded by endless sea… She ignored what she might need to face soon…

Amber went on like this for a while, staring at the Gadget, not paying any attention to Koko. It was only much later— many minutes or hours—that she saw Koko was asleep, so she relaxed a little.

There was no more sign of the Worms.

But the moment she heard Koko's breathing grow heavy and deep, it was like a small barrier broke. Just as when it had been injured and she had been all alone. When, like now, all her feelings and thoughts had flowed out at once.

And now she couldn't help them from coming.

Things nagged at her, like what Koko had told her in the forest…

Maybe, you can't know what is real—

The thing is, the Mahou energy—it's just strange!

Its voice still echoed in her head.

Amber did not agree—or want to agree—with Koko's ideas and thoughts. They caused a lump in her throat.

Koko was just paranoid, she told herself.

As her eyes were still on the Cat, trying to focus on something else, she caught sight of another thing.

She had almost forgotten them. The stars.

Amber had ignored them the first day, never having thought she would need to see them again. She had never thought she would spend yet more nights out at sea.

Now, she tried her best to ignore them, but from the corner of her eyes they sparkled, and she gazed up to where they were splattered across the sky.

They looked a little like deformed starfish: all organically shaped, different from one another, but containing at least one triangle. They blazed and burned in blues, pinks, and greens, in the black, so far away. They reminded Amber of sweets.

This last thought also made her recall the sweets Halfmoon had stuffed into her pocket. She pulled one out, and held it in her hand, not taking off the wrapper.

As Amber watched the stars, something in her eyes prickled, but not *only* at their glint or the way their warped bodies twisted and turned.

Instead, the look of the faraway stars made her think. Of this journey. Of everything.

The Gadget seemed to have turned itself off.

She had never seen such stars on Earth. *If they were stars, that was, and not more creatures, flying in the sky.* Still staring up at the night sky, she wondered whether the sun and moon she saw here were the same ones she saw from her bedroom window. It was just one of the many things that hadn't been explained to her.

Somehow, Amber found her thoughts drifting back to what was really happening, the truth.

What was she doing here? She was out here, on a vast, open sea, propped on a tiny boat, with a talking Cat. A few days before, she would have regarded this nonsense. She would never have believed it.

But somehow… in a way, in its own funny, crazy way, she liked this. Sometimes, Amber kind of liked this whole thing, because it meant she didn't have to go back home for now. Because she was elsewhere, and things were happening.

For a moment, she wondered. *This world, this journey, could it…* She didn't like the thought. *Could this be that* change, *the one she always wished for?*

No, no, no. Amber shook her head. *She was here, doing the exact same. Trying to understand, giving up when it all was too confusing.* Trying to get back. Back to something better, from before.

Her depressing life in Japan indeed felt so distant, like it was a life that was not hers. Or rather, as if the *present* were memories being shown to her, a dream. It almost felt like she was lost, sleepwalking and blindly stumbling through this journey. Maybe she was—even if she never would have admitted it.

But when she turned her attention from the sparkling stars back to the Gadget, she knew, at least, *they couldn't be completely lost*. After all, *Halfmoon* didn't seem lost.

And there, indeed, was a final message from Halfmoon. *Believe in my plan, just follow, follow me, kiddo.*

Amber finally unwrapped the candy. And so she sat, eyes flicking from the screen to the stars and back, repeating these words to herself, as she ate the piece of candy, the blueberry taste so similar yet so different from the ones in her town…

CHAPTER 11 – THREE DAYS??

Again, she had no memory of ever going to sleep. Or of any dreams. All she could remember was the dreamlike, fluffy, cotton atmosphere of the Gadget.

Sitting up straight, she ignored Koko's loud snores, which rumbled into the morning stillness. The Stars were gone. Again, she had that feeling. That soft, dizzying sensation of waking up properly. A slight, nauseous feeling. Almost like… a numbness. As if she had fallen into some kind of doze, a slumberous dream *inside* the Gadget, and was waking up now. Waking up to the sea roaring on all sides. She shook her head; *perhaps she was still tired.* She rubbed her eyes. And convinced herself it was nothing.

Beside her was breakfast, clattering quietly with the sway of the ocean: a small, delicate bowl of rice mixed with some scrambled eggs. It was still warm.

Amber held it up to her face as she ate from it with a spoon, her eyes still gazing into the distance, as if they had never left that spot in the sky where the Stars had been. She realized that the sun she could see here *was* the same one from Earth, or at least looked like it.

Her mind was indeed still filled with the same thoughts from last night.

As she looked out at the slow rocking of the waves, the happy lift, the heavy fall, she couldn't help but think, again, of her town's sea, her small apartment. *What time was it there now, and how long had she been gone?*

When would she be back?

At that moment, the Gadget glided down. Instantly, she saw a new message, a mind reader.

I know you want to leave.

And another.

Should I tell you when you can leave?

"What?" Amber whispered to the Gadget, placing the bowl back down. "I…? Of course I want to leave!"

A single number, rather than a word, appeared on the screen.

3.

It blew softly into her ears. Along with the rest of Half-moon's words.

Three days. Three days, and I swear not much more, and then you will arrive at DragonFree Haven.

"Only three days…" Amber mumbled to herself.

This unusual, new sense of time sparked something else in the back of her mind. Something she hadn't done yet. Before she could make sense of this, she found another quick message on screen.

Have you seen the Teleclock's numbers?

"Yes," she mumbled. "Yes. I've seen them, but never properly. You told me not to worry about them yet."

She had been hesitant, but she had fallen in love with the

strings, and how could this be different? After all, they were all Halfmoon's inventions, things which she knew could not hurt.

For the first time, Amber observed the clock-part of the Gadget. Numbers 1 to 14 circled around, but instead of clock hands, the number 8 was underlined in red.

Kiddo, these are very special things. They are simple things, too, and I know you will be able to understand them. They show you how much time you have. They show how many days you have left before the Terror will come.

But beware, they might change a little in a day. The Teleclock might say you have 8 days in the morning, and in the afternoon of that same day, say you only have 7 left! It changes as the Teleclock re-calculates the most accurate number every few hours, based on the location and speed of the Terror.

Amber nodded to the Gadget, in case Halfmoon was watching her.

Three days, out at sea, with Koko and with whatever could appear from the depths. Three days, and all she needed to do was hold on. She grinned. She needed to keep herself together, and avoid the terrors, so that she could follow the plan, and get to the new islands. So that she could finally escape this world.

And she had to be back home—she *would* be back—before eight days. Or at least that was what the clock said now.

All Amber needed to do was to avoid things. Avoid scary things. Scary, like the talking House, or the dying Fox cub, or the childlike Doodles. Anything that could eventually drive her insane.

For if she didn't, her mind would try to understand it, then fail, slip… But she could *not* fall into restlessness, confusion. She could not pass out and sink into the snow, like she had on the Wacky Winters… *Oh no, that could not happen again.* She needed to stay safe and sane, steady her feelings. All she needed to do was *avoid.*

But before she turned to the strings, she observed the clock a little longer. There was a spark inside her that Halfmoon had evoked. A need, an urge to know as much as she could about the things that she *could* know about.

She stared until her eyes felt sore at the unchanging number 8.

It took what felt like hours until she was reassured enough; it wouldn't change too much, she was safe.

So, on Day 1, Amber finally looked at the strings.

She watched them twist and take the shape of skies. Skies that looked like they were painted. She was sucked into them, their scene…

They looked like painted skies—all drawn out, but flawless, with perfectly round, spongy clouds. She was gliding swiftly. She could see her little bird feet beneath her, walking on air and wind. Simple, little, normal bird feet.

She knew exactly how far she was from the ground, how many feather-lengths she was from every house below, and every other flying creature in the sky. She knew.

And she steered herself like a self-assured captain, a steady aeroplane, diving in and out of the clouds. At her own will, her own flight, her own power.

As that little bird, she was happy. For this was all she could wish for.

* * *

Just as Amber was feeling quite steady and distracted, Koko awoke.

It took a while for her to notice, but when she spotted the thing that was staring at her out of the corner of her eye, her gaze and steadiness dropped.

Immediately, she was no longer in the skies as she recalled their conflicts and Koko's tears yesterday. The Lizard. The fear, the almost-guilt. Things she'd rather avoid.

She wanted to look away.

"Amber!" she heard its sudden, funny voice cut through her, almost like waking her up from a dream. "I—Iwantto add something! Our talk about theLizard never got clearedup—"

"*No*," Amber cut in. As she looked at its face, she couldn't find a trace of anything besides fury.

"But there was something I wanted to add!"

"Koko." She kept her features steady, steady, steady. "Don't you see? This will only result in… fights."

"Fights?" Koko frowned, as if the word tasted sour in its mouth.

Amber pulled away the receiver to lock eyes with Koko properly. Lock eyes once, then not again.

"It wasn't *fair*." Its voice broke. "It reallyreallyreally wasn't. You're not saying I *deserve* that, are you—?"

There was an odd sound. Amber knew Halfmoon was calling. Koko was about to protest, but she picked up the Gadget.

"Please, Koko, please. I saw what happened with your Lizard, and for you, I am sorry. But I must remind you, or tell you, that such a creature was not what you think it was. How did I forget… to *warn* you? That Lizard, it was a toxic type. The—the ones, when touched too often… explode! Oh yes, they explode *everywhere*, and—and the juices that—that come out, well, they are toxic. After an hour, they kill you. Koko, I do promise, it would have ended your lives eventually. So forgive Amber, please."

Koko frowned and nodded, biting its lip in concentration. Amber couldn't tell whether it was trying not to laugh or cry, or a mix of both. It reminded her of the sounds the Cats always made.

"Oh, *Amber*! You too are here." Halfmoon suddenly exclaimed, as if she could be elsewhere. Something about Its tone made her recall the way It had talked to her in Its cabin. *The average intelligence in Catslaughter Island is very low. I did not expect you to get that.* "Well, I just wanted to say, I'm so glad you like the Gadget. So glad—so very glad. Remember, it never ever harms, ever. Cats and people change, I know, and some anger and blame for things are always inevitable. But remember, you always have the Gadget."

In the exact second It hung up, Koko's eyes grew themselves wider, neither them nor its lips withholding anything, as it dissolved into giggles and giggles and giggles.

Amber scrunched her face up at the sight of this, even more as tears flew out of its large eyes.

But then she found herself joining in, somehow.

At the sight of her laughing and laughing and laughing too, something about Koko's expression grew a little gentler.

"They explode," it said between snorts.

"They *explode*!" Amber cried, tears pouring out of her eyes as well.

"And out of the explosion, come juices…"

"…that kill within an hour!"

Amber was laughing at Halfmoon's words, without even understanding them.

Although this time, things were *different*; it was a new feeling.

This time, she was neither laughing into static silence nor causing a dozen screaming Cats to collide into each other. She was not Amaya now, laughing to pretend. Here and now, she felt actual amusement.

After a moment, she asked Koko, "But… why would Half-moon say that?"

It slowed, then stopped its giggles. And smiled. "I guess to, I dunno, make me forgive you, so we don't argue or whatever." It shrugged.

"Hm." Since Amber said nothing and only closed her mouth after laughing, she still wore an unwanted grin.

"Well, those were lies, weren't they?" Koko asked innocently.

"Well…" Amber grew aware of what was happening. "Wait… Halfmoon wouldn't lie, but I guess—"

Something flashed across the Gadget's screen. Something Koko could not see. Only her one ear still pressed to the receiver, connecting her mind.

The world may be full of folly, but I am not, kiddo.

And, recovering herself, she drew back her smile. She remembered what she needed to do, and who she needed to listen to. She wasn't laughing anymore.

"Koko," she said. "We shouldn't laugh at Halfmoon."

Koko had side-tracked her, dragged her into nonsense.

"What?"

"I said, we should not laugh at Halfmoon!"

"But that was *funny*…" Her tone clearly caught it off guard. "Wasn't… wasn't it?"

Amber made no reply, and a cold silence stretched out. Something had happened, something between her and Koko, but she knew she needed to forget it.

After a moment, Koko gave in, a strange emptiness in its voice, "OK… I guessHalfmoon's right. Ishould forgiveyou. I'm sorry. That Lizard wasn't reallymine, anyway. I'd foundit in the snow on the Wacky Winters…" It sighed. "I guess… I guess I'mjustlonely."

* * *

Amber avoided scary things for the rest of the day.

For a long time, she only existed in the sea and sky within the Gadget.

The *real* sea and sky around her were starting to fade away into the back of her mind, somewhere hidden. But as hours and hours trailed by, her eyes occasionally flitted anxiously from the frame of the screen. They studied the setting sun, the rocking waves, and she could not help imagining what huddled in those waters.

The more often she did this—observe the fall and rise—the more something grew heavy in her stomach. She didn't know how to describe it, but she was so *annoyed* with the sea. She grew restless, she grew bored. Hours and hours ticked by… and she was still in the same place.

But, she reminded herself. Three days. Three days, *and I swear not much more.* Just three more days of this. And she found herself constantly checking. Checking the numbers, although she knew they wouldn't change too much.

8, underlined, remained for many hours.

She couldn't describe it, but somehow, the number on the Gadget *not* changing scared her a little. Nothing changing, even though it was the same day, hearing nothing from Halfmoon.

Amber sat and sat and stared and stared until her head hurt and there was a red line beneath 7.8.

It has not yet moved much. And I doubt it will move more today.

* * *

She was a bird.

Again, she flew.

The bird whirled in circles and loops, making gentle movements with her wings.

But then, she looked down. *For the very first time.*

She looked down at the distant world below. It was maybe a new island.

But she was too high up. The fluffy clouds blocked the ground from her vision, and she could barely make out a few dark spots. Brown, dry soils and small mushed-up greens. Possibly plants. And white. A very new place.

Although she couldn't see clearly, she was sure she under*stood everything about the place. And yet, it scared her. Because she wasn't entirely sure yet of what lay below. She didn't know, not completely.*

She sharpened her eyes to see, then dived...

The ground looked murky. The land was rotten. What she had mistaken for plants were not plants at all, but an oozing slime, seeping through the muddy ground. And something else. The white was snow. *Bitter, deadly snow. Like the one on the Wacky Winters.*

She decided to reach back up into the carefree clouds. Fly at her own will, not letting her wings get caged by what lay below...

* * *

Amber flew in the blue skies all afternoon, not once looking down again...

Then she looked. At Koko.

It was staring at her, screaming or talking to her.

"Iwanttotalk!"

Startled, Amber jerked, and it did too.

"W-what?" she asked.

"I said, I wantto talk!" Again, its voice woke her up. Woke her from her blue skies. That feeling she had come to face again.

"*What* do you want to say?" she asked, louder than she'd meant to, head still diving through a cloud.

The world around her swam into proper focus, and her eyes weren't used to the rich light of the intense afternoon sun. Koko was crying.

"The…Gadget…" it croaked. "You're so obsessed."

"Obsessed?" She frowned.

"It makes you… confused," it said with an unnatural squeak.

Amber made no reply. Biting her lip, she tried to focus on the words, but it was as if, while she had been flying through imaginary clouds, the real world had been flipped onto its head. As she continued to stay quiet, Koko let out a sudden sob and turned its back towards her, leaving the words hanging in the cold, approaching evening air.

Before she could make sense of this, she realized how much her eyes stung, and how *odd* she felt.

Amber felt numb, like she had when walking in the Wacky Winter's forest. Lost, in the surreal scenery, watching the world with a dim, discreet fear, but otherwise indifferently, like a film. Although she sometimes liked this feeling, now it made her feel lost and out of place in a way she had never intended.

The Gadget floating above her again, she snapped back to her senses. Koko was *crying*.

Silently, the Cat's eyes were streaming tears as they stared into the distance. And she knew *this* couldn't be right.

Amber knew she needed to do, do something…

She followed Koko's gaze out at the still and black sea. The sea seemed strangely darker than usual, as if it were an omen of things to come. But she did not feel the terror that she might have felt. *Could this numbness have been caused by the Gadget?* This last thought scared her, a little.

She said, "OK. Koko. I'll prove it. I'm not obsessed. I won't use the Gadget for the rest of today."

CHAPTER 12 – OWNER

For a moment, Koko studied her intensely. Its messy face was lit by the last rays of the sun, but there was something about the way its eyes were twinkling, perhaps in fulfilment, that seemed to come from deep within. "Does that mean we can *talk*?"

"Talk? Well…"

Amber knew she had no choice. She was planning to avoid the Gadget for the day, and this would keep her busy.

As she stared into Koko's teary eyes, she realized she barely knew anything about this Cat, which was one of the main reasons she always felt so tense when she looked at it. It was that mystery, not knowing where it had come from, what it really wanted.

So, maybe, she could understand it better.

She raised her eyebrows and forced a smile, which fortunately she was good at. "Anything you want to talk about specifically?"

Koko froze, its jaw dropped a little.

"What?"

"You want to talk!" Its voice was croaky but expressed pure joy.

"Yes, well. I do," she replied, flatly.

"All I'd really wanted to say was, it... it doesn't matter anymore, the Lizard, stuff."

She sighed. "Then let's forget it."

Again, Koko smirked and laughed, as if it couldn't believe it. Amber was starting to get annoyed by its enthusiasm.

It started crunching on its Cat Improvement Pills from the sack, not having anything else to say.

She started, "So, there is something *I'd* like to know about." When she wasn't terrified, she was desperate to under-stand Koko's unorthodox life (*while* she was terrified, too). *But how could she ask about it? How could she get it to explain its existence, as Halfmoon had tried?* "I'm honestly curious. I'd like to know about... life. On, er, Catslaughter Island."

Koko's ears dropped a little, yet it kept on smiling. "Oh, life... *mypersonal life?*"

"What? Well, no—"

"I'll tell you the storyof how I came to Catslaughter Island..."

"Well, all right." She tried not to eye the Gadget.

Koko smiled sadly, suddenly blinking out tears. It was full of energy and joy one moment and sobbing the next. It took another few CIPs. Amber wasn't sure if she still wanted to hear what it had to say.

"When I was just a kitten, I got lost on the streets. My parents—who knows. I was soso small, and roaming around everywhere on the streets of Japan, and... *all by myself.* I could never now. But back then, I was unaware of the dangers. It was a terrible time of my life. I soon found the Portal, I guess. I met Halfmoon, and the strange new land was scary, but soon I… kind of got used to it.”

It was odd for Amber to imagine that Koko had also once been new to the realm.

“You mean you weren’t born here?”

“Oh, yeah.” Koko gulped. “A whole lot of stuff happened before I camehere. I…” Its voice trailed off.

“But…” Amber could not help herself. “When you lived in Japan, weren’t people…? Did anyone see you? I mean, was anyone scared—?” Her skin prickled at her own words, and the image in her head.

“Oh.” Koko’s eyes were full of hurt. It pointed at its face. “You mean *this*? Us?! Us, Cats, not cats, *weird* things?”

It had not answered the question that Amber had not asked, not even touched on the things she really wanted to know. Silence stretched out, until Koko finally added in a quiet voice, “I don’t know if I’m allowed to talk about this…”

“About what?” Amber bit her tongue, hating her ignorance. But a chill crept along her back, making her shiver. She cursed herself for having brought this up.

“How the Mahou energy, the realm works…”

For a moment, there was only silence.

“But anyway, I *wasn’t* always such a Cat, no. I really… used to be more of a *cat*. You know, a cat. But that’s the thing…” Koko’s voice broke.

Amber tried to ignore its awkwardness and focus on its words, listening closely. *Only a few more hours.*

“What happened?” she asked. *Apparently, it was something terrible. Something when it had been just a cat.*

“You… can’t… imagine…” Koko went on, and as it spoke, its face and lips swelled. “Iwas all alone. Onthestreets… But I soon… metthisreally kind person… Or so they seemed. Then they did terriblethings. To me."

At this point, Koko was no longer in any state to talk, and Amber didn't push any further. *So, some person had tortured it.* She didn't know what to say.

Perhaps she would even have felt some kind of sympathy for Koko in that moment. But she remembered all their circumstances and still felt quite numb. She flinched at her own urges, trying to resist looking at the Gadget's beautiful strings to work out for herself what Koko had said… And the things that it had *not* told her were also swirling around in circles in her head.

"I'm listening," she said. But still, Koko could not answer and was caught up sobbing and choking in its own world.

It seemed that a long time passed, Amber trying to swallow up her confusion and urge to use the Gadget, until Koko muttered, "Yep, I wasbetrayed. Andthat'sthe reason why… It's always *so* hard to trust things." It had stopped crying and looked exhausted.

A thought struck her. *So, Koko was betrayed and tortured, which led to it finding it hard to trust.* A guilty relief washed over her. *Perhaps this was the reason that it believed in things like illusions. That it thought some things weren't real, that it sometimes doubted Halfmoon—it was paranoid! Maybe,* a small, small hope rose in her. *Maybe, the world wasn't as complex as Koko made it seem. Maybe it was just its complex feelings.*

At least she hoped it was true. At least the fact that it was a vulnerable, paranoid, ignorant thing was somehow a comfort.

But then, as Amber observed the small fluff and mess of fur and tears, she remembered why she had wanted to talk to

Koko in the first place. It was sobbing again, in such intense pain from what it had experienced. And yet it had told her.

Amber frowned, struggling to think of what to do. And she did feel them; the emotions were there. She did feel a small ache at the sight of it—guilt and another feeling—for what had happened to it, for how this creature, though odd, was feeling.

"Koko…" She did *want* to, want to connect. But it felt like her surroundings were all out of place, she was not present in her body, and she was perhaps not really there. It was that same feeling, which she hated when it came up unexpectedly, because it left her clueless about what to do. She wanted to feel bad for Koko, but she could not connect with it—with Koko, with her own emotion—no matter how hard she tried.

A few minutes passed. Amber sat stationary on her end of the boat, trying not to look up, occasionally attempting to say something to Koko, to set things right. It seemed Koko deeply regretted having trusted her with the thing that so upset it.

Soon, Amber found there was no point in anything either of them was doing, sitting around awkwardly, trying to understand each other, until Koko cleared its throat and mumbled, "Sorryaboutthat…"

Amber decided just to shake her head.

Koko munched more medicine, and instantly its face and lips returned to normal size. "Hey, Amber…" it started. "I'm also curious. If it's not toomuch to ask, can you tell me something aboutyourself? It would… makeme feel better."

Amber bit her tongue again; Koko wanted her to speak of her life now. She knew what it meant. It was almost like revenge. *No, not revenge; it was as if Koko wanted fairness, for them to be equal.*

"What do you want to hear?" she asked, accidentally raising her voice a little. She noticed a prickling on her skin.

But she knew it didn't matter, anyway. Anything, *any* detail of her ordinary life, let alone her life before Japan, brought back unpleasant feelings. Anything did—it was all the same.

Koko still looked at her with a hurt expression, as if it wanted something more. Something to get rid of its own awful feelings and replace them.

It wanted to talk to her, to share its feelings. But *she* couldn't. She couldn't even understand it. She couldn't even quite feel right now.

"I don't know what you want," she snapped. "The story of my life? I was born in England and moved to Japan. I was honestly doing fine before I came *here*."

Of course, this was a lie, as in Japan she had been anything but fine, but it helped to keep her distance for further details.

"Sounds pretty… nice."

"*Splendid.*"

"What?"

"Nothing!" Amber said, wanting to escape the situation. "Look, I don't want… to talk about this." She sighed. "I know *you* can easily talk about your feelings, any of them. But I… I'm different."

Koko looked at her with weak, teary eyes, ones that made her chest feel tight and made her clench her fists.

Memories started rushing back to her; she recalled it all. *Memories Koko had provoked.* The joy, then the shock, the breakup, the change, the new, the hurt, the shame, the confusion. She stared at her knees, her own body, trying to look at anything but Koko.

But *it* seemed to be breaking. Its constant sobbing was starting to stir something up in her.

Their boat shook.

Amber lurched to the opposite side of the boat. Water splashed onto her, hurled by the waves. Koko cursed quietly.

She only managed a gasp when she saw it coming. And then she went silent.

Amber was unsure of how tall *it* really was. But a long, slim, slimy pole of flesh emerged out of the sea, a sickly shade of green. *Was this its neck, or its whole body?*

Assuming what she saw was all there was to it, it looked like a Snake. Except, it had the wide jaw of an alligator and the teeth of a blood-sucking vampire bat.

A part of it did not even look like an animal at all. Rather, it looked like a pole of flesh, a stick that you could reach out towards and hold and twist.

But this wasn't what mostly disturbed Amber, what made her break into a cold sweat and her lips tremble so terribly as they never had before—so terribly that they nearly detached and fell off her mouth.

It was its *face*.

The creature's eyes were huge and sticky-looking, the size of deflated basketballs. And they were so round—its eyes were *so* round—and they popped and glowered and loured at her. The eyes were swollen with *tears*.

It made a quick, high-pitched sound that could have been both a giggle and an awful sob. Then, something below its streaming eyes that looked like a chin moved and twisted into an upside-down smile. Except it had no proper mouth. But it was making bubbly sounds.

It was a crying Snake. A *crying* Snake! It was so *true*, to Amber, the Snake felt so real. There was so much emotion, messy, unnecessarily awful, unfair agony within it, that Amber started crying herself. This creature, this horrible, horrible sobbing creature was emotion; it was suffering; it *was* vulnerability, in the shiny glint to its wet skin or the mournful, almost lyrically poignant melody of its cries.

It almost reminded her of Koko.

After a last hiccup escaped its jaws, it slowly slithered back to where it had come from, into the deep ocean.

Amber started to laugh. She giggled and kept herself in place, not daring to move. She could feel sweat all over her body, which felt tense and sore. She wanted to be sick but did not dare duck over the boat's edge.

For a long time, they sat in silence. Amber bit her lip to stop it from trembling, and Koko's gaze wandered into nothingness. They barely moved.

Eventually, she tried and started to talk, but few good words escaped her mouth.

"That random thing, it… it *must've* been a bad dream…" But she didn't manage to convince anyone.

And Koko only wore a clouded, perplexed expression as it said, "I'venever seen such a monster before! But don't worry, there aren't *too* many monsters in this area, although, really, we can't everbesure… Noteven Halfmoon can know."

Amber wanted to cover her ears.

Maybe Koko could relate to her fears, but it handled fear in a way she did not and could not.

So, their conversation was pointless. She couldn't understand Koko, and Koko couldn't understand her.

Because there was nothing of meaning or comfort they could say to each other, now shaking terribly, Amber couldn't wait any longer, and she needed so desperately to distract herself. Even *if* she experienced a small feeling of numbness, for whatever reason. *The numbness*, Amber knew, *was not as bad as the monsters. It was the only refuge she had in this world. There was no point in proving she had the Gadget under control, as it had her under control! And the Gadget could not hurt her, like Koko could.*

CHAPTER 13 – FOLLY FOX GLITCHES?

Amber knew that the Gadget could not hurt, but on Day 2, from the moment she awoke from the Gadget, she could sense that, somehow, things were getting weirder.

Her feet struggled as they paddled beneath the weight of her body, trying to lift her up, trying to reach the surface. Everything around her was almost pitch black, and she could hear the noise of water entering her ears. A deep, tingly feeling made her panic as she peered down and could only see the endless bodies of water, the depths that held secrets. She knew there was something below her...

Amber remembered what she was doing.

She'd been staring at the strings for countless hours. The heavy night sky was starting to get lighter and there was a feeling of bitter unease in her stomach. This time, it felt as if she'd had a nightmare. *Of course, a good nightmare, removing anything bad she was feeling and converting it into strings.*

As Amber observed her surroundings, it felt as though her body had really fallen asleep, as it was insufferably frozen, almost paralysed. She had felt so *inside* the Gadget's image, the blue strings of the ocean. She also noticed a throbbing pain in her forehead. *It couldn't have been caused by the Gadget, could it?*

With her eyes half-open, face half-numbed and asleep, she continued to observe her surroundings.

The sky was a tender, empty pink, the colour of melted candyfloss, a colour she knew came rarely, right when the sun was rising. A thing she could only catch a slight glimpse of if she were fortunate, for usually she liked pink skies. But now it felt wrong, somehow. *The sky, the ocean, it all looked...* She searched for the word. *Simple.* Her vision was a little… *smudged.* Everything looked a little like a painting, a depiction.

As she stared up at the sky, perhaps the same sky as the one above Japan, she felt that numbness. Like there was something *wrong* with the way the boat rocked very gently, almost soothing, as if she were in a cradle, and the way she couldn't feel any wind.

It almost felt like the strings were more real than real life.

Amber turned back to the Gadget to check the days. It read, 7.54.

She spent the next few minutes just looking again, impatient to see if the number would change again so soon.

But after a while, she felt a knot in her stomach.

She looked at her painted-looking hands and saw they were shaking. It felt like there was something in the air, some force, that made her hands shake, because they shook against her will. Amber clasped them together, trying to stop the tremors.

But as she stared at the screen, she realized there was something happening. Even if she terribly wanted to deny it.

The screen had turned a horribly bright, eye-stabbing shade

of blue. For a moment, she caught her breath, puzzled, until something appeared in the centre.

Though it was blurry, Amber could tell it was some kind of creature. It had legs as skinny as the trees on the Wacky Winters, the sharp snout of a carnivore. Its eyes were unfocused and googly, as if it had been dead for days, like the Cats'.

And yet it moved, growing bigger and bigger on the screen, making squelching noises, as it crawled closer to her face.

Then, it jumped. The image sharpened; Amber's stomach lurched as the wild, deadly eyes seemed to stare directly into hers. Only a screen separated her from it.

It gave a scream. The sound was muffled, like it was trying to speak, but also wrong, like the Cats. It clearly wanted to communicate, to yelp out something, but the words were wrong. There was no Halfmoon to give it permission to speak.

She didn't want it to speak.

The eyes, with huge pupils yet slit in an almond shape, glared at her with tears. Barely moving, Amber turned off the Gadget. She was still holding the receiver to her ear.

The screen was black. It was what felt like a few minutes later that she dared exhale.

She felt numb. Amber had no idea what to do.

The Gadget could not hurt, could it? But she was starting to feel less sure... Then, she hated herself for even asking again, as she knew it was the best thing she had.

After a moment, perhaps unconsciously, she turned the Gadget on again. Her heart stopped as she saw the same bursting blue. But no creature.

Instead, there was a message. Halfmoon.

That was not meant to happen.

The Gadget made a noise. Halfmoon was calling her, and then appeared on the screen.

"Amber," It spoke to her.

She spun around, afraid Koko would wake.

"Oh, Koko's sound asleep. This will only be a short call," Halfmoon said. Then Its face darkened. "Terribly, terribly, terribly sorry about what happened. Did that frighten you?"

"I—well, yes," she stammered.

"Completely understandable. That was… funny, wasn't it? But do not worry, that was just a little… glitch. In the system. The Gadget. Nothing to worry about. Believe me, I will take care of it."

Amber nodded. "You'll take care of it."

"I will not let the Teleclock show you anything upsetting ever again. I promise."

"Thank you."

"In my Paws, I promise."

"You promise."

Before she could say anything else, Halfmoon's image and voice disappeared from the screen.

This time, as she fluttered in the sky, a memory, an image, arose from the depths of her mind: how last time she had wanted, wanted, *to fly down. But when she'd neared the land, she'd seen that green, melting liquid and the snow…*

She watched it now. It was probably dangerous. After all, it was completely unknown to her.

The land was scarcely visible from the weak gleam of what seemed to be sand shining through the covering clouds. She could make out only some browns and greens on the ground, which she knew well enough now were not plants.

And there was a curiosity burning and growing inside her. She hovered in the air, watched the land, and considered. For a moment, she needed to flap, flap, flap *as her small bird body almost dropped, so deep in thought of what to do. Wind from above also tried to blow her down, but she stayed a safe enough distance away, to observe…*

She wanted *to dive again. She wanted to see what was there, what could live beneath the rolling clouds and peaceful skies. She needed to. She knew she needed to.*

But she was frozen, as if standing on air; she couldn't bring herself to do it.

What if she fell? What if she fell into the ocean instead? What if she did not land on the surface—on an island—but drowned?

* * *

The Gadget couldn't possibly hurt. Could it?

It was afternoon. Amber's eyes prickled because she wouldn't stop staring at the clock-part.

7.54. 7.54. 7.54, and no change.

7.54, 7.54, 7.54 and no more from Halfmoon, either.

She dug her fingernails into her skin. Watching the strings, looking at the numbers. Waiting, waiting, waiting.

For the first time since using the Gadget, she was distracted. Her eyes kept flitting from the screen to the real ocean around her and back.

Her thoughts—those horrid, stomach-churning questions and strange ideas—pulled her eyes to the waves. As if she could find it there: her simple, straightforward answer.

Ever since she had seen that creature that morning, something was different.

In a way, now that the *strings* had shown her that they too could be scary—that they could show her unwanted creatures—they somehow felt more real, causing the real now to feel fake and distant. So, Amber looked for the fake, to distract from the real pain.

Eyes on the dull, wobbling waves, she tried to reassure herself by saying, *It was just a mistake. Just a mistake in the usually well-working system.* Or perhaps *the strings were doing what they always did—taking bad things from her mind.* But Amber hadn't been thinking of anything too bad. The creature in the screen had seemingly appeared all by itself.

So, she waited hopefully for more messages, more explanations, more reassurance from Its words.

While she waited, she kept herself distracted with the strings, so as not to be alone with that one thing, that one question in her mind: the one always there, but just out of her sight…

What if there was something more *going on?*

But somehow, the question was even in the Gadget. *What could be beneath her, in that strange land, if she left the blue skies?*

And it was all around Amber, too. *What could lurk in the seas?*

She didn't want to think about it. For she couldn't ever give up the Gadget.

"Whoa, are youOK, Amber?" Koko was looking at her.

"Yes? Why?" she replied.

She knew Koko hadn't even noticed what had happened that morning.

"You look… dehydrated. Sad. Are youhomesick? Do you

need water or something?" Then it laughed quietly, its eyes on the sea, but looking anxious itself. "There's *a lot* if you like!"

She ignored its comment. Although she did feel that for some unknown reason, her head hurt.

"Why are youholding it like that?" Koko asked, frowning.

"What—the Gadget?"

Amber realized what it meant. Instead of letting the Gadget drift on its own as usual, she had scooped it up closely in her hands, as if to steady the thing—whatever it was—that had gone wrong with it that morning. *Good Gadget, Good Gadget. You'd never hurt.*

Amber shrugged in reply.

When she couldn't ignore the way Koko was still watching her, she turned towards it completely.

 Its face had darkened.

"Really," it muttered. "Don't you *ever* get bored of it?"

Every inch of Koko was facing her.

"Well," Amber replied in a voice equally quiet. "What else should I *do*?" She knew what Koko wanted, of course.

"Talk to me," it said. "I dunno…"

Amber frowned, knowing very well what happened when she did. "Well, Koko… don't *you* ever get bored? Of… doing nothing at all? Of staring at the same old sea?"

"Amber." Koko's lip twitched. "The images, the ones in the Gadget, they're literally the same ones as the sea around you, of the same sea, except they're *just* images and the sea is real."

"Exactly. Neither you nor I know what might… arise from the ocean." She gulped. She preferred the depths inside the Gadget, the strings. The real depths scared her.

"Yeah, but, you know, sometimes us Cats, we just do nothing."

"Well," she snapped. "I can't *do* nothing."

"Why not?"

Amber clenched her fists and resisted the urge to say something that would make Koko cry. "I *can't.*"

But Koko's mouth hung half-open. She needed to keep going.

"Listen," she said, trying to keep her voice steady. "Even if after a long day, say, I get bored of the Gadget…"

"What?"

"I don't *have* any other choice." She shook her head once. Then again, harder. "No choice but to… keep using it."

Koko still wore an innocently puzzled face. "Why?"

Amber's breath caught. She needed to give in.

"I'll… I'll lose my mind," she whispered, not actually wanting Koko to hear. Her voice trembled. "I'll simply… *lose my mind…*"

Her vision blurred, hot and wet, and then she raised her voice. "I'll lose my mind without the—without the Gadget, and I'll lose my mind with this sea, and with these—these… Oh, these horrible, horrible CREATURES!"

Through her thick tears, in that moment, all Amber saw in her mind was the bird. She knew, if the bird dived too far from the blue skies, she would drown.

If the bird dived too far from the blue skies, she would drown.

Koko flinched. It looked at her as if she were a monster, a Worm, a Doodle herself. "Oh."

Amber shook her head at it but didn't want to let herself cry.

"Well…" Koko sighed. Its eyes were wide with more than shock. "OK. It *really* does keep your mind off things. Doesn't it?"

It coldly turned away from her, sniffing. Amber shivered at her own words, the dreadful things she'd let escape from her mouth…

Something startled her out of her thoughts. There was a new message. At last.

They were two words, two words stuck together like the Cats' speech, against the blue backdrop of the strings.

Helpme.

Then, *Kiddo.*

Amber's eyes widened, as if to understand the words the best she could, trying to catch a second thought, perhaps a new message that would clarify everything. But this time, nothing changed at all.

"Halfmoon…" she mumbled. "*What?*"

The Gadget could not possibly, possibly hurt?

"Hello, Amber."

This time, she did jump a little, and her breath stopped for a few seconds.

"Oh." She sighed. "Halfmoon."

The face on the screen nodded slowly, Its eyes twinkling.

"Sorry if I frightened you!" It cried.

Koko turned as it realized what was happening. "What?"

"I decided to call to check in on you both." Halfmoon smiled.

Amber smiled back. Either It had listened to her thoughts, in whichever way It did with the Gadget, or this was a coincidence.

"I'm… fine," Koko said. Then its face swelled with tears.

"Halfmoon," Amber said. "What did you mean by your last message?"

"Which message?"

"The one you just sent before calling m–"

"I didn't send any! Perhaps your eyes tricked you?"

"Well…"

"I promise I will look into it, Amber."

Only Amber, never kiddo. As Halfmoon's face vanished, she realized that It never called her kiddo while calling her, only ever in the depths of the Gadget.

* * *

Halfmoon sent her another message that afternoon.

There, Amber, my newest invention. I know I have been giving you lunches and dishes already, but now finally, you can serve yourself. The sack, can you see, it's filling up? It's full of all the food in the world, *absolutely anything you could wish for, kiddo!*

"Wow!" Koko said. "That is a lot of food. So, so, so, so much food."

"It's… It's almost scary," Amber said, staring at the slowly growing sack. She forced a laugh to sweeten these words, but she had spoken them.

"Scary?" Koko tilted its head in such a way that Amber knew she had said something stupid.

"Well." She sighed. "It's… too good. Too nice of Halfmoon. And it's like there's nothing stopping me from stuffing my face with food all day and night!"

Koko still looked confused. "*I* couldstop you? Or…" It let its gaze wander off, as if imagining Amber stuffing her face. "Just *don't* do that. I don't understandyou."

"What I'm trying to say is, it's endless. The food is literally, magically, infinite. And the thought—it almost scares me. It overwhelms me." Now Amber made more of an effort to laugh. *This was a joke. It was very funny to have infinite food!*

"Well," Koko replied, a look of something like jealousy in its eyes. "OK. But, isn't… isn't the Gadget also infinite?"

Amber's stomach churned. She didn't know why, as Koko hadn't said anything wrong. But for some reason, this made her bite her tongue.

"But that's… different. I could eat food night and day. Because it's so good. But it wouldn't be good for me. I'd be sick. That would be the consequence."

"The consequence?"

"But the Gadget doesn't *have* consequences like that."

Koko watched her, eyebrows furrowed.

It shook its head. "OK," it said.

It must've been early morning of Day 3, for the gathering beams of light in the sky showed the sun was rising.

That night, she hadn't used the Gadget. And she'd had a nightmare.

As she awoke, she remembered it in detail almost more vivid than the Gadget's screen.

In her dream *she'd been running, yet it was impossible to say from what. But something, many things, were coming from the sides, from above, from below. There were gurgling, hissing, and sizzling sounds. The sounds of chaos. The ground was dark, dusty rock, and even the air carried a heaviness, as if there was something in it blocking it from entering her lungs. Amber didn't know. She didn't understand. There was no way for her to know anything.*

She didn't know how it was possible that the ground crumbled *and deformed beneath her feet. She didn't know how she was feeling. She didn't know what colour the sky was. She didn't know anything, anything, anything.*

There was no escape, and she was exposed to the world of things she did not know.

But at least now her head did not hurt.

Sitting up, Amber shook the memory of the dream away. She would be there, on DragonFree Haven, today.

She pulled the Gadget down to her now. The number had finally changed.

7.211. *Explore depths.*

This time, she couldn't ignore it. The way that every time the number changed, there were more decimal places. Somehow, the more digits the numbers got, the more she felt… *that* feeling. Not only the numbness, but with it, that bit of fright. Like she had when Halfmoon had called out of nowhere.

As if a further explanation to *Explore depths*, additional words popped up on screen. *Since the Gadget re-calculates a more accurate number every few hours, the more you look, the more it opens itself up.*

Before she could process this, a playful sound of splashing made her turn her head. Something in the water was floating past her.

Her back prickled, and she felt vomit rise in the back of her throat as she realized it was skin. The skin of some dead animal.

As she observed the shrivelled-up features, a part of her mind started analyzing, drawing conclusions. *But no*, she told herself. *No, no, no. It was not the same creature. Like Halfmoon said, it was just a glitch in the system. Nothing to worry about.*

She kept her eyes closed until she was sure the thing in the water had floated past.

It was not the same. It was not. It was not.

When she opened her eyes, her whole body convulsed.

That did it, she thought.

Amber had wanted to just forget the creature from yesterday, to leave it, again, all up to Halfmoon.

But now, after she had seen the things she had, she was sure of it…

There was a truth—some horrible truth—that she could not shrug off in any way.

She knew there were things in the depths that she did not know of. She knew there were those words, those words that Koko did not speak.

Amber missed the way she used to feel.

What the strings used to be for her—a home, safe from anything in any way strange or unexpected. She even missed her life before Japan, when she had understood absolutely everything. When she had still been Amaya, clutching her pencil tight, forcing a smile on her face and making things all OK. Or Amaya, safe inside the Gadget. Because now, Amaya was slowly losing her mind… And *Amber* missed understanding.

She remembered how, when Halfmoon had sent her on this journey, It had said, *I will make you understand. And I promise I will.*

But It hadn't. She didn't understand yet.

Since there was something, something perhaps about the Gadget, that Halfmoon did not tell her, perhaps she needed to figure it out for herself.

She thought of the bird, the skies, the mysterious land. Maybe, if she were cautious—very, *very* cautious—she could explore it.

In the blue skies, she dived down.

CHAPTER 14 – LURKING IN DEPTHS??

It was Day 3, the day she had waited for. She knew she had a few hours left. So, if she could find out a little, only a little, about anything that was happening, to explain the weird creatures, to prove the Gadget could do no harm, all would be fine…

The sack moved towards her. She knew it was filled with Halfmoon's food for her, but she was supposed to serve herself. Not hungry, she pushed it aside.

Amber thought back to the overwhelming hours she had spent on Catslaughter Island, meeting the beasts themselves, the talk with Halfmoon, the table of sickening food, and Frog. She thought of Frog's Teleclock. Petal. Petal's leather jacket. She tried to recall exactly what had happened.

When Koko was awake, she called its name.

She felt sick as she watched it slurp up food loudly with its jaw wide open, bits of it flying everywhere.

But it stopped when it saw she was talking to it. "What!" it said, almost an exclamation. It seemed that now it had fully given up trying to talk to her, having always been the one starting their awkward conversations.

"Can I… ask you something?"

It turned its body to face her completely, shyness in its face. "Amber," it mumbled. "I reallydid mean what I told you yesterday—"

"This isn't about that, I guess…" This was a half-lie, as she wanted to be able to explain more about the Gadget to herself. She wanted to slowly fill in the blanks.

"Y-yeah?"

"Why doesn't Petal like the Gadget?"

"What d'you mean?"

"Well…" Amber sighed; what she was doing was incredibly daunting. She didn't know what she might hear. She told herself, *unless she found some horrible, hidden truth, she had nothing to lose*. But she knew this was a lie, as her hands were shaking, somehow knowing there was something. Something.

"On Catslaughter Island, Petal was scolding Frog. It hadn't been listening…" she started.

"So?" Koko looked confused.

"Petal had said something else. When Frog was staring at… at the Gadget, he'd explained that Frog was testing it…" Amber paused, realizing what she had said. "Of course, Petal must have made a mistake, because Halfmoon said Cats had already tested out the Gadget, and that it was safe. But anyway, when Frog was using it, Petal said it *influenced their young minds too much*. He was so… strictly against it."

Koko didn't reply.

"Do you know… why?" Amber's voice had grown weaker, hoping they weren't talking about anything Halfmoon disapproved of. She didn't want to say anything bad about the Gadget.

Koko shot her a dark look. But she knew it had *strange* thoughts about the world too. It had told her about illusions, that *maybe, you can't know what is real*, and she was sure it knew quite a lot about the way things worked on Catslaughter Island.

"Amber," it started. It reached for the sack and took more Cat Improvement Pills. "First of all, Petal would never be wrong."

Amber changed her tone. "Koko, I didn't mean it that way."

Koko sniffed.

"There *is* a reason, right?" she forced herself to say. She forced a laugh. "It's because… Petal, he seems like a control freak—isn't he? Protective of Frog. He is just one to do his own thing, hating being told what to do or being influenced by anything else. Isn't that why he always wears that jacket? It must be, because Catslaughter Island is always warm, so it can't be that he's cold. He just loves Frog, right? *That's the reason*."

Koko's gaze burned into her skin. Its googly eyes still unnerved her. Even if they felt more neutral to her since she had first met it, she could rarely read them.

"Petal is the best," it said quietly. "Petal is a great Cat. And I don't mean power. His jacket looks great onhim."

"All right." She nodded. "But I mean… Petal couldn't have made a mistake for no reason. And… it's probably how overprotective he is."

"Petal made no mistake!" Koko hissed, its lips trembling. "I know Petal very well, and I care for him, and I know he is not stupid!"

Amber jumped at its tone.

"Don't talk about Petal that way. You don't know how

much I trust him." Koko's voice shook, so fragile and easily broken.

Amber bit her tongue, regretting what she had stirred up. "But Halfmoon *knows* what it talks about. It's Halfmoon's Gadget, after all."

Still, Koko wore a face of pure dread. "You're so sure of everything," it said. "So why are you asking me?"

She knew she had stumbled upon a pitfall. Something that, in their conversation, was pointless. And her time was limited. So, if she couldn't ask about Petal, she needed to ask about the Mahou energy.

"Fine," Amber said cautiously. "Then I want to know something else. I'd like to know how and why you even came to exist."

Koko chuckled nervously, when it had been crying seconds ago, and said, "That's quite *philosophical*, isn't it?"

Amber sighed. She knew she had to be extremely cautious with what she asked. Not to say anything wrong, or bring up things that were *wrong. All she was trying to do was find logical explanations.*

"I mean, when did you come to this realm, you Cats? I want to understand. When did you make Catslaughter Island, *if* you made it—?"

"Oh. History." Koko's face got paler, and it smiled nervously. "Well, fromwhat Halfmoon's told us, a longlong time ago, cats found the Portal. Normal cats from Japan. They-came one by one. They found *magic* in this realm, but nothing more. Then... the cats *adapted* to the Mahou energy and picked it up eventually, and yes, with newabilities, created land. I guess that's when webecame Cats. We grew our own plants. And that'sit."

She remembered Halfmoon had mentioned this. Amber

scrunched up her face. "But, what do you mean *that's it*?" she asked.

Koko's expression was neutral. "That's it. That's all I know."

Before Amber could ask any more, it explained, "My ownknowledge of *how we came to exist* is kindalimited… You see, Halfmoon keeps some secrets and stuff. But It does gather us together every once in a while, and shares things It has spotted with its Eyes, or tells us about otherislands."

What secrets? But maybe it was best she did not know. "Tells things… like about the Doodles?"

Koko nodded. She noticed its face had gone chalk-white and sweat dripped down its face. Then it coughed terribly and took more medicine.

"It has Eyes everywhere, doesn't It? Watching things?" she asked. She couldn't help the way her voice sounded unnaturally flat. But the idea of the Eyes warmed her slightly.

"Yeah. Don't ask how It got them there, though. Seriously, I don't know."

Amber forced another laugh to make everything cheerier, because they both seemed rather jittery.

Because she realized that there was something that even Koko did not know. Perhaps things that no one knew. Or perhaps things that only Halfmoon knew.

But she kept going, her chaotic thoughts trying to arrange themselves into sense, before she slipped into complete nonsense again.

She was going to have to ask about Halfmoon.

"So, Halfmoon has *abilities*, It has told me, right?"

"Mm. Halfmoon's so full of power… It can do anything It wants, to be fair. It says It's blessed with Mahou energy, and we all know that's true…" Koko's voice was clearer after taking medicine, but there was a tiny bitterness, a jealousy in the way it spoke the words. It shook its head. "It's great! Halfmoon's an amazing inventor, always doing what is right for the island. Although, It always tries to beat the Mahou energy."

"Beat… the Mahou energy…?"

Koko shook its head again. "Forget that. Forget that! Well, I mean, Halfmoon sometimes… It likes to show It can do well *without* needing Mahou energy! I guess trying to be modest. Its inventions, It says, only use a little bit of Mahou energy, nothing more. That's really all I meant."

Amber smiled.

"The other Cats don't really *have* Mahou energy… Here is where this becomes very complicated. Halfmoon says the Mahou energy can, well, bebeyond ourunderstanding…" Koko coughed.

Amber bit her lip, fidgeting with her hair. There was a lot she did not know. But she told herself it did not matter as *Halfmoon knew it all.* She wanted to use the Gadget, then and there, but Koko's words stayed with her. *She just needed to go a little further, expand her small knowledge a little more…*

"It gets complicated?" she asked. "Well, but don't all Cats have a *touch* of—of magic?" And then she asked, "Why are Cats' lips so swollen and they—and why—?"

"Amber, I've told you that." It shot her an almost sinister look. "It's becauseof speaking. Cats can't—"

"No, I know! But… you're so *long*… You don't look like normal cats…"

Amber gasped, wishing her mouth would stop. She had slipped on words.

For a second, she was sure she had asked the unexplainable.

Yet, Koko said, "It's just like the speaking."

"It's… *just like the speaking*," she repeated. "What?"

But her stomach churned as she looked up at its face—it was… so, *so wrong*.

Koko twisted into something alien. Amber watched its chalk-white face darken; she watched the small, harmless crinkles in its face that usually appeared in its smiles grow grotesquely huge, casting exaggerated shadows around all its features, which gave it an appalling, almost comical effect, as if it were a cartoon character painted hyperrealistic. Something was out of line.

Amber's neck prickled, but she continued watching as Koko's eyes scanned around, as it lowered its voice to a whisper, as its voice broke. As Koko gave her an answer.

"Amber. I reallyhate this, but look… I wannatell you. I have this belief, this theory, that the Mahou energy is *toxic*. The air is full of it. The air we breathe in right now is toxic. It's very *strong*, the Mahou energy to the Cats. Too strong. And it's just like with speaking. It's *just* like with the speaking. Halfmoon ignores this. And that's thething. The Mahou energy isalways tricking us. Amber!

"This, *this* is exactly why I didn't give you a coat on the Wacky Winters, even though it seemed socold and you were shivering so terribly. Halfmoonhad packed one, but I held the sack as closed as I could with my Paws, so no coat could escape. And even now I think that the snowwas *fake*. You weren't supposed to see any of that, feel that coldness or see that snow. Halfmoonalways ignores this, tries to show It can beat themagic, but—but…"

Koko let out a head-splitting cough and reached for some water to drink. An instant look of shame and deep regret settled on its face.

Amber sat, paralyzed.

Suddenly she realized what Koko meant. *It was just like the speaking:* the Mahou energy, the fact that the Cats did not look like real cats, was like their speaking. *Speaking, something Cats weren't biologically made for,* broke their jaws. *And they were not meant for magic, either.*

In panic, Amber broke into uneasy breaths, almost gasps, unable to understand completely what Koko had said.

It was exactly what she had feared—to hear something dreadful, something dreadful that frightened her so badly she was forced to avoid it all.

The Cats weren't meant for magic. It broke them. It broke them. It made them strange.

After the thought passed through her head one more time, she said, "No, no, no."

When she laughed, it was not forced. It was a proper response, the only response, to the nonsense she had heard.

"Koko," she cried. "That's… funny."

The idea of it made tears form in her eyes. For a moment, she kept her gaze fixed onto the faraway distance.

When she turned to look at Koko again, it immediately blurted out an apology, "Sorry. I'm reallysorry. That was sosostupid to say. It was just something I'dthought to myself after a long time… I'mstupid. I made a terrible mistake; I'm not allowed to talk about that. I'msososorry."

For the first time ever, Koko's low and insecure tone almost stirred something up in Amber. She almost didn't like how badly it thought of itself, how it bent and shook its head, as if it were bowing to her.

She nodded. "Thank you… And I don't need to understand the magic, if Halfmoon already does."

She remembered Halfmoon had said *There are a lot of things on our island that—how should I say? … Are just called.* Amber knew that some things *were just*, just implicitly understood by Halfmoon. She did not need to know everything, and it was enough to believe Halfmoon's names for things, for it made perfect sense to believe It, so she did.

"But there is something, one last thing I'd like to know." Amber was torn, but she wanted to understand, at least a little. She had a final question. "Where do you get… all this information from?"

Koko's eyes widened for a few seconds. Then they became somewhere near normal again. "Halfmoon, ofcourse. Well, except that last thing I told you. But I'm not allowedtotalkaboutthat." It coughed. "Things are as Halfmoon says, and It constantlydoes things around the island, for the island. I think… It cares about us, so why would It lie? It has so much power, and I trust It, because It helpedme."

"It helped you?"

"It helped us." Koko sighed. "Things aresocomplicated and rough, they can hurt, but Itcan protect us."

"Protect you? How—from what?" But Amber knew she had taken this too far. She realized she was trembling all over, eager to know, but also terrified.

Koko shook its head, as if getting annoyed. "Monsters. I mean… from bad things. Scarystuff. But most Cats don't ask twice, Amber. You just haveto know everything, do you? And then you… *don't even listen…*" But then, as if feeling bad for its tone, it added, "It's justthe way thingsare."

Amber gave a smile in return. "Sorry. You were right. I don't always need to know everything. I can… like you said Cats do, just do nothing."

Koko opened its mouth and gave her a look as if it wanted to say something, but Amber shook her head dismissively and that made it stay silent.

Finally, she opened the sack and got out what looked like a bento box Halfmoon had made for her using magic. Without even properly looking at what Halfmoon had put in it, she stuffed her face with what tasted like a type of sweetened rice cake. Solely to avoid further conversation.

And then Koko started to cough horribly anyway, wheezing, trying to swallow down water. But it was not taking any more medicine to speak. Amber knew it was uncomfortable; it would speak no more. She knew she was missing something. Yet Koko was not speaking—it did not *want* to speak—and she knew it was only because of Halfmoon that Cats even could!

This world was, as always, so odd, but it was easier to believe Halfmoon.

Since Koko believed Halfmoon was right, and Halfmoon said it did not harm, she continued using the Gadget. She would stare at the strings, and stare at the strings until they reached DragonFree Haven.

She needed to clear her head of all this nonsense, these meaningless words. Because Amber would hear no more.

But, the strings only showed water. Lots and lots of water, and bird wings splashing and splashing, trying desperately to reach the top, trying to reach the surface again, but already too deep down… *drowning*.

CHAPTER 15 – BACK IN BLUE SKY

When Amber saw it and looked up from the screen, she wanted to pretend she never had, but now it was too late; Koko had seen it too.

"Is that…?" it cried.

Amber yelled at it to stop, but Koko leaned over the edge of their boat to get a better view. Then it fished the horrible thing out of the water with its Paws. And brought it on board, right next to Amber.

Amber gagged at the scent of dead and burned rubber.

"It's one of Halfmoon's inventions!" Koko cried.

It was broken and wrong. The thing looked only half of itself, with wires sticking out, sparking. Then came a robotic voice. "Open fields," it said. "B-b-beware o-o-of the open f-fields."

"Get that away!" Amber shrieked.

Once Koko had got a better look, it tossed the Eye back into the ocean.

Only a second later, the Gadget rang.

"Amber, Koko!" Halfmoon's voice and image joined them.

"Did that Eye startle you? I must apologize, when you are so close to your destination!" It took a moment to catch Its breath, for It had been gasping. Then Halfmoon gave a hearty laugh. "Almost as much folly as one would find on the Folly Teplaytides!"

Amber exchanged a look with Koko, puzzled.

"Why, Amber, hasn't Koko told you about the Teplaytides?"

"Er, yes," she answered. "The island where the other Portal is."

Halfmoon nodded. "I am sorry about that Eye. I do not remember ever sending an Eye to where you are, since—since I steer where they go. Very, very odd. I did not *see* through that Eye. But it's just a glitch, a malfunction in my usually well-working system!"

Amber returned the nod.

"You will soon be arriving at DragonFree Haven," Halfmoon went on. "No more than four or five hours from now. You have a, er, friend there. I wish you luck!"

Just like that, Halfmoon hung up.

For a moment, all Amber could do was laugh and turn to Koko.

"A friend?"

"I have no idea."

When the two had a rushed lunch a bit later, Amber refused to touch her fried fish.

It was as if there was a black, buzzing cloud inside her, draining all her feelings except for the occasional knot of dread in her stomach and the frustration of not knowing. It was as if she was avoiding it all by avoiding her food.

Koko shot her a rude, questioning look. "Why aren't you eating?"

After a moment of silence, Amber explained, "I don't really eat when I feel… When I'm… I don't feel hungry when I'm confused."

"Confused about what?!"

* * *

Two more hours. Three more hours. Or perhaps five. She didn't know exactly.

She told herself she was *not* unknowing, told herself she was *not* trapped, told herself she was *not* scared.

But she could no longer hold on.

Somehow, everything that she had bottled up ever since the event with the Doodles was suddenly bursting free, as much as she tried to withhold it.

It had all caught up with her. She was finally making a short visit to reality. She tried to keep herself from really losing her mind, but perhaps she was, and there was nothing else to it.

With her hand clenched into a trembling fist, pressed down on the wood of the boat, she cowered and tried to look away and shut her eyes and feel all right and not cry. *She had to keep herself as stable and steady as she could, of course.*

As usual, she hated that this was the truth, the actual reality that she was living in, letting time pass in. Everything was far too much; everything was either sickening and gruesome, or something that caused her hysterical outbursts of laughter. Yet even laughing was hard now.

Amber shook, wishing she were in another place, wishing she felt safe enough to open her eyes, wishing this were not the reality she was in. She wished all this had not happened, but guilt made her eyes teary. She knew the hard truth, that *wishing never changed a thing.*

Fortunately, through all her chaos, Amber had the Gadget. It was her light—her direction—in the endless sea. The world around her was terrifying, she felt restless and outraged, and it was all absolutely *unacceptable*… but she had the Gadget.

It even helped her forget anything weird about it, anything that was a little frightening or odd about it. Its beauty and comfort almost helped her forget the prickly headache and numbness slowly spreading in her body. Almost.

Amber noticed Halfmoon had sent her a message.

I know funny things happen, but remember, it never harms to use it! If you are ever bored with the way life works, swallow it all up, use the Teleclock!

Its messages always filled her with joy. The joy never lasted for long, but she still liked the way the comforting words flowed into her.

For a few seconds, they made her forget absolutely everything.

Painted-looking skies, all drawn out, but flawless, with perfectly round, spongy clouds… Today, it was all the same.

She swooped and flew through the clouds with a light feeling of nothingness and an empty heart. She remembered it —perhaps she shouldn't have, but she did. When she'd been arriving on the Wacky Winters, approaching the new land, she'd felt that same emptiness. Except now… all was good. This time, she felt that the land really was empty, and there was nothing in front of or beneath her.

She wanted to stay here. She wanted to believe this. She didn't want to go anywhere else, not ever again.

She felt happy, trying not to eye the land below.

Once again, she was an ignorant, yet somehow an omni-scient creature, knowing exactly which direction to follow in the sky.

Then, perhaps still streaming unconsciously in the strings, the bird, or even Amber, began to wonder. How could she always *be a bird, so carefree? How could she get rid of that terrible, ever-present urge to dive low? Was the answer, as always, distraction—knowing she could be pulled back up again by some external force?*

* * *

When she awoke from the Gadget, it really was as if she had been woken up from sleep, simply by the real company of the ocean.

Somehow the sight of the ocean overwhelmed her.

For a moment, she wondered if she had actually fallen asleep, for her body still felt like she was dreaming. She almost felt a bit lost, as if she had accidentally overslept during a weekday, mistaking it for the weekend.

The first thing Amber noticed was the pain. The sickening, throbbing pain in her head. It was as if she had finally paid the price after having excessively watched the strings.

She had lost track of time, but she knew they would be there, on a new island, soon. Soon.

There was a new number on the Gadget. 6.7234.

It made her jump again. The numbers now only reminded her, pressured her, no longer reassuring. Somehow, the longer the numbers got, the more she dreaded them. After observing 6.7234 for a while longer, she made up her mind; she didn't want to see another number ever again.

Amber grew aware of the tears on her face, but she did not feel sad. *What was wrong? What was happening?*

Koko yawned beside her.

Amber was sure her burning eyes were bright red. She looked into the distance, restless, trying to catch the slightest glimpse of the new land, but there was none so far. However, as she squinted her eyes, she saw the thin outline of something fly past, very high in the sky, dancing on the clouds and nudging the sun. It was coming from the direction of DragonFree Haven.

"What is that?" she asked Koko. She pointed as it soared past her.

Koko frowned. "Isn't it obvious? It's a dragon, from DragonFree Haven!" It seemed it had, as always, forgotten all their previous days' conflicts.

Amber could not believe Koko's words. She looked up to see if she could spot the flying thing again, but it had already passed.

"So, dragons exist?"

Koko snorted. "That's… ridiculous! Well, no—I mean yes! Well, maybe."

"So? *What was that?*"

"Well, you know you can see for yourself when we get there! Let's say that was a Dragon!" And it left it at that, which made everything much worse.

As Amber sat idly with her eyebrows twitching, Koko asked, "All right, and what's up now? What's wrong?"

Amber shook her head. "Nothing is wrong. Or, I don't know…" She wasn't lying.

"Hmm," Koko replied. "So, something's wrong andyou don't know what! Trust yourgut feeling…"

"Yoghurt … feeling?"

"No!" Koko snorted. "Not yoghurt feeling! I said, trust your *gut*, with what's wrong, I mean. You know, intuition."

She looked at it. "What? No, *no…*" Amber knew that her head had always been most sensible, but she craved information, and feelings were always in her way.

But now, everything felt so distant. There was a deep, dizzying numbness all over her, choking and drowning her.

"I just… *really* want to arrive, finally," she said, almost robotically.

Her head fizzed and buzzed; she could not think straight. She felt barely anything. She really *had* paid the price now.

Amber wanted this feeling to go away. *If she could not make sense of things, she wanted to, at least, feel real.*

The pain in her head intensified and she felt her skull would split at any moment.

She swallowed. She knew Koko was watching her.

Amber didn't know what was happening to her. But it felt like her head was being punched hundreds of times.

Now, there was only one clear thought in her head. *She would do* anything *now to free herself from the feeling.*

Amber leapt into the ocean, with her clothes and shoes still on.

She heard the violent splash of the waves, felt water filling her ears, and burst up to the surface again, gasping for air. It was icy-cold and stung.

Koko beside her looked horrified. "*What* are you doing?!" It mumbled something like a swear word. "Amber, I don't know ifthat's safe…"

Then she remembered. The rippling waves. The bubbling water. The ocean itself was fizzing and buzzing as well. She felt it brush against her, tickling, yet not hurting her much.

"This isn't going to kill me, is it?" she said.

Koko did not answer.

But it was working; it was taking the feelings of boredom and dryness away. The ripples and sensation of the waves were waking her up properly. The few days she'd spent out on the sea had all felt like one clouded, dizzy dream, but now she was leaving it behind. Amber smiled, for a fleeting second. She had been getting so restless, trapped on the boat.

But she knew she had to return. Now perhaps in a more conscious state, she remembered how dangerous this was. An emotion filled her, and she was finally feeling again. She swung her arms back onto the boat, and Koko grinned nervously. Amber grunted, trying to get back up, but at that moment, her stomach gave a funny flip as something grabbed her whole leg, forcing her head back underwater.

She was scared now. *Very* scared. She knew she was back in reality.

Frozen, she let herself get pulled down. There was no time to think. She was being swept away, stolen from the world above, down, down, each second becoming more aware.

* * *

Whenever it was that Amber opened her eyes, her surroundings made her want to shut them again.

She felt horrible, but she knew *this was all her fault.*

She didn't know why or how it was possible, but she managed to draw unsteady breaths again. She was breathing. No water entered her lungs. Yet she was still underwater.

Looking down at her legs, she realized her vision was not blurry. Her paddling feet were in sharp, vivid focus, struggling and kicking beneath her. Except it felt more like she was *floating in mid-air* than swimming.

She tried to reach back to the top. But a concentrated, throbbing pressure on her whole body pulled and chained her down. It seemed to be some new, invisible force that kept her stuck, rather than the friction of the water itself.

The water was cool and lively, flowing around in its own freedom, unlike her. Perhaps the cold should have made her skin feel numb, but all it did was make her feel more alive.

Amber looked up at the light shining in from the sun. She saw the shadow and the outline of their boat. *What could Koko be thinking now?*

As her eyes travelled back down, the black space beneath her was no longer empty water. There was a monster.

Amber screamed and was shocked that she could clearly *hear* the rawness in her hoarse voice. Her rushed gasps that followed echoed throughout the whole ocean. She screamed and screamed again, her feet in a big mess as they tried to steer her away, though she could hardly move.

It looked up at her and stared, the thing with black eyes and a deep gaze.

The creature had a slight, skinny build. It was the size of a horse. In fact, it looked quite like one. A Horse.

Amber tried to catch her breath in the strange air source, dread spreading through her whole body. She could breathe, but each time she did, her chest hurt a little more.

Then, the force dropped. She breathed in small amounts of water. It was as if the creature had stopped this force, and even the sea felt *denser* now.

Her eyes lost focus and started stinging as the taste of salt came into her senses and she could no longer see the Horse's face…

Amber kicked and swam away, water entering through her mouth and nose.

She noticed that the further she distanced herself from the creature, the more entered her face. She tried to hold her breath. The creature was bribing her with air.

She didn't have time to turn back and find out whether she was being followed—she needed to escape.

All she could see was a dark, blurry body of water. At one point, she caught a glimpse of things floating around her and a pair of wide, golf-ball eyes, but she could not make them out and swam past.

Now Amber no longer heard herself breathe. She could barely see the flesh-coloured blobs that were her hands. Her vision blurred and darkened. There were quick, sharp, hammering thumps in her chest. She had to breathe.

She had to breathe.

Amber had no choice. She turned back, making it to a place where the water grew a little thinner, and a bit of oxygen could enter her lungs. It didn't make any sense at all. But, seeing she was alone, she stayed there to catch her breath.

At the edge of her vision, she saw a shimmery light shining in from a small tower of rocks beside her. They formed firm stone walls in a wacky circle, almost ritualistic or occult-looking. Seeing that she would fit, she swam inside the circle. That was when she spotted it.

It was another bright crystal-blue X.

Amber reached out a finger towards it. *Well, it wasn't duplicating.* Nothing strange was happening. She moved closer. She laughed with relief. *This was fine.*

It happened again.

Her extended finger felt it first. But soon her whole body was thrown backwards. Thrown with immense force away from the Portal.

She felt the same force again as the Portal disappeared.

Gasping for air and catching her breath, her blurred vision finally focused on what was in front of her. The Horse. It had got her again. She would not swim away this time. She had no escape.

Unmoving, she was staring straight at it, when she heard it speak.

"*Hello*, Amber."

CHAPTER 16 – HOLLOW HORSE LIES OF FOLLY?

I t giggled.

The Horse was pulling Amber towards it. As she saw it close up, she admitted that, somehow, it was quite beautiful. It looked delicate. Only a little crazy. And yet, still like the type of broken creature that could duplicate and bleed from the sky.

It had sharp, steady hooves with fins growing out of the sides, and a long flossy tail. Both glimmered in a godly amethyst, the same colour as its mane. The rest of its body was angel-white. Its ears were fox-like and pointy, and its face looked frail and hurt. A silver half-moon marked its forehead.

As she observed it further, she realized it was not a Horse, but a Fox. Amber didn't know what to think.

It took a minute for her to realize that there was something happening to it. Every few seconds, the creature's image had a habit of flashing in a whirl of colours and becoming strangely distorted. It was as if its image was *glitching*, like a broken video game. *Or, like the glitches in the Gadget...*

Amber moved back.

She had thought only Cats could use human language in this world. Again, she heard English, never Japanese. It was like the creatures that could speak spoke English so that she could understand them better. But Amber did not know what they all wanted from her.

She found herself unable to leave due to the magic force, and all she could do was stare, open-mouthed, watching. Although she could, she did not dare breathe.

Amber knew they were supposed to arrive at DragonFree Haven sometime today. But she had been so close to the other Portal, and she knew that she had to get to *any* Portal as soon as she could.

The creature was still watching her. She could almost feel the deep, penetrating eyes cutting through her.

The creature spoke no more, and Amber filled the silence with an almost-scream as the words escaped her mouth, "Please, leave me alone, *sea monster*."

"Much o-obliged…" came the creature's reply, with a stutter. It spoke much clearer than the Cats, she noticed, and sounded less forced. But still not like it was a creature *meant* to speak.

Amber gasped and her eyes widened as it went on, "…but first, m-m-may I have a word? And also, I would not think I deserve my s-spot in that… *monster* category of y-y-yours."

"I don't have much time," she squeaked.

The creature's eyes widened as well, but as if raising its eyebrows. "Oh? Dear, of course you do not *have* time. Time is not of your b-belongings. Also, I have f-frozen time." It giggled again.

Frozen… time? Amber thought not even Halfmoon was capable of something like that. *If it were possible, that was.*

It explained, "A very powerful magic. You see, everywhere

in this realm M-mahou energy flows. But in the ocean, the Mahou energy flows more solid than ever, as liquid, not gas. So, it is much e-e-easier to use it. What I have done is I have f-frozen the *life* in the ocean, temporarily. No one else can, especially not on land. I tend to get my energy from the m-m-moon, or stray Mahou energy in the sea, although I do need Mahou energy in the *first place* to do so, which comes from myself. I personally always carry a lot of m-m-m-magic with m-m-myself…"

Then, the creature crouched and performed a type of bow, glitching while doing so. Her thoughts drifted unwillingly back to the Fox cub on the Wacky Winters.

"A-allow my introduction. I a-am Timeravel, Amber. Or, at least, that is what I call myself."

Amber stumbled backwards, unsure. She didn't know what was being said. She was standing, her feet felt floor beneath her, and they were about to run away. Then, she felt an odd tension holding onto her body, forcing her to keep still. She struggled in the grip of invisible hands. She knew this creature —*Timeravel*—was doing it.

"How do you know my name?" she burst out, now trembling, as her only choice was to look at the creature.

"I h-have watched you closely," it replied. "I watch things. See, I watch time, some would say I *unravel* time, but I will not be explaining in *which* way. Over time, I have found just as much use of the ocean. I unravel it, study its Mahou energy. M-m-magic flows everywhere, and I use it wisely."

Amber forced a funny grin and nodded. In that moment, she felt a weight appear beneath her and turned to find a small wooden stool in the middle of the ocean.

"Sit," Timeravel commanded, and she did. It felt as if she were sitting on regular, solid ground.

Timeravel crouched down beside her, bending its front legs. "I *saved* you. This o-o-ocean is full of, well, *things*. When you fell into the water, when you *entered* the w-water, putting yourself into a very v-v-vulnerable position, you would have been attacked. But I saved you by bringing you down here, where you are safe. I used the opportunity to talk to you, as I have things I want to say. But a-all right; if we must hurry, be it so."

Amber knew exactly what it meant with *things* but had no reason to believe it. She regretted ever having left the boat.

"You have… things to say?" she muttered. "To me?"

Timeravel smirked.

A deep dread had manifested in her stomach, but she decided she would let it talk. *She would let it talk, let this happen, and when it was all done, she would be able to escape.*

"You n-need to be aware; I could very easily kill you if I liked."

Amber gulped, the threat catching her completely off guard. Again, she started to feel like the whole experience wasn't happening to her. *But she had to stay and listen.*

"What do you want?" she asked.

"Like I said, a w-w-w-word…"

Timeravel's image glitched terribly, and Amber waited for it to stop. It got up again, smirking, and started, "M-many years ago, the C-cats came to this world where they *picked up* Mahou energy. They became, well, powerful, and owned some Mahou energy. They created land. C-correct?"

Amber remembered. "Yes. That's right. I've been told."

Timeravel glitched and made the sound of a sigh. "I believe I can sense the big problem. It is easy to… persuade you. Many are."

Amber got up from her stool and took a step back as she processed these words. "What are you saying?" *Timeravel had repeated what both Koko and Halfmoon had told her about the realm. Now it was saying they were wrong.*

Timeravel looked at her and gave a manic laugh.

Her hands turned into fists, then opened again. She couldn't do anything about this, but it hurt.

"What do you mean, it is easy to persuade me?" Amber repeated, shakily.

Timeravel laughed again before disappearing from her view.

Amber's seat collapsed under her weight, but instead of hitting the hard ground, she slowly sank in the water. This time, she was still breathing.

Then, she felt ground again. Beneath her feet, she now saw a slightly see-through floor but carpeted in something dark-red and fine. She didn't take a single step forward, and stayed where she stood, waiting for the scene to settle, but it did not; in front of her, rose tall, black shelves filled with many books.

Exactly as it had with her, an unseen force made them stand on the ground, disregarding the underwater norms.

The image spun in her eyes, and she fell back onto an uncomfortable skinny stool, dizzied. *Why was there a library underwater?*

The scene fell apart again, and she was back swimming in the ocean, her chest hurting more than ever.

Something sparkled. The second she saw the blue out of the corner of her eye, she knew what it was.

Amber dived towards the Portal, relieved. Her *exit*. Finally. When it disappeared yet again, the next thing she knew, she was back on the stool in the library of books.

Amber was breathing heavily now, trying not to fall apart

like the fast-paced scenery herself, wishing she could stay by the Portal. She tried to ignore all the books and shelves around her, but failed, and started hyperventilating, ignoring the tears in her eyes.

Timeravel was with her now, glitching.

"Be cautious," it said, as if she had been the one who had created the two images.

"What… just happened?" Amber groaned, her mind not being able to quite grasp the truth behind this strange ocean place.

"As I said," Timeravel replied. "M-mahou energy flows in the water. Plus, I have M-m-mahou energy myself, and I know how to use it. But your eyes… Be—be cautious. Be cautious with your e-eyes, what they tell you."

"My… eyes?"

As if this were all a hilarious joke, she saw something in the distance in that second. It was, in fact, an eye. Of some beast.

Not Halfmoon's Eyes, but the strange outline was of something large—small at first, then zooming closer, closer, until the whole eye was bigger than their library, slamming right into them…

Amber shut her own eyes, burying her face with her arms. She did not want to see.

When she came back up to find the eyeball gone and Timeravel giggling manically, she burst into tears, waiting for whatever was to happen now to happen.

However, when Timeravel saw her tears, it stopped smiling and the same dull seriousness as before came to its face. "S-s-sorry," it said, with a glitch. "As I was saying, be cautious with your eyes. For instance, that *Portal* you saw, know it w-was an *illusion*, all my Mahou energy and a t-trick to your eyes, a false signal to your brain.”

Amber looked directly into its face. “*Which* Portal? When?!”

“It depends. You could say I am generalizing.”

A fresh wave of tears came to her as she struggled to understand.

Timeravel scoffed. “The P-portal, for instance, you saw minutes ago. It was, after all, the s-same one you saw earlier, after falling into the ocean, when you were escaping from me. The same i-i-image, re-used.”

“An… illusion? The Portal I saw in the ocean, it was an illusion?” Amber felt like she had been lied to. She still hated the idea of the illusions, of not knowing.

Halfmoon had said the idea of the illusions was nonsense, and she always knew It could tell whether something was real, but It had never explicitly said they did not exist. Her head was full of questions.

“An illusion,” Timeravel repeated.

“But how?” Amber asked, her voice desperate and grating. “You *make* them?”

“I cannot explain this in simple words, but yes, essentially. Essentially, I do make images with my Mahou energy. I am full of Mahou energy, p-protecting it from harm. But sometimes it does what it wants, Amber. Although, I do *have* to use it often because of this realm that we have all created. For e-e-example, I made this area here safe. For you. I used the Mahou energy because you are here. The oxygen you breathe in now is healthier, more natural—I am m-m-making sure of that, I am *making* it.”

“I don’t understand…” Amber replied. “You’re making the air healthier, more natural, than what? Than the air outside?”

Timeravel shook its head, suddenly not meeting her eyes. "Y-yes, I am sorry, Amber, but this is the way it is. This is the reality of the realm, of the world we have c-created for ourselves. The Mahou energy, the energy that flows in this realm is, simply, not always good. I can control it a little, make it healthier than the Mahou energy that is not controlled, as that one is simply not meant for your l-l-lungs…"

Healthier? Timeravel could control the Mahou energy in the realm a little, to make it 'healthier'? Amber shook her head. "And what do you mean, the *world we have created for ourselves*? Who has?" She was crying properly now.

Timeravel still refused to look at her, as if uncomfortable. "I *have* to use the Mahou energy, protect the Mahou energy, in today's world. The world that so much has happened in… But it does not matter for n-now. I see you need a break. Let us talk of something else for a while, shall w-w-we?"

And just like that, Timeravel let go of the terrible topic of the illusions and the magic. Amber sighed. It felt like there was magic *inside* her—struggling in her grip, squirming, chaotically reluctant to be compressed into a clear explanation in her head. Perhaps it was all too complicated for her to understand.

Timeravel walked across the carpeted floor, as if in thought. Amber wanted to shout, shout at all the things she was being told, as she did not want to hear. But she knew she *had* to listen. She had to watch, hoping she could use the Gadget later.

"Putting what I just told you aside," Timeravel said kindly. "There is something e-e-else I would like to show you."

It pointed straight at one of the black shelves, at least seven feet tall, and filled with endless books, all different covers, yet with no titles.

"Look, this is a s-special library," it explained. "Amber, this library contains books which spell out your f-future, your whole life. These b-books are very important, *yours*. All an illusion, of c-course."

Amber gave a small laugh, like she had on Catslaughter Island. "This is all *nonsense*!" She didn't know what else to reply. "How can books... determine my future? Are you saying those are all fully written, with every mere *detail* of my life?"

Timeravel's image glitched to show unexpected sharp teeth. "No, they are not fully written. They do not have to be— and they are not always—books. This is my p-personal choice of presenting them to you. These are the factors that make up your l-life and show your destiny."

Amber's gaze slowly moved down to her shoes, and Timeravel started talking about the library again, about how important it was, and how it represented her destiny, without getting across any proper point. All nonsense. She didn't even know what Timeravel was talking about anymore.

Eventually, even Timeravel gave in, "You do not seem to understand. L-l-look."

It took a second, then the library was gone. Instead, the ocean floor was replaced with shiny, glassy, black tiles, and dozens of canvases were displayed, each with a white cloth thrown over to hide what was beneath.

"You d-draw," it remarked.

Amber tried not to think about how it could possibly know this.

"Think of it this way. It is not your book; it is your canvas. *Your* canvas."

Now, there was a spark of recognition in her mind. She

understood, perhaps. Amber reached out and pulled a white cloth off a canvas.

It remained white.

"Where's. My… destiny?" she said, eyes growing wider at the blank canvas.

Timeravel grinned. "This shows your destiny; you have none. It is still wordless or still waiting for colour. You cannot tell the future. It is i-i-i-impossible."

Amber put the cloth back on, hands trembling. "And what are you trying to say with this?"

But Timeravel only smiled. "It is your canvas."

Amber stood looking at the canvases for a bit longer, eyebrows twitching, trying to digest everything she was being told. Silence stretched out.

Then, Timeravel studied her with an odd expression, and muttered, "Perhaps there is still hope. But otherwise, you will make the same mistakes… face the same doom as I have…"

"What did you say?"

"Oh." Timeravel's face flushed a little. "I had not meant to say that a-aloud. You were not meant to hear that. Best you forget you heard that."

Amber nodded, a hysterical smile on her face. Then, the words burst out, "So, what is it that you want to tell me? Just do, please, whatever it is!" She could not bear it any longer, and somehow, this was like it was with Koko; she wanted to know, wanted to understand what others thought, but was utterly terrified.

Timeravel sighed with a grin and walked closer to her, so that its eyes stared right into hers.

"L-l-let me open your mind, Amber. A little…" And it started as she listened. "We are, as you know, in a realm parallel to Japan. But it all began with an empty dimension, occupied purely by air and sea, and lively energy streaming everywhere. As well as four F-f-foxes, who existed before anything else. Four creatures, not quite *foxes*, but taking the form and life of Foxes…"

Amber *could* believe these words. "Then, the Cats came, and adapted to the Mahou energy and created land, right?" she pressed, something rising inside her.

"N-no." Timeravel looked stumped.

"No?" Amber asked.

"That is incorrect."

"*What*?"

"The C-cats never created land; they came much later. *It*, all of it, *everything* started with four Foxes, and I am one of them. We possessed great, great powers, because we came from—we were *made by*, perhaps—this energy. We created one big land. But then we fell apart, so we split up, each Fox taking their own part of the island, creating their own, new l-l-l-land.

"Only *then* was it that other creatures arrived. The C-c-c-cats, for example. They came through from Japan and started inhabiting my island. And I chose kindness: the most ignorant thing I have e-e-ever done. You cannot be kind in these years, can you? This was long ago, but as I continued to share my Mahou energy, to use it in the wrong way for them, terrors came. Terrors came from the Human w-world.

"I protected our land, and all the creatures, and even made a spell of time. I made time tick differently in Japan than here, to distance the two realms, to prevent terrors from coming unannounced. It did not even work completely, I believe, but when I was of no m-m-more use, they drove me off their l-land…" Its gulp was very audible in the stunned silence.

Amber felt sick. She started to shake her head. "I don't

know why you're telling me this… but that can't be true! How *can* that be true? I know it's not!" She clenched her fists. *She had no reason to believe Timeravel.* "I won't let you… *persuade* me of such random things!"

"Oh," Timeravel replied. "But are y-y-you not already?"

Amber shook her head again and stated, "I trust Halfmoon." *She had already decided to stick with It. She had already decided. She had already decided what to do. And she didn't need things to be more complicated than was necessary.*

Timeravel scowled. "And *why*? Things aren't always what they seem to be, A-amber."

"I know. I know that! I know…"

"You don't know very much, do you?"

The words cut very, very deep.

"How can I know, then," Amber replied, fighting tears. "If it's true?" *Of course, she believed Halfmoon, and nothing could change* that.

"There is not a way for the definite answer… But look me in the eyes," Timeravel answered.

Amber did so. The eyes were deep, cold, and held many things.

"Now, can you trust me?"

"Based on… your eyes?"

Amber wasn't going to say it, but the eyes, penetrating, and even empathetic, did *look* trustworthy. But she knew by now that eyes could lie—Koko's had. Its big, creepy, goofy eyes had not shown the soft, fragile thing it was. *So, Timeravel's eyes, with so much power, could definitely lie.*

Then, Timeravel started glitching, though Amber could tell that there was more it wanted to say. It fell to its knees, no longer able to control itself, the Mahou energy inside it seemingly pouring out.

"*W-w-wait*," it screeched.

Amber covered her ears.

Yet not only because of the horrible sound.

"I-I need you to k-k-know! This was n-not s-so long ago, when I-I was u-used, used for only *t-t-t-their* purpose. Now I have to pro-pro-protect so much M-mahou energy in the ocean, for t-t-the C-cats, as they do not know how to h-handle i-it!" It seemed to be drowning in memories and magic, but gasping, trying to tell Amber a final thing.

"It was not so l-lo-long ago!" it gasped again. "Not s-so lo-lo-long—"

It glitched, trying to speak, but Amber felt the force sending her up perhaps accidentally, the ground dissolving beneath her feet. She couldn't breathe anymore as she was swept up and rose.

Amber left the unexplainable experience behind in the depths of the ocean.

She didn't know if time had been frozen for Koko as well, but she knew it ticked normally when she saw Koko stir at her return.

CHAPTER 17 – MOVING ONWARDS??

"Amber…"

Its voice sounded croaky and dim, jittery and worried. Mixed with a sigh of great relief.

"Amber!" It sprang up towards her head slowly appearing out of the water. "Come, hold my Paw!"

But there were more things, many things that Amber didn't know.

She wanted to find out what the last thing was that Timeravel wanted to tell her—perhaps to show herself that there wasn't an even worse horror, hiding, right beneath the surface.

She took a deep breath before quickly pulling herself back onto the boat—but only for a moment.

"What are you doing?" Koko sobbed.

There was no time to explain anything, so with a swing of her arms, she jumped back into the water, leaving Koko there, shaking.

She swam with all the strength in her body, down, down. Only blackness filled her vision, and she could not even see her arms stretched out in front of her. In fact, it was almost as if, when Amber had been here with Timeravel just minutes ago, there had been a light turned on. A grim, ugly, alarming light, but some sort of clarity nonetheless. Maybe it had something to do with being able to breathe with Timeravel. Because now, Amber was running out of air. And she couldn't see anything at all.

But when she kicked herself as far down as she could, and some of her last bubbles of breath rose up, she realized how stupid this was. *Exactly like with the House.* Really, she was putting herself in danger.

She couldn't find Timeravel anywhere, only some small, tall, dark outline in front of her…

Amber got closer, squinting, as if squinting would sharpen her view. They were small rocks scattered together in heaps; a huge, neatly stacked pile reached out from the black depths, perhaps from the bottom of the ocean. She peered into them, kicking her legs to come closer. But then her knee hit one of the rocks and the pain was deep and white. She opened her mouth to yelp, only for the sound to be muffled and for her to lose all her breath.

Amber swam up to the surface to find Koko waiting for her to get on board, watching a few drops of blood from her knee grow into what looked like a huge pool by her side.

It did not even reach out to help her. Maybe it was too afraid. Maybe it thought anything it would do was useless, anyway.

When she was back on the boat, she lay still for a couple of seconds, her breaths returning in small, gradual puffs.

"You could've been eaten!" Koko screamed at her. Then it pulled her into a hug that she could not fight in that moment.

Her knee stung and the water had made the slight scrape look much more dramatic than it was—blood pouring and spilling across their boat when she only slightly shifted her leg.

Koko shrieked and wiggled away from it, releasing her from its awkward embrace.

She also finally noticed a terrible prickling on her skin. All over her body, there was a tiny, stinging rash, probably left from the ocean.

Then, as everything replayed itself in her head, she spluttered and gasped and cried.

Koko spoke quietly, wanting to know what she had seen.

But all Amber could do was shake her head. And then, with a horrible, sudden lurch of her stomach, she ducked over the edge of the boat in time to be sick into the swirling dark depths.

Koko did not speak to her anymore, then.

When she weakly looked up to get her Gadget a few minutes later, her stomach dropped, but not because she'd swallowed a lot of seawater.

The Gadget was not gliding above her.

She asked Koko about it, but it shrugged, mumbling some indistinct excuse.

She... she must've left it in the ocean. How had she forgotten it?

The tears continued to fall now, with no clear beginning or end; she could not catch them with the Gadget, could not even distract herself now.

The present moment, the events of the day, and the plans of the future all blurred into an unintelligible non-chronological mess in her mind, all the terrors absorbed by the Gadget now bursting to the surface once more, as if she were reliving them.

She was trapped. Trapped in this reality, with no more

escape. Amber knew she had to act; she had to do something…
but there were no strings she could stare at now.

With her hair still dripping wet, her eyes streaming salty
tears, her lips still quivering and there being no end to her feelings, she listened to Koko meow uneasily. It was the first time
she had heard it meow. It stared at the bleeding injury on her
knee. "Is it… OK?" Koko asked, coming closer.

"Er, is *what* OK—?"

Koko stuck out its rough, sticky tongue and began to lick
her knee. She jumped back. However, after a moment, she
allowed it, knowing its licking could likely infect her, but she
had worse things happening in her head. There were worse
things than Koko.

And there was nothing now playing in front of her eyes to
replace and soften the memories and memories playing in her
head—of all the nonsense, the illusions, the strangeness, the
library, the blank canvases, the pressure, the dread, the truth,
the idea of the uncontrolled Mahou energy, the story of the
Foxes, the story of the Cats…

She ran out of breath and pinched herself, overwhelmed by
everything. She didn't like admitting it, but without the
Gadget, this was what she was.

Amber tried to make sense of things. *Timeravel was a
creature that had watched her, that had things to say to her,
some of which she had not even heard. It lived alone in the sea,
filled with Mahou energy that it claimed was* healthier *than the
version found in the air. Things she did not even want to try to
understand. It claimed that the realm had started off with only
four Foxes. And it claimed other things too, including words it
had never even brought to life…*

Amber kept shaking her head again and again, so hard that
with each shake she felt the throbbing pain in her forehead

increase, as she tried to shake out the truth, not wanting to accept any of it.

But then she decided she wouldn't accept it. *She did not have to accept what she had witnessed as being what had really happened.*

"Surely Halfmoon can send us a new Gadget. Right?" she pressured desperately, her throat dry and sore.

"I don'tknow, sorry…"

Amber looked into Koko's eyes as deeply as she could. She knew she needed to say something. She did not know what details she was or was not going to tell it, let alone what she was allowed to tell. She almost wished that Koko could somehow steal her eyes from her and be able to sink *into* them, seeing exactly what she had seen and understanding exactly what she had understood. About everything.

But then again, she did not want that. She did not want to think that everything she had seen had been true, let alone real. She had never been more open to the idea of illusions.

Amber waited in the torture of silence and thinking. She had felt numb most of the time while listening to Timeravel but found it impossible to feel numb now. The numbness and distantness would start again soon, she knew, but now she felt lost at sea. It was like she was unable to decide how to react to this reality—this reality that she was unsure of, of what it meant, what was right, or how she could know anything at all.

But Amber knew she had to tell Koko something, and so she explained, "I'm honestly… *unsure* about what happened, myself. But there were sea monsters, I think. Yes. And I met this creature—it—it could talk. But I'm almost convinced that it was an… an illusion." She was still choked up and felt awful, but forced out her voice.

"An illusion?" Koko asked. "You actually believe in illusions?"

Amber grew tense at its careless tone. "Yes. But still, I do think Halfmoon can *tell* whether something is an illusion or not." *And she would leave it at that, not defining what an illusion even was.*

When she was about to snap completely, Koko exclaimed, "Look, it's an Eye!"

At the word, her stomach churned, remembering the last time she had seen one. But this Eye was not broken; Amber saw it was flying in the air! The Kitten Robot levitated towards their boat.

And… *it was carrying a Gadget.*

Without even managing a smile, Amber took it and instantly started looking at the strings, at the images of deep waters and blue skies that were so familiar. She looked at skinny trees where she did not know what was behind each one, at talking Houses with voices that she could not explain, at creatures from far below that weren't even *supposed* to exist in her mind…

After a while, she caught Koko mumbling, "That's odd…"

She shot it a curious, yet horrified, look. It caught her eye for a second, then explained, "Halfmoon, from what I know, rarely has Kitten Robots go near the ocean. It usually has them in the clouds, or at the entrance of new islands…"

Then, they both saw it: there was a dense fog in the air, moving to the side at that moment to reveal their arrival to new land.

"Oh!" Koko cried. "That explains it."

"But… how did It get a second Gadget?" Amber asked.

Koko shrugged. "Halfmoon's ways."

Amber opened her mouth to reply but thought better of it.

She could sense that Koko was shaking lightly with nervousness. They were here.

There was no more to say, except to herself. *She knew she trusted Halfmoon. After all, she was here on this journey because of It, or at least, had a lot to do with It. She had no reason to trust Timeravel, suddenly, randomly.* Amber didn't even know who—let alone *what*—Timeravel even was, and who else agreed with it. Many Cats agreed with Halfmoon, and she liked to stick with others' opinions. It was safer.

Amber knew, or she thought, or she really knew, that *there was a reason for everything.* And *she would not trust Timeravel because of a gut-feeling, that its eyes looked kind, for that was ignorant.* It was ignorant to believe Timeravel, and what she knew about it was limited, *if it even existed, that was.*

It was ignorant, and Amber had little choice anyway. She didn't have the freedom of a decision as big as whether to trust someone, nor did she ever want it.

* * *

Again, it was cold. But it was hot, too. Somewhat chilly, mixed with a scorching warmth.

Amber shuddered, taken aback by the unusual temperatures. But as they started walking a few steps into the new land, it almost worked well. Like sipping cold juice on a summer day. Or like taking a hot bath on a winter night.

Then, Koko stopped and turned back slowly. "I almost forgot. We're gonna have totake our boat with us!"

As Amber looked at it, she noticed she couldn't see clearly. There was something in her view, making it foggy. Scanning the whole place, she saw it was everywhere, but she could not tell what *it* was. It could have been a list of things: mist, fog, smoke, her own frozen breath…

It took her a moment to realize what Koko was talking about. "What do you mean, we're going to have to take our boat with us?"

"On land, with us!"

"We won't be leaving this island by boat? What are you saying?" Amber grew impatient.

Koko grinned matter-of-factly. "We won't really be leaving by boat, no… So, we kinda need to send the boat back toHalfmoon. Man, I've not thought this through…"

Amber sighed, remembering that she didn't know every detail of the plan. But she was sure Koko hadn't ever mentioned anything like this.

"But *why* can't we leave the island by boat?" she asked.

The corners of Koko's mouth twitched upwards. "It's complicated. *Trust* me! Let's pull our boat with us on land—"

"But—"

"Trust me!" Koko yelled. "I've talked it through with Halfmoon."

So, Amber decided simply to go along with Koko. She knew that was what she had to do here, anyway—the plan was that this was a small *break*. This island was their break, and they had to use the brief time they had to explore it.

All Amber wanted, of course, was to be happy. She wanted to feel happy and real, avoid thinking about anything that caused distress, listen to Halfmoon, and just get on…

Koko managed to lift the boat out of the water and onto the land with her help. To Amber's surprise, it weighed barely anything. She remembered it was alive, and as it steered *itself*, she noticed its jerky movements only slightly resembled signs of protest.

As soon as its base scraped the mossy ground, its height decreased a little, and instead its width expanded. The boat created a long, flat surface underneath itself, perfect for sliding down hills.

Koko caught Amber's eye and smiled. She almost smiled back. They both jumped right in, with the Gadget following along. That was when the boat started to move. It was as if they were still sailing out on water. In fact, it felt smoother, a heavenly, comfortable ride.

Amber's eyes captured all they could of the place as they made their way towards wherever it was their boat was taking them. The ground had caught some of the moisture or heat, or whatever had resulted in the smoke or the fog; it looked damp, or dried, and the closer she looked at the ground, the more of the substance was gliding around. It was soft when she touched it—it seemed to be moss, or a type of grassy herb.

They were skidding up a slope, and the more they advanced, the closer the resemblance of the place grew to a quite peculiar flower garden. It was a glamorous sight.

At that moment, Amber felt a sudden tug to the right. It was like a force pushing their boat to the side. Their boat seemed to fight it at first, then gave up and continued upwards, now completely to the right. They were heading northeast, and the scenery blossomed into something yet newer as the images flashed past Amber's eyes. A scent filled the air, too.

"It smells of… plants!" Koko announced cluelessly, raising its voice a little over the air that blew over its face as they raced onwards.

Amber thought it was right. That was how she would have described it as well. It smelled fresh, but not the kind of fresh that was brand new and perfect, but like the fresh that had lingered on for ages and never got boring. It smelled of weeds and planted seeds, of growth and a calming space. But Amber was not calm. Rather, the smell made her heart thump rapidly against her chest. And the temperature was so balanced that she should have neither sweated nor shivered, yet she did both. The fog especially got on her nerves—she didn't like not being able to see what was ahead. Still, she tried to pull herself together, to *simply get on.*

Despite the speed they were going, Amber stood up to lower the Gadget. She held it in her hands for a while, still standing.

"You don't need that *now*!" Koko called out.

"Sorry," she said. "What am I doing? I meant to… grab the map."

At that moment, the boat lurched awkwardly and Amber tumbled out of it onto the grass—and was incredibly surprised by the soft landing. She still held the Gadget in her hands, and for a moment, all she wanted was to close her eyes and feel the comforting warmth of the plants and the wisps of the substance protecting her; it felt so delightful, she could have kept her eyes shut and fallen asleep. But then the sensation startled her, and when she heard Koko's edgy voice asking if she was all right, she experienced a similar feeling to when she awoke from the strings, when she was pushed back into reality.

Amber saw that the boat had stopped but still drifted very slowly, very slightly towards the right. *Probably by a magic force...* The sight made her gulp and her stomach churn. Because it reminded her of what she had seen earlier that day.

She got up and noticed the peculiarity of the surrounding plants. She had never seen such on Earth. A sudden realization hit her. "These are the same plants as on Catslaughter Island."

Koko leapt out of their boat and onto the meadow with her, to see. Amber wished she had not even mentioned it.

"Really? I've never paid attention to them." Koko reached out and then rolled around on the softness of the crocodile-green ground.

"This is also the same grass," Amber observed. *It was the same one behind the blueberry bushes in Japan.*

"Really?" Koko got a closer look but seemed uninterested. It stretched out comfortably. "Grass. That means, you know, lots of Mahouenergyaround…" it muttered.

"Sorry?" Amber asked.

"Didn't Halfmoon explain?" Then Koko started to giggle. "This issofluffy!"

"No?"

"*Of course* thisisfluffy!" Koko yelled. "I've never-touchedthis before! But I love, Ilove this. I've never felt anything likethis—!"

"I meant Halfmoon. *What* were you saying about the Mahou energy?"

"I *love* plants!" Koko shrieked. "IloveIloveIlove!"

Amber's skin prickled; there was something strange about Koko. It was acting unusual, and although it lay on its stomach with its back to her, she could hear its voice sounded, some-how, distorted.

"Koko? Answer me!"

Koko's voice made her heart drop. "IloveIloveIloveIlove-IloveIloveIloveIloveIloveIlove!" it repeated over and over, swallowing words and air.

"Er," Amber cleared her throat. "*Koko*?"

"IloveIloveIloveIlove…" It slowly turned its head towards her, and when it did, she screamed.

Fifty times more than usual, Koko's face was swollen. Its lips were bulging; its eyes were twitching. "Whatsup?"

But at the sound of her scream, Koko fell back, alarmed.

Amber got up and ran a few steps backwards.

For a moment, all she could do was stare.

"Passmethesack!" Koko gulped. "Passmethesack!"

It took a moment for her to understand what it meant. Although incredibly squeamish at the sight of it, she forced her legs to take her to the boat, and she threw the sack over to Koko. It got up and started chewing Cat Improvement Pills.

For a long time, Amber stood unmovingly and stared at her feet and at the crocodile grass.

It took several minutes before she dared look at Koko. She realized it had climbed back into the boat and was waiting for her.

"Really sorry about that," Koko's more neutral face spoke to her. "That was weird."

Amber didn't meet its eyes. "Yes. It was. But what were you saying?"

It thought for a moment, then replied, "The Mahou energy. I meant, well… I don't know much about this, but all the energy, as Halfmoon said once, is more concentrated on some things than others. And grass is just packed with lots of Mahou energy. At least the one on Catslaughter Island. I didn't know DragonFree Haven also had this much grass." It shrugged.

"Oh," Amber said. "The grass is full of Mahou energy, and —and it… made you…" Her voice trailed off, but she forced a smile. "I see." She pinched her skin, forcing her mind to *stay in place*.

"By the way," Koko said. "Did you notice something strange is happening?"

"What?"

"I don't *know*, our boat—why is it heading—?"

"You're heading north too, Koko. Look at you!"

Amber pointed; Koko's body was, as well, slowly falling

in one direction as it was nearly pulled out of the boat. It shook its head. "Let's just follow this—this *force* andsee what we find, I guess. Yeah. Let's just *go*."

Both now back in the boat, ignoring what had happened with the grass, Amber checked the map.

The map was different.

She had thought that, aside from the vague spiky outline, there was nothing drawn on the map to give guidance for DragonFree Haven. But as she narrowed her eyes, she saw there were three faint lines marking three separate sections of the island. She didn't understand how she had not spotted them before, and saw they were, in fact, labelled A, B, and C. They were currently in C. The map showed that most of the plants ceased to grow in the middle B and in their place there was a small clearing.

It was as if the more she looked at the sections, the more details appeared. She flinched, trying to ignore this fact, for something about it unnerved her slightly.

B also showed some sort of small houses, symbolizing some type of civilization. *New creatures, new life.* This was when Amber put the map away, pretending she had not seen what was on B at all.

As they rode on over the green, healthy land, the grass blades grew up yet taller until it looked as though they were sailing through a moss ocean with little waves of them. The plant smells increased and mixed with a satisfying sweet scent that Amber had never encountered before: it was like honey, mixed with a hint of wildflower and hay, and perhaps some juicy fruit.

All the powerful senses mixed queasily with her twisted feelings.

She couldn't help but notice that the aroma was coming from section B, which was also where they were headed.

Amber was on the verge of panic, wanting to be able to prepare herself and not let the seemingly sentient boat determine the speed—currently fast—that they would approach section B in. But then she realized that section C was very large, and they were still far away. *Or, at least, it said so on the map.*

Trees, plants and all types of fantastical things began to crowd them on all sides. New scenes were seemingly born at every turn, and all in what was meant to be part of grassland section C. As the realization struck Amber, perhaps to emphasize the fact even more, their boat stopped in its tracks…

The map was wrong.

Amber felt dizzy.

As the small meadow of grass went on, the area flattened down into a texture made up of something that looked like some new, scientifically discovered fungi. It seemed to be moss at first glance, but as Amber fixed her eyes properly on the small, spiral-like way it was growing, she knew no moss looked like this. It was hugging the whole rest of the island. On top of it, more recognizable mushroom types and flowers grew (or at least Amber thought that was what they were).

The honey-wildflower smell increased and the fog substance still glided in the air, but for no apparent reason, here it parted in two. Amber noticed both parts were crawling past her, one on either side for as far as she could see. But what really made the view here so new and distinct was what was perhaps a dozen feet away.

There were creatures of all types. They walked, and trotted, and flew on all sides, for the area was not too big. Amber stifled gasps at things and creatures that she had never seen before on Earth. It was almost inconceivable to think that the creatures here could think for themselves, just like the Cats, crafting their own homes and rules. They were not like the Worms. The word from earlier struck her again. Civilization. *New, strange life.*

But Amber could not help noticing how *clearly* they were not like the Worms—how apparent their intelligence was to onlookers. As she neared, she was at first stunned by the obscure sounds of what seemed bird-like peeps or rodent-like chitters, and pungent, musty smells, and many different things, but she already knew *this*, she could already feel *this*, only by observing the ways in which they moved.

Amber felt nauseous as the force pulled her out of the boat and closer towards the things; this was like discovering Catslaughter Island all over again. Except, this time not even Halfmoon could guide her.

CHAPTER 18 – CONTROL CIRCUS

When in doubt, Amber, or *Amaya*, sometimes liked to flip things over, to look at them from a different view. She liked to look at things and find *shapes*. She had to, anyway, when making guidelines for her drawings. In this world, or even in Japan, these shapes were, in fact, her real-life guidelines. She liked to find boxes. In her head, she liked to fold things up into a neat, tidy box. Something digestible that she could understand.

Catslaughter Island, Left Ear, had been a triangle, but the way the camp was set up was like a big, friendly circle. What she saw of DragonFree Haven now looked like a wide, grassy square filled with flowers, heading up to an oval. Then, a rectangle upwards… *mountains*.

Before her and Koko was the oval. It was filled with life, plants, scents, sounds, and something else—*fire*. Amber's eyes tried to identify the flaming red that was burning off the ground yet leaving it unharmed.

The force pushed her. She stuck out her heels and pressed

them into the ground, but only managed to drag down the force for a few seconds.

She coughed. The place's previous scent was now mixed with a new one of burned coal or smoke. Something about it hurt her lungs. Her coughs were short and bark-like, turning into raspier, yet steadier ones within just a few seconds.

As she came involuntarily closer, she wanted to shut her eyes. But a part of her needed to see. And again, she was observing.

Somehow… it all looked very *lovely* together. In front of her was a mix of all the elements, and although there was a lot going on, there was no conflict to be seen. Nothing outrightly wrong. Amber could already sense it; there was a clean sense of system or organization in the air. Of, in some playful and messy way, order.

Catslaughter Island had been lovely, *too. Lovely and fake, a lullaby sung wrong. The Wacky Winters had been cold, numb, and terribly confusing. And this place… it was, but somehow it was not,* lovely.

She hated the idea of the Cats, because they were Cats, and not regular cats. And she knew cats. *But this place was completely new, with not even a touch of familiarity. Just entirely alien.* She could picture it in different ways—lovely, or not.

Koko beside her studied the creatures' every move cautiously, which almost looked like fascination or awe. But Amber had no way of knowing what was passing through the Cat's mind.

Everywhere she looked, she saw the incredibly soft fungi ground. She reached out her hand to touch it, then instantly pulled it back. It had felt spongy, uncomfortable, and alien.

Stationed on the fungi were what she thought were everyone's houses—but these were even less like *houses* than the Cats' ones. Flower petals and supplies that looked like they were from the meadow in Section C made up little nests.

Some of these nature beds were empty, while others housed sleeping creatures Amber had never seen before. Some creatures looked artificial, almost fabricated, as if, like the Doodles, a small child had dreamed them up, while others closely resembled animals she knew from Earth—though never as much as the Cats. Some looked like lions, birds, insects, serpents, and more, but somehow entirely different...

She caught sight of what looked like a cute, funny-shaped chair, set randomly in the centre of it all. It took her a moment to realize it was a throne, and that the rods on its back were long and had crown-like spikes suggestive of royalty, peeking up into the sky.

It stood on top of a tiny hill in the ground, higher up than everything else.

Beside it, there were two more hills double the size with two other thrones. This confused Amber. *Were there three leaders?*

Leadership, like on Catslaughter Island. Ruling. Clearly a sign of organization. *There was something here that Halfmoon hadn't mentioned.*

And then and there, she could not stop herself from being hit with the deep, prickly dread she was trying to suppress. Of questions, everything she wanted to know. Of illusions.

A shrill, quiet shriek came from somewhere in her throat. Koko shot her a concerned look as the force placed them even closer, and everything looked sharper and more realistic. Almost, completely real.

There was a soft sound of heavy footsteps in the grass. Amber turned her head.

A creature was walking towards them.

It was tall. Very tall. Its legs were long, giving it a sense of uncanny unnaturalness. Its eyes gleamed in a way that suggested it knew exactly what it was doing, a certainty running across its face. Its tail was long, swift.

It was a Fox.

Fresh feelings attacked Amber's insides, and she heard Koko squeak beside her. *It was its legs, its legs!*

Koko started running past the creature, past the whole area.

But Amber didn't have much time to make decisions, and she ran a little too slowly, too late, not being able to move properly. It did not matter.

The dim north-east force that had earlier been quite notice-able, with so little going on, came back intensely.

It felt like Amber was losing all the control over her body as she was pushed violently to the side. It was the same form of Mahou energy Timeravel had used.

"Ugh, letmego!" Koko groaned, trying to fight the force.

But fighting didn't seem to help.

Then, it seemed like the whole world flipped. Something happened that Amber could never have described. It was a very unworldly feeling. For a second, it didn't feel like *any* world anymore. She was falling senselessly through empty space.

The force got so strong that it seemed all the gravity had gone and been replaced with something else. In fact, it felt exactly like she was falling to the *side* instead of down.

She heard Koko scream faintly the moment this horrifying sensation began but could barely hear it over the gushing of blood in her ears or rushing into her head as she was hurled upside down.

And then it stopped. The world shook back into its place, and they were thrown against a wall.

It took Amber a moment to regain her senses. The world still seemed to shake, her eyes swimming out of focus. She had to shut her eyes and clasp both hands over her mouth to prevent herself from vomiting.

Koko beside her also turned an odd shade of green.

It took Amber a moment to realize that they were pinned against something. They had been placed on two of the three thrones.

"Scary!" Koko laughed, regaining its trembling voice. "What was that for?!"

Amber shook her head as she saw the long-legged creature that they were meant to be hiding from turn up in front of them.

Many pairs or trios of eyes were watching.

It was the third Fox she had seen so far in this world. She hoped it was a coincidence. But she didn't like that it was a Fox.

Yet, unlike the first Fox cub, this one wasn't small and tiny. Unlike Timeravel, this one wasn't short and stunning. Amber had had some trouble identifying the other two as Foxes, but this one was barely recognizable.

Then, Amber cursed herself; *why was she linking them? They had nothing to do with each other. Nothing at all. Even if they were all, somehow, Foxes.*

Its body was quite lithe, with enough flesh to appear well-fed and strong. Its bushy tail was huge with fine, reddish hairs, reaching quite far up to the creature's head level. Its legs, of course, grew down in a very slender, long, almost grotesque way, and instead of normal Fox paws, it possessed something almost like hooves—*Paws*. Like Timeravel.

The Fox's colours were swirled all over in a chaotic mix of reds in tones of wine and fire, a shimmery emerald green, and some oranges and yellows resembling the sun.

The only actual things about the creature that seemed fox-like were its pointy ears, snout, and face. Not even its expression was fox-like. It held its chin to the sun, and if there was one word to describe the way its eyes shone, the way its smile was just a little too wide, it was *prideful*. And Amber could not help the fact that its eyes reminded her of Timeravel.

Grass was growing out of its back.

Before Amber could do or say anything, the creature spoke, "Hey, Amber! Hey, Koko! Halfmoon's told me *all* about you!"

Then, it giggled.

She thought of Timeravel.

The way Amber would have described its voice was clear, bright, and incredibly boosting. Energetic, and extremely overwhelming.

It trotted even closer and looked directly into her eyes. Something about the Fox made her think of a very big little boy who'd had too much sugar. She shuddered.

"You might've not heard of me though," it went on. "I have… er, siblings. Sibling Foxes. Heard of them?"

Amber froze. She still felt dizzy, and this all *meant* something.

Sibling Foxes. Another Fox.

It was the second creature who had mentioned sibling Foxes. Two creatures, two of the Sibling Foxes, said the same thing. *It made sense.*

So, Amber trembled just thinking of it. *Perhaps Timeravel wasn't an illusion after all—perhaps it was right.*

And if Timeravel was right about the Foxes... what if it were also right about the story of the Cats?

Amber shook her head, to no one in particular. *No, no, no. That couldn't be.*

For that would mean...

She'd been wrong the whole time.

The next thing she knew, the Fox's voice was fading, and her eyes lost focus as she melted into darkness.

* * *

Koko stared at her with its googly eyes.

"Wonderful! She's alive!" the thing that was a Fox cried. "Nothing to worry about! Some creatures aren't used to this force! Let's give her a moment."

Amber noticed she was still sitting on a throne, and Koko was holding an unidentifiable bottle in front of her face.

"That's Mushroom juice!" The creature laughed. Its laugh wasn't fox-like nor hysterical, but simply wild and glad. Like it was enjoying itself. "Drink it!"

But she pushed the strange liquid away and stood up. She still felt quite weak and trembled in fear and giddiness.

Koko only smiled at her.

Then, the Fox turned around like nothing had happened and flattened out the beds of the other creatures with its Paws. It started humming to itself.

Koko looked a bit nervous but kept on smiling. *So, everyone was pretending she was all right.* Amber sighed. *But that made it all easier.*

"We need an introduction!" came the Fox's voice, although it had its back to them. "I guess you can refer to me as the 'Tall Dragon King'! My makings call me that, see. Not that I'm any better than others, well, no. You know, any higher up or worthier than them. But my makings, they like to compliment! Flattering!"

It took Amber a moment to understand what it meant. "Is that what your *creatures* call you?"

"Yep! Tall Dragon King! I keep our island in order, keep everything lovely. I love taking care of us!"

The Tall Dragon King turned around again, its weight on its front legs, as if to play.

"Anyway, to clear things up, this… Cat called Halfmoon rang me on this weird device… It's called a—a—"

"A Gadget," Amber chipped in. "Or a Teleclock." Then she spotted that a Gadget of its own was gliding above the Fox; she hadn't noticed before because of its height.

The Fox expanded its already wide grin. "I *love* that thing… Truly an amazing invention."

Koko shuddered.

It looked up to its Gadget and held it down in what seemed deep admiration. "Halfmoon told me some Human, from the other world, was coming to attack your island. I guess you could say DragonFree Haven and Catslaughter Island are friends, so I figured I'd help! It said the two of you had to get back to the Human world to stop them somehow. And that you needed, well, a small place to *rest* and someone to show you the island as a quick stop!"

Amber froze.

Koko, beside her, shivered.

"I dunno if we can trust it," it whispered.

Amber pretended she hadn't heard it.

But when she forced her voice out to speak, the words

came out a mumble: "Halfmoon… It hadn't told us we would see you."

Only after she said this did she recall the vague mention of a *friend* they would see.

The creature's look turned a little blank, a little guilty and hopeless.

After the encounter earlier today, Amber's whole world was flipped on its head, and she grew more paranoid than Koko. *But then again, this creature had a Gadget, meaning it wasn't lying about knowing Halfmoon personally. And Timeravel had been something completely different.*

Yet still, the question seemed to almost escape her lips, and Koko's eyes watered slightly as it mumbled half of it.

"But… how canwe…?"

The Fox looked down at Amber, rather than Koko, although it had been the one who had spoken. It looked and smiled at her with eyes full of hope, full of goodness and understanding. Then, Amber realized. *So* that *was the trait that so resembled Timeravel!*

Its eyes looked like Timeravel's, something she would not base her opinion on. If anything, it terrorized her.

The Tall Dragon King seemed to understand. "How can you… trust me? Believe me? I—I don't know," it gave in with a sigh. "But listen, sometimes you don't need to *know* to trust. Sometimes all you need is your heart, and your soul, to feel. So, I guess that's your choice, Amber."

Amber bit her tongue.

Even Koko gave a nod and failed to stifle a snort. "It doesn't… workthat way."

The Tall Dragon King sighed again, but then forced a huge smirk back on its face and sprang up, reminding Amber of a funny circus show she had gone to when she was very young. "All right!

"So, I could share some of our food supply, because, really, we've got a lot! I could show you some great sites if you'd like to go for a picnic up in the mountains—a beautiful hike! We could have so, so much *fun*! Or we could go for a stroll in the forest. I doubt you've ever seen anything like it! Oh, excuse me, I really love this place. When making it, I put so much effort into *everything…*"

"You made this place?!" Koko spoke, its mouth hanging slightly more open than usual.

"Yep."

Amber saw Koko trying to catch her gaze, impressed, but she looked away, her stomach churning. She knew Koko still knew as little as she had the day before, but now that this new Fox was here, everything was different. There was another Fox here, and Koko could see it.

Then, without saying anything else, the Tall Dragon stopped smiling and turned its back to them again. It pulled down its Gadget and started looking at the strings. Amber and Koko were still just sitting there.

Again, Koko stared at her, as if to communicate something privately, but she shot it a glare, which instantly made Koko turn away. Both of their gazes wandered into the distance over the whole scene again, as they remained sitting awkwardly and unmoving on the thrones. Amber could have laughed. That same weak feeling of dizziness from earlier came over her again. The two didn't know what to do but wait.

In that moment, Amber decided to stay happy and to deal with her true feelings later. Or, she had to, at least, stay only neutral.

After what felt like a few minutes, the Tall Dragon King

still absorbed in its own world, she cleared her throat. She thought about their next move.

The Fox did not look up from the Gadget.

She cleared her throat again, this time louder than before.

"Yes?" came a quiet reply.

"We left our boat there in the fields. Would you have a way to keep it safe for us?" Her voice quavered slightly.

"Yes... Oh—yes, *sure*!" It seemed the Fox suddenly realized who was talking to it and what was happening. It spun around, and for a second Amber swore she saw its face flush.

"Sorry about that," it added, flatly. "I'm trying not to use it that much anymore."

Amber gave a hurried nod.

Then, with apparently only its mind, the Fox pulled their boat to where they were. Amber could see it come flying from the distance, then turn abruptly in the air, with a sort of *screech* —as if the boat had caused friction with something invisible— before landing softly into the mossy ground beside them. Even Koko gasped.

"We could definitely hold on to this till you need it later! Or, if you like, we could send it off to Halfmoon directly!"

"Maybe send itoff to Halfmoon?" Koko replied.

Amber said nothing, but the Fox nodded.

Then, its voice made her jump. "What would you like to eat?"

Before Amber could reply, it raised its Paws and made some food appear out of thin air. At least *food* was what she thought it was.

The mixture was arbitrary, and it was like with the creatures—some features, some things Amber recognized a little, others were completely unknown.

There were fungi, some toadstool-like with cap and stem,

others looking like strange multi-coloured moulds. There were fruits, or berries, recognizable as juicy from their gleaming skins. Some were protected by squiggly rods of spider-web-structured things, others by long-reaching vines or menacing spikes. Some resembled tiny trees, others had quite organic shapes.

Amber didn't want to try most of them.

The Tall Dragon King kept creating more food, its Paws raised in a fixed posture, clearly in concentration, as more and more food and dishes appeared.

"Thank you for all of this food," Amber said. "Really. But you don't *need* to put in all this effort. Halfmoon, you see, has this new invention. We have literally *infinite* food! We can share some." She smiled, expecting the Tall Dragon King to look, at least, surprised.

However, it just shook its head. "I *like* putting effort into things. It's fun. Try some of this."

Amber opened her mouth to protest, but Koko turned towards her. "Amber. Comeon. Try somethingnew."

"The food is even for Cats to eat." The Tall Dragon King winked. "It's not poison!"

That moment, a crowd of creatures encircled them, snapping their teeth and widening their jaws for food. But not one leapt onto the table, nor touched another. Amber accidentally let out a scream. She gave a weak smile at the sight. *They were trying to behave themselves.*

"Excuse me!" scolded the Fox, though rather softly. "I'll care for *you* later!"

One by one, like animatronics programmed to do so, the creatures scattered away. Perhaps they were disappointed.

Amber's eyes moved back and forth from the strange food to the strange creatures with all number of arms, legs, eyes, and heads. Even as they retreated, no two creatures looked the same from the back. She watched the distinctly coloured and shaped blobs become smaller and smaller as they moved away in a squirming, almost rhythmic pattern. A few of the creatures had tails—some like crocodiles', others almost like Cat ones—which they wagged to and fro as they crawled or trotted.

And in their colourful chaos, there was something about the funny messiness of the scene that… Amber gulped. That did not look or seem but *felt* pretentious.

Something—about these creatures and their island—reminded her of a big, put-up circus show. A tent built only for entertainment, even though an outside place existed past the curtains.

The creatures were like something fun and chaotic and loud, blocking out all the quiet background noises from the world outside. In a way, this whole scene was created to keep your eye off something ugly, keep it distracted. As if someone had stuck a big plaster over a broken knee. Sprinkled pink glitter over a cluttered, filthy surface. Pointed at an interesting bird in the sky.

And the Fox fit in flawlessly. Amber could almost hear it say, *Turn up the music, widen those smiles, come on, let's have some* fun*!*

DragonFree Haven had a much wilder, energetic atmosphere than Catslaughter Island. Catslaughter Island had carried this—she couldn't describe it any other way—this *stillness* with it. This cold stillness, and yet this deep comfort. This intentional fakeness: they were all Halfmoon's tricks, intended to make it all *easier to process*... And yet, it did not, at least not as noticeably, *distract,* or stick a plaster over broken bones.

Except…

Here, use the Teleclock!

Amber's stomach churned. She didn't know where that last thought had come from, out of which terrible part of her incautious mind, but she didn't like where this was going.

The creatures were gone.

After seeing the Fox draw a perfectly round small basket by Mahou energy to store the food, Amber watched one last tiny creature stay staring at the table, hesitantly.

It was about two feet tall, with a gigantic head for its puppy-like body. Its eyes were too close together, like two huge ovals with stick eyebrows. It wore an enormous automatic grimace, with nettle-like teeth and an uneven chin. Rose stems popped out of the sides of its head, and its whole head was covered in spikes. Three vibrant roses grew out of its head, like a crown.

It was a poor, rather uncanny-looking, one-armed creature, waiting desperately for attention.

And it got it immediately:

"Hello, Rosy Little Goblin, and you, Crystal!" cried the Fox, turning its head.

Amber looked around. The Fox had addressed two beings, but she only saw one.

"I see you've finally dared to come out of the volcano." The Fox gave a really encouraging smile and turned its body completely towards the creature.

Then, Amber saw what it was. It appeared to be a small living gemstone in various colours, with a long piece pierced in the middle like a sword. It sat, rolling around, right next to what the Fox had called the 'Rosy Little Goblin'.

The creatures shrank back a bit, as if shy, squealing.

"Shhhh, it's OK," calmed the Fox. "These are just visitors. I promise I'll help you out later. Why don't you go play in the volcano?"

The tone it spoke in was so kind, so soothing. Amber gulped.

Its Paws busy packing up food again, the Tall Dragon King laughed. "Always need me, don't they? My makings," it cried, as if to Amber and Koko. "Well, I created them. All of them! I want to help them, to make them have the best life possible."

The best life possible. Amber watched carefully as the Rosy Little Goblin and Crystal rolled and limped away, side by side. They joined the others, the other creatures with all the erratic, nonsensical features and strange stretches of skin. *I want to help them.* These creatures weren't even consistent and nearly identical like the Cats, but they were so *randomly* unique. And there were so, *so* many of them. Something about them made Amber shudder and her skin crawl. It was almost like she didn't even want, or dare, to understand them.

"Is it hard," she asked, dumbstruck. "To care for all those creatures?"

The Tall Dragon King grinned. "Just have to feed them, and love them, which I do! And have fun! I love adventures, and my creatures do as well!"

"But why make so many of them?"

"What do you mean?"

"Isn't it hard to care for all of them, so many? If you, alone, own an island, why don't you create creatures to help you?" *It had so much power over the land,* and Amber found herself biting her tongue more.

The Fox's reaction was hard to read. It now faced them, a coldness in its eyes. "As slaves?"

Amber shook her head. "I didn't say —"

"Listen," it said, slowing its voice and looking down at its feet. "When I create my makings, I'm creating lives. And of course, I don't create lives for my benefit…"

"Of course." Amber nodded.

"I mean," the Fox went on. "Just imagine, imagine existing, just existing to exist, for some purpose that you never chose. Never *had* to be, but now you do…."

The image of Timeravel's—*her*—empty canvases flashed into Amber's mind, but she instantly shook the idea away.

"My creatures, they… they grow by themselves. They live by themselves. And… if we were only here for the sake of it, not for living, I would have given up so long ago…" There was something new and twisted in its voice.

The Fox was turned away from her in a way that made Amber think it was hiding its face. She wondered if it had started crying but could not make it out.

"But?" she asked.

A moment of silence passed.

After a while, she realized the Tall Dragon King was, again, staring at its Gadget.

As it caught her staring at it, it exclaimed, "Oh, I'm *so* sorry! Really can't resist sometimes!" This time there was visible redness on its face.

Amber frowned. *Even* she *didn't look at the strings in the middle of conversations.*

"But I chose to live," it went on, as if nothing had happened. "I chose to grow my legs taller, taller."

Beside her, Amber heard a noise that sounded as if Koko was suppressing a laugh. "*Taller… legs!*" it cried.

But after repeating its words in her head, Amber realized there was nothing funny about this.

This was kindness. The creatures had a leader who cared and wanted the best for them. *There were three thrones, two for anyone to join. Because there was no purpose and there was no role.* But it was more than kindness.

With all its Mahou energy, the Tall Dragon King could do whatever it wanted. Everything she'd seen today, probably it had made and designed itself. It designed everything, and all by choice.

The Tall Dragon King had control. Had control over its land.

But Amber knew, she knew, *not over itself.*

CHAPTER 19 – SURFACE-LEVEL ODDITIES?

Go on, listen to Halfmoon, stay happy.

As Amber followed Koko, who followed the Tall Dragon King, she kept getting lost. They were walking to what the Tall Dragon King claimed as one of its favourite spots, and Amber followed the map to detect when they would cross from Section B to C. Section C went up, all the way into the mountains, which seemed to be the direction they were headed.

But she found the map was inaccurate to their surroundings. *Or rather*, she told herself, *the surroundings were inaccurate to her map.*

Soon, when she accidentally walked into something like a tree, the Tall Dragon King laughed and grabbed her map without asking.

"Excuse me!" Amber cried out, furrowing her eyebrows. "Give it back!"

Its smile left its lips. "I'm sorry." It handed the map back, which Amber snatched instantly. "But the Cats got the map wrong."

Amber groaned. "No, they have nothing wrong!" And her tone made the Tall Dragon King leave it at that.

She felt funny. Amber felt funny because she had trusted the map to be right all along. She felt funny because the Tall Dragon King seemed kind, so kind...

There were things inside the picnic basket that Amber was not eager to try. It was one with a very long handle and swung over the Fox's shoulder like a shoulder bag.

As they marched, Koko had got over its shyness and looked at the Tall Dragon King with more than nervousness— something like awe. However, the awe was buried beneath its sharp look of hurt and betrayal, puzzlement. "I'm justcon-fused," it said to the Fox. "How Halfmoon's *never* mentionedyou."

Amber stiffened as the Tall Dragon King replied, "Koko, you're right! That's very odd, very odd! Are you sure It hasn't? I've known Halfmoon for years!"

Amber cleared her throat and quickly added, "Maybe... if It told Cats too much about other islands outside of Catslaughter Island, it would only excite them. And, since, clearly, the journey isn't safe, it would put them in danger." She picked the excuse at random and was quite satisfied with it. She would have said anything besides the true reason Half-moon had never talked about it.

But Koko appeared deep in thought, as if believing her.

Every moment or so, they caught glimpses of creatures running by, then hiding in the shadows.

"Do you have names for all your makings?" Amber asked the Fox, trying to fill the silence herself, so that no one else could, and their conversation could not go in the wrong direction.

It shook its head. "I don't name anything. I simply *made*

the place. Just for it to live and my makings to have fun. I don't need to name fun."

"But, I heard you call one 'Rosy Little Goblin'?"

"That's just a nickname!" the Fox snickered. "I love that guy, and I like to call him that!"

"So, what about the 'Tall Dragon King'?" Koko wondered.

Amber was glad it, at least, took her side.

However, then Koko said, "But I like that, honestly, not naming fun."

The Fox cracked up. "To be honest, I was joking with that! My makings, they like to flatter me. But well, if you really want to call me something else..." Its face coloured again. "I guess you can call me... Quirkstride."

"Quirkstride?" Koko repeated. "Where does *that* come from?"

"Oh." Quirkstride forced a laugh, but this one was small. "Weird, yeah, I know! It's a nickname. Actually, it's what my siblings used to call me."

Amber stopped in her tracks and did not look at either of them. They were back there, *talking about the siblings, Foxes.* Her heart skipped a beat.

She was about to speak to try to soften Koko's reaction to the words, but it had heard them.

It was curious, and it was ignorant.

"Siblings... You've mentionedthem before," Koko acknowledged, then smirked. "Tell us about them!"

Quirkstride stopped laughing, and it was like their cheery background music had dropped. "I mean... the other Foxes. Bet you know what I mean?" it said. It was clearly struggling to keep its voice flat of any emotion.

Amber wanted to pretend she did not know what they were

talking about, and walk ahead, but at the same time, she had to listen.

"No? Halfmoon, It… It hasn't told me about you." Koko watched Quirkstride with something like suspicion, and its eyes flitted from it to Amber, probably now aware that it was the one who hadn't been told anything.

No one moved anymore.

Quirkstride made a soft crying noise. Then a noise like it was trying to stop. "It doesn't matter. Let's not talk about sad things…"

Amber nodded, shaking now, but Koko came closer to Quirkstride, placing a Paw onto it. Quirkstride flinched, its grin long past, but not daring to cry.

"I guess you haven't given in to your feelingsyet," Koko said.

But Quirkstride walked away, frowning. "What?"

Koko seemed eager. "To… to be able toaccept, you need to hate *first*. I always feel better aftercrying."

Quirkstride looked at Koko for a moment, eyes wide and mouth half-open in an expression that Amber hadn't seen before. It shook its head, shaking away Koko's attempt at comfort. Then it laughed. Then, it put its grin back on and said, "Let's have our picnic!"

Quirkstride's favourite spot was on the left edge of the island, surrounded by forests, and at the foot of the mountains.

Sheltered, it was a collection of tiny moss hills, peering down into a waterfall, which started as a weak stream drizzling down tenderly and then dropping.

The ground felt even softer under Amber's hard school shoes than it had at the edge of the island.

The restricted sunlight here made the moss glimmer,

dancing along with the water in a dazzling show. The water was even clearer than on Catslaughter Island.

This time it wasn't the chatter of life or the freeness of the land, but rather the silent privacy, hugging everyone close together. There was not much space.

It smelled of crisp, sweet forest air, and a bit of the breeze from the mountains above came down.

And it was all like one big forest family; the trees were all friends, and the flowers looked like siblings. Amber went along.

Again, there was an almost-natural air to the place… That feeling of *organization* she had got earlier.

It was a bustling, yet quiet, noise. As though this all was some big event that everyone was keeping up with. Everyone was in on something unspeakable. Amber and Koko, they were now part of the circus.

Quirkstride set out a blanket. It appeared to be knitted out of grass, with a few holes in it. Then, Quirkstride unpacked all the food and set it into these holes, on display. It rested its long legs in the moss. They did not fit on the blanket.

Koko's eyes wore that bitter, perplexed look again, almost as if it wasn't used to a creature so much taller than itself, but Amber pretended it had laughed. She put on *her* happiest face.

And then they ate. Amber decided to try different foods. She tried unusual berries and food in flames or spiced fruits. The food was good.

With her left hand clasped around her hair, Amber felt good, telling herself she *did*. Everyone was smiling and ate peacefully.

They all felt the warmth of the sun stroke their faces and let their legs dangle and splash into the water stream, which Amber thought was refreshing. Then, they laughed, and their conversations trailed off to random things and they told jokes.

So, no one acknowledged them—the things that floated right beneath the surface, very, very close.

Everyone avoided them, for individual reasons, pretending they did not see when those things swooped over them, danced above and around their heads, and were reflected in the water stream. *Because the things... they weren't* really *there.*

Amber talked and talked and talked about the most random things, anything to keep the noise going.

After a while, she suggested, in order to have something else to do, "Let's play tag!" And for a moment, she almost gasped, *for how would they, such different creatures, play?* It only reminded of how odd it was for a Cat, a Fox and a girl to spend time together.

But Koko smirked and Quirkstride laughed, and they agreed.

So, they started. They made their way down the small hill they had sat on, walking around the shimmery water to drier areas, and then into the forest.

As soon as they entered it, they started their game. They chased after each other for a while, everything outwardly simple and happy as they passed by tree after tree, until Amber felt a heaviness inside her, and yet still they ran. She looked up, forcing herself to grin, and saw Quirkstride's extremely long, skinny legs direct its unnaturally large body around trees and bushes. It grinned too, giving her an awkward, proud look.

She nearly tripped and fell when she saw it run, the long legs spinning in breakneck motion, reminding her of daddy longlegs spiders. But she held onto herself and ran too.

They raced the wind, and Amber did not let her heart stop when she saw Koko's face, as it was, occasionally appearing from behind thick trees. It was swollen—twice its usual size—and worsened every time it passed through the grass. But Amber kept her smile. For nothing bad had happened.

"You know, I don't think I've been this happy in a long time! Or *ever*!" Koko yelled through the entire forest.

"Me neither…" replied Quirkstride, but Amber saw its eyes trail down. Then, its eyes trailed up again.

When they grew tired, they rested again on the grass. Koko seemed still full of energy, eager to talk, but Quirkstride stared at the strings of its Gadget, seemingly swallowing up whatever it was that it had almost let out a while ago.

Amber mimicked it and turned hers on as well. The images of flowers and fields on the screen reminded her that nothing bad had happened. She especially didn't want to talk to Koko alone, for the skin around its mouth was still bulging and fat.

Just then, she received a message. But unlike any others, this one seemed… *rushed*.

Amber. Time is running fast. Remember, Teplaytides is a strange place, and you must be prepared. You must be happy when coming there, or things will go wrong. Because… there are lies. Lies of such folly, as vicious as… horses. Lies as vicious and attention-seeking as horses, yet with bones as hollow as the ones from birds. I am the only one who is right.

Amber's hands trembled as she turned off the Gadget, but she pretended she had seen nothing. *Vicious as horses.*

She knew little about Teplaytides, but *would it be enough if she came numb? Did she really have to* feel *happy?*

And by now, she thought, *did Halfmoon know about Timeravel?*

She tried convincing herself It didn't, or that she had no way of knowing if It did, but the more she thought about the word *horses*—the more she thought about Timeravel's mane, its hooves—the more her chest hurt.

Amber laughed, mostly to herself, trying to completely forget the message. *She never saw it.*

She was still too afraid to look at the numbers, the clock part of the Gadget, but told herself *they still had a lot of time.*

"Is everything all right?" Quirkstride asked, and she realized they were both looking at her.

Koko nodded, as if it had been addressed, and Amber replied, "Yes, everything is amazing."

And she *almost* felt quite alive.

* * *

They wandered deeper in, catching the views of new plants and life. Amber was watching a couple of tiny insects climb up a tree when Koko snuck up to her and whispered, "Psst, Amber, see that Cat-thing over there?"

"Isn't that a lion? Actually, no, it's not a lion." Amber knew no normal lion would have flowers and plant-like vines growing out of its body, forming a mane. The Lion sat licking its fur, a few feet away, in the spotlight of some light beaming in through the trees.

Koko's eyes were shining in fascination, and a dreamy smile brushed its face. Now also watching the Lion, Amber had to admit it was quite a sight; it was a dark green shade, with lots of miniature flowers and petals blooming on its long, heavy fur. It looked interesting. That was what it was: neither lovely nor unlovely, but just a thing, a thing amazing to look at.

Then, she noticed that aside from its admiring gaze,

Koko's ears were all floppy and its head was down. Its lip trembled.

"What's up?" Quirkstride asked, joining them.

"I think… I'm going to take a break from exploring, and return to the spot," Amber cut in, now trying to avoid any more emotional outbursts from either Koko or Quirkstride, as they were all here together again and not engaged in running.

"Sure," Quirkstride said, and she stumbled away, leaving them behind some trees.

She could still hear Quirkstride's voice: "What's with that bitter face, Koko?"

"Uh, nothing…" came its low stammer.

Amber increased her speed, trying not to listen to their conversation.

A fallen tree was in her way, and so she stepped over it, but that was when she overshot her stride and face-planted directly onto the grassy ground.

When she got up, she realized how unnervingly similar her surroundings looked, and she grew unsure where their spot at the stream had even been. All she knew was that she was not yet near enough to hear the water flowing, and she could still hear Koko and Quirkstride talking.

She looked around for a while, trying to get back on track. Time ticked by unnaturally without her noticing, but soon, every fallen branch, every loose twig, every spot of shadow or light on the path was exactly the same, even as she kept walking.

A few times when it looked difficult, Amber came to a stop and got down the Gadget, stared at it for a few seconds, then put it away again.

But eventually, she had to accept that she had lost her way, and that she needed to get back.

Amber didn't know why she had escaped the scene so suddenly in the first place. As she thought about it now, it seemed so silly to her, as nothing bad had occurred. All she'd really wanted was a break from them.

But she knew this wasn't true. She couldn't describe what it was exactly, but something about Koko's dropped ears and face had stirred something up in her. She remembered its swollen face, full of grass. She remembered their conversation with Quirkstride on the way to this part of the island. Amber shuddered.

There was some tension in Koko's voice that she didn't like—that scared her. Something bad and dark. Something she couldn't understand. Whatever it was.

Amber found her way back and discreetly started passing by the spot where she could hear Koko and Quirkstride talking.

"But why are you so upset now?" Quirkstride sounded extremely uncomfortable.

This time she could sense it, stronger in the air than before. It was in Quirkstride's tone as it said this. *Something was wrong.*

She tried to rush away, but she could hear them, loud and clear.

"I… liketheway that your creatures *are*…" Koko sounded odd, not like its usual self. As if it were trying not to cry, which was something it usually never tried to hide.

"Well, then!" Quirkstride forced a chuckle. "You like them. That's great!"

Silence.

Amber gulped and wanted to flee. But as she started running, she heard Koko's voice again, in a mutter. This was like with the Doodles; she was torn—not knowing if she wanted to know what was happening or not. And she stood still.

"It's just… IwishI could use the magicthat way."

"What do you mean?"

"Yourcreatures… yourlegs… It's all so cool. I wish I couldjust grow myself taller whenever I wanted…"

There was a noise like a sigh. "Oh, Koko, you clearly don't understand!"

Now Amber knew she was trapped; they left so much silence between their words that the slightest movement would draw their attention. She held her breath, hating herself, trying to cover her ears.

Quirkstride's voice was much deeper than usual. It was the first time she had heard it talk with no enthusiasm, no joy. "It's not all sunshine and rainbows, you know—Oh, sorry!" Its voice went back to normal. "I hadn't mean to say that aloud…"

Koko sobbed quietly, and Quirkstride cleared its throat. "What I meant was, I had to grow myself taller to… Well, to see from a better view."

"And what about the thingsaround you?" Koko asked.

"What things?"

"Your old, other view. Didn't you… *miss* it?"

Quirkstride gasped. "No, of course not. I'd like anything in the world but… face that again." For a second, Amber swore she heard its voice break. "Koko, you've got to understand, it's something that I had to do. Growing my legs, taking the responsibility of this island, it was barely a choice."

Koko was still sobbing, and Quirkstride added, "Don't waste time wishing for things you'll never get. It's my Mahou energy."

Koko's sobbing stopped for a second. "So, Halfmoon could also—?"

"I don't know what Halfmoon can or can't do. But growing my land with the Mahou energy is simply something I can and *had* to do. I keep things great, don't I? I need to stay in this position; this is what I've been doing. I've started this wonderful land, and I won't stop. Who else would take care of this island, keep the Mahou energy safe? Keep the Mahou energy from… harming others? And I don't miss my old ways, no."

Amber took a few steps back, trying not to make sense of the words, as they mentioned the things below the surface. But she heard Quirkstride's last words.

"It's not always what it seems, you know. It's not easy. To always stand tall, use the Mahou energy this way, be such a role model."

CHAPTER 20 – TRUST??

The screeching of creatures tore her free. Her breathing rapid, her heart rate too, she sat up straight, knowing everything was fine.

She had just woken up and was already lying to herself.

They had slept through the night in this place. Amber was covered in grass. It was unintentionally scattered all over her like a blanket and stuck in her hair. She could feel some moss on her face.

Brushing it off, she got up when she heard Koko groan and swear beside her. She knew instantly that something was happening.

Koko was fighting something, pushing against it. It was the Gadget.

Quirkstride was not with them. Quirkstride was not there.

She heard the Gadget make that same noise it made when Halfmoon called.

"Koko! Why aren't you picking up?" she said, without thinking. A call from Halfmoon was probably important.

It gave a guilty shrug. "Amber, youdon'tunderstand…"

She frowned. "*What* don't I understand?!"

"This… really annoys me. I don'tknow howyou put upwith It. Halfmoon… isn't It always bossing usaround?"

Amber winced.

She snatched the Gadget out of its reach. She picked up the phone, but saw it was already picking itself up. She heard Halfmoon speak in a grumpy voice.

"Koko, I know you are present."

Koko, a few feet away, turned red.

"You have failed me greatly. I cannot believe it. You act so carelessly… And time is running out. We are almost completely out of time. Now, you have only three days left. The Gadget reads *3*! Three days. But I have seen you, and you are *so* careless… useless."

Koko grabbed for the Gadget, but Amber ran a few steps away, wanting to hear the rest.

"You have had your… share, I should say, I must remind you. So, I hope you are happy enough to come to Teplaytides. If not, pretend. Do not get all emotional; it just makes everything unnecessarily complicated."

Amber shot Koko a puzzled look as her feet felt lighter. "What share?"

"Oh!" came Halfmoon's voice. "Amber, why—hello!" It sounded uncomfortable, forcing Its voice to remain cheery and bright.

"Halfmoon," she blurted. "Do you—?"

"I assure you I have it all in my Paws! Well, perhaps in Koko's Paws, too, a little, I should say… But not to worry! I know exactly when the Terror is coming, no more surprises! But, er, it would be best if you arrived there as soon as possible —today."

"T-today?" Koko asked. "It's a few daystravel!" Then it

covered its mouth, as if having said too much.

"Oh, Koko, *do not exaggerate*!" Halfmoon sounded dumb-struck. "If I send, well, a bit of magic your way, I bet it will all be quicker!"

Amber did not know what this meant but sighed, somewhat in relief.

"But yesterday the number was still somewhere on *6*," she added.

Halfmoon smiled but made the sound of a shrug.

"We need to leave," Amber said.

"Indeed you do," Halfmoon said. It hung up.

Koko fixed its gaze on the ground, tears glinting in its eyes.

Since Koko was not doing anything, Amber instructed herself that they would wait for Quirkstride to appear again, to tell it they were leaving. She used this as an excuse to turn to the strings—but really, Amber knew she *had* to use it. She had to use the Gadget now to move on from some of the things she had overheard. *It was all meaningless*, she told herself.

All the things she had tried to lock up in her subconscious were scratching at the walls of her mind, wanting to come out, but with the help of the strings, she could pretend they were not there for a bit longer.

After a while of Koko's crying and Amber's watching, she said, "I don't think Quirkstride's coming."

Koko shook its head and replied, "I'll get it. I have a plan. Trust me."

Amber waited, and in that moment, she did not know what to trust. All she knew was that they had to do as Halfmoon said, and she had not meant to overhear it. It should never have happened. Whatever it was.

A while later, Koko came back with Quickstride, whose

eyes were sunken in disappointment. "Leaving already?" it said. "Oof, I wanted to spend more time with you. But all right, I wish you luck with your… journey."

Amber looked at Quirkstride, and as she realized she would never see it again, she found she was startled.

"Q-Quirkstride," she started, not knowing what to say.

Koko still seemed hurt, but she saw something new flash in its glare. "I thought we had to go!" it cried. "I can't believe this…" But even it stared at Quirkstride awkwardly, and mumbled, "You know, itwas really… *cool* meetingyou."

"Aww, I liked meeting you too!" Quirkstride called after Koko, who stumbled away, sniffing.

Amber did not move. She knew she had to go.

Then, she realized.

It was there; there was a rightness in its eyes. She had seen the same thing in Timeravel's…

As she observed Quirkstride, she could feel that it was different. Quirkstride felt different to her. *It almost felt like a human, more than a thing. It was that rightness, that sense of being…* It almost felt wrong to call it 'it'. There was something more about Quirkstride, about *them*, than… just a Fox.

Amber said, "I think I believe you. About everything…"

"What do you mean?"

She could not reply, as she herself was unsure of what she meant. She wished she could take the careless words back, but she had said them.

"Forget it," she mumbled, bewildered. "Thank you." She started running.

Amber reached Koko, who stood waiting at a tree.

"*What* do you believe Quirkstride about?" it asked.

Amber's neck prickled. *Great.* "Nothing. And… what did Halfmoon mean by *share*?" The words flowed out naturally.

Koko turned pale. "It's not really a share… onlyalittle reward…"

"For when you're done with this?"

Its eyes swelled with tears, as always. "Yeah, when I'mdone with this." Then it wiped its face and said, "Amber, stay happy."

"Then don't get emotional," she snapped. "So, where are we going?"

The journey was not as long as expected. They were walking, half-jogging up steep hills and slopes, eventually leading up to proper, enormous mountains and chasms. Koko was in the lead, carrying the map between its teeth, carving paths through nature. It was running.

Then, they were there, on the second tallest mountain of DragonFree Haven.

Koko grinned and, still leading, pushed aside a concealing branch. It trotted aside to show the view of the entire island.

And there, there was something else…

Amber couldn't even speak, say a word, when she saw dozens of them. She'd only caught tiny glimpses of them before.

"I talked to Halfmoon and Quirkstride," Koko explained. "And Itoldyou to trust me. So, here, Amber, I present… the true Dragons of DragonFree Haven."

The creatures weren't real dragons.

They were Dragonflies. The size of cars, trucks.

"They'll take us to Teplaytides."

They did not look wrong; Amber was relieved. They were utterly unremarkable aside from their size. She ignored their slightly longer tails and crystalized-looking wings.

"OK, which one are we riding on?"

"Do you like them?" Koko asked.

"Er—yes, Koko. Which one do you want to ride on?"

It scanned all the Dragons. "The red one."

She shot it an anxious look; the red Dragon was at least three times the size of her bedroom.

"Are you sure?" she asked. "It's… the biggest."

"Scared?" Koko asked. "I *want* the red one."

"I'm not *scared.*"

Amber took down the Gadget to hold it during the flight, and they helped each other climb onto the colourful beauty, gripping its bulky insect features. It felt more comfortable than Amber thought it would, sitting on a Dragonfly. She could feel its insect-like body as something soft and flat.

Another heavenly ride. *To hell.*

A few seconds later, they were lifting off the ground, preparing for blastoff.

The other Dragons around them all went up at the same time. Amber had never been on a rollercoaster before, but she imagined it felt like this.

When they were in the sky, her eyes were already shut tight, and when she opened them again, her gaze was aimed exclusively skywards, rather than downwards. She held one hand over her Gadget, the other on the Dragon.

"Amber, are you OK?" Koko asked, although its own face was chalk white with a touch of green. Its claws were out to secure itself better.

But she could not reply and simply held on.

Soon, they were up high above the clouds. Amber looked around to see the sky turn a bright red that met orange, a chaotic pop to the easy clouds' almost picturesque softness.

The Dragons all slowed, and the ride became gentler.

Amber finally dared to use the Gadget.

She expected, somehow, to find another message of Halfmoon's. But they usually appeared right after she turned on the screen, and she sighed, seeing none. She was almost disappointed.

But this disappointment soon ebbed away as she sucked herself into the screen.

* * *

She was back in the sky again. Not the real sky around her—but the perfect sky, as a bird.

Except, she wasn't quite a bird now. She was soaring, and she steered herself not with wings, but with... her bare, fleshy arms. She could see her naked elbows drawn out awkwardly in front of her face. In fact, her whole body was naked. And it was quite cold, up in the clouds.

A sudden cloud appeared right in front of her. She passed through it. Thousands of microscopic wet ice needles punctured her unclothed skin. She shivered just as much as wiggled her body, positioning herself into a very wrong motion for flying. She was not a bird. She looked more like a caterpillar—torn out of its cocoon half-made, with the beginning of wings, but ugly, the exact mixture of newborn and old, and still yet a caterpillar.

It was like trying to fly an airplane underwater. Trying to steer a ship through the crust of the Earth. So horribly wrong.

Now, there was nothing in her mind but three single questions.

Where was she going?
What was she doing?
Why was she flying?

* * *

Amber's heart soared; a new message had appeared.

Halfmoon froze even the scene in the Gadget.

Hello, Amber. Things must absolutely stay in order. Things should stay all right. Now, some advice for when you arrive at Teplaytides: just enter. See it as bad, skin-burning poison, a place you must enter with no hesitation. Leap right into the poison without even noticing it, for it will give you a push, surely, to teach you to swim!

Amber nodded to the screen. *She would do so.*

But first, before they arrived, she would use the Gadget for a little while longer, the stress-sucking comfort she could not live without…

Just when her mind had drifted from the ride, she felt Koko tugging at her.

"Amber," it spoke softly, though its face was scrunched up. "Stopthis." It coughed. "Why are you *always* using it? This Gadget, Halfmoon…"

"What about Halfmoon?" Amber slowly turned towards it.

"You know it's not real, right?"

She removed the receiver from her ear to properly look at Koko.

"Themagic in it causes illusions, so whatyou see of the Gadget is not completelyreal." It gulped.

"What do you mean?" she said slowly. "Of course the images *inside* the Gadget aren't real."

Koko shook its head. "You don'tunderstand—"

"What don't I understand?"

It sighed. "No. Forgetit—"

"No, seriously!" Amber raised her voice. "What don't I understand?"

Koko watched her blankly.

Her whole body shook now, so sick of Koko and the things

it claimed. "Why are you like this? Why do you always tell me such… *things*?" She spoke each word quicker than the last, carrying a new level of exasperation. "You always tell me such… *nonsense*. I don't know why you do."

Koko was about to open its mouth when she added, "But I've no reason to listen to anyone but Halfmoon."

And she left them there; the words stuck.

However, after a while, she heard Koko say, "This *is* all becauseof Halfmoon, right?"

She furrowed her eyebrows. "What?"

"You clearly don't… trust me. And it'sbecause of Half-moon. *Only* ever Halfmoon. Isn't the onlyreason you decided to trust Quirkstride, because you realized Halfmoon did? Youonly went with me, because ofHalfmoon? And now that Halfmoon no longertrusts me, you don'teither."

"That's nonsense," Amber said. "*Nonsense*."

But now she wasn't sure herself. She wasn't sure of anything anymore.

CHAPTER 21 – ORDER??

As the minutes or hours passed and they rode the Dragon—Amber had completely lost track of time, but everything seemed to feel slower than it was—she distracted herself from Koko, though she felt a deep numbness spread. The consequence of all the feelings and things she had avoided.

Panic set in when she could not get rid of the feeling. She knew that although doing so had been a mistake, she could not jump into the water here as she had on the boat. But that was exactly the thing that started to bother her—falling. She could barely feel her body now and thought about what might happen if she lost control and slipped…

The Dragon was not helping, either. For quite some time, it had peacefully glided, but now it dropped much lower, or wheeled its way upwards and crashed into the clouds. She could only admire the other Dragons' easy, softer movements in jealousy.

Then the Dragon turned right, abruptly halting in the air, and Amber nearly flew off its side. The Gadget was knocked out of her grasp, but instead of staying in the air, it fell and hit the sack beside Koko. The sack fell off the Dragon.

Amber froze. The Gadget tumbled into the waters below.

"Oh. The food's gone," Koko said.

Her hands shook, and she grew dizzy as she looked down at the endless falling space.

Now, for many painful hours at least, she would not have Halfmoon with her.

Amber pulled a big, false smile. "Oh, why did you have to choose *this* Dragon?" It seemed pointless, but she couldn't help gazing at the other Dragons' easier, steadier flight. "We could have gone by boat."

Koko shrugged, but when it spoke, its voice had lost its usual spark. "I chose this red one because it's my favourite colour."

"*What?*"

"I said, because it's my favouritecolour."

"How is that... a valid answer?" All she could do was laugh.

"My... feelings aren'tvalid?"

Amber couldn't resist rolling her eyes. "Oh, Koko... Koko." She forced a smile, although her eyebrows twitched together. *The Gadget was gone.*

That moment, she spotted something odd out of the corner of her eye. In the distance, half-hidden behind the clouds, she caught sight of something red and small flapping around in the sky. Something flying. Whatever it was, she could see there was a group of them, slowly floating towards their Dragon like a flock of birds. But their shapes didn't make sense, for they looked like small strips of skin or pieces of a person.

Amber instantly began to sweat, and her heart palpitated as her whole body knew that *they were coming.*

She knew that things—in the bleak absence of the Gadget—were much easier to be aware of. *It seemed they were getting closer to Teplaytides, or maybe this was Halfmoon's magic...*

"Can I tellyou something?" The tone Koko spoke in made her turn her head. Its voice carried an unusual depth; it was not too emotional and to the point, but restrained, as if concealing something else.

She knew instantly from its voice that it was hiding something big. And then she wondered, *what choice did she have, really?* Her numbness didn't allow her to think straight, but she could see Koko looked serious. *Very* serious.

Amber didn't want to know about the red flapping things. And she didn't want her and Koko to fight again—it would only be inconvenient and waste time as it always did. *She had to keep order,* she remembered. *Things had to stay all right. Everything needed to be all right.*

"OK?" she answered, deciding it was best not to turn her head away from Koko anymore. "Tell me."

Koko swallowed audibly. It sounded almost disgusting.

Amber kept staring at it.

"I knowyoudon't... trust me..." Koko started. "Iknowyou... you probably thinkI'mridiculous." Then its eyes gazed into the distance, as if recalling something traumatic. "I knowImean nothing toyou. I knowI'mjustaCat. But... evenifyoucan't understandwhy, Ijust... want you to hear me. That'sall."

Then, Koko refused to meet her eyes at all. Amber sighed. *Did it really want to make her guess what was on its mind?*

She reached for the Gadget, only to remember that, because of Koko, it was now gone. She clenched her teeth.

Koko finally mumbled, "Theskies were dark..."

"What?" Amber asked. "When?"

She was losing her patience, and the only reason she listened was because of Halfmoon's message.

Koko reached into its own fur and pulled out a fistful of old Cat Improvement Pills. It took a big bite, crunching on them slowly. Only then did she notice its puffy eyes and trembling lips. But it didn't even look like it usually did. Its face was almost chalk-white, pale with something she had never seen before. Koko wasn't even crying.

"I was a kitten," it spoke, its voice a whimper. "Alone on the streets."

She waited.

"I always watched the streetlights, was my own guardian, watched over myself every night. Made sure no car could… run me over. So, I watched every car pass. Every traffic light turn from red to… that awfulbluish green colour. And every green meant a screech of tires, a chance of a car turning and ending my life." It gulped. "Every red meant a chance of that not happening. Became a sort ofpassion, I guess, not dying. It was like ahobby. I'd stay somewhere near the streets, because that's usually where there was leftover food. Or *roadkill*. And I'd count every time a car passed, every time I didn't die. Two points for green light, one for red. Red, my favouritecolour…" Koko let out a really unnatural snort that made its whole face twitch upwards.

Amber wanted to scream.

"I lied," it said, its mouth relaxing again. "I said I didn't know what happened to my parents. But… Isaweverything. And all I remember… is that I was alone. The skies were dark, and humans couldn't see where they were driving."

Finally, Koko broke into tears. Koko, who usually cried over small things, had suppressed them.

Amber didn't know what to say. All she knew was that since the horrible words had escaped its lips, there was a black, unsteady noise of deadly silence in the air. And she could think of a single solution. She knew, as always, *she had to fill it, keep busy.*

Her eyes became focused on something behind Koko's shaking outline. The red flapping things had returned. They were coming closer.

She tried blocking them from her view.

"Koko," Amber started, fixing her eyes entirely on purely its face. "Why are you telling me this?"

It looked at her with the eyes of a poor creature, a thing that had suffered. But all she could really see, in its tears and mess, was vulnerability.

The image before her frightened her, it bewildered her, it drove her insane.

Yet, Halfmoon's message was still clear in her head.

So, Amber said, "I think I know what that must be like."

Koko gave her an expression of both interest and bitterness. "I don't thinkyou would…"

She pretended she hadn't heard. "My cat, Ichigo, died. I was about eight years old." She pinched herself, trying not to let herself get lost in a trail of memories and tears.

"Really?" Koko gulped, but its eyes were crowded with a new suspicion that Amber couldn't quite explain. "I didn't-know you had another Cat! Did you have others?"

Amber sighed. "It wasn't a Cat. It was a… *more normal* cat. I think you can't imagine it, but I really did like cats. I was kind to them. I used to love cats, actually."

And then she thought of the *other* small kitten. The faded feelings returned instantly, and it was almost overwhelming. In those times, Amaya had started to sense her parents' marriage falling apart. Gradually, she had distanced herself from them and needed someone else to spend time with.

"I swear," Amber repeated. "I used to like cats. That cat was... Kamiko."

Koko's eyes prickled with so many things it did not say. "*Kamiko?*" Its voice was unnaturally high-pitched. "I knew youwere... thesame," it said slowly. And then it said, "So. It was youwho left methere."

All the colour drained from Amber's face. She laughed. It was now a natural reflex. "*What*? What do you mean?"

Koko glared at her with a raw, bitter intensity. Kamiko.

Memories started rushing back to her. She started feeling very sick. *Everything that had happened in her happy times, she had left behind. To rot. For so long, she had been living only in her worst times, the darkest versions of her past.* Never *in the happy times.*

"But that's not the worst part." Kamiko winced. It swallowed a couple of CIPs, and for a second it seemed to be stuck in deep thought. "What—what *happened* to you? You really did used to be kind to cats...

"And no, you don'tknow what that's like. You lost Ichigo, a pet. A thing, an object, and that's all I am to you, right? It's what you view us as—things? *Things!*" It coughed and wheezed horribly at the last word, turning it into an odd exclamation.

Amber almost covered her ears.

Her eyes tried to rinse out the guilt she now felt all the way from her stomach, tried to roll it away down her chin, but even when the tears fell, she felt the same. She couldn't look at Kamiko.

In all that she was feeling, Amber turned away for a second.

And now they were here. Now she could see them.

The red flappy things had almost reached them, and the clouds had all disappeared.

They looked like… lips. Real, fleshy, blood-filled, human-like Lips.

The group of Lips were closed tightly and floating by themselves, as single, bodiless tissues in the air in the near distance. Yet, they were less like *human* lips than the Cats' ones.

Because blood was drooling slowly down, all over them, bottoms and upper halves. They were bleeding Lips. But they weren't *just* Lips. Rather, they *were*, in fact, as Amber had thought previously, small lip-shaped strips of moving flesh twisted into slimmer, longer shapes at the sides. It was almost like they were Lips with tiny angel wings making them float.

They almost looked like birds. Faceless, featherless, bleeding bird Lips.

Amber cried out, but before she or Koko said any more, the Dragon dived low, and a rough landing followed into an awful slimy stench of land. They left the sickly Lips there in the sky.

Amber realized she hadn't kept track of the days. *How long had they ridden the Dragon? How long had she been talking to Koko? How long had she been on this horrible ride?* She couldn't remember.

But somehow, they had now arrived at Teplaytides. She was blinded by light and sudden confusion.

"Koko," she started. "*Kamiko—*"

Kamiko would not listen and broke into a coughing fit. Amber knew it had spoken too much.

There was no more time to speak.

There was no more to say.

They both managed to smile and pretended there had been no tears, that there was order and not chaos.

Because Amber knew Teplaytides would be a *strange* land.

And it didn't, but somehow it did, make it all OK again. Make things stay in order.

CHAPTER 22 – A WORLD OF CHAOS???

Everything was blue.

Although it was a small space of land, all she could see were blue, cloudless skies. It was like an open field of rocky ground, and it seemed not much more existed in this world—as though she were in some video game.

Amber heard Kamiko slip off the Dragon and swear. Its eyes watered at the brightness of what lay ahead.

The Dragon was gone. Vanished, as if they had been alone all along. There was no trace of life anywhere. Amber saw that even the direction they had come from was blue, and blue only. It was as if everything was rich sky, and anywhere they walked was simply an extension of it.

Lost, her heart flew against her chest, and she grasped for Kamiko. She had never done so before, but she wanted to hold on to something.

Kamiko, however, shot her a dark look and shook free of her hold. Yet it, too, was trembling.

Though everything appeared deserted, she could occasionally catch glimpses—small shuffling sounds and faint movements of beings. Shadows and spine-tingling flickers of black against the blue. But nothing else.

Amber stopped and glimpsed at Kamiko with exhaustion. "Oh, I wish we hadn't lost our—"

"Why doyou want that Gadget *now*?" After all its crying, Kamiko's voice sounded empty and dull. It almost scared her.

"I don't," Amber snapped back. "But our things—our only *direction* was in that sack, in the map, when it fell…"

"Oh."

As she watched its hopeless gaze, it was as if Kamiko's eyes reflected their shared ignorance.

There was a rush of wind, the foul breath of a breeze. And a loud, clanging voice filled the air.

"Hurry, hurry now. You are but nearly too late."

"Halfmoon!" Amber gasped, while Kamiko shook its head. She noticed its teeth were chattering.

Her vision was spinning, eyes on the alien land all around. She did nothing but stand there, listening for Halfmoon, in whatever way It did it, to tell them something else. Halfmoon. She was unsure what she was meant to think of Halfmoon, but remembered she was here, here to do what It had instructed her to: simply find and enter the Portal. And before she could manage that, she had no time to worry about what came afterwards.

Amber shrieked at finding Kamiko suddenly standing in front of her face.

"What?" it asked.

She shook her head.

"So, are we just… walking there?" it muttered.

"Well, how else?" But Amber too had got a headache,

staring at this sky. Halfmoon wasn't giving them any more guidance. It felt like they were in a sort of dream—aimless, numb, and blind, yet searching for focus, for a direction.

"I don't knowhowIfeel about those shadows..." Kamiko was watching something in the distance.

"Ignore them," she stated. Amber knew they had to stay together so that they could both survive. Kamiko probably hadn't forgiven her for anything, but what mattered now was success. She reached out her hand, and hand in Paw, they paced along on the rocky ground. It gave the sensation of dissolving beneath her feet, so Amber began to run. She was still holding Kamiko's Paw, but it seemed to slip in her grip at times, into nothingness.

"We don't exactlyhave anydirection," Kamiko whimpered. "You know."

"Ugh, stop it!" Amber yelled. She changed her expression to a forced grin. "But yes, yes—we do."

She pointed straight ahead, but it felt like the world was spinning, so she pointed left instead. There was no direction, and she wouldn't let herself believe it.

She started running, running straight into the blue. This was exactly as Halfmoon had suggested; a quick leap into the horrors would give her a push, helping her to swim faster. *She would get this done quickly.* Amber did not dare stop.

All she saw was sky. All around her was sky, as if swallowing her. She ran, ran into what she did not know, hoping she was still dragging Kamiko along.

Why was it so bright here? She was trying to find the end, but it seemed the light only got brighter the more she ran.

And then, the slurred voices started. Whispers. There were hallucinatory sounds in her head. One of them was ear-splitting and made her reach out her hand, crouch, and bury her head in her arms.

"Kamiko!" *Was it hearing them too?*

But Kamiko was gone.

There was something… a coldness running down her back, a funny, fuzzy feeling felt in her throat, blocking it with the clogging of air. There were things around, behind, and in front of them—there was no doubt about it—waiting for the perfect moment to make an appearance.

Amber stood up and saw she was alone. Except now there was something coming towards her, a few feet away. It was water. A tide was coming in, slowly rising, then falling, each time a little closer.

More voices.

She covered her ears.

They're not real. They're not real. They're not real, she told herself.

But the shadows from earlier had returned. Much larger than before, they twisted into the gnarled shapes of faces. Faces she had not seen in a long time.

Amber shut her eyes. *She didn't want to see* these *faces, if any at all.* And yet she heard their hushed, whispery voices reach out into her ears.

A force came. It ripped her eyes open so fiercely that they stung, and she couldn't close them again. Tears ran down her chin and she tried using her hands to cover up the sight, but the next thing she knew, she was staring right through her hand—right through her flesh.

She tried to shake free of the force, of the Mahou energy, but every move only threw her back. The faces' eyes popped out of their sockets with high-pitched squeals. They came out with memories.

The faces remained suspended, without Amber being able to make sense of *why* and *how* they were there.

Around her, she could hear the roar of the approaching waves. But she could not move. She made no move to run. In her field of view, aside from the faces, she saw a staircase in the distance. Long, winding. Final.

When her eyes trailed back to the faces, tears were already streaming down her cheeks.

As she saw the Gang.

As she saw her parents.

As she heard the voices.

To her horror, not even her tears were normal. Down her face was running *salt*. Amber had no choice but to wipe it off with her hands.

This was the worst type of pain. This was worse than suffering, than being afraid. This was worse than having to hide; she was facing it all now. She was facing all the things that, as much as her brain worked and worked, it could not make any sense of or come up with any reassuring explanations that could help define their logic.

She was reminded *of the time when she did understand. When everything made perfect sense. When even her emotions were under her control, and everything was predictable.*

But then she was reminded *of when the unexpected came and tore everything apart. When she'd learned how to fear, and how to hide, how to laugh at everything.*

The faces giggled and giggled at her, like the Cats. Eyes popped out, tongues lolling, their twisting shapes crawling towards her. They laughed and laughed and laughed, and the sound stayed in her head as a muddled, misty cloud.

Amber could not stop them—this was just like with the Cats; she could not close her eyes at the sight. But this time, she could not even use her hands to cover her vision. And there was nothing she could do to avoid what was in front of her.

Amber screamed. The tide came in.

She saw only one more face now. It was her mother's. The sparkly eyes, the blissful smile—the one she *hated*. Amber looked away. Her mother's face, even as she fought it, did not respond. It continued to laugh.

A trail of memories ran playfully across her mind. *She did not even respond, in fact, to the pain, to the change. She waved it off with the flick of her hand, her forced grin...*

Amber opened her eyes and got down on her knees, her breathing shallow, as she held onto the filthy ground underneath her hands.

She realized that this Mahou energy, unlike the one on Catslaughter Island, was less concentrated on specific things, but rather diffused and random, entering her mind at its own very will and even further disorientating her. So, here she stood, in a world of illusions, of lies, having no control of her own.

She shut her eyes to the chaos. *Enough... nonsense!* she thought. She felt her body run into the water to get through it quickly. Then, like she used to as a little child, she let a smirk spread across her lips and gave a manic laugh, mimicking the faces. She tried to forget what she had seen, and ran right into the black, oozy water.

But when it reached her waist, she knew that whatever swam in it was unknown to her. It was just one of the things she had no control over in this shifting world.

She didn't know what this all meant—or if it meant anything at all.

Her eyes lost focus on the world around her, and her consciousness was lost there, too, in her eyes, as she saw her life reflected in them again. She was only aware of the voices in her head, but they slowly dimmed.

Water gushed from all sides into her ears. Black water, not allowing her to see what lived in its depths.

Another voice joined her in her head. She wasn't sure where it was coming from, if the Mahou energy was telling her something, or if it was Halfmoon speaking at that very moment. All she could do was try to push through, because Amber was still, after everything, looking for an explanation. Another Halfmoon, someone or something providing reassurance and information. Something that told her that everything was, in fact, all right and in order.

She's drowning, claimed the voice. *Poetically. In thought, so lost. My point is, I know how these young Human minds think! Whatever she is sad about, helping us might make her, well, proud of herself.* Whatever it meant, Amber knew she was not proud of herself. She still did not understand.

Because chaos was too much; it could not be folded up and put into a box. Chaos was wild, something too complex even to grasp. It intimidated her, mocked her.

Trying to swallow it all up with a quick leap, she almost drowned in it all.

* * *

When Amber opened her eyes, she was lying on rock. She felt as though the sea had washed her here and saw that her knees were bloody and scraped.

Gasping, she vomited out all the water she had swallowed.

It was grey and murky, the colour of the previously dusty ground.

Slowly, she got up, the blue light stinging her eyes. She saw that the sea was coming back, waves slowly crawling towards her.

It was a strange land, and she would not let herself cry. She would not let herself accept it, for it was wrong. It was weird. Unacceptable. She forced another laugh. *This was not real. This was not real. This was not real. She must have been dreaming.*

Just as she remembered that there was a place she needed to go, a task that she needed to complete, she spotted it a few feet away, perhaps also washed up by the tide.

A Gadget. She knew this precious thing so well. Perhaps it was the same one as before. Or maybe Halfmoon had sent a new one.

Through all the chaos, she had a Gadget. A comfort.

Amber turned it on, knowing she would only use it for a little while. She was taken off and away by the hypnotizing strings.

She watched the image of flower fields. Multicoloured, almost unnervingly straight rows of them stretched out as far as she could see. She watched as the mellow warmth of the morning sun beamed over dozens and dozens of bright pink flowers. She turned to look into the distance, to meet skies still yawning and clouds rolling away. For in that moment, she really seemed to be standing and living there inside that scene. Instantly, the sweet image clutched her and took her away to a land of its own, where it absorbed her and she was unable to leave. The flowers were all identical and had a rhythmic swing to them as they danced to the beautiful day. It certainly was a safe space. And yet…

Even as she sat there, unaware, unconscious, hypnotized in her own world, she felt a vague pang of pain in the pit of her stomach. The feeling she always avoided. Intuition, instinct. The yoghurt feeling.

There was something wrong with the flowers. And she didn't think this because there actually was, or because she saw how they were different, but simply because she *felt*.

She came to the guilty realization of how stupid this was, using the Gadget *now*. She knew, really, deep, deep down, that she shouldn't be distracting herself. She and Kamiko needed to hurry. Halfmoon had sent them here for a reason.

But... what was *that reason again?* All she knew now was that she could not keep her eyes off it, the amazing Gadget. She was sucked right back into its beauty, its glory... The place where nothing scared her, where all her feelings were in an invisible grip, where she was sure of everything, and nothing mattered.

Time passed strangely, but as Amber's consciousness drifted slightly from the Gadget, she found herself soaked in water. A small tide was rising, higher and higher, going above her waist. Amber *wanted*, of course, to stop it, to fight the Mahou energy, but she knew it was no use. She knew this was better. And she returned to the Gadget.

But then there was a scream.

It echoed into the nothingness. Something about it trapped the air in her lungs. It sounded raw and hoarse. Crying and panicking.

Amber lifted her body out of the water and saw Kamiko in the distance. It was lying down, staring at the unknown. It took the image of Kamiko, half-dead and on the ground, for Amber's attention to shift and for her to finally let the Gadget go.

She didn't know what was happening, only that Kamiko was suffering.

As she walked towards it, her body slumped beneath her weight like a corpse. With all her human strength, she pulled herself to Kamiko, although the forces around her were stronger.

She could tell its pupils had enlarged. Its shaking was raging and intense, and its knees knocked together. The hissing sounds escaping its mouth were clearly directed at whatever lay in front of them.

Amber scrunched up her face in concentration, but all she saw was the eye-stabbing blue. All she saw was a screaming Cat, and blue.

Kamiko was seeing things she could not.

Amber gulped and knew she had only one choice. *She had to enter its mind somehow...*

Again, she thought she was crying, by the sensation of something cold running down her face, but she gasped as she remembered the salt.

It was as if she could not even control her tears. This place was taking over her body, exerting its control over what *she* herself could do.

She shook her head. *Enough nonsense.*

She called out, "What are you seeing, Kamiko?"

But suddenly it came to her, as a coldness in her face, a blow to her chest.

She realized properly, for the first time, that Kamiko was *alone.*

Kamiko was all alone, and aside from, perhaps, Petal, it didn't have anyone at all. And now she saw what, over the drudgery of the years and years, it had become without her. Amber realized that she had left it—to rot. She had done *this* to Kamiko, everything that was playing out in front of her now. *She* had done this to Kamiko.

Perhaps through her realization, she saw the thing. Her mouth went dry, as if all her words had been stolen, her voice to scream had been sucked away.

It was taller than she was. Taller than Kamiko.

It was a traffic light, with a long wiry body and flashing lights. The lights turned towards her as if observing, deciding something.

This was not an ordinary traffic light. The lights blazed all green. A wrong, muddy green.

The traffic light swayed to the side and bent itself to dangle down in a droopy, bored position. Then, the long wires from its body split and lengthened as a pair of arms and legs sprouted from its sides, also at an unusual angle.

As it stepped closer, it came to trap them with its electric body, waving its slender arms around. It pulled them closer, and Amber's whole body prickled, petrified.

It did not fit in with the blue angel skies. This was a dark thing.

There was the bloodthirsty sound of a failed attempt to break, then a car crashing into something in the distance.

Amber watched Kamiko's distant expression—as if through an exaggerated lens—and its quivering lips and face expressed more than pain—insanity. There was also salt beneath its eyes. Its ears were droopy, its fur stuck up, and Kamiko was drenched in sweat. But it wasn't trembling. Only screaming, silently.

Another screech of car tires.

And there was a car that came. A big, bulky, dark green, almost turquoise car. The car's lights turned on, lighting up the whole blackness with bright yellow, bold, blinding rays.

A bare second later, the car's engine did something. Or perhaps the noise was still coming from the tires advancing, but from somewhere erupted a gut-wrenching *vrr-rrr-vroom*!

The sound felt thick, packed with things out of nightmares, blaring and horrifying. Kamiko shrunk back into its fur, as if to protect itself.

Amber watched with horror as the car drove backwards, which looked quite wrong with the speed it was going. An intense stench of gasoline reached their noses. More noises boomed into their ears as it drove much too fast, and another crash told them that the car had slammed into something.

It must have been quite similar to this, Amber pictured, glaring at the blue-green lights, *for Kamiko, when its parents had been run over.*

She shuddered as she heard Kamiko start sobbing, though this was natural behaviour for it. Kamiko fell down, crouched on the ground, and howled. It howled desperately, helplessly, watching as the car drove in circles around them. It watched the traffic light. It resembled the tiny kitten it had once been— and still was—stood alone on the lonely streets.

Amber shook her head. But this single action wasn't *doing* anything. She dug her fingernails into her skin.

She felt sad, like she wanted to cry, but also numb, as she knew tears would not help. She wanted, wanted so badly, to do something.

She ran up to it, and touched it, but her arm waved through it, right through the Mahou energy around them. Numb.

"Ka…miko…!" she said. Her voice was so broken, so poisoned. The Cat did not turn to look at her; it was her fault. *She sounded strange.*

This *was* real; there was no pretending to it. She had let

time pass and had got distracted, but it was all here, happening. She realized that now. Bad things *had* happened.

She wasn't real. She was recorded. She was the one who did not act, who ignored, who pretended.

And all she could do was wait. And watch.

It reminded her of her mother.

Because there was nothing, nothing she could do.

CHAPTER 23 – TRAPPED EYES????

Kamiko whimpered. It tried to get to its feet. But its legs shook, and it fell limply onto its face, banging onto the rock ground. And yet again it tried to stand up, even when a rose-coloured liquid ran from the top of its face into its eyes, which were now glued shut in grief and horror and its breathing was laboured, yet very alive.

Kamiko was forced to watch the green lights for a final time. Then it tumbled backwards.

Its eyes remained closed. The traffic monster melted away. Now, there was deserted blue sky again.

Amber stumbled, and then her tears ran down faster than she'd thought, faster than her legs. When she reached Kamiko, she was panting hard, as if she had run a race, although she had only run only a few feet.

Still, she could not touch it.

As Amber watched Kamiko, the Cat who, after everything, had some hidden courage, after everything had still tried to be kind, her feelings collapsed together.

As she observed the figure, the figure who rarely hid things, the figure who expressed its emotions naturally, she realized Kamiko was more than a victim. Kamiko was *so* much more than just a victim.

Kamiko was not even *it*—but *he*—and she had been so cruel in treating him as a thing, a useless object with no grip on his wild feelings.

When Kamiko exposed his wounds, let her see inside, it hadn't been weakness only, a lack of self-control. Rather, he had expressed himself as vulnerable on purpose, to state a greater trust, a conscious choice of his show of emotion.

Amber stared at the dreamlike image of Kamiko's body. She knew he was alive. She tried to nudge him, but it did not work.

Were they too late? Perhaps the question was also present in Kamiko's head, chasing itself around, trying to snatch its tail. They really should have been there by now. But none of that seemed to matter much anymore. Still, there was a pressure, a pressure she felt everywhere, of how she might have failed to fulfil her one and only purpose...

Although the whispery voices had all dimmed, Amber could still hear some in her head. The voices told her to cry, so she gave in. She cried and cried, and the salt ran down all the way to the ground. And now she could not deny that all this... made her sad.

"I'm sorry, Kamiko," she muttered. "I'm sorry for what I did. And your Lizard. And everything." *What could she say? She had got distracted.*

Amber sniffled and sobbed. There was nothing for her to do or to say anymore. She could only wonder what was next.

After crouching over Kamiko for what felt like a long time,

there was a familiar ringing noise. Amber scoffed but knew it was important and blamed herself for not thinking of it before. She picked up the phone of the Gadget and watched the screen present Halfmoon's face.

As she examined It closer, she saw Its face was scrunched up and Its eyebrows turned down, like knives.

"Amber." Its voice was firm, urgent, exasperated, almost.

Out of the corner of her eye Amber watched Kamiko's body slowly rise again and sit up.

He frowned, seeing the Gadget on and beside him.

"Oh," said Halfmoon. "Is that Kamiko I see? So, both— better."

Without saying anything, Amber stared at the screen, glad that she could not see the real Halfmoon, wishing she could escape from here, but knowing that it was impossible.

"Do you two realize," It started, "what *nonsense* this is?" Halfmoon almost smiled.

Amber exchanged a glance with Kamiko. "I do," she said, emotionless. "I do, and I'm sorry. I know we were supposed to hurry and—"

Halfmoon laughed without it reaching Its eyes. Suddenly, It raised Its voice. "What have you been doing... for the last few *hours*?!"

"Battling for our lives..." Kamiko mumbled. "And our sanity."

Amber felt the palms of her hands sweat.

"Because of you... It is now too late."

No one replied.

"My Eyes show me the Human; they are basically already inside our Portal."

"But," Kamiko squeaked carefully, trying to keep his voice steady, ignoring what Halfmoon had just said, "Areyousure that your Eyes are… completely accurate? The Terror, have you seen it in real life—?"

"*Kamiko.*"

"Y—yeah—?"

"You *do* realize that Catslaughter Island may die." It looked deeply offended, clenching Its teeth. They even glistened, as if ready to tear out Kamiko's throat. "And you will be lonely. You will not have *any* home to return to. You will also die. It is not as if your fellow Cats *like* you. I trust in my devices, much more than I trust in you."

Kamiko took a step back and sat quietly on the rock. He did not cry. Instead, he stared at the Gadget's screen.

"And you, Amber," Halfmoon shook Its head. Its voice was strange, unnatural, almost scared. "I do not know what we will do now." Its left eye twitched.

The human was probably already standing behind the blueberry bushes.

"*You* have wasted so much time. I guess you really are just an ignorant, useless child."

The words cut. Amber felt more salt beneath her eyes.

"I must decide what to do now," It said finally. "But I doubt you can make it to Japan before the Gadget shows 14. Perhaps, it is best if you don't even try." Halfmoon shook Its head again and hung up.

* * *

No one spoke.

Amber noticed that, for the first time ever, Kamiko used the Gadget himself, solely to distract himself from this place. She knew he didn't want to exist, exist in this reality. And she let him escape it and exist somewhere else.

So Amber sat, watching Kamiko watch the Gadget, thinking that someone, someone so small and vulnerable as him, did not deserve this. *This was so cruel.*

But she knew this was her own fault, mostly.

She did not hate herself for failing Halfmoon, but she blamed herself for allowing this to happen. She had been so lazy, so scared, letting everyone push her along, letting everyone use her, out of fear… fear that she, in fact, had no direction. That she didn't understand. But all this was meaningless. She'd had no say in the plan, although she could have. And so, all she'd done was give others the control she did have. Like she had let the Gang use her.

Kamiko had suffered because of her.

Just because she had been scared to admit that she was scared. For that was all she was: a useless little girl who knew nothing and was afraid of admitting to it. Lost in this world.

"You know," she heard Kamiko's voice come from behind her. It was the first time he talked to her normally since the realization of what she had done to him. "It's kind of myfault. That you're here. It'sonlybecause of me, that you're evenin this plan."

Amber didn't know what to say. "How?"

"Youknow how much Halfmoonloves Its inventions…" Kamiko reached into his furs and pulled out a few saved CIPs. "Oh, by the way, I'm running out of these. Not sure how much longer I can talk." He gave a shrug, eating more. "It got some warning that the Terror—some Human—was coming, all one random day. It called out a bunch of Cats—I was one of them —to help It. I think It wanted us to give It ideas, as It's… it's so useless, isn't it?"

Amber could almost hear the lowercase. She had never

heard Kamiko talk about Halfmoon in this way. But remembering the phone call, she said, "It is."

"Halfmoon showed us a view of the Eye. Now that I think of it, It was, I guess, displaying what It could see from the Kitten Robots, so that we could see it too. On some invention, It showed us the Eye's street view of Japan, near the Portal, where the Human Terror would soon be seen. Basically, It showed us a camera of the whole street. And that moment, in the street, I sawyou."

"Are you saying, I was in the Eye? That must have been before I entered the Portal..."

Kamiko took what seemed to be the last Cat Improvement Pill. "Well, messed up with all my feelings, I was a total loner. My feelings took over as I recognized you. I had to see you, even if that doesn't make sense, as I didn't know if it was really *you*. But it was *almost* like before. Almost, you see. Even if, at the same time, I knew it wasn't really likebefore. It wasn't the same, and it made things easier if youcalledme Koko. It was like before, but different.

"So, I guess Halfmoon realized then that preventing the Terror from even coming, from outside, was a good idea, and that you'd do the job. But part of the plan was also so I could... see you, feel less lonely, even for just a while.

"That's what Halfmoon meant with my share. Sorry, Amber. I really am... pathetic. If I could have had the slightest bit of self-control, maybe you'd never be involved in *this*... And we wouldn't have been used this way..." His voice was lost.

Salt ran down Amber's chin. "I don't blame you, no, not one bit, Kamiko. You couldn't have *controlled* your feelings, I..." She paused. "We—we are not the ones here with control over the situation. Halfmoon, It—It—*It* does, and we're just the slaves. There's nothing we can do anymore. Nothing. It's probably too late and besides, the Mahou energy, it does things to our minds. I don't even know what's real anymore…"

She paced around them, Kamiko not even looking up from the strings. She wondered if he had even heard her at all.

And without waiting for his reaction, she told him; she told him about Timeravel and what it had claimed about Catslaughter Island, how, not too long ago, it had been thrown out, likely by Halfmoon Itself. Whether the whole story of the Cats and the Foxes was believable or not was not something she could judge now. She just needed to get the words out.

Still, Kamiko did not look at her.

Amber started crying again. She did not sob or gush uncontrollably, but her eyes simply grew moistened, stinging, almost clumpy, as if this time all the remaining salt within her was gathering, ready to be dissolved or flee through the few tears she let escape, silently.

Finally, Kamiko looked up. She stood there motionless, looking at him. Lost for most words but at the same time with so much to say.

And she knew he was, too. He was lost, still lost on those horrible streets.

* * *

The Gadget was ringing again.

There had been silence between the two for many minutes now.

Amber groaned and walked towards Kamiko to tell him to ignore it, when he picked it up.

His eyes got a new glimmer to them, but also darkened. "Petal," he said, not removing the receiver from his ears.

Amber could hear Petal's voice, "Koko—I need to tell you. I don't quite believe the Human is there yet. I overheard Halfmoon talk to you. But, did you know, the Gadgets have Eye views on them? It turns out that we can also see what Halfmoon's Kitten Robots can see of the street view! Do you remember when Halfmoon gathered us all, when we were deciding the plan? I think It was showing us the back of the Gadget!

"Recently, I have also got a Gadget. Honestly… It's better than I thought. Oh, Koko, I think I've been wrong about it! And on the back, there's a button. If you press it, you can see the view, and from what I see, the Human is not there yet. They're *three streets away*. I just want to say… Halfmoon seems to be wrong. At least, we can't know It's right. I would not give up, if I were you."

"T-thank you, P-petal," Kamiko mumbled.

"And, also…" There was a sudden shift or drop in Petal's tone.

Amber saw the face in the screen look at the ground. She'd never heard Petal's voice sound so small. And so distorted.

"I… let metellyou why I wear that jacket. I know you've wondered about it… I do wear it because, yes, I don't like being like the otherCats. I *do* think they're all boring. But, there are other reasons. I was hidingsomething. Inside the jacket. I stole a Human watch. I… I've really tried, but Ican't read the numbers. Halfmoon's never taught us how to. But that's exactly *why* I stole it. Idon't knowwhat'shappening to me now. To us all. Something is. I want you to keep the watch. Amber, Ican't read the numbers, so Ican't tell you what time it is in Japan. But, it seems more time has passed than youthink. There's something… sosostrange happening. To me. Toeveryone who usesHalfmoon'sinventions. Please, please, Koko, *comeback—*"

His voice was gone. It was clear they could not reconnect with Petal.

Then Amber watched with pity as Kamiko's eyes swelled with tears. "Petal!" he shrieked. His eyes had lost their usual gentleness, and his lips began to bulge.

Amber's own lips trembled; Kamiko looked terrifying again.

"What's… happening?" she whispered, startled.

Kamiko stared at the screen. He did not look at her, but instead his eyes stayed fixed to it.

"WhathappenedtoPetal?" he cried. "Whatwillhappentohim?"

Amber watched the screen, too, and all she saw were erratic, jagged, unnatural lines that seemed to snap together. Then the screen turned blue. It was the same blue as when she had seen the creature on the screen. It was also the same blue as the skies around them.

"Kamiko…"

He was ignoring her, salt dropping from his eyes onto the screen. It was using him. She knew it now. His mind was trapped inside it.

She took a step closer, and carefully tried to take away the receiver. It did not come off with a gentle pull, so she tugged at it harder, but it still stayed glued to his ears.

"Kamiko! Stop it!" she yelled. "Don't you know what this means! I still need to stop that human! Petal said it's not too late!"

But Kamiko was not like before; he was broken.

As she watched his profile, goosebumps spread over her whole body. He did not look right. He looked awful, like he had when they'd first met on Catslaughter Island. Like when he'd rolled in the grass, when he'd been full of the horrible, toxic Mahou energy. When she looked at his eyes more carefully, she noticed they were not just swollen—they were twice the usual size. They almost seemed to be coming out of their sockets…

Amber stood frozen as his eyes were sucked out, leaving empty spaces behind. Kamiko was eye-less. His eyes had been sucked into the screen. And she saw them there, shown-off, displayed like some macabre taxidermy exhibition, staring at her, crying, through the screen.

Amber gagged but her body was frozen to the spot, and she could not move.

Then, Kamiko, his eyes still inside the screen, started swinging. His limps lifted themselves, but as he rose, it looked as if the skin and fur did not belong to him. He swung around, his loose body being thrown to all sides, as he danced, and danced, and danced.

It looked like… he was being pulled upwards by a string.

At first, she couldn't accept it. She could not accept Kamiko in this way.

But then she was reminded of how cruel, how cruel this was, not to her, or to anyone else, but to him.

Catslaughter Island being put into potential danger was a pain.

Halfmoon's plan not working out was a pain (*but It shouldn't have relied on only them,* Amber thought, *anyway*).

But Kamiko was suffering. He was actually *suffering,* probably feeling worse and feeling *more* than Halfmoon had Its whole life. Amber knew that, at least in that moment, Kamiko's life was more important.

The image hurt her. *They had been pulled by strings.*

And then she saw the previously unquestioned feature that all the Cats had; their long, string-like fingernails. Kamiko's, right now, were lifted up, doing as the Mahou energy pleased.

As Amber saw how Kamiko's slack, small body almost willingly stayed in place, she realized he was *allowing* this to be done to him, because he searched for distraction; he was in pain. This was exactly like with the Gang.

And with her emotions… all her efforts to try to suck her feelings up, to contain them, or to force them into artificial shapes, were wrong. Because she could control and reject them only for so long. For all that she—that Kamiko—had control of, were their reactions, and *not letting.*

Otherwise, if they allowed it or let themselves get distracted, it would be their own fear, their own fear and pain, pulling their strings…

Amber stood up straighter and stared at her friend. *Maybe there* was *something she could do.*

So, she spoke.

"I'm sorry," she said, her voice raw and weak. "I'm so, so sorry. I didn't want to hurt you, and I didn't want to ignore you. Although, that's what I ended up doing. I'm sorry. After things… changed, everything slipped out of my own hands, out of what *I* could do. Or at least, what I felt I could do. I had to leave you there, and I had to return. My parents—they wanted that, they decided, they did that, they didn't let me keep you. But I shouldn't have ignored you on this journey. I know you wanted to see me. I've been so awful to you. Kamiko, I'm sorry. After everything that's happened in the last few days, and all these—these monsters, I was just so frightened. And not only of the monsters, Kamiko. I'm afraid of being afraid. I'm scared of not knowing anything, not knowing the smallest, slightest thing in this realm, or even in my own world. I'm scared of *being* small. Now, I just want to get back home… But really, Kamiko, I swear, I do trust you. I do trust you."

She sensed the eyes trapped in the Gadget glance towards her, and it didn't take long until they came back out in reverse, and Kamiko's body fell, slumped, onto the rock ground, but free.

CHAPTER 24 – REALITY

If what Petal had said was true, they still had time.

"I need to go home." There was so much Amber needed to fix. Although much had changed, they could still only see the same sky and the same rock. As if nothing else existed. But it did: there was a real, living, magic-less, whole other world outside, waiting.

After Kamiko had fallen out of the Gadget's grip, Amber had not picked him up yet, afraid her slightest movement could harm his fragile body. He really was a small—but brave—*cat*. And she knew he needed to get back to Catslaughter Island. It was his only home, and he needed to get back to Petal. There was no point in him going to Japan with her.

"Thisplaceisdrivingmecrazy," Kamiko muttered. Both his and Amber's eyes widened at his voice. He sounded croaky, almost like he had when he'd rolled in the grass.

"Kamiko," Amber started, "do you have any more Cat Improvement Pills?"

"Allgone!" She saw him flinch, probably in pain.

She didn't know what to do.

"But…" came Kamiko's desperate tone. "ThingsI-wanttosay."

"Yes. I know. I *want* you to talk!" she cried back.

"Youneedleave. You—"

"If it hurts you, stop talking for a moment!"

He managed a nod.

As she watched Kamiko still on the ground, she knew that after all he'd been through, with all that this place had done to him, she had, she *had* to understand him.

"ThingsIwanttoknow." He gave a cough.

His eyes were still full of hurt, and Amber thought she knew. She *understood*. Everything about him.

She stood up straighter, took a few steps back. Kamiko was still collapsed. After everything, he was left bruised and weakened.

But she refused to help him up.

Kamiko frowned, and a bitter expression spread across his features. Yet still, she refused to help him, although it was clear what she needed to do.

He opened his mouth, but his words never came. He watched as Amber stood and refused, as he lay there broken and shattered, and she did not even lift a finger.

But then, whatever darkness had slithered into his eyes cleared and brightened. He seemed to understand.

Without Amber's help, Kamiko had no choice but to lift his trembling limbs and stand up all by himself. And he managed.

Amber smiled. "You just have to trust, as Quirkstride says," she said, watching his confidence in his shaking legs steady, his posture settle.

A new alien sensation of hope shimmered in his eyes. "Amber…" His voice sounded wrong, and she knew he could no longer talk.

She needed to speak *for* him.

Amber, perhaps for the first time, genuinely smiled at him. "I do trust you, I swear. And yes, I promise to see you again."

This Cat was going back, all alone, to Catslaughter Island. He could make the journey. She knew he could do it.

And the look she gave him showed that. He could finally completely believe it, believe that Amber believed in his strengths. He no longer cried now, but fought through everything the best he could, this time knowing he was not alone, believing in his own power. The change he could make.

Then he laughed. And then he was off and gone, random shadows sprawling where he had stood mere seconds before, into the blue. Only one thought struck her: *This could never, ever have been Kamiko days ago.*

Amber started running herself. For a moment, she shuddered. *What if she got lost?*

But then she saw it again—that winding staircase in the distance. Not too far. Stairs, against the skies, uneven and steep. Stairs leading into the sky. It almost looked like that was all there was—sky and stairs. But she already knew now that when she walked up those steps, things would change.

Amber ran.

She knew she could not afford to lose herself. Not when Kamiko and her whole world were waiting.

She knew if she did lose herself, if she fell into the madness surrounding her and let it swallow and devour her… she would be stuck. Stuck in this wretched land of boredom, forever and ever. With nothing but the Gadget.

The same sudden buzzing noise entered her head again, as did the vicious voices that sent chills into her skin.

As she ran, Amber tripped on a bump in the rocky surface,

and caught herself, but barely. Her feet quickened beneath her stumbling body, but she continued going, and as she did, it seemed the scenery fell apart into something new. It was exactly like what she had seen happen in the underwater world with Timeravel: illusions, change.

Things around her started to shift and transform without warning, leaving her heart thumping against her ribs, her head feeling faint in disorientation. The blue skies faded, and dark, coiling wisps of smoke replaced them, now crowding over everything.

Amber heard laughter and screams, seemingly there just for her, coming from above, as if from some kind of distorted angels. She covered her ears.

When she tripped a second time, it wasn't the ground she was tripping on, but… Flowers.

They were the same Flowers she had seen in the Gadget. But now they danced not to the flow of the wind nor the sweetness of the early morning sun, but to the sharp, blood-curdling rhythm of children's laughter and screams. Of things that *had* been but were no longer. Of memories that should have dissolved with the blue sky but sneaked their way back into her mind.

Amber lifted her foot off the Flower she had stepped on. A weird, light-headed sensation fizzed up her leg. She felt jittery as she saw the Flower lift itself up; it was almost like she was watching a person, the back of their head, the body she had stamped on.

And as the Flower turned towards her properly, she saw it did, in fact, have a face. It had what seemed like two monstrous, hefty lips squashed together, with a pair of cartoon-like eyes emerging from the upper one. Its petals were crumbled and crushed and popped out of the Flower's face like spikes of a crown. Its body was a skinny long stem, bent in the middle like a human body, and at the end of it, thin, slippery fingers as a hand.

The hand grasped at her, and Amber's feet stepped onto the stem body once again with force, squishing the plant as it split open and splashed her with the green, mushy insides of the Flower. She gagged and scurried away.

As she looked back, she realized she was being chased. But now by more than one Flower.

There were rows and rows of them, soldiers marching to war, but looking beaten already. Their eyes had a slight glow to them as they came, an army of zombies.

Panting, she raced ahead, not daring to even turn around. She heard the buzzing noise, then individual voices and shattered pieces of statements in the back of her head.

Amber stopped.

In front of her, there was something new. Its posture was dry and droopy, and she knew it was the same creature that she had seen before in the Gadget. And now she realized this creature was also a Fox.

The Fox stumbled towards her, and with each step, its weight shifted so much on one side that it nearly tumbled over.

Amber stood for a moment. Then, she gave her skin a small pinch and walked to the side in an attempt to casually move past.

But the creature stopped her. Once again, as it had in the Gadget screen, it opened its mouth as if preparing for speech, but no sound escaped. Just a small sigh, a raw exhale of air. Monsters, creatures, animals, *Foxes* weren't meant to talk.

It observed her with its horrible eyes. That was when she screamed, and when she slid right through the creature's body.

Amber headed straight towards the stairs. She thought

she had left the horrors behind her when a slight weight brushed her shoulder. Her skin prickled, and she saw the end of a Flower, a hesitant hand reaching out to touch her. Beside it, dozens and dozens of hands came to take her with them.

"No!" Amber screamed. "I need to enter the Portal! Let me go!"

One Flower studied and considered her, tilting its head. But then its lips split open to reveal sudden, hidden, carnivorous teeth. They sank into her flesh, and a throbbing sensation climbed up her arm.

"Ugh, leave. Me. Alone," she bawled. There was now salt down her chin, and each intake of air caused a sprouting pain in her chest. Again, it felt like there was something toxic, perhaps about the Flowers, that she was breathing in.

The Flowers, they were like the blueberries. Amber had a lot of memories of flowers from her early childhood. Those were the small details that she could remember. The small scents that she had held on to.

But now, in the active, immediate present, Amber wanted to let the Flowers go. Otherwise, she would be too late.

Summoning the last bit of her strength, she came free of their hold and her legs carried her until she was almost climbing the stairs. She halted at the bottom. It was as if she could feel it; the Portal was on the last step.

Amber took the first step. Nothing. Her foot did not meet the marble surface. When she jumped to start on a higher step, she managed to stand with both feet. She took the next step, but tripped in the empty air, and she fell back to the first step. This time she could feel it as she took the next.

Cautiously, Amber proceeded upwards, much faster now. All she had to know was that these stairs were like anything else on this island—sometimes appearing real, other times false. She gulped but knew it was true somehow.

She had tried to find logic, but now she tried to find her own way of dealing with the nonsensical things. The awful ones. That were here.

Narrowly managing the painful climb, her head almost burst as more voices broke in. With every step, her shoulders grew tenser, she became stiffer, and a new level of terror was dropped onto her like a bomb—with every step, she was more aware of what she was about to face. *Or* what she did not know she was about to face.

With her hands out in front of her, testing the trueness of the next few steps, Amber almost climbing up on all fours, she did not even want to look up. But she did not look down either, or to the sides, where the hands of Flowers and faces of other things all came whispering and reaching out towards her.

She was still making her way up through pretty angel skies, when black, fuzzy things entered her vision, appearing like tiny little flies swarming around her, obsessed. She heard a buzzing noise, and then a thousand voices spoke at once in her head.

It was as if her eyes had been blinded by sound, like in the talking House.

She felt her weight crumble beneath her, and she tried to keep herself upright. Her ears were too loud. Her eyes were too wet. Some voices were familiar in the back of her mind, others were not.

Although she deeply recognized those voices, those frightening scenes, the memories had one strange touch to them, a touch of unreality. Things seemed… fake.

Amber unexpectedly grabbed her chest. Or her stomach—she couldn't feel or see her body anymore. Something felt uncomfortably empty inside her. *As if this were the first time she were really alone.*

But it was.

Still, she knew Kamiko deserved for her to try. For his sake, she would not use the Gadget.

Amber raced up the stairs, not paying attention to anything, only letting herself get lost in her task of narrowing down the Portal hole.

Even when she caught a glimpse of those goofy faces and what looked like the same floating Lips, now all screaming out *words, words, words*, and water rising to her knees, she would not give in to what the voices told her.

Amber thought what she was doing was different from before, but then…

She stood at the end of the stairs, on an elevated level.

Amber reached the Portal. It was, again, an X.

She shook her head and took a leap straight into it.

Her body was thrown back.

Salt ran out of her eyes as she remembered what this meant.

"No, no, no," she whispered.

The Portal in front of her had an unvivid outline, and all the colours and everything slid out of place before her.

Whatever she did, it did not let her pass through.

Amber sank to her knees, not daring to touch anything anymore, not even tremble.

Her worst fears were confirmed.

She really was here now, alone, stuck now, trapped. With no options or freedom, in a world of chaos with no explanations, in her lonely dread and confusion. And with… *numbness* —the only company, the only thing Amber had, the only thing that made the things around her less scary. She didn't *want* to turn to the Gadget, of course, because she now knew that it could harm, that it was bad, but Amber did not understand how she could possibly control herself in a place like this. *How could this be expected from her—from a child?*

She let out a scream. It was in protest and fury, for she would not let herself scream in fear.

But then, for a moment, she did. She admitted she was scared. And she let the darkness, the voices, the Flowers, the illusions, and everything else around her sink in.

Then there was silence.

A few seconds later, when the voices and everything started once again, it all seemed... more real. Amber was no longer suppressing anything. The sky turned white.

The Portal in front of her looked different, much clearer. She could see the defined transition, where she needed to go.

She realized that it was because she'd been rejecting its presence—*that* was why she hadn't been able to enter before. It was the same thing Halfmoon had been doing. The same thing It had told her to do.

She had been rushing, trying to *get this over with as quickly as she could.* She had tried to *leap right into the poison without even noticing it.* She had believed Halfmoon, blindly, submissively, refusing to see. But Amber needed to *see* things —the Portal, this whole world—for what it really was. If she didn't, her eyes would trick her, and then her mind would follow.

Amber understood. What she was truly afraid of wasn't being trapped here.

It was losing herself, her sense of who she was, letting the Gadget and the magic nibble at and eat it, slowly, gradually, until there was nothing left.

She reached out to the Portal. There was still a mild force. She understood she needed to stop, if only for a few minutes.

She let the memories, all the pain, sink in even more.

Then she tumbled down, letting herself fall off the staircase. She knew below her there was water, and she trusted she would be caught.

And indeed, she was swept into the small sea and pushed along with the streams. But now she did not drown herself, and did not fight the sea; now she just swam, and swam. Knowing she had the control.

The Flowers left her alone now, yet she could still hear her own memories speak to her. She listened.

Soon, Amber came up the stairs again and was ready to enter the Portal.

CHAPTER 25 – FAMILIAR FACE

It felt weird being back on Earth. It was like the world had flipped in its place, and everything was different now that she was back. The paved ground felt hard and bumpy beneath her feet, and it hurt to walk.

Although she'd known she was going to end up in this place, for a moment Amber was so bewildered by her surroundings that she tripped and fell forward.

She was back, she was back.

And suddenly, she wondered whether she had imagined the whole thing… She knew she had probably imagined some of it on Teplaytides, like the illusions of the faces or voices. For many things she now had no explanations.

She had sprung out of the X and was now climbing out from under the bushes.

How long had it been? A week or so.

A week, and only a few seconds.

Her eyes lost focus as she thought about her mother. *How much she wanted to see her, and to think she was so close now…*

Amber felt very different. So much had occurred in her head. Now that she was no longer using the Gadget, there was a white, illuminating space inside her mind slowly growing larger; it was not quite an emptiness, but empty of things that were not her own thoughts. It was eating away at the Gadget's marks that were still etched in her brain.

Yet, she was not done.

If there was still a threat around, one that she had taken such a long journey to prevent, she had to try, try to protect Kamiko.

She scanned the area for any sign of life but found again peace in the streets. She needed the Gadget, but as she looked up, she found nothing but the sky, which she realized was darkening. *How many hours had she been gone?*

Amber pushed the thought aside as her breathing quickened. She stumbled back to the blueberry bushes and found her Gadget right there. As she observed it, she swore it had shrunk in size, to go more unnoticed, perhaps. Even its bright orange colour seemed duller than usual.

Trying her best not to use it, she searched for the thing that Petal had described. The Eye street view. Her fingers traced along the Gadget's perfectly smooth surface. On the back, in fact, there was a button. She'd never noticed it before—she had always been distracted.

As she pressed it, a whole new small screen emerged on the back. It was a view of the street from above, made by Halfmoon's cameras, Its Eyes, Its Kitten Robots. Amber remembered what Kamiko had told her about the grass carrying magic, and she was sure the grass near the X was the same as the one on Catslaughter Island, meaning it helped Halfmoon's inventions work. She guessed the Eyes—or Kitten Robots— were hidden in the blueberry bushes, since Petal had said they usually lived in plants or trees. They probably crawled out and explored the place, at the fast speed of Catslaughter Island time.

The screen displayed the entrance of the Portal behind the bushes, and a large space of street around it. Amber saw a small figure and knew it was herself. But there was a yellow blob a short way off. It was the Terror slowly walking towards the Portal.

She set off with a sprint, crossing the road with the Gadget in her hand, eyes on herself as her figure neared the blob.

She didn't know how long she was running, or how much progress her feet were actually making, but her eyes were now fixed only on the almost still, stationary blob and her organic, moving figure. Soon, they would clash.

Then, just when the human was three streets away, the sun came out.

Before, her numbness hadn't allowed her to feel it. But now, what had been weak, false light, turned hot—scorching hot, and *bright*, and she had to squint.

Somehow, as she felt those sweltering rays fall onto her and the Gadget, the Gadget felt lighter in her hands. Amber stood very still. The warmth was sharp, almost biting. In that moment, it was like the sun mattered more than the human.

She shook her head, pinching herself to focus. Her forehead gleamed with fresh sweat, but she wiped it off. The blob advanced on the screen.

She gulped; according to the Gadget, the human was now suddenly a much shorter distance away. They had come to her.

She raced past a single house, and then, then…

Amber could already see them. See them, according to the Gadget. But in front of her, as the yellow blob came yet closer, they were not in her view. Even when she was supposed to be standing in the exact same place as the human, she saw nothing.

It couldn't be too late, because the Gadget said the human was still in Japan!

But when Amber raced around the whole neighbourhood, she did not find the Terror. She did not find *anyone*—the streets were completely empty.

Now, as she stared at the blob on the screen, she found it hardly looked like a human or any Terror at all. It could have been anything: a smudge, a mistake in the system, an error in the energy, an overconfident Halfmoon…

And she saw it was a lie. The Gadget had lied. The Mahou energy, like the energy from Teplaytides, was unpredictable. *The Gadget had lied to her thoughts.*

She clenched her fists, standing where she was. She didn't like this. How not only she, but her mind had been used, and even more that she had allowed this…

Amber's lower lip started trembling, in the same way that Kamiko's did before crying.

It had stolen her brain power, she thought. *The Gadget had taken her* energy, *sucked it out of her mind while it sucked the horrors of her nightmares… And yet they were* her *nightmares, things she was* supposed *to feel. She deserved to* not *feel numb. She deserved to experience those emotions—of fear, dread, confusion—as much as any other feeling, like joy.*

Was that why the Gadget had left her so… numb? So bored, in a way, so empty and drained, with a vast space unfilled by the big feelings and thoughts that, naturally, should have been there. Was that why she had got headaches? Because the Gadget really had, in some literal, but to her unexplainable, way stolen the power of her mind?

Amber wasn't sure if Halfmoon was even aware of how

her thoughts had been sucked into this device, or of what had happened to Kamiko on Teplaytides. With the way It had made all Its plans, inventions specifically to stop the Terror, she was almost sure It had believed the Gadget, too, all along.

Just an ignorant child. Now, she wanted to admit it.

But any way that it was, all she knew was that she had to go home. Amber *wanted* to go home, and so she headed off running.

On the way there, she walked closer to the beach, to a spot along the railing where there was sea, and sea only, below it and no ground or road could be in her way and interfere. If someone or something fell, it would be lost to the ocean forever.

Amber checked behind her that no one was in sight. The streets were empty.

She flung the Gadget onto the ground. Then came her legs; swift and steady, she kicked and stomped with all the force in her body, smashing it beneath her feet.

She frowned when the Gadget made a tiny, final sound. A low hum or tune. And then she shook in horror as she saw one last message. The screen was blue, the colour of the Teplaytides skies. Perhaps because she was not holding the receiver, she could not quite make it out. It said something about *strangeness, things happening.* A message sent by Half-moon, begging Amber to return to Catslaughter Island.

She decided she would do so—for Kamiko's sake. But she had to see her mother first.

With trembling hands, she slowly picked up the biggest piece of the Gadget, swallowing a curse, hoping it was still in use. But it wasn't. So, she kicked the rest of it off the bridge and into the swirling waters. She reached into her pocket, grabbed all the sweets she still had from Halfmoon in one handful, and tossed them, too.

Then she ran towards what she had really come for, to what was really important, to what she had neglected.

She was already crying as she ran, because of what all this Mahou energy had done to her, because of what it had shown her, but she found her mother there, also crying. The familiar face of a stranger. The face was still blurred and unfocused, but seemed in tears, speech-less, as the familiar stranger leaned against the doorframe of the apartment.

* * *

They were at the table, the same table that they'd had lunch on, yet with such a different conversation from their last.

From what she was now told, and the way her mother's voice shook, Amber knew she had been gone for much longer than just a few minutes—what she was supposed to have been. There was something terribly wrong with the way the time and magic worked on Catslaughter Island, something that Petal hadn't been able to tell her. But none of it mattered now.

She knew she had to return to Catslaughter Island as soon as possible, for something strange was happening. But, that moment, this was more important.

Her eyes were on her fists, which slumped onto the table, not daring to look up.

She knew she had to tell her mother everything. She needed to tell her what had happened, what was happening at school. She had to.

And to do so, she needed to unclench her whole body, look up, and acknowledge what was in front of her.

But why was she even so scared? When Amber asked

herself this, it all seemed so silly. But she couldn't help trembling.

Amber observed the figure before her ever so slightly. Her eyes scanned her mother's end of the table, the crossed arms, the tight jaw, but moved up no further.

She could not tell whether her mother was upset with her. Amber thought, although she wasn't sure, that she had seen her mother in real tears when she had come home. Maybe she'd only imagined it, maybe everything that had happened the last few days was all only one muddled dream… but even if her mother *hadn't* been crying, in that moment when she'd come home, Amber had known that her mother had been worried sick.

The whole time she'd been in the Cats' realm, the thought that her mother was *worried* about her had not once crossed her mind. After all, *how could she have been worried—how could she have even* known? *How could she have known that Amber was so, so far away?*

Maybe it didn't quite make sense, but as Amber watched her, it was almost like she knew that her mother had, in some way, worried. Maybe, although she couldn't have known, she'd *sensed* her daughter's distance. For it was odd to imagine that she had been in another realm, and her mother hadn't even *noticed*.

Amber now felt a dreamlike memory of something like homesickness or a distant longing. As if, even if she'd never dared to admit it, she'd missed her mother, too, all along.

As she faced these feelings now, it was such a scary idea, to a child, to have been so far from home. She had experienced many days, all alone, in another *world*.

At that moment, her mother asked her, *why was she crying?* and whether *there was anything she wanted to tell her?* and that it would be *really good* if they could *make it all up.*

Amber kept her gaze exactly where it was, not moving and not responding. Because it would mean, if she told her mother how she was feeling, that her feelings, that everything, were real. It had always been her fear, accepting the truth for what it was.

But she knew she had to. She knew it was all real.

Amber's eyes moved up. The first quarter of her mother's face.

The mouth was closed and silent. Especially without the rest of the face, Amber almost did not recognize it. For a second, a strange fear gripped her, and she pictured that above the mouth, if she lifted her head, she would see the face of a monster, a Cat. She was scared that if she looked at the face, it would be alienating, the face of a stranger. Somewhat familiar, but stranger than what was completely unknown.

But then she noticed how the mouth was simply waiting calmly, listening. For the first time in forever, her mother was open-minded.

So, Amber gave in. She started talking. She told her exactly how she felt.

How she... hated the move. How she hated all that had occurred. How she hated how it seemed that everything in her life had fallen apart, and that she had been caught so off guard. How she missed her old life, sometimes just wanting it back, but her mother always had the attitude that it had never happened, that she should pretend, that she should suck her feelings up—

And then she paused. And sighed.

She finally looked up at the whole face, to see her mother was crying too.

And there was nothing *wrong* with this face.

Her mother seemed so… small. Her face was not covered in fur, and she did not have googly eyes; her jaw was not too wide, and she was not a Cat. She was just… her mother. The living, breathing human that she could talk to. Someone who existed in the here and now, with Amber, in the present, and not in the past.

As Amber looked at the carved face, she noticed the move had shaped her mother's face too. It looked paler, much slimmer than she'd ever remembered.

Amber realized that she had never cared to ask about her mother, how *she* was doing. The move, the change, it had made her weak. Like when cold skin was less sensitive to pain, or when thirst was less noticeable when swimming in water. It had made Amber neglect what mattered.

"Oh, Amber," her mother said, half-whispering, voice seemingly at the edge of breaking. "I'm sorry. Thank you for telling me." Her tone was not harsh. In fact, it was soft, a comfort she hadn't heard enough.

Amber looked her directly in the face. So directly, in fact, that her mother broke the eye contact.

"I'm so *sorry*," her mother repeated. "You know, Amber, let me tell you something of my own…"

Their eyes met again, and as the voice spoke, this time Amber listened too.

"I've also been… scared," her mother said. "I *am* so scared. So, so scared, and I don't think you can imagine. After your father and I… After everything, and being back in this apartment, but living here, not only for the summer… I don't know what to do with us. Sometimes in these months, yes, I do *pretend*. That we're still here on holiday. That we are happy. But then I realize how much has changed. And it's not really anyone's fault. Life has happened, and we must move on. We need to accept this new life as our… fresh start." The corners of her mouth lifted gently.

Amber smiled back.

"But… what I really want to tell you is that… it…" Her mother sighed. "That it was an illusion."

Amber started at the word. "*What?*"

Her mother's face betrayed her surprise at Amber's tone, but after a moment, a smile crossed her lips. It was quite a sad smile.

"Amber," she said slowly. "We weren't happy. We never were, really. Maybe it felt like it sometimes, or we were happier than we are now… But it wasn't *real*."

The words came sharply. They struck Amber's memories. They made them fall out of her sturdy grasp and held them shakily in a trembling, unsteady hand. She didn't know what to say.

Yet, there was something about her mother's way of speaking that kept her listening attentively, that made her look right into her eyes. Something very real.

Her mother half-smiled, but with eyebrows drawn together, almost piteous. "I've never told you this, Amber. But your father and I, we've always… fought. We had these arguments. They were very long and went on forever. Ones we always hid from you. We really weren't such a happy family as we often seemed to be. So, for years and years, I knew that *this* was going to happen eventually. When it all escalated and happened, it… It really was no surprise." She sighed but forced a smile.

For a moment, Amber looked away. Then, blinking back tears, she stammered, "But, I don't understand. You—you always pretend to smile the way that you used to smile. You pretend that things are OK, like they *used to be*. Were we not… happy?"

She shook her head. "Amber, when things were OK, that *was* me pretending. In a way, there were always these… conflicts present. And it's life, but Amber, I'm sorry. The life we used to have wasn't real. But I never *pretended* to care about you. I really *did*. That's exactly why I pretended, why I hid things from you. I didn't want you to see those fights, Amber, I was trying to create the best life I could for you. I should have been honest. I'm sorry. But now, *this* isn't real either, it's not right, not talking to each other, avoiding each other, not being true."

Amber smiled. "Then let's create a new, *real* life," she said.

She told her mother all about what was happening at school. As she said these words, they seemed to stumble out of her mouth hesitantly, as if it was the first time she had spoken in her life. They had a shaky, almost awkward touch. The words were newborn, small babies scarcely learning to walk.

Amber had to look away. But she knew what she was doing was right, and in a moment she'd look at her mother again.

When her mother replied, she said she would support Amber with every step now, that she could not stay at this school, and that she would create change in her life.

But Amber shook her head; *she* was going to create the change, and make an effort, stop relying on others.

And then, they talked more and more, and they found their minds opening to new possibilities.

Amber had always felt at least a little numb around her mother, rejecting her presence, avoiding, pretending. But now this all felt unreal, because it felt real. More real than ever. It was something new. And the opposite of numb.

But soon, Amber had to stop. When her mother stood up to get a glass of water, she remembered Kamiko. She could not leave him alone if he had indeed made the journey back to Catslaughter Island. Tears started collecting again in her eyes, and suddenly she was hit with the urgency of leaving. She had known, really, she was going to have to return to the terrible place, just for him. But she would do it. Kamiko deserved the world.

Another thought hit her. Time difference.

Thirty seconds in the human world meant a day on Catslaughter Island. Her heart stopped.

Maybe it was because the rules had always seemed slightly off—nothing she had been told had ever been quite exact, never strictly accurate—that she had forgotten. Amber bit her tongue. Everyone was probably waiting for her. *For years.*

A light tremble overtook her. *How much time had passed? How many hours and how many days had Kamiko been waiting? Was he still waiting?*

Amber cleared her throat, stood up, and pushed in her chair. "I'm going for a small stroll before the sun sets completely."

"Sure."

But before she was out of the door, Amber sighed. "This afternoon has felt like days have passed."

Her mother smiled. "Hasn't it?"

* * *

When she was back alone outside, she had no choice but to get her bicycle. She wouldn't be fast enough on foot.

As she rode it, she struggled to balance; it was the first time she had used it in at least a year. And yet, it worked to get her to the bench, to the bushes, the gap, the X. She left it right there and, panting hard, let herself fall into the X, with no time to think.

The next moment, she was lying on grass.

Amber took a few deep breaths before getting up. She really was back on Catslaughter Island. Back in this terrible place. She hoped she had made the right decision.

But she told herself she was conscious; she knew what she was doing. She knew she wasn't coming to Catslaughter Island this time to prove that it wasn't real, to prove that she was not scared. But because she knew what was wrong, she knew Catslaughter Island was a strange and scary place, but she was no longer afraid to be scared, to not understand. And she was going to see Kamiko.

As she got to her feet, a chilly shudder went through her. But it wasn't fear. There was something new in the air.

As she started walking, she felt the sensation again that nothing was like before. Her eyes were on the grass on the ground. Its colours were distorted and dull, and it looked even less real than last time, more like something she would have encountered on Teplaytides. She could still hear the fake noises, except now they fit even less. Last time, they had helped her to convince herself that this was not real, they had softened the truth, but now they just seemed what they were— fake, an imposter—to her very real feelings and to the truth. She was now trying to stay completely in reality, but she knew it was impossible with the illusions.

As she found the main path and was walking beneath the sign, with the camp in the distance, she realized that every inch of her body was shaking. It was as if she hadn't noticed. As if her body were aware of something that *she* was not.

As she stepped out into the camp, Amber realized. All

around, the camp was crusted with a thin, slippery layer of frost. It definitely hadn't been there before. There was a light, sometimes stronger-growing breeze blowing what looked like small flakes of snow onto everything and everyone.

Even though Catslaughter Island wasn't entirely covered in snow, like on the Wacky Winters, and it didn't *look* very cold, the sensation Amber now felt of almost freezing to death was far, far worse.

Amber trembled, and in her rage, too. She had been lied to, had believed lies and lies the whole time, and had let them influence her choices. She had made so many mistakes, and yet she was not the only one who had done wrong.

Teeth chattering in the unexplainable temperature, not even trying to understand it, she ran for him, Kamiko, wishing and praying he was still, *somehow*, alive.

She could now see cold houses, which still stood in crisp, empty sunlight and on what was now stone-hard, frozen jelly, and Cats, and many other things. The same unreal sounds and smells filled her senses and mixed with her twisted feelings.

For a moment, a second before she saw everything, Amber had to shut her eyes. She had to stay still and wait for the feeling to pass. Because she was so scared to open her eyes and find Kamiko gone.

But she knew that was what was *meant* to happen. It was the thing that made sense, the logic in the situation, the unexpected, that she simply could not understand. Even if now, it was out of her control. She was so scared, but also so bored with making the same mistakes. So bored with being bored with life, waiting for change. But she knew now how change worked. Amber knew she had to face it; she could not hide anymore.

What she found when she opened her eyes was Petal. Petal

on the ground, a few feet away, staring at an identical version of Amber's Gadget, staring so intensively that his eyeballs were coming a bit out of his sockets.

His eyes had changed. Amber saw a weak, unreal glimmer in them as his body collapsed to the snowy ground, eyes still on the screen. It was the same look Kamiko had given her when all he wanted was to stare at the strings.

Amber stepped closer, lightheaded.

And there he was, Kamiko, standing next to Petal, shaking, trying his very best to be a comfort, but with no effect. She almost smiled, because *he was alive, and she was almost glad that it did not make sense!*

Other Cats were there, too, but none dared touch Petal. Amber spotted Halfmoon facing the other side, pacing around, looking somewhat nervous. Its face was redder than usual, even in the cold. Amber could hear It mutter the same phrase over and over: "Reality is frightening. Reality is frightening. Reality is frightening. Reality is frightening…"

Suddenly she felt odd, and her cool skin prickled. *Was she dreaming?* Kamiko was *supposed* to be dead, of course, *supposed* to be gone. Many years should have passed for everyone, but everyone was still here.

Thirty seconds in Japan were a day on Catslaughter Island. But everyone was here, as if only one day had passed.

She was glad Kamiko was alive, and she knew that this was what she had come for, anyway. She had come to see if he somehow still could be, although there was no reason he should. And yet, here he was. Alive.

She would have been perfectly fine, but her head still swirled in confusion and wrongness. She hadn't thought she'd ever feel like this again. But she knew the feeling was temporary. She knew it was natural in a world like this.

Catslaughter Island did not *look* normal. Aside from the falling snowflakes and crust of ice, colours swirled everywhere —bright, random tones and all kinds of illusions. The lightly drizzling sky had turned the same broken shade as on Teplaytides. Amber saw half-images floating everywhere, more Cats suddenly seeming to be standing somewhere they were not, the same staircase as the one on Teplaytides positioned somewhere random—before vanishing. In fact, everything seemed to be shifting and bursting and turning all around, thousands of things occurring at once.

Her eyes tried to follow everything, and the chaos became unbearable. The next moment, she was seeing Fox cubs, Houses with eyes, Eyes themselves, Doodles, even the tide from the ocean...

Dizzy and unable to feel her body anymore in the cold, Amber focused on Petal. He was bent unnaturally over the Gadget, in a slumped position she never thought she would see someone with such a strong posture be in. He was completely ignoring Kamiko. But Amber knew, by the looks of it, that *Petal was not fully in control of himself, then and there.*

Her stomach dropped.

"PETAL!" Kamiko was screaming, trying to push Petal away from the sickly position he was in, while the other Cats around sighed and shook their heads—if they weren't joining in with the screaming, crying, or laughing.

Amber stood there awkwardly, not knowing what to do. But she remembered how on Teplaytides she had taken it slower, not trying to suppress any feelings, and therefore, made sense of things in their own way.

So, she approached the scene calmly, getting used to this new situation, although everything was spinning, and she felt sick.

Petal and Kamiko were next to the floating table. Amber was about to approach but decided against it as she came closer, and Kamiko's face became sharper.

Kamiko was properly sobbing now, and his tiny cries even froze out the voices of the other Cats. His face was chalk-white and sweaty, his body was cold and wet. He clung onto Petal tightly, pushing and kicking him and wanting him to face anything but the Gadget. Wanting him just to look at him.

But he wouldn't. Petal was not meeting Kamiko's eyes.

The sight of the scene made tears roll down Amber's chin all over her already damp, frost-covered uniform. But it wasn't only Petal who she hated seeing like this—it was Kamiko.

And then Petal's glassy eyes looked at her, over Kamiko's shaking shoulder, with not a hint of anything she had seen in them before. But then she recognized it as a much duller and sadder version of Petal's usual expression of strength and ambition.

His eyebrows twitched together and his lip trembled, and yet his eyes still wore that glowing, steadfast, though now distant and almost empty look of wanting to keep going, to fight what this Gadget was doing to his body.

With what was perhaps his last bit of strength, he screamed, "IT'S ALL AN ILLUSION!"

As he said this, an ugly, beastly shiver ran through his whole body, but Amber's gaze was fixed on his jacket.

Petal's face was drained of his usual self, but his jacket looked exactly as it had before, possibly the exclusive thing on Catslaughter Island that did. It was as though the jacket was protecting Petal a little. From the Gadget, from the cold.

Then, Amber had to take a few steps back when she saw it happen.

As it had happened to Kamiko.

Petal's body slowly rose because of the tension, the darkness of the Mahou energy, and he was lifted, higher, higher, until he no longer touched the ground. Amber knew. *He was being pulled by a string.*

Kamiko shrieked and grabbed his legs, but then Petal's eyes narrowed, and they were sucked into the Gadget.

The eyes stared back at Kamiko.

Amber's chest felt tight, and her feet started steering her back in the direction she had come from.

But a dreadful sound made her turn around.

It was the sound of more sucking.

Petal's body danced all over again. And the whole of Petal was sucked into the Gadget, as easily as a piece of dust by a vacuum cleaner, as easily gone as a small fly slapped by a big human hand. He was just gone.

For a moment, Amber swore she saw the expressionless eyes inside the Gadget widen even more, and break into tears. She swore she saw the whole Gadget moisten and small drops of salty tears ooze down, and grains of salt pop out from the screen, causing the Gadget to break into several loud, stomach-churning noises.

Amber had to cover her ears at Kamiko's awful screams to prevent herself from breaking down entirely as well.

But when Petal's body was completely gone, he left something behind. He left something behind, and Kamiko saw it.

They were two items. His jacket. And a wristwatch. It was the watch he'd talked about.

The sight of the jacket there by itself reminded Amber of something. The cold. The snow and awful weather here right now. Petal's last scream of *IT'S ALL AN ILLUSION!* was still ringing in her ears.

Could Catslaughter Island's constant sun and warmth have

been an illusion? Just like Kamiko had said the Wacky Winter's coldness was an illusion? Could the Cats have always been constantly cold, and Petal knew, so he'd worn a jacket to keep warm?

Amber moved closer.

She was about to do something—lay a gentle hand on Kamiko, hug him, try to reverse Petal… But as she stood there, a few feet away from Kamiko, she saw from behind how he trembled. How terribly and helplessly he trembled. Many Cat eyes were now on her, and for a moment there was silence. She stood and stared, arms limp at her sides, exactly like when she couldn't stand up to the Gang.

Amber retraced her steps, heading in the opposite direction.

She didn't like this. This was wrong. She wouldn't allow this to happen, she was going to take action, she *was* going to help Kamiko—but she needed to focus, she needed to escape first.

In this situation, there really wasn't anything she could do. There simply *wasn't*. And this time it wasn't her fault, but she wouldn't do any good standing there when Kamiko turned around; he would only be in more shock. If Petal could be saved from his grotesque fate, Kamiko was the only Cat she could think of right now who could even do or say anything.

She followed the short, now frosty, mossy ground to where the grass was long and up to her knees. Except, now it had died and become flatter, for here there was actual, ankle-deep snow. The snow crunched in an unnaturally loud way as she stepped, unlike the silent, probably fake one on the Wacky Winters. She was in the random patch of nature at the side of the island. But when the ground turned sandy (or when there was sand *beneath* the heavy snow), and she neared the seashore, she stopped abruptly.

There, face bulging like a swollen, fleshy balloon, was Frog.

"PetalbrainmeltedintoGreatMoonvention," Frog croaked, sniffling. "PetalgoneforeverPetaldead?"

"I'm sorry, Frog," Amber said, realizing her voice was hoarse and raw only after she had spoken. "I don't know what happened to him exactly."

"Petalbroken?" Frog shrieked, desperate.

"Yes." Amber gulped, shaking all over. "I think Petal is broken, Frog. I'm sorry."

Then, after letting out a trembly sigh, she wildly ran off, perhaps because large tears had formed in her eyes. For some reason, she didn't want Frog to see them.

Clumsy, tiny footsteps followed her. With a sniffle.

Amber turned around and held out her hand, as if to stop it. But Frog had followed her closer than she had thought, and in that fraction of a second it bumped into her, smacking its face on her hand. It fell over into the snow, in a sobbing heap of skin and bones.

Amber gasped. "Sorry, Frog!"

Frog screeched, its whole face a tsunami of flush and tears. And salt. The sound must have caused a flock of birds to fly off, except there were no birds here.

Not looking back, Amber slowly turned again. After a few steps around iced-over plants, she was already at the beach.

She wanted to take off her shoes and walk in her socks, run along the shore again, but she needed all the extra warmth she could get, in this weather. Pacing along the coast for a while, she tried to decide what to do, a feeling of helplessness in the pit of her stomach.

She watched the plain, fake, now wintry beach, but found it looked more real than before. *If Halfmoon Itself lost all sense and meaning, would this beach still look as fake as it did now?* Amber thought it wouldn't, as, using Mahou energy, Halfmoon seemed to be the one controlling the image. It wasn't a natural or a normal beach, after all.

She gave a long sigh again and watched her breath become visible and float away from her into the air.

And she began to think. Kamiko had lost Petal. Lost Petal to the madness of the Mahou energy.

Again, she knew that reality, and whatever the Mahou energy was creating—illusions—were incredibly hard to distinguish.

And she remembered how Petal's—how Kamiko's—body had slowly risen, then danced around, pulled by the strings on his Paws, his eyes getting sucked right into the screen, then peering out with that same chilling, wide, grotesque expression and very thin pupils. Amber shuddered. Again, she felt a deep sense of unfairness, and for a little while she let it all out through tears, naturally. She was just so afraid of this place. She was afraid, but she knew it was true—at least, as illusions —and she would accept it. She needed to stand here for a while longer, shivering in the frosty sand, and some time before she could do anything. Time to consider what was true to her.

A part of her mind was still scared, still scared of not understanding, of being useless. But she would not let the feeling take over anymore.

CHAPTER 26 – SEWING BUTTONS

mber heard voices nearby. They were familiar, and she recognized the tall legs, as well as the small, bent-back figure of Timeravel standing next to them.

A light feeling of relief and something else brushed her face and made her smile as she ran towards the two familiar Foxes.

"Quirkstride!" she said and sank into the depths of their eyes, not caring about the legs. The sight of them no longer caused her stomach to lurch.

"Hello, Amber!" Quirkstride's grin hadn't changed, but their face looked different, more like when they had been crying.

Amber waited for Timeravel to speak, and then they—she knew the Fox beings should not be called *it*—looked up. "You must wonder how and why we are here."

She shook her head. "Actually, I *hadn't* wondered. I'm…" She struggled to find the words. "I'm glad you are here."

Timeravel stared at her for a while. "A-amber, I can

explain it all. I will; I know things are odd. But first, you're all shaky and your nose is blue. Do you need a jacket?"

Then she noticed that both Quirkstride and Timeravel were wearing jackets. The jackets were bright blue and made of leather… They were the same as the jacket Petal had worn.

"Oh." Somehow the sight of them brought tears to Amber's eyes. "Well, yes. I'm freezing. I'd love one. But how—?"

"We made them," Timeravel cut in. "They're special jackets. They protect against this awful cold weather."

"We'll make you one now," Quirkstride added. "We'd love to."

"What?" Amber said. "Now?"

"Yes. Now." Timeravel smirked.

"Using Mahou energy?"

"No, actually," Quirkstride replied. "We're kind of trying to avoid relying on magic that much. We make them by… getting stuff from Japan. Of course, we use Mahou energy to do *that*, but the rest is all up to our Paws."

"It's very real," Timeravel said. "Very real. We need real materials and real effort to create real things. Now, before we start, and before I explain things… I wanted to apologize about something."

Not knowing what to say, Amber listened.

"When I met you in the ocean," Timeravel started. "I had not intended to frighten you—in case I did. I had not intended to *criticize* you for the mistakes, the same ones I-I made. That was, of course, the reason I wanted to talk. I knew everything, everything that was happening, and I wanted to warn you. And I did not want to be too straightforward, so I was almost speaking in code. But… sorry."

Amber recognized the face, the ambiguous expression of

fear, of guilt. She answered, "That's all right. Thank you, thank you for trying to tell me what was happening with, well, *everything*. I know there's something wrong with the Mahou energy, and the Gadget ..." Her voice trailed off, for only a moment. "But... thank you."

Timeravel smiled nervously before dropping their smile and looking down.

"Your voice," Amber noticed. "You sound so... *clear*." Timeravel sounded like when Kamiko took Cat Improvement Pills. More human. But in a different way to Halfmoon. They didn't stutter like before, either.

"Oh." Timeravel's face twitched. "Yes. It has to do with the Mahou energy."

They stared at the ground again, and Quirkstride did the same.

For a moment, Amber waited acceptingly. And in that moment, she did not feel that same impatience, that anger or annoyance when others got emotional. She didn't feel that old, old feeling of dread she'd got at Kamiko's tears. Because she knew getting so emotional was a thing she did, too. A thing they all did.

Again, Amber was hit with the reality of what had happened with Timeravel, and this time she was no longer so scared. *Others* had done wrong... and then there was Timeravel, trying to tell her this, probably trying to warn her of making mistakes and of getting it all wrong. The idea almost made her cry. She felt so *grateful*.

Timeravel turned to look her in the eye again. "Now, let me explain a few things. When your Cat friend arrived here from Teplaytides, he found me, and together we froze time. We managed to temporarily stop the time difference spell—the one that I had initially created—so your friend could still see you.

Time is odd. Apparently, Koko and Halfmoon are *immune* to any time spells *anyway*, and so—"

Amber had let small tears spill from her eyes, and splash down all over her cheeks. "I don't care, I really don't care about the rules of the Mahou energy right now!" she burst out, never having thought such words would escape her mouth. "I'm glad you're here. All I know is… that I believe you, and that I trust you!"

Quirkstride giggled. "Let Timeravel talk!"

"Oh—*sorry*…" Suddenly, Amber laughed, too.

"No; it's all right," Timeravel replied, smirking. "It *is* very complicated, the Mahou energy, that is. Put simply, Koko and Halfmoon seem not to react to the time difference, and age as if they were living in the Human world. Essentially, Amber, Quirkstride and I want to reunite with the rest of our siblings. Quirkstride and I had not spoken to each other in… *years*. Many. But here we are now to see what is happening."

Amber gave a weak smile. "Well, I'm glad you made it. Really, I am."

"Then why are you crying?" Quirkstride asked, a look of concern on their face.

Amber was about to open her mouth when Timeravel smiled. "No, we know. We saw what happened with that Cat Petal. Horrible."

Quirkstride suggested, "While we make your jacket, why don't we take a stroll here at the beach, to keep our legs warm?"

* * *

To make a jacket out of nothing and air and random bits and pieces of stolen objects, lots of passionate effort, little time, and *some* Mahou energy, Amber soon learnt, the first step was to create the base of all the sides.

She wasn't entirely sure how or where the Foxes got their supplies from. She guessed maybe they had pre-stolen them, or even used the Mahou energy to create them. But all she knew was that she trusted them.

What looked like a few sheets of scrap paper, some brown and yellow felt, lots of fuzzy cotton stuffing, scraps of fabrics in brown, green and blue, purple leather, googly eyes, and a handful of buttons were produced silently by Timeravel and Quirkstride as they walked. Then, some scissors, pins, needles, and different coloured strings and thread.

Amber wondered how beings with fox-like Paws for their front legs and hooves for their back ones could sew. She didn't understand how they, for the occasion, walked on two legs like the Cats, and made these objects float in the air. But she didn't ask questions.

Amber wanted to help. She wanted to help, and didn't want to sit back this time and watch and wait for the whole world to turn and change for her. She wanted to do something. She wanted to work with her friends.

The Foxes assigned her the task of sewing a strip of blue fabric onto a large brown one.

As the Foxes started attaching the paper with the felt and the fabric and the leather, making the dimensions of the jacket, and she helped, they walked in focused silence. The silence was focused, but also caught up and full of unspoken shared thoughts.

Their feet all passed over the same white, perfect sand, the one that was trying to be real, trying to pretend. They were surrounded by fakeness. But they were here together, Paws (or hands) all busy together working on the same thing, and they were not fake; they were no longer pretending. They were here together, and they enjoyed the view they had. Away from what was happening at the camp.

"P-petal was not a Cat who deserved that," Timeravel started into this silence, still in shock—but also acceptance—with what had happened. "I watched him. He was strong, he stood up for himself, and he cared for his sibling, Frog. Petal was kind. But… this is not about deserving or kindness even, to be honest. Petal was, well, trapped."

"Sucked in with the Mahou energy and all," Quirkstride added in a low voice, not looking up from their sewing. "I got so confused when I saw that happen—I didn't know the Mahou energy was capable of something like that."

"Yes." She remembered the big, poor eyes trapped inside the huge screen, the Mahou energy. But she did not picture Petal's eyes. She pictured Kamiko's. "I hadn't expected that either." And her voice exposed her slight tremble.

Amber let go of her needle, and it glided beside her in the air. Then she bit her tongue to stop herself, but loosened up at the faces around her, letting tears fall, and not by accident.

"But is he really… gone?" she asked.

Quirkstride shook their head hopelessly and met her eyes, before returning to Amber's jacket. "Until we saw you a moment ago, we were still watching. After Petal got lifted into the air, and, well, got *into* the Gadget, the Gadget… it turned *blue*, and that's when the Mahou energy really escalated. You can hear it now. The sound of Mahou energy." They stopped for a moment, and Amber could hear the same Catslaughter noises of silence, louder than ever.

"But I'm *still* confused," she admitted. "*So* confused. By all of this, as there is so much I still don't understand. After

Petal… after what happened, he left behind his jacket. You saw that, didn't you?"

"Yep," Quirkstride replied, pausing their sewing. "Amber, what we all need to understand is that what Petal did was astonishing… Absolutely *amazing*. He had such a powerful mind that he actually *manipulated* the Mahou energy. He used the power of his mind to make himself the jacket. And the watch. Because Petal couldn't have stolen the watch. He couldn't have travelled all the way to one of the Portals to get a watch from Japan. Either he entered a Portal from *here* by himself… basically by breaking the Mahou energy and *creating* a Portal, so to speak, or he *made* the watch. Well, the Mahou energy did. It's hard to explain. But Petal was very strong."

"As strong as us," said Timeravel with a slight grin, eyes also still focused on their thread. "He must have made the jacket the way we're making yours."

Amber broke into a fresh bout of tears. "Then, what happened to Petal now, exactly—do you know?"

Quirkstride looked up again. "I was talking about that to Timeravel! It's really just… the Mahou energy. The odd, strange, weird, bizarre Mahou energy! It's a wild energy, and was never meant to be used the way it has been. That's why it made even a Cat as strong as Petal lose control. This is just the consequence of what's happened."

Timeravel scoffed, and in that moment, Amber saw the same arrogant creature she had met in the depths of the seas. She did not blame them.

"That Halfmoon… it thinks it knows everything, thinks it's the most powerful. But it—such a useless thing—is anything but powerful, with the childish ways it uses the Mahou energy. It makes these inventions. It claims to use its own talents, and yet it hypocritically creates inventions almost purely with Mahou energy, misusing it, of course. Halfmoon tricks everyone!

"Amber, this is what I attempted to tell you when I saw you in the ocean. We both were used. Amber, I was too kind. We both were s-squeezed into the wrong places, into areas we were never even meant to go. I was banned from Catslaughter Island, and it was Halfmoon who made that horrid decision." Timeravel stopped in their tracks.

Amber stopped too, needle and fabric still floating in front of her. *So, it* was *Halfmoon. Halfmoon had done it all.* She looked down at the sandy ground. They were now talking about the *things*. The truth. But she was ready to hear it all. See things in their true light, the light that she *could* see things in.

"Yes, Amber." Timeravel noticed her frown. "Halfmoon lies all the time. It is not what it presents itself to be. It itself might be an illusion, a trick to the eye. I could not care less. The Cats used me, forced all my Mahou energy and power out of me, to protect the land that really was my own, the one that they had stolen. It was not fair, but I gave in, and I-I let them. But I am tired of being a victim, and I will not fight them, and not help them either, but I will stand up for myself."

"I'm sorry about what they did to you," Amber mumbled.

Timeravel smiled. "I could control them all, too, make them my little puppets, make them obey me. But I will not. Power does not mean greatness. That exactly is the thing—the Mahou energy was never supposed to be used in this way by the Cats; it is *wrong* to control the Mahou energy."

Quirkstride gave a laugh. "The Mahou energy does weird stuff! We think it sucks in and steals beings' power over themselves, the control over their own brains. This Gadget…"

Quirkstride's gaze shifted away for a moment, and Amber followed it to their own Gadget, still above their head. "I better get rid of this thing!"

Amber agreed.

Timeravel went on, "When trying to use the M-mahou energy for their own use, the Cats really are damaging themselves. The Mahou energy toxifies them, the air they breathe in. It changes their looks." They rolled their eyes.

"I think I understand," Amber cut in. "The Cats were never supposed to come here. This should never have happened." Again, she trembled, the image of all the Cat faces still twirling around in her head. She knew she might never get rid of the horrific pictures that her eyes had absorbed over the last few days. But she didn't want to get rid of them; they were her unique experiences.

She picked up her needle again and continued stitching into the brown fabric. "And there are illusions," she added, her voice breaking slightly. "We're surrounded by lies."

"Exactly!" Quirkstride said, but Timeravel shot them a glare, for them to be more cautious.

For a moment, she was still someone in confusion, in helplessness. But as she finished sewing the blue onto brown, she remembered that Timeravel and Quirkstride were here. And they were busy making a jacket for *her*.

"Don't see it as lies," Quirkstride assured. "It's just the nature of the Mahou energy."

"It is just what it is," Timeravel spoke. "I see the madness of the Mahou energy in the camp now, and there is something I could do, but I need to wait for it to settle down. And I have only so much control over the land. This is what the Cats have done to themselves. We do not know exactly what this all does to them, what consequences and long-term effects it really has, but here we are now, to see. We've made it here to see! The Cats look weirder and weirder, and we can see what happens to them in the next age of Cats, I should say.

"The Mahou energy is powerful. See, Amber, this is why I sound *clearer* now. I was suppressing and hiding all that Mahou energy inside my Fox body, the form I present myself in, so Cats could at least not steal that from me. And a lot of Mahou energy can make anyone g-g-go—" For the first time since Amber had seen Timeravel in the ocean, they glitched. "– c-crazy. But fortunately, I am more cautious in using it now. Instead, it flows around me. The Mahou energy, we should let it be free, and I rather would not touch it…"

Amber gave a genuine smile. "I understand."

Timeravel grinned back. "I see you have finished your jacket piece. Give it to me, and I'll attach it to mine."

She did so, and watched Timeravel start the mixed media back of the jacket, while Quirkstride worked on the sleeves.

"Also," they went on. "There is one more apology I must make. The sea monsters, as you call them, I am also responsible for them. If I'd wanted, I could have held them back completely…"

Amber shook her head, but they continued, "Amber, Halfmoon *sent* those sea monsters for you. At least, that is what I believe. It's so obsessed with its inventions, wanting to develop them. The Cats and you are its test subjects, its guinea pigs, its lab rats, for its experiments. I can't say for certain, but I believe that Halfmoon, with its Eyes, is always watching you. It brought up sea monsters to your boat, to scare you. The monsters, they never hurt you, did they? They left you alone, never *killed* you. If it was Halfmoon behind them, it wouldn't have wanted you dead, but the monsters were intended to make you need a comfort, force you to turn to the Gadget. I saw how many sea monsters were brought to the surface by Mahou energy forces. Almost as if Halfmoon was keeping them there, in case it needed to bring one up to scare you."

Amber shook her head, almost in disbelief, although she did believe the Foxes. She remembered the Worms and the green Snake. "Thank you so much for telling me. So, Halfmoon's always been watching me, tried everything to frighten me, make me *need* the Gadget?"

"We can't be sure if this is true," Quirkstride said. "We don't know how much Halfmoon really knows, what's on its mind. We don't know how much it's the Mahou energy doing something and how much it's an individual creature. We'll never know for sure, but then again, it doesn't matter that much."

"I should have told you this before," Timeravel insisted.

Amber shook her head again. "You've done nothing wrong, Timeravel. *I'm* sorry for thinking *you* were a monster! Well, what even is a monster?! I know they're... illusions, right?"

"I say they are. They are a way in which the Mahou energy represents itself. I do not recommend trying to understand it."

"I won't." Amber nodded, yet there was one more thing, one thought that had clawed itself into her mind. "But there is... something. Something I saw. It looked like... a Fox."

"A Fox?" Timeravel lifted their eyebrows.

While the Foxes attached fuzzy, loose pieces onto finished, bigger ones, front Paws working at a quicksand speed, Amber told them about her encounter. How she had seen the image of it inside the Gadget, before seeing what looked like its body float past in the ocean, then seeing it on Teplaytides.

After a while, Timeravel concluded, "It must have been

one of our siblings, somehow. At least one of them. They must still exist, somewhere, s-somehow."

"But that couldn't *possibly* have been the same thing I saw floating in the water, could it?" Amber asked.

"I think our siblings were also trying to warn you," Quirkstride cut in. "Of, you know, bad things that could happen. Did you see anything else like that?"

"What do you mean?"

"See anything, especially weird?"

Amber laughed. "A lot."

"Anything that seemed to *call out* to you?"

At this, she recalled something. Something that, because of the Gadget, had completely left her mind. "On the Wacky Winters, as Cats call it, there was this House, where a Portal was kept, and I heard this voice…"

"A voice?"

"It was a song. It did seem to be specifically for me. I also saw *other* Foxes." This time recalling didn't cause her any pain. "A Fox cub. I think it tried calling out to me."

"Those must have been our siblings!" Quirkstride exclaimed. "Trying to help you, probably. We can only *hope* they're safe, but we need to find out…"

"We're going to look for them," Timeravel said. "Since we were the first thing—we Foxes, or whatever we are—that ever existed in this realm, we are as good as part of the Mahou energy. It cannot harm us, but we can harm it. And we share many memories, as siblings, as small Foxes. But, as I mentioned before, we fell apart. It was our own selfish fighting, and the Mahou energy, that caused misunderstandings between us. Quirkstride and I will look for our siblings to be together again."

Quirkstride nodded in approval. "But… before we leave…"

Again, they looked up from their sewing, at the Gadget, and snatched the invention into their Paws. But Timeravel had already awakened some force in the air, and the Gadget was hurled into the ocean with a *splash*. Amber heard a strange muffled buzzing noise as it sank.

She could only smile.

Laughing, Quirkstride turned to face her. "Hey… You know, all that *standing up taller* and *growing longer legs* stuff, it was stupid. Koko's right, you know. To accept, you really do need to *hate* first. Only then should you grow yourself legs like mine!" Quirkstride snickered.

Amber joined in.

She realized suddenly that Timeravel was beaming, holding something up to her face.

"Finished!" they exclaimed. "Amber. What do you think?"

* * *

The finished jacket was a chaotic collage.

Yellow, cat-soft felt wrapped half the left sleeve, sliced through by a scratchy strip of violent green fabric. The other sleeve ended abruptly at the elbow, but was blue and puffy, almost bird-like. Layered, crumply purple leather formed the main body of the jacket. A beautifully neat collar—purple, green—sat at the top. Below it, three mismatched buttons marked where the jacket could be opened and closed: one square and grey, one orange and intricate, and one tall with tiny illegible text printed on it. Ragged cut-outs of shapes that desperately tried to be stars and hearts completed the look. The

Foxes had sewn on some extra buttons and glowing googly eyes.

Try it on! Quirkstride had said. Amber hadn't taken the jacket off since leaving the Foxes.

Pieces of her skin itched and throbbed; others were soothed and warm. Random things, both soft and rough, were sticking into her from all sides. Yet each bit was stitched with wild, loving care.

She shuffled along the beach in discomfort. The left sleeve was much too tight, though the rest of the jacket fell too loosely over her body, and the collar stuck strangely up into her neck. A button fell off by her slight touch, into the sand.

Amber picked it up.

But the Foxes had made it, just for her, she had to remember, because she was cold.

This is... more impressive than any of Halfmoon's *inventions*, she'd told them.

They had made it, using their big, messy Fox Paws, with not *even* a touch of Mahou energy, limited to the skills they had already. In this world, they had helped her, and they were on her side. And she had helped them make it.

Before Amber had left, Quirkstride's face had darkened a bit, and they'd said, *Maybe we'll meet again someday.*

Timeravel had gone on: *But it is useless to sit and wait for life to change, Amber—this is what I meant with the c-canvases, the books. It is your canvas; paint it your own way. And remember, you may never truly know reality.*

She had given the unusual creatures a hug, then. *Thank you. I know.*

CHAPTER 27 – RAINING TOADS

She ran back all the way she had come from, back to where Petal had vanished, where the Gadget still was and where Kamiko was bawling and screaming.

As she approached him without saying anything, she gave him a look, and in their eye contact they both knew that, with Petal gone, there was no one left for him. Kamiko shivered but smiled at her jacket. She could not leave him like she had before.

And not crying any longer, gazing into space, he did not protest as she picked him up and carried him. Not because he allowed this mindlessly, but because it was exactly what he wanted. Exactly what he needed.

Amber felt a small drop on her shoulder.

She turned her head and squealed in horror, seeing a fat, slimy toad sitting on her back. Kamiko leapt off her and tried hitting it away with his Paws, when Amber saw there was a toad on his head, too. The next moment, there was another on her face!

Amber took a jump back and the toad fell off her nose.

With her head tilted in this way, she faced the sky. She saw hundreds and hundreds of small black dots falling from above.

"It'srainingtoads…" Kamiko muttered, although she could tell he could barely speak.

More and more tiny beasts landed on their heads, startled and confused.

"Come on." Amber hopped along the ground in a zigzag pattern, avoiding fallen slimy creatures. "They can't hurt us. But before it gets heavier, *let's go*."

She pulled Kamiko with her, and the two started dodging more toads as they slowly marched towards the island's entrance.

But Kamiko stopped and held out a Paw. He gazed at the camp, the ruined camp, the chaotic place, yet something that had once been his home, for a final time.

"Amber!" The sudden call of her name sounded sour, dull, but also frightened.

She glanced around for a moment, using her hands to hit any toads out of her vision, and Kamiko turned, too.

She saw Halfmoon, the one who was screaming her name.

Except *it* wasn't Halfmoon, but something else.

What had been its head was unsteadily bobbing on top of its upper body, which had also largened and widened. What had been its neck was a long, fat tube, as tall as Amber, reaching out like a tree branch out of its trunk. What had been its eyes were empty sockets—for its true eyes had sprung out, although they still hung on by a skinny red string.

And somehow, it *did* still have kind eyes. Eyes could lie, but also tell the truth. But its eyes weren't its true ones. Amber knew where its real Eyes were—all around everything. Always watching her.

It was not even quite a person or a being. It was just a

thing, a lie, an illusion, a fake. A monster creating more illusions. Something Amber had never quite trusted, but just believed, listened to, never questioned, simply obeyed. It was not a Thing, but a *thing*. A thing: no more than the Gadgets themselves.

And Amber knew much worse things existed in the world than things that did not look right. Quirkstride and she were both very tall, and Quirkstride was perhaps a bit *too* tall, but it wasn't something of much importance now. Quirkstride and Timeravel looked real enough for her to believe them. It was their truth; it was what they were. But this was different.

Amber clenched her fists and simply stared.

"Amber," it started again, gasping for air.

"What do you want?" she shouted back.

"Asmalltalk! Why, girl, child, *kiddo*, don'tbeshyofmylooks!" It now sounded exactly the same as when the other Cats were trying to speak.

Amber shook her head. "Leave me alone."

"ButAmberkiddo! DoyoureallythinktheGadgetcanhurt, Amber? Why, thatwouldbeanawfulmisunderstanding!"

Amber covered her ears at the dreadful noise. "You're not supposed to speak!" she screamed. "And I am *not* your kiddo!"

"OfcourseIcanspeak!" But the thing that was Halfmoon flinched as a toad landed right onto its eyes.

For a second, as the toad fell off, Halfmoon's image flashed, and it was once again the same as before. Its voice cleared.

"My Gadget's design is an achievement, Amber. And some things may be so devastating that you may laugh, some things so spectacular that you may cry. But Petal's accident is no laughing matter, and my achievement is nothing to grieve about."

Amber furrowed her eyebrows. "Petal's *accident*, as you call it, was your fault."

Halfmoon paled even more.

"What are you even trying to say?"

"My point is that we should see things for what they are, and not just… feelings!"

She thought for a moment, then said, "I know you just feel scared."

Halfmoon froze. "What?"

"Well, of course, you're scared!" Amber went on. "Exactly like everyone else, all the other Cats, as you make them be. You feel scared."

"AndwhatwouldIfeelafraidof?" It made a ridiculous face, as its new looks returned.

"The Mahou energy. You pretend you can use it well, that it's all in your Paws. When really, you can't admit it, the fact that you're weak! That it's impossible for you to master it or know the way it works!"

Halfmoon gave a scream excruciating to her ears. Its eyes widened, the corners of its open mouth trembled, and for a moment it stood screaming with its head turned towards the sky, shaking it at what Amber had said. After a few minutes, it kept on muttering its phrase from before, "Reality is frightening… Reality is frightening… Reality is frightening…"

Amber let it sink and drown in its chaos as she ran away with Kamiko.

As they made their way to the Catslaughter Island sign, neither of them said a word, but both smiled. Amber didn't know exactly what to do—where there would be a Portal, how they would escape—but what she did know was that she'd now learned *how* to enter Portals, and that Kamiko trusted her.

For a while, they searched. They didn't dare listen to the

horrible noises back at the camp, and focused only on what was in front of them, looking for an X.

But then Amber realized that perhaps it was impossible to find it. *Perhaps…*

She reached out her hand slowly in the air and was sure she felt something. *Something*. An idea hit her. Perhaps *anything* could be a Portal, and they were always connected. Perhaps the X Portals were a piece of design, fakeness, slapped on top. Perhaps there was always an opening. That was what Petal had discovered; he had, in some way, used the Mahou energy.

Below her feet, Amber found a hole, as deep and black as a grave. She took Kamiko by his Paw and leapt inside without hesitating.

The next moment, they were both sitting back in Japan on the grassy ground.

"Well…" Amber sighed. "That was weird."

As she looked at Kamiko, she realized he looked different. He had certainly shrunk in size and looked almost like an ordinary cat. He still had quite an outstretched jaw, and his eyes looked a bit human-like, but he was, still, just a small cat. And now he walked on four legs.

Kamiko met her eyes and forced out his voice. She could tell he was having trouble speaking, and yet his words were different, not stuck together in the same way as before.

"Amber," he said. "I want you to have Petal's watch. Here, put it on."

She shook her head. "Petal said it was for you."

"No, seriously." Kamiko laughed. "It's really weird for a cat to wear a watch. And to talk. So, take it to make me shut up."

Amber returned the laugh, and slid the watch off Kamiko's

paw, which was quite easy as it was much too big. It fit better on her human wrist.

Then, she spotted a small kitten—she knew it was one of Halfmoon's Eyes, or Kitten Robots—crawl by her legs, clearly having followed her from the bushes.

It was smaller than Kamiko had been when she'd found him as a small kitten—much smaller. Too small. It seemed innocent and vulnerable and tiny and useless. In a way she knew it was—its creator was.

She stomped on it, smashing it with her foot. She heard Kamiko make a noise like a laugh.

As they made their way out of the blueberry bushes, Amber reflected on Halfmoon's last words.

My point is we should see things for what they are, and not just... feelings!

In a way, Amber thought, *it was right.*

They should not see the Gadget as only a distraction from pain, or the Cats as something scary. They should not avoid the truth because of fear, and avoid fear itself, for fear was a creature they had to let out. But often, feelings were what things were. After all, how could they know what was true in a world of illusions, if not by trust? Judgement and logic had clearly failed.

CHAPTER 28 – EMBRACING FREEDOM

"**I**know a path to the beach."

Kamiko was still beaten and tired, but even he had to admit the sky looked gorgeous as there were still a few strokes of light in the setting sun.

And Amber needed time to think of how she would introduce him to her mother. She knew, deep down, she had loved the cat—but would she recognize him?

Her bike was still right where she had left it by the bench. She strapped Kamiko onto it and rode all the way into town, where there were people and life. In the past, she had always loved cycling in the evenings. She'd loved going out by herself, with the freedom of deciding where to go. And she realized she still did.

She passed a corner, knowing Kamiko still sat safely in the small basket of the bike. A few people stared, a few people pointed at the unusual tabby cat, but she could only grin back at them.

Then... she felt that familiar sensation of her stomach

lurching. They were still there from hours before, even if it had been days for her. The Gang.

She was about to press the brakes when she realized she could cycle past them, if she wanted.

As she stared at the distant faces—the astonished faces, the confused faces, the strange faces—it was as if she saw them for the very first time. Now she looked them each directly in the eye, as if they were something new. Riding the bike, she was much taller than them, even more than she usually was. And she saw that same expression of fear. Trapped eyes.

Finally, she could understand them.

One of them, for a second, tried intimidating her. But Amber had never seen the girl from this angle before. She'd never properly looked at this fragile, vulnerable face from the additional height of her bike.

The individual face, usually part of a joined-up monster, said, evidently trying hard to force a sarcastic smirk, "Nice… *jacket*." But her lip curled up all ugly instead, and her voice broke.

"Thanks!" Amber grinned.

And she realized they were just as much puppets as anyone. They had held themselves back, by their own fears. Fears of the different, fears of their own insecurities. At least some kind of fears.

An even deeper smile spread across her features as she went past them. *Experiences could make people make the wrong choices.* But Amber knew now that memories were, in fact, not just thoughts. They were fears. And fears, when suppressed, could hold her back. She couldn't rush this either, and *leap right into the poison,* swallowing fears up. She needed to set them free, or else they would trap her. And being trapped by her own fears and prevented from action was even worse than being kept in a wacky, nonsensical world with Cats. Much worse.

Soon, they arrived at the beach. It was a small one. Amber parked her bike right beside the staircase leading to it, carrying Kamiko with her, until the ground turned soft.

A whirl of wind washed over their lively faces as they heard the seagulls scream and the real waves crash down into smaller ones. The real air blew salty and crisp, alive.

Sweat ran down Amber's face. She wiped it off with her new sleeves. It was so hot here—real, flaming summer. And she could feel it.

She realized that moment, as she looked down at the sewn-on buttons and googly eyes, that it was the first real thing she had worn this summer. The first real thing. Besides her now sea-washed, sandy, frosty uniform.

Amber liked her new jacket. She had worn nothing so messy, so strangely uncomfortable and so eye-catchingly flashy in a very long time. And she hadn't worn anything so special, so special to *her*, ever before. It was wrong-looking, in the best way.

Still, she did not know completely what was real and what was not. What had been cruel and what had been *wrong*. All she knew was that the Foxes had been kind. The Foxes had tried to help her. And Kamiko knew she trusted him.

"Honestly, I like thisplace." Kamiko managed one final clear sentence. "It's real, after all, Amber."

"It's beautiful." She gave the sweetest smile. "But you can call me Amaya."

And they never spoke again. For words were just one way that Halfmoon had controlled them—not a way in which their small, nonsensical universe should have been described with. Kamiko was not meant to speak. Their universe did not need interruption, distraction… In their own freedom, and her acceptance of their truth, it just *was*.

Amaya observed the blue sky one last time—the natural sky, containing no Mahou energy—and knew now, there were no more Eyes. *You cannot watch me anymore, Halfmoon, I am alone and free.*

ACKNOWLEDGMENTS

I want to thank my very first readers, especially Liza, Guido, Frankie, Kim, and Anna, as well as everyone else who offered feedback and suggestions on my later drafts, particularly Wendy and Bunny.

A big thank you to my cover designer, Jack Hillside, for creating the stunning design perfectly reflective of my novel's spirit.

My deepest gratitude goes to each and every one of you who donated to my fundraiser page (you know who you are), as well as to anyone else who has in other ways supported me with this passion project.

Finally, a huge thank you to my parents for their help with everything and maintenance of everyone's sanity throughout this very winding journey.

But most of all, I want to thank Taylor. She stayed at my side through my most dramatic rewrites and every hour spent at my desk (literally).

ABOUT THE AUTHOR

M. Minji Jacome is a writer living in Spain with her multilingual family and her delightfully strange cat Taylor. *Trapped Marionettes*, her debut novel, was published when she was 14. Minji is autistic and an advocate for neurodiversity. She likes coffee, classic literature, jellyfish, and the wonderful whimsy of Tim Burton films. Passionate about art and self-expression, she enjoys writing and sharing the wacky creations of her mind.

Instagram: @minji.writes

THANK YOU

Thank you for purchasing this book. Please consider leaving a review on Goodreads or Amazon.